PRAISE FOR TAH(

"BEGINNING TO READ TAHOE HIJACK IS
BOARDING A RACE CAR... RATING: A+"

Kittling Books

"A THRILLING READ... any reader will find the pages of his thrillers
impossible to stop turning"

- Caleb Cage, The Nevada Review

"NOW I'M HOOKED...Borg not only offers a good mystery, but does a
terrific job with some fascinating California history that is both enlightening
and gripping"

- Sunny Solomon, Bookin' with Sunny

"THE BOOK CLIMAXES WITH A TWIST THE READER DOESN'T
SEE COMING, WORTHY OF MICHAEL CONNELLY"

- Heather Gould, Tahoe Mountain News

"A FASCINATING AND MUCH RECOMMENDED NOVEL"
- Midwest Book Review

"I HAD TO HOLD MY BREATH DURING THE LAST PART OF THIS
FAST-PACED THRILLER"

- Harvee Lau, Book Dilettante

CHOSEN FOR BOOK DILLETANTE'S LIST OF

BEST CRIME READS OF 2011!

PRAISE FOR TAHOE HEAT

"IN TAHOE HEAT, BORG MASTERFULLY WRITES A SEQUENCE
OF EVENTS SO INTENSE THAT IT BELONGS IN AN EARLY TOM
CLANCY NOVEL"
- Caleb Cage, Nevada Review

"TAHOE HEAT IS A RIVETING THRILLER"
- John Burroughs, Midwest Book Review

"WILL KEEP READERS TURNING THE PAGES AS OWEN RACES TO CATCH A VICIOUS KILLER"

- Barbara Bibel, Booklist

"THE READER CAN'T HELP BUT ROOT FOR McKENNA AS THE BIG, GENEROUS, IRISH-BLOODED, STREET-WISE-YET-BOOK-SMART FORMER COP"

- Taylor Flynn, Tahoe Mountain News

PRAISE FOR TAHOE NIGHT

"BORG HAS WRITTEN ANOTHER WHITE-KNUCKLE THRILLER... A sure bet for mystery buffs waiting for the next Robert B. Parker and Lee Child novels"

- Jo Ann Vicarel, Library Journal

"AN ACTION-PACKED THRILLER WITH A NICE-GUY HERO, AN EVEN NICER DOG..."

- Kirkus Reviews

"A KILLER PLOT... EVERY ONE OF ITS 350 PAGES WANTS TO GET TURNED... *FAST*"

- Taylor Flynn, Tahoe Mountain News

"PLENTY OF ACTION TO KEEP YOU ON THE EDGE OF YOUR SEAT... An excellent addition to this series."

- Gayle Wedgwood, Mystery News

"ANOTHER PAGE-TURNER OF A MYSTERY, with more twists and turns than a roller coaster ride"

- Midwest Book Review

"A FASCINATING STORY OF FORGERY, MURDER..."

- Nancy Hayden, Tahoe Daily Tribune

PRAISE FOR TAHOE AVALANCHE

ONE OF THE TOP 5 MYSTERIES OF THE YEAR!

- Gayle Wedgwood, Mystery News

"BORG IS A SUPERB STORYTELLER...A MASTER OF THE GENRE"
- *Midwest Book Review*

"TAHOE AVALANCHE WAS SOOOO GOOD... A FASCINATING MYSTERY with some really devious characters"
- *Merry Cutler, Annie's Book Stop, Sharon, Massachusetts*

"EXPLODES INTO A COMPLEX PLOT THAT LEADS TO MURDER AND INTRIGUE"
- *Nancy Hayden, Tahoe Daily Tribune*

"READERS WILL BE KEPT ON THE EDGE OF THEIR SEATS"
- *Sheryl McLaughlin, Douglas Times*

"INCLUDE BORG IN THE GROUP OF MYSTERY WRITERS that write with a strong sense of place such as TONY HILLERMAN"
- *William Clark, The Union*

PRAISE FOR TAHOE SILENCE

WINNER, BEN FRANKLIN AWARD, BEST MYSTERY OF THE YEAR!

"A HEART-WRENCHING MYSTERY THAT IS ALSO ONE OF THE BEST NOVELS WRITTEN ABOUT AUTISM"
STARRED REVIEW - Jo Ann Vicarel, Library Journal

CHOSEN BY LIBRARY JOURNAL AS ONE OF THE FIVE BEST MYSTERIES OF THE YEAR

"THIS IS ONE ENGROSSING NOVEL...IT IS SUPERB"
- *Gayle Wedgwood, Mystery News*

"ANOTHER GREAT READ!!"
- *Shelly Glodowski, Midwest Book Review*

"ANOTHER EXCITING ENTRY INTO THIS TOO-LITTLE-KNOWN SERIES"
- *Mary Frances Wilkens, Booklist*

"A REAL PAGE-TURNER"
- *Sam Bauman, Nevada Appeal*

Titles by Todd Borg

TAHOE DEATHFALL

TAHOE BLOWUP

TAHOE ICE GRAVE

TAHOE KILLSHOT

TAHOE SILENCE

TAHOE AVALANCHE

TAHOE NIGHT

TAHOE HEAT

TAHOE HIJACK

TAHOE TRAP

TAHOE TRAP

by

Todd Borg

THRILLER PRESS

Thriller Press First Edition, August 2012

Library of Congress Control Number: 2012937739

ISBN: 978-1-931296-20-5

Cover design and map by Keith Carlson

Manufactured in the United States of America

For Kit

ACKNOWLEDGMENTS

In the spring of 2011, I was contacted by The League To Save Lake Tahoe about participating in their big Oscar de la Renta fundraiser, the famous Tahoe fashion show sponsored by Saks Fifth Avenue. The show generates a great deal of money for The League To Save Lake Tahoe. With this annual show, Mr. de la Renta and Saks have done a great service to Lake Tahoe.

No, they didn't want me to strut my stuff down the runway - bummer! - but they wondered if I would be willing to auction off character name rights to a character in my next novel.

Hey, if I can get some hang time with the guy who put gowns on everyone from Jackie Kennedy to Cameron Diaz, I'm in. The show is a great mix of good environmental causes and fashion.

Okay, so I didn't get to meet Oscar, but my books were there at the estate on Tahoe's West Shore.

The person who won the auction is Pam Sagan from the Bay Area. Thank you, Pam! Your contribution is hard at work funding efforts to keep Tahoe clear and beautiful.

Pam, and generous people like her, have been critical in the effort to protect Lake Tahoe.

For my part of the deal, this new novel features a character named Pam Sagan. I should point out that I have never met the real Pam Sagan, and I made no effort to shape the book's fictional character in relation to her.

Thanks to Pam, and thanks to The League To Save Lake Tahoe! It was a fun project!

As for the other people who deserve my boundless gratitude, no book can shine without the assiduous efforts of its editors. I benefit from several, and I can't thank them enough.

Liz Johnston, Eric Berglund, Christel Hall and my wife Kit. If this story pulls you in and gives you a good ride, it is in large degree to the spit and polish of these four stellar wordsmiths. They are experts in multiple arenas, and I'm a lucky guy to have such help.

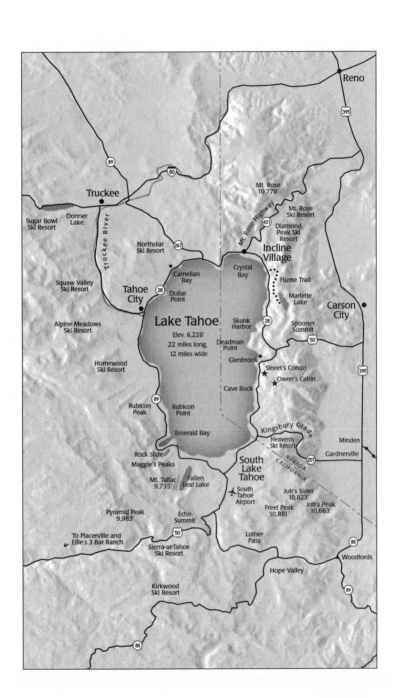

PROLOGUE

Paco Ipar awoke to the night fear.

His throat hurt. It was hard to swallow. Harder to breathe. His heart thumped as it did when he was younger and he came out of a nightmare, yelling, soaked in sweat. It should have been different now that Paco was ten years old.

It had been years since Paco was afraid of the dark. He was too old and too tough for the night fear.

Paco stared up at the ceiling of the van, remembering where he was.

They'd left home in the middle of the night. He remembered the glowing numbers on the dashboard clock turning from 2:59 to 3:00 as he watched. Paco had slid into his sleeping bag on the van floor and had gone to sleep.

It felt like he'd been asleep for a long time when he first awoke. He looked out as they drove by the empty farmers' market parking lot in South Lake Tahoe, lit by yellow streetlights. The lot was empty. There'd be no more tables and tents until next summer.

Then Paco dozed off again.

Awoke just now. Afraid.

It was still dark. The dashboard glow silhouetted Cassie, Paco's foster mom, up in the driver's seat. She turned the wheel fast to the left, then jerked it to the right. The van bounced on uneven ground. She braked hard, came to a quick stop, swore.

Cassie never swore.

Paco lifted his head. "Cassie?" he called out.

"Stay quiet, honey," she said in a harsh whisper. "And stay down. Don't let them see you!"

She punched in the headlight switch and turned off the engine, leaving the key in the ignition.

"I mean it, Paco," she whispered. "Stay where you are." She opened the door and got out, slamming it behind her.

Paco sat up, his sleeping bag gathered around his chest. He rolled onto his knees and rose up just enough to peek out the van windows.

Off to the side of the van was a rocky cliff where two flat walls of rock stood at an angle that formed a corner. To Paco, it looked as if Cassie had parked inside a big box. Closer to the cliff and facing the same direction as the van, there was a big pickup truck with a topper. Its lights shone on the vertical rock. Both of the pickup's doors were open. Between the truck and the van, two men stood near the driver's door. They were huge. Like in a comic book. Facing them, her face lit by the reflected headlights, was Paco's foster mom.

One man was pointing his finger at Cassie. His hand moved up and down like he was pounding a hammer right in front of her face. His finger almost touched her nose. He shouted, but Paco couldn't make out the words.

He couldn't quite see her face, but Paco could tell that she was frightened by the way she flinched. She gestured with both of her hands out, palms up, pleading.

The man slapped her face!

Paco slid out of his sleeping bag. He could run over and punch the man. Kick him. Maybe he could make the man stop.

Cassie had told Paco not to let them see him. But they were hurting her. Time to break her rules.

Paco reached for the side door, then had a thought.

Cassie's purse was still between the front seats. He reached into it and pulled out her cell phone. He couldn't call 911. She'd made that very clear. She didn't have the right papers for Paco. She said that they lived under the radar. She told Paco that any contact with the government could get him sent back to Mexico.

But he could call that man she'd talked about, the private cop. Paco looked back out the window.

Again, the man struck his foster mom! Harder.

She stumbled back.

Paco nearly cried out. He put the phone in his pocket. There wasn't time to call now. He had to go help her.

He would run up from behind. Surprise them.

Paco reached up and slid the inside light switch to full-off, then opened the side door quietly, and stepped out. The night air was very cold. Mountain air.

Paco slowly shut the van slider. He ran silently through the dark, over to the cliff, and came up behind the pickup.

Paco looked out from behind the truck.

One of the men pulled out a gun! There was a crackling sound. A blue light.

Cassie fell. Her scream ripped through the night.

Paco ducked back behind the pickup. What could he do against a gun? He couldn't breathe, he was so terrified.

Paco looked out again. The man was still outside of the headlight beams. He lowered the gun to Cassie and fired again, another blue flash in the night.

Paco stared as Cassie writhed and jerked on the ground.

One of the men turned back to the pickup.

Paco jumped back behind the pickup's tailgate.

They might have seen him!

He had to run. One side was the cliff. On the other side, the van and the dark forest. If Paco ran to the van or the woods, the men would see him. Paco was a fast runner. But he knew the men would shoot him.

He crouched down in the dark. Waiting. With Cassie dead, they'd drive away. Never see him crouching behind the pickup.

"I'll check her van," said one of the men. "Maybe the kid is hiding in there. You take care of the woman."

Paco looked at the van and realized that when the man walked over to it, he'd be able to see Paco behind their pickup. Paco was trapped against the cliff. There was no escape.

He climbed up on the rear bumper of the pickup. Turned the latch on the topper gate. It swung up and open.

Paco stepped over the tailgate into the pickup bed, careful not to make a sound. He pulled the topper gate shut behind him. He looked out through the smoked windows of the topper. Saw movement. A flashlight beam. The dark windows of the pickup topper made the light look dim yellow.

The man looked through the van, came back to the pickup, and stayed nearby waiting for the other man to return.

Paco waited a long time, maybe fifteen minutes or more. He cried silent tears, one hand clamped over his mouth so they couldn't hear his whimpers, the other wrapped around his body, trying to clamp down on his violent shivers.

The second man came back. Paco could hear him panting. The two men said something, mumbled words.

One got in the van and started the engine. The other got in the pickup. It rocked as the man slammed the door. The engine started. The van drove away. The pickup followed with Paco hiding in the pickup's bed.

Terrified, Paco had no idea of how far or where they had gone when the pickup stopped, the passenger door opened, the pickup rocked again. The door shut and the pickup raced off with Paco still hiding inside the topper.

ONE

"HELP ME!"
      The voice on my phone was young. Terrified. A boy, I thought. Frightened to the point that his voice trembled.

I'd gotten up before dawn to do some bookkeeping and get some bills into the mail before heading down the mountain to meet Street Casey. She'd been to a bug conference at Sac State, and their closing dinner went late the previous evening. So Street stayed overnight at the Hyatt. I decided to drive down and join her for a nice breakfast and then take her to visit the Crocker Art Museum to see their new modern addition.

I'd just poured my second cup of coffee and was writing out my third check when the phone jangled on the kitchen counter. I looked at the clock as I answered the phone. 6:30 a.m.

"Owen McKenna."

When the boy cried out for help, I said, "Who is this?"

"Paco."

"What's wrong, Paco?"

"Come get me!" The boy's voice was a shouted whisper, taut with fear. Behind Paco's voice was background noise, a dull roar that sounded like machinery. Or a windstorm.

"Where are you?"

"I don't know. In a pickup. In the back. I opened the back door and climbed inside."

"The pickup has a topper?" I said. "Can you climb back out? Or is the topper gate locked?"

"It's not locked. But the pickup is going fast."

"If you go to the front of the pickup bed and pound on the wall, the driver might be able to hear you. If he hears you pound, he'll stop."

"I don't want them to hear me. They'll kill me."

"Why do you think that?"

"They shot Cassie."

"Who's Cassie?"

"My foster mom."

My heart made a heavy beat.

"Is there a window? Can you see outside? What do you see?"

"The windows are dark. I can't see anything." His voice quivered.

"Is the hatch unlocked? You could jump out when they stop. Jump out and run away."

"We're going faster."

"Paco, what is your last name?"

"Paco Ipar."

"Paco, I want you to hold on while I see if I can find out where you are. Give me a minute. Don't hang up!" I set the phone on the counter.

I pulled open the front door of my cabin and ran outside into the cold, rainy, dark November morning. My Harlequin Great Dane Spot bounded at my side. I jerked open the door of my Jeep. The interior light doesn't work, so I reached in and felt along the top of the dash. Found the cell. Raced back, flipping it open as I ran back into the light of my cabin.

Once in the door, I hit the button to turn the phone on. The keypad lit up and the phone began the slow process of coming alive.

I grabbed the other phone off the counter. "Are you still there, Paco?"

"Yeah." His voice was meeker. More fear. It sounded like he was crying.

"Good. Don't go away. Don't hang up. I'm getting help. I'll be right back."

The cell phone finished booting up. I dialed Diamond Martinez.

He answered.

"Sergeant, I've got a kid on my land line. Paco Ipar. Says he's hiding in the back of a pickup that is currently in motion. He's using a cell phone. Says the men driving the pickup shot his foster mom."

"You believe him?" Diamond said.

"Maybe. Where are we with tracing cell phones? Cell towers, or GPS, or whatever."

"In the movies, good. But in real life, when time is critical? Not good. We can skip the court order requirement with emergencies. But they still need three cell towers to pick up the signal before they can triangulate it. As for GPS, the satellite connections are often blocked by the mountains."

"You're saying you can't trace the kid who called my land line and then get his location off his cell phone's GPS," I said.

"Sí. Not soon, anyway. The best thing is to get as much information from the caller as possible."

"I'm going to put my cell phone close to my land line earpiece so you can hear this kid," I said to Diamond. I held the two phones together and spoke. "Are you still there, Paco?"

"Yeah."

"Paco, what is your cell phone number?"

"I don't know! It's Cassie's phone."

"Paco, how old are you?"

"Ten."

"Where do you live?"

The boy was silent for a moment. The roar of wind and road in the background was like pressure over the phone. I felt the tension of fear, the strain of the boy's terror.

"I live on a farm," he said. "In the valley."

"What is the closest town?"

"Stockton. We live an hour away."

"Which direction is your farm from Stockton?"

"I don't know."

"Is there a smaller town?"

"Sort of. Mostly, there's just farms."

"Is the pickup you're in near your farm?"

"No. It's in the mountains. There were tall trees. And it's cold. Not like where we live."

"What school do you go to?" I asked.

"The elementary school."

"What's the name of the school?"

"Aggie's Green."

"Aggie's Green?" I repeated to make sure I had it correct.

"Yeah."

"Where's the school?"

"Over by McDonald's. A long way. I ride the bus."

"How did you know to call me?" I asked.

"I looked in Cassie's phone. She said I'm supposed to call you if something happens. She says we can't ever call the cops. I don't want to go to Mexico."

"Paco, you called my land line. If something happens, I want you to be able to call me back on my cell phone. Does Cassie's phone have my cell number?"

"I'll look." Paco didn't speak for a moment. "I don't think so. It just has your name and one number," he said. "The one I called."

"Let me give you my cell. Can you memorize it? Or write it down somehow?"

"I can put it in her phone."

I gave him the number in segments. Area code. Prefix. Last four. I repeated it three times. "Call my cell, first, okay? I'll be out on the road, looking for you."

"Okay," he said. His tone didn't give me confidence that he'd gotten it correct. But he was too scared to project confidence about anything. I hoped that he was like most kids and that working with electronics was second nature for him.

"Do you know where you were when your foster mom was shot?" I asked.

"No. I was asleep when Cassie drove. Then I woke up when she stopped. Someplace near Tahoe, I think."

"What makes you think that?"

"When I woke up once I saw the farmers' market."

"Do you know which one? South Lake Tahoe? Or Truckee?"

"South Lake," Paco said.

"Are you sure? There's no farmers' market now," I said.

"I saw the parking lot. We used to sell our tomatoes and

peppers there in the summer."

"Which way were you going when you saw the farmers' market?"

"I don't know."

"What side of the car did you look out to see it?"

"Right side."

"When your foster mom was shot, can you remember seeing anything?"

"No. Just some cliffs."

"Do you know what kind of pickup you are in?"

"No."

"Do you know the color?"

"No. It's dark out. Maybe gray."

"Is the topper gray, too?"

"It's white."

"The man with the gun," I said. "Is he driving?"

"I don't know. Him or the other guy."

"Does the pickup belong to the men?"

"I think so."

"And it's still driving fast?" I asked.

"Yeah."

"What car did your foster mom drive?"

"She drove our van."

"What kind of van is it?"

"Chevy."

"Color?"

"Brown."

"Do you know the year?"

"I don't know. Kinda old. The pickup is slowing down! They'll hear me talking!" His voice radiated terror. The phone went dead.

"Paco? Are you there?"

But he was gone.

TWO

I hung up the land line, and picked up the cell.

"I gave the boy this cell number," I said to Diamond. "I'll call you back on my land line."

I hung up the cell, dialed on my other phone.

"Could you hear what the boy said?" I asked when Diamond answered.

"Missed some words. But I heard enough to know that the boy didn't give us much to go on."

I thought about the phone conversation. "Paco said that the South Lake Tahoe farmers' market parking lot was out the right side of their van, which means they were heading northeast as they went through town. Sounds like they may have crossed the state line into Nevada and Douglas County."

"Making it my jurisdiction," Diamond said. He was a sergeant with the Douglas County Sheriff's Office.

"Maybe. When I asked the boy if he knew where his foster mom was shot, he said no. But he knows the area well enough to recognize the farmers' market in the dark."

"When he had just awakened," Diamond said.

"Yeah. Then he fell asleep again, which makes me think that they ended up some distance away from the lights of South Lake Tahoe."

"Like these guys met the foster mom in a deserted spot," Diamond said. "She could still be alive. If only we had an idea of where to search. But without a make and model, or a plate number, we're out of luck. We can't put out an Amber Alert unless we have enough information to meet the criteria. We can't even prove that the boy has been kidnapped, whether intended or not."

Diamond paused, then said, "Maybe I can get something generic up on the signs. Dark pickup. Light topper. Wanted for questioning."

"But the men don't know he's in the pickup," I said. "The sign shouldn't say anything about a missing child, otherwise it will tell them that the kid is a stowaway in their pickup."

"Good point. I'll hold off for now. I'll contact the other county sheriffs. You want to call SLTPD? Tell Mallory about it?"

"I could," I said.

"That a problem?"

"You would probably get a better reception with the commander than I would. Even though it's been over a year since that no-knock entry his boys made on my faulty information, Mallory and I are still on eggshells around each other."

"Good time to reconnect," Diamond said. He started to say something else, hesitated, then spoke again. "We should consider that the boy was maybe still sleepy when he called you."

"Like he had a bad dream and his story may not be reliable?" I said. "Could be he had a nightmare about his mama getting shot. But he sounded lucid. I'm willing to bet that those men fired a gun, that the boy is in the pickup as described. Of course, the details of a crime are always different in reality from what is initially reported, but the kid's trauma is real. I think he told the truth as he knows it."

Diamond made a slurping noise on the phone. Coffee, probably. "I agree," he said. "Unfortunately, there's a lot of dark pickups out there with light-colored toppers. Not going to be easy."

"Right. But if we see one, we could follow it and look in the back when it stops."

"Hard for me without a warrant. Not so hard for you, a nonofficial law guy." Diamond said. "But call me, you find a pickup that matches the description. Always good to save a kid, warrant or not."

"You open the back of a pickup," I said, "and you find and save a kid, no one's going to worry much about warrants."

"Sí," Diamond said. "Let me know if you see or hear anything."

We hung up.

Because I'd told the boy to call my cell first, I used my landline phone to call Street on her cell.

"Learn anything new about bugs?" I said when she answered.

"Nothing I can't tell you over brunch at the bistro," she said. "But the fact that you're calling makes me think you can't make it."

"Right." I told her about the kid named Paco, supposedly trapped in the back of the truck of men who shot his foster mother.

"My God, Owen! That's horrible! What are you going to do?"

"I don't know. Wait and be ready in case he calls again."

Street was silent for a moment. "What can I do to help? I could come up and help organize a search."

"Thanks, but Diamond is going to alert the other sheriff's offices. Eventually, every cop in the area will be looking for the pickup. We have no information about where to look. So another searcher probably wouldn't make any difference." I paused. "I'm sorry that this happened."

"Owen, you can see me anytime. You wait on this kid. Let me know whatever happens. I'll be leaving shortly. I heard what I came for, and without you coming for brunch, I'll head home. If you can use any help, call me at my lab. I'll be there in a couple of hours."

"Okay. Thanks."

We said goodbye and hung up.

THREE

Ifelt a terrible sense of helplessness when I hung up the phone. I believed the situation was serious. But I was powerless to do anything about it.

I called Commander Mallory of the SLTPD.

"Mallory," he said when he came on the line.

"McKenna here. Wondering if you had any reports of gunshots this morning."

"Not that I know of. Why?"

"Got a situation you should know about." I told him about the phone call from Paco and how the boy's foster mother had told him to call me if anything bad happened.

"Let me see if I've got this straight. You're saying that there may have been a murder or attempted murder of a woman whose identity we don't know. You have no idea of where the crime took place. The woman's foster kid is claiming to be in the back of a pickup, and he's saying that the driver or drivers murdered his foster mom. And you have no idea where the pickup is."

"Yeah," I said.

"But it's not a kidnapping," he said, "because the kid voluntarily got in the back of the pickup, and the men don't even know he's there."

"If the men in the truck knew the kid was in back, they would probably tie him in place. Then it would be a kidnapping."

Mallory paused. I heard the pop and hiss of one of his everpresent Cokes. "And this is all based on what the kid said. A kid you've never met. You can't vouch for his credibility. And you have no evidence. You don't know where the kid lives. The kid doesn't even know where he lives. You don't know the foster mother's last name."

"Correct."

"How old is this kid?"

"He said he was ten."

"Ah," Mallory said in that tone that just misses condescending. "The perfect age for telling the truth."

"He sounded pretty stressed," I said. "I'm inclined to think he's telling the truth."

"I should get the troops ready on your inclination? I've been burned doing that before."

"Just doing my duty as a citizen. Your call on how you respond."

As we said goodbye, I knew that Mallory would in fact let his troops know about the possibility of a kid in crisis somewhere near South Lake Tahoe.

I next called Special Agent Ramos who runs the FBI's Resident Agency in Tahoe. I told him the same thing I told Mallory. Like Mallory, Ramos was skeptical, but also, like Mallory, he took all possibilities seriously. Murder, kidnapping, and the possibility that men had taken a kid across state lines, were all FBI territory. Ramos said to stay in touch.

I pulled out my topo maps of the Tahoe Basin and started with the farmers' market location in the middle of South Lake Tahoe. Moving my finger northeast from there, I imagined the path that Paco's foster mom may have driven. Paco had said that the pickup was parked near some cliffs. I looked for places where the topo lines were stacked close to one another, which would indicate very steep, rocky areas.

The topo map showed multiple rocky projections that might look like cliffs to a Central Valley boy. Some were in areas inaccessible to a van, but I found lots of accessible places, far too many for the map to be useful. And even if I went to the right cliff, I might never know it unless I found the woman's body or the van.

I called Diamond again.

"The boy call?" he asked when he answered.

"No. Wondering if you heard anything or had luck with the vehicle."

"There's a lot of dark pickups out there with light-colored toppers," Diamond said. As he said it, my cell started ringing.

I shouted. "My cell is ringing." I picked up the cell and held it next to my land line phone so Diamond could hear.

"Hello?"

"It's me. Paco."

FOUR

"Paco, where are you?"

"I don't know! In the forest." His breath was short. Like he was gasping for air. I realized that he was running.

"Where was the pickup when you climbed out?"

"On the side of a road." The boy was panting. "I jumped out and called you." He was panicked. "But they saw me. They're chasing me."

"Two men?"

"Yeah." Pant. Gasping pant.

"What can you see?" I said.

"Nothing. Just trees!"

"Keep looking," I said. "If you give me a landmark, I can come get you."

"They're getting closer!" A whispered yell. A desperate plea. The boy was grunting with effort.

"Paco, keep running. Don't give up." I wanted to say something that would give him confidence. "Men can't run through the forest like boys. If you dodge around trees and jump over boulders and logs, they can't catch you! You can get away! Dodge through the forest!"

I wanted it to be true, but the image of two men chasing a young boy choked off my air, squeezed my heart and lungs.

"Don't talk, Paco, just run!"

Paco's short frantic breaths became low volume as if he was no longer holding the phone to his head. I heard a throbbing wind noise.

Although the sound was soft, it came in a fast, rhythmic pulsing. I visualized him holding the phone in his hand as he sprinted, arms pumping. I didn't dare call to him or ask a question. I needed to wait and give him a chance to do what boys are often great at, running and evading and hiding. If he could hold onto the phone, if the battery still had power, if he could get away for a moment...

Maybe he could tell me something that would give me a clue about where to find him. I spoke into my land line. "Diamond, I'm going to hang this up and take my cell in my Jeep. I want to be on the road when Paco sees any landmark. I'll call you when I can." I hung up.

I trotted to the front door and opened it. Spot was already up, sensing my stress. He came outside with me into the rain. I let him into the back of the Jeep, got in the front, and started it.

The private drive I share with my upscale neighbors is almost always deserted because my neighbors are almost always in Los Angeles or New York or Miami or Frankfurt or Rio. I drove fast, but slowed hard before the curves so I wouldn't spin out on the rain-slick asphalt. I was down the mountain and on the highway in a few minutes. Paco could be in any direction. I turned south for no reason other than that Paco's only known location was at the South Lake Tahoe farmers' market.

I drove fast in spite of having no destination. I held the phone to my ear and listened to the hyperventilation of a terrified boy.

Paco's huffing got louder and quickened as he became exhausted. The pumping wind sound sped up. It sounded like he was running even faster then before.

The boy screamed. Loud enough to rip my eardrum.

I jerked with adrenaline.

"Paco, are you there?!"

I heard Paco crying. I couldn't tell if his pain was physical or psychological.

"Paco?"

"I fell!"

"Get up, Paco! Keep running!

I heard faint, high-pitched cries. The rhythmic pumping was back. He was still alive. Still running.

"Do you see anything now? Any building?"

His grunting was extreme, each exhalation marked with a

desperate cry.

I wanted him to concentrate on running. But I couldn't get to him until I knew where he was.

"Let me know the moment you see anything," I said. Maybe he heard me. Maybe not.

I had witnessed fear before. But a terrified child on the other end of the phone line was a much higher level of gut-wrenching emotion.

Another scream. Louder than before.

"Paco! Are you okay?" Adrenaline had my nerves burning as if from electricity.

I heard a heavy, whimpering grunt, a percussive exhalation.

"Paco, can you hear me? Are you okay?"

Maybe he was wounded and had collapsed. More sounds came. Exertion, as if Paco had climbed over something and then jumped to the ground.

The plastic of my phone made a cracking sound. I realized I was squeezing it like a vice.

I heard him moving. Still panting. Still alive. His cries were continuous. If I kept focusing him on looking for landmarks, maybe that would help control his fear.

Or my fear.

He hadn't spoken after the last scream. I wanted him to say something.

"Paco, do you see anything, yet?"

"I see the bubble cars." Paco's voice was wheezing.

"What are bubble cars?" Maybe I heard him wrong.

"Bubble cars. Gray ones." His panting was so loud I could barely understand him. "On the sky ride," he said.

The Heavenly Ski Resort gondola.

I stomped on the gas. I was going south toward Round Hill. My speed climbed to 60, then 65. I let up to take a curve. Then I came to the hill going down and the long straight before the stoplight.

Puffing, sucking air, he said, "The bubble cars are in the woods."

"Paco, run to the gondola. The bubble cars. Stay in the trees for cover, but follow the cars down the mountain, not up. Do you understand? Go down the mountain. You will come to a road. I'm going there now. I'll look for you."

I sped up to 70, slowed as I went past Kingsbury Grade. At the next intersection, I turned left to take the back road around Mont Bleu and Harrah's.

As the gondola comes down the mountain, the first street that it soars over is the one that runs behind the casino hotels. Just past Harrah's was the gondola. I skidded to a stop at Heavenly Village Way, turned left, and rushed into the new Van Sickle Bi-State Park.

I drove up to the lot, parked, and jumped out. I let Spot out of the back and sprinted toward the mountain.

We ran up the lift line, under the gondola.

The lift maintenance workers keep the lift line free of major trees, but it was not an easy run. There was a trail in places, but in other places nothing but boulders and impenetrable Manzanita bushes.

I wanted to call 911 and get patrol units to the scene, but I didn't dare hang up on Paco.

"Paco!" I shouted into my phone. "I'm at the road below the gondola. I'm running up the mountain. Stay in the trees." But my phone was silent. I looked at the readout. I had battery power, but no connection. Maybe Paco's phone had gone out of range. Or he could be out of battery.

Maybe the men had caught him.

As I ran up the gondola line, I scanned the trees looking for any movement that could be Paco or his pursuers. I saw nothing except Spot trotting in front of me.

The gondola was stopped for fall maintenance, and the cabins, Paco's bubble cars, hung motionless and silent in the air above me. I stopped, cupped my ears, and listened for any sound that could have been Paco up the mountain. There was no noise except for Spot's panting.

A snapping sound came from up in the distant trees. Not a gunshot. More like a breaking branch.

Spot stopped and stared, eyes and ears focused.

I stared at the open line where the trees had been cleared. It was a wide, straight path a couple of miles in length and rising 3000 feet in elevation. But the rain had increased, and the dark clouds had lowered so that the gondola disappeared into the gray blanket just a third of the way up the mountain. There was nothing to see but green pine needles and the dark umber of wet tree trunks and gray boulders and gray sky.

Then a splash of blue color flashed from one tree to another, over logs, around boulders, just to the side of the lift line. The blue grew into a jacket on a small boy. He came down the mountain like a running back down the field, stiff-arming boulders and logs as he vaulted them, dodging trees, his feet churning as if to run through and over anything that would stop him.

I ran toward him.

I didn't call out. I didn't want him to get a false sense of security and come out into the open line where he would be an easy target. I saw no pursuers. But they might still be out there.

As I got closer, I realized that Spot might frighten him, so I called him to my side and held his collar as we ran.

When Paco was close enough that we might startle and scare the boy, I called out.

"Paco, it's me, Owen McKenna!"

He kept running toward us, over rocks, around bushes. He reached out and grabbed the trunk of a sapling as he went past it. He used it to swing himself around the tree and off in a new direction.

As his face came into focus, I saw the unmistakable fear, the stretched grimace of terror.

"Paco, it's me," I said again as he approached. "It's okay. You're safe now."

But he blew on past us, feet churning, unthinking panic driving his flight.

"Paco!" I lunged, grabbed his arm. Pulled him to a stop. "It's okay. You're okay."

The boy's eyes were wide, the terror obvious. Blood from a scrape ran down his brown cheek. He struggled to pull away from me, straining to look back up the mountain, panicked whimpers coming from his throat.

I pulled him to me. He was a tiny kid, hard and wiry and soaked wet with rain. His head barely came up to my navel. I knelt and held him, forcibly quieting him.

His panting breaths caught, and he began to cry. In a half-minute he was sobbing and clutching at the front of my shirt. I held him until he calmed a bit. Then I stood and took his hand. His hand was small and sweaty, his skin as rough and callused and scratchy as that of any adult laborer.

We trotted into the trees and hurried the rest of the way down the mountain, staying in cover. I held Paco's hand. Spot walked behind Paco, sniffing him.

Periodically, I glanced behind us, checking the woods for movement or sound, but saw nothing.

A minute later we were at the Jeep. I thought about the men back in the trees, maybe watching with binoculars. I thought it was best to not indicate that the Jeep was mine.

So we walked on past, moving fast, staying in the trees. When we got down to the road, we darted behind buildings and followed a weaving path toward the shops and the gondola's base station in Heavenly Village.

FIVE

I watched Paco as we walked. He frowned, deep and intense. He kept jerking and twisting to look back behind us, his fear so great that he didn't seem to notice the giant dog sniffing him.

While we walked, I called Diamond, told him I'd found the boy, asked him to inform other law enforcement. I told him I'd call back when I knew more, and I hung up.

I worried about Paco having some kind of emotional meltdown. He'd witnessed the shooting of his foster mother. He'd been trapped in a pickup and chased by men with guns. How much trauma could a kid take? I expected some serious fallout as he coped with the enormity of what had happened. But he just did a fast walking trot, his body stiff with tension, his teeth clenched, his eyes twitching.

I tried to gauge when the big reaction would come, thinking about how to keep him distracted for a while longer. Spot was the most obvious vehicle for occupying a child with other thoughts. Spot had walked behind and next to Paco. After a hundred yards, Paco still hadn't acknowledged him. As we got farther from the men who chased him, Paco glanced less behind him and more often at the dog who was the same height as he was and three times as heavy.

At the gondola base station, we stopped.

"Paco, you should meet my dog." I turned the boy to face Spot.

Spot wagged, curious about the boy. Spot had rarely seen me hold a young child's hand.

"Paco, meet Spot. Spot, meet Paco."

Spot stuck his nose in Paco's face. Paco jerked back and used his arm to wipe off his face.

I grabbed Spot's collar and held him in position. "Spot is friendly. You can pet him. You can even ride him."

Paco gave me a quick glance, then looked over toward the shops that were between us and the mountain. His eyes flicked around, taking in the milling people, looking at the corners of buildings as if he expected men to jump out.

I wanted to get Paco to change his focus.

"Go ahead and pet him," I said, gesturing toward Spot.

Paco put his hand behind his back as if for safety. He telegraphed discomfort, did a little rocking motion.

I knew that a connection with a dog could help, so I pressed. "He's waiting for you to pet him," I said.

Paco looked at me. "I'm afraid..." he paused.

"You don't need to be afraid," I said. "Spot is very friendly."

"No. I'm afraid I'm going to wet my pants."

This was new territory for me. I took a moment to think. Ten-year-old kids usually have pretty good control, but this boy may have been holding it since they left Stockton nine hours before.

"Okay, Paco. Just hold it a bit longer and we'll go into a store."

I told Spot to stay, and we went inside a sports clothing shop.

"Can I help you," the purple-haired clerk said, her tone wooden.

"We need to use your restroom, please."

"We don't have public restrooms."

I grinned at her. "Perhaps you'd like to make an exception to your rule, so we don't damage your carpet."

She looked at Paco who was doing the rocking motion again, his hand at his crotch.

"Left rear corner of the store," she said, a touch of alarm in her voice.

"Thank you."

We found the door behind a rack of ski jackets. Paco looked

at me. I wasn't sure what it meant.

"You, ah, don't need my help, right?" I said to Paco.

He frowned. "I'm ten years old," he said.

"Just checking," I said.

When Paco came out, he looked relieved but still scared. He rotated, looking around the store. I thanked the clerk, and we went outside.

Spot was waiting. "He's still waiting for your pet," I said.

Paco looked up toward the mountain and over at the other buildings, then reached out his hand, holding it high. Spot lifted his head to sniff it. Paco raised it higher. Spot lowered his head to sniff Paco's chin. Paco stepped back. I reached for Spot's collar.

Paco slowly lowered his hand to Spot's head.

The moment his hand touched, Spot launched into a pant. It looked like Spot was smiling.

"Ready to go?" I said, thinking that I had to get Paco to a place where I could ask him questions.

"Where?" Paco said. He looked worried.

I remembered that Cassie had told Paco that they couldn't go to the police. "My cabin. I can make some calls, get you back home."

"I don't want to go to a cabin."

"A cabin is the same as a small house. It's where I live."

He took a step back from me. "Cassie said not to go with a strange man."

"Okay, good rule. Tell you what. We'll go to my girlfriend's lab." I pulled out my cell phone to call Street.

"What's a lab?" He sounded suspicious. His frown deepened. I was going to have to think before I spoke.

"Lab is short for laboratory. My girlfriend is an entomologist. That means she studies bugs. The lab is where she works."

"I don't want to go there. I don't like bugs."

"I don't like them, either. Don't worry, they're all in containers. You don't even have to come inside if you don't want to. You can stay outside with Spot."

I dialed. Street answered.

"Hi sweetheart," I said. "I found the boy."

"That's fantastic. Is he okay?"

"Seems like it. Back in town, yet?"

"Just got up a little bit ago."

"I need your help if you can spare a few minutes," I said.

"Sure, what?"

I moved a few steps away from Paco, turned a little so he couldn't hear me. "I have a situation. I don't know what to do with him. I was going to take him home, make some calls, see if I can figure out where to take him. But he doesn't want to go. You could probably help with this."

"And you're calling me because..."

"Mostly because you're a woman. And he's a kid. You'd be better at this."

"You think women can work some kind of female magic stuff with kids?"

"Yeah. That's exactly what I think and need. Female magic stuff. I don't want to call Glennie. She would turn it into a news story."

"You know I'm not a normal woman," she said. "No kids. Strange job. No access to the typical village of support."

"Still a woman."

"Okay, bring him here."

"Thanks. We'll be there in a few minutes." I hung up.

I turned to Paco. "C'mon," I said. I pointed to Spot. "Bring Spot."

The kid looked at me like I was nuts.

I pointed. "Take his collar. He'll walk next to you."

Paco didn't move.

I walked over, took Paco's left hand, lifted it up and put his fingers around Spot's collar. "He heels. On your left side."

Paco looked down to his left. "He has paws, not heels."

"Sorry. I meant that he likes to walk on your left side. Like this." I reached and held Paco's hand as he held Spot's collar. We walked. Spot heeled. I let go. Paco and Spot kept walking, Paco very stiff.

I knew it would be good for Paco to walk with Spot. But he kept frowning.

We walked to the main boulevard. I kept watch around us. No big men caught my attention.

We went into one of the shops. The counter clerk stared at Spot, clearly amazed at his size.

"This is the boy's service dog," I said to the clerk.

The counter clerk kept staring but didn't speak.

I spoke to Paco, louder, so that the clerk could hear me.

"I'm going to leave you and Spot here for a few minutes while I fetch my Jeep. I'll pull up outside. Don't let go of Spot for anything. And don't leave this store until you see me. Spot will protect you."

Paco's trauma was still obvious on his face.

"Did you hear me? You'll stay here until I come back in a few minutes?"

Paco slowly nodded.

I went out and took a different route through the village, into the parking garage and out the back side, found a little-used path that got me behind the commercial district and into the forest.

I got into the Jeep, drove down to Lake Tahoe Blvd., and pulled over in the bus-stop lane. I ran to the store and brought Paco and Spot out to the Jeep. I let Spot into the back seat, put Paco in the passenger seat, and went around and got into the driver's seat. I put on my belt, started the engine. Paco didn't move except for shivering from being wet. I turned the heater up high.

"You should put on your seat belt," I said.

Paco shook his head. "Cassie says they're dangerous."

"They protect you if you get in a collision," I said.

"They trap you in a collision." Paco's manner was set. No point in arguing.

I drove over to Street's lab. Let Spot out. Opened Paco's door. He stayed in the seat. Spot came up and sniffed Paco.

"I'm not going in a lab," he said.

I counted to five. "Okay. Stay here for a minute and pet Spot."

I left Spot with Paco and went inside.

Street looked up. "Hi, sweetie." She raised up on tiptoes and kissed me. "Where's the boy?"

"He won't come in. He's suspicious. He won't go to my cabin, either. He was obviously taught not to trust strange men."

"Smart," Street said. "But they shouldn't stop at the strange ones. The ones kids know best are often the worst. Women, too. I'll go talk to him." She put on her rain jacket and went outside.

I followed her, but stayed back as she walked up to the Jeep.

Street stood in front of Paco's open door, her hand resting on Spot's back. Casual. Friendly. I'm in way over my head when it comes to kids, but it seemed easy for her.

I hung back by her lab door, under the overhang, waiting. A Douglas squirrel started chirping at me from up in the Jeffrey pine above me. He came down the trunk in jerks and starts, his chirps turning to screams as I refused to move. Spot swiveled his head to look, then turned back. Street was still standing in the rain, talking to Paco. She pulled a tissue from her pocket, touched it to the wet windshield to moisten it and wiped the blood from the scrape on Paco's cheek.

The squirrel advanced on me, upping his volume. I was so impertinent for invading his territory. When he was six feet above my head, I couldn't take the noise anymore.

"Okay, you win," I said. I moved away and sat on a boulder under the leaky rain cover of another tree.

The squirrel came down, looked at Spot, then started advancing across the ground toward me, screaming louder than before.

Eventually, Spot couldn't stand it, either. He trotted over. The squirrel jumped back up onto the tree trunk, went around the back side, screamed some more.

Street finally came over. "Paco understands that he can go with you, that you're safe."

"All because you said so and you're a woman," I said.

"All because."

"I don't know how long it will take to find out where he's from," I said. "I don't suppose you would take care of him in the meantime?"

"Why me?"

"Well," I said, "the woman thing, I guess."

"But if I took him, then you wouldn't bond with him."

"Why do I need to bond with him?"

"Because it would be good for you," Street said.

"For me?"

"Yeah. I also found out he's starving. I told him you would get him a burger."

"No doubt thinking that lunch would be a good bonding exercise," I said.

"Partly, yes. And you need to get him warm and dry. I tried to give him my jacket, but he wouldn't take it."

"What about the trauma of the shooting he saw? How should I handle that?"

"Don't think about handling it. Just let it be. He'll talk about it eventually. You'll answer his questions. I mentioned it, and he was okay with that. I think that he wasn't especially close to his foster mother. He's only lived with her for a year and a half. So it hasn't hit him as hard as it might have. It's still going to be very difficult for him. But he'll get through it with your help."

"My help? This is something for his family to help him through."

"Well, I didn't get his entire history," Street said. "But it sounds like he has no family."

"Friends, then."

Street nodded. "Yes, his friends are going to be critical over the next few weeks. But until you get him back to his friends, it's you who are critically important."

"Not my strong suit," I said.

"Stop thinking like that. Now go. Eat. The rest will come." Street gave me another kiss, and went back into her lab.

SIX

I turned toward Paco. He was still sitting in the Jeep, door open, probably shivering again. From a distance I could see deep vertical creases on his forehead and the bridge of his nose. If the kid frowned any harder, he'd get stretch marks on his scalp and temples.

Having seen his foster mother shot, he was doing an amazing job of being tough.

I let Spot back into the Jeep, and we drove over to the Riva Grill at the Ski Run Marina. I told Spot to be good, and Paco and I walked into the restaurant.

They gave us a table by the window.

Sitting close to the boy in the enclosed space I smelled the same rich odor that I'd noticed inside the store where he'd used the restroom. It was the smell of un-showered boy, bathed in sweat from sprinting a long distance, and shot through with terror from being chased by armed killers.

"Hey, Paco, let's go get washed up."

"Why?"

"Because you've got even more dirt on your hands than I do."

He held up his hands and looked at them. The deep veining of dirt in his skin looked permanent. He shrugged, pushed back his chair.

In the restroom, Paco scrubbed with vigor, but it didn't appear to make much difference. His hands still looked like they had been dipped in black paint a few days before.

Back at the table, Paco stared at the other diners, looking from one to the next. I realized that he was studying their meals. He reminded me vaguely of a hungry coyote that had been hanging around my cabin, wiry thin, and sufficiently motivated to steal food off my barbecue if I went inside for more than a minute or two.

Paco turned away from the other diners and looked down at the table. He touched a finger to the table cloth, then rubbed the cloth napkin.

A waiter came and handed us menus.

Paco held his, but didn't look at it.

"What can I have?" he said.

"Whatever you want."

"I can order anything?"

"Yeah," I said, wondering if it was a stupid thing to say. I pointed on the menu. "They have an entire lunch section."

He glanced down at the menu. "Can you read it to me?"

"You don't read?" The surprise in my voice was obvious.

"Not really. I'm dumb." He set the menu down and stared at the table.

"Paco," I said, fumbling, realizing I'd made a mistake, "if you can't read, that doesn't mean you're dumb. It just means that you haven't learned, yet."

"All the other kids read."

"Maybe they had better teachers," I said.

"We had the same teachers. I'm just dumb. I can't do anything."

I was striking out. "You're not dumb. And you can do lots."

"Like what?"

"Well, for one thing you do an incredible dodge."

"What's that?"

"When you came running down the mountain. You dodged around trees and boulders. You jumped over logs. It was impressive. Even though those men could probably run faster than you, no way could they have caught you."

Paco looked at me. "I still can't read."

"Okay, let's skip the menu." I set mine down next to his. "What is your favorite meal?"

"Cheeseburgers."

"Then let's order a cheeseburger."

"At McDonald's, Cassie only lets me have one little cheeseburger. But I can eat four." Paco looked at me, waiting for my reaction.

"Burgers here are four times the size of burgers at McDonald's."

Paco nodded, thinking. "What if I could eat more than one?"

"Maybe start with one. If you're still hungry afterward, you can get another."

The waiter came by. He turned to Paco. "Are you ready to order, sir?"

Paco looked at me, frowning. He said something so soft I couldn't hear.

"What?" I said.

He spoke a little louder, stress in his voice. "Cassie always orders at McDonald's."

"This isn't McDonald's. Besides, you are growing up fast. Time to order your own meal."

Paco gave me a long, hard look. "I get a Big Gulp at 7-Eleven."

"You can get any drink you want."

Paco looked skeptical, like he didn't believe it was true. Then he turned to the waiter and spoke in a soft, tentative voice. "Can I get a cheeseburger with everything on it?"

"Yes, sir, you may," the waiter said. "What would you like to drink?

"I'll have a Big Gulp Coke and a large chocolate shake with whipped cream and cherry. And super-sized fries."

The waiter nodded and turned to me. He was grinning as if he'd heard the world's greatest joke.

"Same for me but hold the Coke, the shake, half the fries, and add a milk."

The waiter left, and we waited. I looked out at the boats in the marina. Paco looked at the food that other people were eating. A woman at the next table got uncomfortable at his stare. She eventually changed chairs so that she sat next to the man she was with instead of across from him. Now Paco couldn't see her eat.

The waiter brought our food. Paco looked at his burger the way a ravenous raptor looks at a rodent. He lifted the bun, shook out a quarter cup of ketchup onto the ketchup and mustard that were already there. I didn't think his mouth was big enough to get around it, but he showed no mercy as he squeezed it down to a manageable height.

It wasn't exactly like watching Spot eat, but it wasn't unlike it, either. Paco had eaten all of his food before I'd gotten especially familiar with mine. He moved his straw in circles to chase the last drop of shake around the bottom of the glass, making a loud slurping noise. The nearby woman turned around and scowled at us. I gave her my best grin.

"You want another burger?" I asked.

Paco shook his head.

I drank some milk.

"Cassie says that milk is for kids."

"True," I said. "I like it, too."

"She says adults can't digest it right."

"Works for me," I said.

"Still not good for you," he said.

"Cassie has lots of opinions, huh?" I said.

Paco shrugged, then yawned. "I'm tired. I want to go to the van so I can take a nap."

"We don't know where to find the van, Paco."

Paco frowned harder.

"Did you get a good look at the men who drove the pickup?" I asked.

Paco shook his head.

"How would you describe them?"

"I don't know."

"Sure you do, if you think about it. Were they tall or short? Big or small? Young or old? Short hair or long hair? Like that."

"They were like superheroes. They had shaved heads. One was a black guy. One was white."

"What do you mean, superheroes?" I asked.

"Jus' superheroes. Like The Hulk. Spider-Man."

"Why do they look like superheroes?"

Paco shook his head. "'Cause they were, like, real big. And muscles." Paco made fists and held his arms bent at his sides in a muscleman pose. "And one had a cape like Batman."

"Did you hear them say anything?"

"I don't know. Jus' stuff. They didn't talk a lot."

"Like superheroes," I said.

"Yeah," Paco said.

"Can you think of any words? Anything specific?"

Paco thought about it. "Yo-pep. One kept saying yo-pep."

"What else did they say?"

"Nothin'."

"What do you think yo-pep means?" I asked.

"I don't know."

"Did yo-pep sound like a place? Or was it something they were looking for?"

"Neither. It was jus', you know, the guy would say, yo-pep."

"Anything else you remember them saying? Take your time."

Paco looked away. "Salt," he finally said.

"Who said yo-pep, the black guy or the white guy?"

"The white guy, I think."

"And the black guy said Salt?"

"Yeah."

"Could be their nicknames. Salt and pepper. When the white guy said yo-pep, was it like 'yo, dude? Like, 'yo, Paco, hi, Paco?"

Paco shrugged. "I don't know. Maybe." He yawned again. "Where will I sleep? My sleeping bag is in the van."

"We'll figure out something. Your foster mom's cell phone," I said. "May I look at it?"

Paco looked worried. He reached up and touched his cheek where Street had wiped blood from a scrape. "A branch poked me in the face, and I dropped it."

"No problem," I said. "When you get chased, you gotta expect to drop stuff."

The waiter came and took our plates. Paco leaned his forearms onto the table, laced his fingers together.

"When you first called me," I said, "you said you don't know the name of the town where you live."

"We live in the country."

"If I drive you home, can you tell me how to go?"

"I know how to get home from McDonald's and the school. But I don't want to go home by myself."

"No, we don't want that," I agreed.

"Who else can you stay with?" I asked.

Paco shook his head.

"Do you have siblings?" I asked.

"What's that?"

"Brothers or sisters?"

"No."

"Who are your friends in school?" I asked.

"José and Rafael."

"Can you stay with them?"

Paco shook his head. "They have big families and little apartments."

"Do you have other relatives?"

He shook his head.

"You mentioned that Cassie talked about staying away from the cops because you could get sent back to Mexico."

Paco looked alarmed.

"If you were born in Mexico, maybe you have relatives there," I said.

"I've never been to Mexico. I don't want to go there."

"Mexico is a great place," I said.

"They speak Mexican."

"Spanish," I said. "Don't you speak Spanish?"

Paco shook his head. "I heard José and Rafael speak it. I don't understand any of it. I'm not smart enough."

"Paco, you need to understand something. What you know depends on what you've spent time learning. It's not about smarts."

He shrugged again.

"Can you ride a skateboard or bicycle?"

He scrunched up his face, suspicious of a sudden, new subject. "'Course."

"So you have good physical ability. It's like dodging. Not everybody can do physical stuff well."

Another shrug.

"Can you remember when you were little and couldn't ride a skateboard or a bicycle?"

"Yeah."

"So you just hadn't applied your physical ability to skateboards and bicycles, yet."

"I was too little," he said.

"Doesn't matter," I said. "You also have mental ability. You just haven't applied your mental ability to learning Spanish or learning to read."

"So?"

"Mental ability is just different words for smarts."

Paco didn't respond other than frowning more.

"Paco, do you know how you came to be a foster child?"

He shook his head.

"Did you ever know your real mother or father?"

"No," Paco said.

"Did anyone ever tell you why you're in the foster program?"

"No."

"The house where you live with Cassie, does she own it?"

"No. She says that owning a house traps you."

"Like seat belts," I said.

Paco nodded. Solemn.

"Does Cassie have a job?"

"Her job is growing tomatoes and peppers. The landlord lets us live there if we grow enough. He gets most of them."

"Does he live nearby?"

"His house is in front of ours."

"Can you live with him?"

"No. He's mean. He hits people when he drinks beer."

"Have you seen him hit somebody?"

Paco nodded. "He hit Rafael once. And he slapped Cassie."

"So you have nowhere to go."

Paco looked out at the lake, his eyes narrow beneath his

frown. He didn't reply.

"Where would you like me to take you?" I said. I was starting to worry.

"I guess I'll have to stay with you."

My worry turned to panic.

SEVEN

When we were in the Jeep, Paco asked, "What will I do at your cabin?" He sounded a little desperate.

"Hang out with Spot?" I said. That wasn't a joke. Spot had rescued more than one person from despair.

Paco went silent. I ran possible housing scenarios for Paco through my mind. I had no long-term solutions and would no doubt have to go to Paco's town in the Central Valley to find them, a town for which I had no name and no location. The temporary housing solutions for Paco mostly involved me, which made my breath short.

"Before we go to my home," I said, "let's see if we can find where you got out of the pickup. We might learn something about those guys who shot your foster mom."

Paco shrugged.

I drove back to Van Sickle Bi-State Park where I'd found Paco, then followed all the roads closest to where the gondola went through the forest. We worked our way up the mountain, exploring the neighborhoods that fronted Heavenly Ski Resort.

At each likely place where the men could have stopped, allowing Paco to escape, I asked Paco if he recognized it.

He said no.

I repeated the process several times, eventually rising up Keller Rd. and then Saddle Rd. where the houses hung on the steep mountainside with unobstructed views across the big lake. We found several possible places where Paco could have run into the forest and made it over to the gondola, but Paco didn't recognize any of them.

I headed back down the mountain and turned north on Lake Tahoe Blvd. We drove through Stateline, then north on 50, up the East Shore through low, swirling clouds. Past Cave Rock, I turned off on the private road that led to my cabin, and we headed up the mountain. I pulled onto my parking-pad driveway. Paco appeared to pay no attention to my excessively small cabin made of big logs, just as he paid no attention to the huge, angular, glass-and-timber-frame vacation homes of my summer-month and Christmas-week neighbors.

I let Spot out, and got all the way to the door before I realized that Paco hadn't come. I went back and opened Paco's door.

"This is my cabin. C'mon in."

He shrugged and got out. The rain had lessened, and the clouds opened up a view across the lake. The mountains were visible on the far side of the water, their tops white with fresh snow. Paco walked to my front door without even noticing the world's greatest view.

Spot lay down on his bed. Paco sat in the rocking chair.

"Why does Spot have an earring?" he asked.

"He got injured, and it made a tiny hole in his ear. So Street got him the earring."

Paco looked at Spot. The faux diamond sparkled, moving slightly with each breath that Spot took.

"You want something to drink?" I said.

He shook his head. His face was blank. He didn't rock the chair. He just stared toward the woodstove, maybe seeing it, maybe not.

I went into my kitchen nook, opened a Sierra Nevada Pale Ale, took a drink.

I sat down across from Paco.

He looked at my beer.

"Don't worry, I won't hit you. I only hit bad guys, and even that is rare and has nothing to do with drinking beer."

Paco didn't respond.

"What is Cassie's last name?" I asked.

"Moreno. But everyone calls her Cassie."

"Do you know her friends?"

He thought about it. "She doesn't have any friends."

"She doesn't like people?"

"She doesn't have time."

"Why?" I asked.

"Too much work. Cassie says that freedom comes with a price."

"What's the freedom?"

"She says working for herself is freedom."

"What's the price?"

"The price is you have to work all the time."

"She works a lot?"

"That's all she does."

"Can you think of anyone I could talk to who knows her well?"

Paco stared into space. "Our clients."

"Are they at the farmers' market?" I asked.

"They used to be. We used to go to a different market every day. South Lake Tahoe, Truckee, Reno."

"Why would you come all the way to Tahoe? Why not just do farmers' markets near Stockton?"

He shrugged. "The people in the mountains like organic tomatoes and peppers."

"It sounds like you help Cassie grow them."

Paco nodded.

"Is that your specialty? Tomatoes and peppers?"

"Yeah. We have the best anywhere. Sungold, Brandywine, Big Beef, Fourth of July, and Better Boys."

I grinned at his obvious pride.

"But our best tomatoes are Cassie's Amazements," he said. "She made them. And I helped."

"You mean, you created a new type? Like a hybrid?"

"Yeah. She says big companies want the secret."

"How did you make them?"

"We get pollen off certain flowers, and we put it on other flowers. Then we grow the seeds."

"So you are scientists in addition to being organic farmers."

Paco made a little nod like it was no big deal.

"And our peppers are Cassie's Vipers," he said.

"What does that mean, Cassie's Vipers?"

"Hottest chili pepper in the world. Over a million Scoville units. Like the Naga Vipers in England. Cassie and me made it. She asked me what we should name it. I said they should be Cassie's Vipers just like Cassie's Amazements."

"Scoville units mean how hot the peppers are?" I asked.

He nodded. "Over a million."

"You said that you used to do farmers' markets. Where do your customers go now?"

"Now we do deliveries."

"Where do you deliver?"

"All over Tahoe. Cassie calls it Field To Fridge. It's our business. Home-delivered produce, seven days a week."

"She works seven days a week?"

Paco looked at me like I was stupid. "That's what I told you."

"What do you do when she's always working?"

"When I'm not in school, I help her with Field To Fridge."

"Her... Your customers here at the lake. Do you know their names?"

"Some."

"What are they?"

"There's Bridgett and Mike and Dr. Garcia and Mr. Schue. I don't like Mike. There's others, too, but I can't remember."

"Bridgett and Mike, do you know their last names?"

Paco shook his head.

"Do you know Mr. Schue or Dr. Garcia's first name?"

"No."

"Do you know where they live?"

He shrugged. "I know the houses when I see them."

"So if we knew where to drive around, you might remember where they are."

"Yeah." Paco rocked the rocking chair for the first time, then stopped it after one oscillation.

"Were any of them on the lake? If so, that would make it a lot easier because we could just drive the lake-shore roads."

"I think they're all on the lake. No, not all. But most."

"I may ask you to help me find some of those houses." I

sipped beer. "Why do you think Cassie wanted to come to Tahoe in the middle of the night? You didn't deliver that early, did you?"

He shook his head. "I don't know why."

"What did she tell you?"

"She just woke me up and said we had to leave earlier than normal."

"You mean, you still had to make your regular deliveries, but she had to go someplace first."

Paco nodded.

"She give you a reason?"

Paco shook his head.

"Did she say anything during the drive?"

"No. I was asleep."

I finished my beer, carried the bottle to the kitchen nook, came back.

"Paco, has anything been different lately?"

"What do you mean?"

"I mean, has Cassie been doing anything unusual? Different projects? Talking to different people? Working a different schedule?"

He shook his head.

"Why do you think she told you about contacting me if something happened?"

"I don't know."

"How did it come up?"

"I don't know."

"Think back. Something made her bring it up. She didn't just say something like, 'Paco, we'll have dinner as soon as you finish your homework, and then I'll tell you who to call in case something happens to me.' She didn't say it like that, right?"

"No. She was, like, upset. I don't know why. She made me sit at the table and she said she had something important to tell me."

I waited.

Paco continued. "She showed me a slip of paper with your name and phone number, and she showed me your number in her cell phone. She said that if anything bad ever happened to her, that I should call you. She said you were like a cop only you wouldn't tell the real cops about us."

"And she didn't want to talk to the real cops because...?"

"Because they would take me away from her. She said that if you don't have the right papers, you have to go to Mexico."

"Did she tell you anything else?"

"No. She took me into my bedroom and showed me where she was going to put a note she wrote you. And your phone number."

"Where did she put it?" I asked.

"She put the note up above one of the ceiling tiles. Then she taped your phone number to the dresser."

"What's the note about?"

"I don't know," Paco said. He looked down at the floor. "I told you I can't read."

"Is the note still in the ceiling?"

He nodded.

"Then tomorrow we'll drive down to the valley and get it."

Paco shrugged.

"Don't you want to go home?"

"Not really."

"You'll miss school and your friends."

"I don't miss them."

He didn't say it with remorse or spite. Except for when he cried after being chased, he didn't show any emotion.

"What do you want to do now?" I asked.

"Eat dinner."

"We just ate."

"That was a long time ago. You asked me a million questions since then."

"So now you're hungry."

He nodded.

"Okay, I'll get going on dinner. You got a preference?"

"I could eat another cheeseburger."

I thought about what I had in the fridge. "Tell you what. Because we just ate cheeseburgers, how about some chicken? You like chicken?"

He shrugged again. "It's okay."

I was starting to learn Paco's vocabulary of shrugs. Some were affirmative, some negative, some in between.

I put some breast fillets in the oven, found an acorn squash, jump-started it in the microwave before adding it to the oven, put some canned green beans on the stovetop on low, sat down on the other chair near Paco.

"You want anything?" I said.

He looked at the woodstove. "That's the furnace," he said.

"Right."

"Can you turn it on?"

"You cold? Sure." There were just a few split logs in the rack. "Let me get some kindling."

I took my bucket outside and got some huge Jeffrey pine cones from the can where I store them in the early fall.

Paco watched as I crumpled some paper, arranged a few of the big cones, set a split on top.

"You burn pine cones," he said.

"Make great kindling."

"We have a thermostat in our house," he said.

"Dial heat is handy," I said. "But I have to do it the old-fashioned way." I struck a wooden match on the cast iron stove, lit the fire, sat with Paco while the fire grew behind the glass in the stove door.

Paco looked around the room. "Where's your TV?"

"I don't have a TV."

Paco stared at me as if I were suddenly an alien. "Everyone has TV."

"Everyone but me."

"What do you do?"

"Work. Read. Go for hikes with Spot and Street. Stuff like that."

"The bug lady," he said.

I nodded.

Paco looked at Spot, then over at my shelves of art books.

"Why do you have all those books?"

"I like to look at them."

"You read," he said.

"Yeah, but those are art books, so they're mostly pictures of paintings and sculptures. You want to look at some?"

Paco shook his head.

In time, I put some barbecue sauce on the chicken, and five minutes later I served up dinner on my little kitchen table.

Paco and I sat on the two fold-up chairs. We faced across from each other while Spot sat on the floor to one side, his head well above the table top. He watched Paco, following each forkful from the boy's plate up to his mouth.

Paco ate his chicken, but left his squash and beans.

"Field To Fridge is all about selling and delivering produce," I said.

Paco nodded.

"But you don't like green beans?"

"I like fresh beans. Canned beans are bad for you."

"Ah," I said. "Like seat belts and milk."

Paco made a small nod.

"You don't like squash, either?" I said. "It's fresh. Relatively speaking, that is."

He shook his head. "Squash tastes bad."

"Okay if I eat yours?" I asked.

Paco shrugged.

I reached for his plate, slid his squash and beans onto my plate.

"Do you have ice cream?" he asked.

"No."

"Cookies?"

"Sorry. I've got pumpkin pie. You like frozen pumpkin pie, or does it have to be fresh?"

"I like frozen pie if you cook it."

"Okay, I'll cook it. Takes an hour, though. You think you can stay up an hour? You didn't get much sleep last night."

He thought about it.

"You could wake me up," he said.

So I cooked the pie. Paco fell asleep in the rocker.

EIGHT

I woke Paco up when the pie was done.

Spot was back at his place at the table as we ate. His tongue made a trip down the right side of his jowls and back up the left. Spot began to quiver when a little chunk of pie fell off of Paco's fork onto the Formica table. Spot looked at the pie chunk, then looked at Paco. Then he trained his big ears and eyes on that chunk as if to vaporize it. Nostrils twitched and flexed. He swallowed. Only after Paco had scooped the chunk back onto his fork, used his finger to wipe the residue off the table, and then licked his finger did Spot calm with disappointment.

Paco was on his second piece when Spot gave up his intense focus, turned his ears behind him, then got up and walked to the door. Spot stared at the solid door, his tail on the medium setting. Eventually came a two-rap knock.

Paco jerked and stared at the door, fright on his face.

"Don't worry, Paco." I pointed at Spot. "It's someone Spot knows. Otherwise, he'd bark."

I knew it wasn't Street, because then his tail would be on high speed, and he'd be doing the stationary prance.

I opened the door. It was Diamond, wearing his uniform.

"Just in time for dessert," I said. "Or are you on duty?"

"Officers on duty still gotta eat."

I nodded. "I've got pumpkin pie." I looked at Paco. "I even cooked it."

"Homemade or store bought?" Diamond said. He looked at Paco. Paco kept his head down, eating his pie.

"Lot of picky people in this room," I said. "Store bought. You think I could make a homemade pie?"

"You made that bread for Anna Quinn's little adventure at the Vikingsholm Castle." He looked at the pie on the stovetop.

"Anyway, preservatives'll keep me looking youthful."

I put my plate in the sink, served up a big piece on another plate, and set it down at the table.

"Paco, meet my friend Diamond," I said. "Diamond, meet Paco."

Diamond nodded at the boy, sat down, forked a big piece of pie into his mouth.

Paco stared down at his pie, not meeting Diamond's eyes. It was probably Diamond's uniform. The boy had been taught to be wary of cops.

"I'm from Mexico City," Diamond said to Paco. "How about you?"

"Stockton," Paco said in a tiny voice.

"Dónde?" Diamond said.

Paco didn't respond.

"You don't speak Spanish?" Diamond said.

Paco shook his head. Always, he kept his eyes down.

When Diamond finished his pie, he got up, washed his plate and mine and set them in the dish rack.

"I'd feed you pie more often if you always washed my dishes," I said.

"Used to be a dishwasher in a restaurant," Diamond said. "Brushing up on my technique."

"Seems like you had every kind of menial service job before you finished your degree and got into law enforcement," I said.

"I was a Mexican immigrant with major work ethic and no means."

"Meaning, you take what you can get and are grateful for any paying work?"

"Sí."

Paco raised his eyes and suddenly watched Diamond as if to memorize him. He focused on Diamond's belt, his gun, his radio, then looked down to Diamond's shiny black shoes, then raised up to the insignia on Diamond's jacket.

"But you were recently studying the French philosophers, right?" I said. "Thinking of a future career change?"

Diamond glanced at Paco. "You want to pay the mortgage, a

law enforcement career beats philosophy," he said. "You want big perspectives on life, philosophy beats everything."

"Big perspectives on life?"

"Conundrums of meaning and purpose. Moral dilemmas. Like that."

"Of course," I said. "Like that."

When Diamond left, I followed him out to his patrol unit.

"You assumed the kid speaks Spanish," I said.

"Brown skin. Work clothes. Skin and fingernail dirt that won't wash out for two weeks. Logical guess."

"Dirt and Spanish go together?"

"Dirt like that on a kid that age in California means field work. Add in brown skin, you got roots from south of the border. Almost for certain he would speak Spanish. So I tried him. But surprise, no Español."

"My thought, too," I said.

"Means this kid is screwed unless he gets some serious help. Probably his mama brought him from Mexico as a new baby. Which makes him a Mexican citizen and an illegal immigrant. Kid grows up speaking American English, but this ain't his country. Without Spanish, Mexico ain't his country, either. Not having a country is a tough gig for anyone, never mind a little kid."

"He told me he doesn't have brothers or sisters," I said. "No family that he knows of. You got any idea what I should do with this kid?"

"Got me. I'm a cop, not a social worker." Diamond got into his SUV, started it, spoke out the open window.

"The boy tell you anything about the men in the pickup?"

"Yeah. Paco said one was black and one was white, and they were both huge and they looked like superheroes."

"You're kidding."

I shook my head. "Said one of them had a cape like Batman."

"Like the guy was wearing an unbuttoned coat?"

"Probably. The only words they said that Paco remembered was the black guy saying salt and the white guy saying yopep."

"Salt and Pepper," Diamond said. "Heard that somewhere.

Something about Vegas, I think. Maybe you should call Agent Ramos." Then Diamond added, "Any chance you saw these guys chasing the boy?"

"Nope."

"So we don't know for certain if they exist," Diamond said.

"Right. But his fear was real. So we should operate on the assumption that they are real."

Diamond nodded. "Keep your eyes open," he said. "Mañana, hombre." He drove off.

Paco was back in the rocker when I went inside. Spot was lying next to him. Between Paco's strokes and the woodstove's heat, Spot was doing his nirvana reaction, thick tongue panting, eyes drooping. Happy as a dog can get outside of eating a barbecued cheeseburger.

"You can turn it off, now," Paco said, pointing at the woodstove.

"Not that simple. Woodstove wakes up slowly, goes to bed reluctantly. You want cool, you have to move out of the rocker and sit over there. Or go outside."

Paco looked at the dark windows.

"Where do I sleep?" he said.

"I've got a sleeping bag and air mattress you can use."

"Where would I put it?"

I gestured at the small floor of my living room. "Here in front of the woodstove is good. Or you could use my bed."

"Then where would you sleep?"

"Here." I pointed at the floor again.

"Where does Spot sleep?"

I pointed to Spot's oversized bed.

"I could put the sleeping bag there," Paco said.

"True. But Spot is a bed hog. He could push you out or roll over on you."

Paco shrugged.

"But before you go to bed, you gotta take a shower."

"Why?"

"Because you need it. When was the last time you took a shower?"

"I don't take showers. I take baths. Cassie..."

"Says showers are bad for you?" I interrupted.

Paco shook his head. "She says that a bath soaks the dirt out better."

"Unfortunately, I don't have a tub. So you don't have a choice."

"I'll take a shower tomorrow."

"Not if you want to use my sleeping bag," I said.

Paco stared at me.

"C'mon," I said. "I'll show you your towel."

He was reluctant, but he acquiesced.

"Got another call to make," I said to Paco before I shut the bathroom door. "I'll be just outside the front door."

I stepped outside into the cold night and dialed FBI Special Agent Ramos on his cell number. I paced back and forth in miniature, two steps each way so that I stayed under the overhang and in from the rain.

"McKenna," Ramos answered, no doubt reading his caller ID.

"Sorry to bother you at this hour," I said.

"You found the boy who was supposedly kidnapped. Reasonable to call about it. Assuming, that is, that he's telling the truth. Has he given you any evidence?"

"No," I said. "A story, a palpable fear, nothing more."

"You believe him?" Ramos's skepticism was as clear as Mallory's.

"I believe something traumatic happened. He did tell me something that I wanted to ask you about. He said that one of the men was black and the other white. The black man said something about salt, while the white man said something about yopep. It sounded to me like names. Salt and Pepper."

"Really," Ramos said. A statement. Disgust in his tone. "Well, then you've probably got something. There's a couple of dirtballs we've been looking for. Two suspects who go by those monikers. Did the boy say any more about what they look like?"

"Just that they were big guys with shaved heads. One wore a cape."

"A cape?" Ramos didn't sound as surprised as I thought he'd be.

"You know them?"

"Heard of them," Ramos said. "They're based in Vegas. They refer to themselves as The Collectors. An informant has mentioned them. He says that they call each other Salt and Pepper. Silly names, but it sounds like they're trying to build a persona."

"What do they collect?"

"Anything. You pay their fee, they collect people, payrolls, guns. Often they're hired to get rid of what they collect."

"Big fee?"

"Medium scale from what we've heard. We believe that these two men may have been involved in three murders. Two of the victims were men who were suspects in other murders. One was a man we know nothing about. We never were able to ID the body."

"How were they killed?"

"It appeared that they were all hit with a stun gun and then wrapped with shipping plastic. Arms tight to their bodies and heads, too. Death in each case was caused by asphyxiation from the plastic wrap."

"By plastic wrap, do you mean shrink wrap?"

"Yeah. The stuff that they put around wooden pallets and cardboard boxes to hold it all in place."

"Anything else you know about these guys?" I asked.

"Nothing except their names."

"The murders you describe, they all take place in Vegas?"

"Probably," Ramos said. "The bodies were found out on the desert in shallow graves. Two in one grave, the third in another grave. Near popular hiking trails. In both cases it was hikers who noticed the graves." He paused. "Hate to think these boys have come to our bucolic mountain hamlet."

"Me, too."

"The thing is, these guys are grandiose. They do stuff in goofy ways that gets media coverage. But that doesn't make them any less dangerous. You watch your back," Ramos said, then hung up.

NINE

When I went back inside, Paco was finished with his shower, and he had put his dirty clothes back on.

"Gotta brush your teeth before bed," I said. "I've got a brand new brush I've never used. I'll get it."

I fetched the brush.

He looked at it with suspicion.

"My teeth don't need brushing," he said.

"Yeah, they do. Don't tell me that Cassie says that brushing teeth is bad."

He looked at me, but he didn't protest.

"Good. She made you brush, didn't she?" At least there was one thing that Cassie and I agreed on. I handed him the brush. "Toothpaste is in the bathroom," I said.

With a sense of resignation, Paco tore off the plastic wrapper, took out the brush and went into the bathroom. A few minutes later, he came out.

I handed him the sleeping bag I'd dug out from the back of my closet.

He put it on the edge of Spot's bed, climbed into it and curled up next to Spot.

I wondered if I should be doing anything else. This was foreign territory for me, but even I knew that a kid shouldn't go to bed without some kind of touch. Especially a kid who, unless he was a world-champion liar, had just been through a major tragedy. So I walked over, bent down, and gave him a pat on the shoulder.

"Goodnight," I said.

He didn't respond.

Sleep came in bits, interrupted by long bouts of stress and worry about the kid in the next room.

In the middle of the night, I finally got up to check on him.

I slipped out of my bed, walked quietly to the door, and looked out.

In the faint light from the LED display on the microwave, I saw him. Paco was sitting up, backed up against the log wall, knees to chest, hugging his knees, the sleeping bag still bundled around him. On his left, Spot's bulk was pushed up against him.

Normally, I wouldn't have been able see his features in the dark of night. His eyes and eyebrows were black on a brown face. But the dim kitchen glow reflected off his wet cheeks.

I didn't want to startle him. So I made a little noise against the doorway before I walked out.

There was just enough space between Paco and the wood-stove that I could sit down on the floor next to him, my back against the log wall. My elbow bumped up against his shoulder. He didn't move. Didn't say anything.

I felt as ill-equipped for this moment as any in my life. What do you say to a kid who has witnessed an assault on his foster mom, a kid who apparently has no relatives, no place to go, who lives with the constant worry that he may get picked up by authorities and sent to a country he can't even remember.

I thought back to when I was a kid his age, tried to remember kid emotions, kid responses to tragedy. But I immediately realized that it was not instructive. I'd been a cocky kid, full of himself, living with my solid, reliable family in Boston. The support within my family home was constant. And outside the home, in a city where several of my uncles were cops, I felt equally self-assured and protected. My entire existence as a kid had nothing in common with this kid next to me, crying in the dark, facing a future that was a giant question mark at best, nearly destroyed at worst.

I'd already learned that Paco was as taciturn as they come. Even if I knew what to say or ask, I knew that he probably wouldn't answer.

"You want to talk?" I said. I knew it was a feeble attempt

before I had finished the question.

Paco didn't speak.

I put my hand on his bent knee.

"You've been through hell," I said. "It's okay to be upset. I know it really hurts."

Still no response.

I waited.

Eventually, he said, "My life is like an empty room."

I didn't know what to say. I realized that my hand was clenching his knee hard. Too hard. I tried to relax it a bit.

"You're a tough kid," I said. "Together, you and I can find these bad guys. We can put them away. It won't make the hurt less. But it will be something."

He sniffled, rubbed his arm across his nose.

In time, his breathing slowed a bit.

I didn't move.

He lay down to the side, away from me, his upper body on top of Spot.

I waited until he was sleeping, pulled the sleeping bag up over him, then went back to bed and listened to the steady drone of rain on the cabin roof.

The next morning, I found Paco snugged up so tight against Spot that I worried that Spot had crushed him in the night. He was tiny compared to Spot, and I wasn't confident that Spot was careful around small bed-mates.

I leaned in close to see. Paco was out, but still breathing. I relaxed. Paco's arm was over Spot's chest. Spot was snoring.

I poured a cup of coffee, turned on my laptop, and spent some time looking for information that might tell me where Paco lived. Then I called Commander Mallory, talking softly so I didn't wake Paco.

"Heard from Ramos that you may have a lead on the men who kidnapped the boy," Mallory said. "And Diamond told me you've got the kid at your house."

"Don't know what else to do with him," I said. "I'm planning to take him home today, ask around, see where he can stay. But from what he told me, it doesn't look promising. No family, no friends with room, no relatives."

"You find out where he lives, yet?" Mallory asked.

"No. He says it's an hour out of Stockton and just down from McDonald's and Aggie's Green Elementary."

"He know his street address?"

"It sounds like he doesn't have one," I said. "He said their house is at the back of the landlord's property. They grow tomatoes and peppers and sell them up here in Tahoe."

"You have a plan how to find the house?" Mallory asked.

"More of a guess. I Googled St. Agatha's Elementary and found one about an hour out of Stockton. It could be the school. I'll let you know what I learn. You haven't had any reports of a van or pickup that fit our description?"

"No. I'll be in touch if I do," Mallory said. We hung up.

Spot had opened his eyes for a few moments when he heard me talking on the phone, but any inclination he had toward waking up was obviously trumped by his desire to stay in Paco's embrace. They were both still asleep.

I did more computer work while Paco and Spot snoozed. Paco finally woke after my third cup of coffee.

"Hungry?" I said.

He nodded. Wiped sleep from his eyes.

"You like oatmeal?" I asked.

He shook his head.

"Cantaloupe and blueberries?"

"Blueberries," he said.

"Coffee and grits?"

Paco screwed up his face, shook his head.

"What do you like?"

"Pancakes," he said.

"I've got buckwheat cakes. Will that do?"

"What's buckwheat?"

"Like buttermilk but with a little more oomph."

"I like plain buttermilk," he said. "With eggs and bacon," he added.

"Tell you what. We'll go to the Red Hut, and you can get whatever breakfast you want."

An hour later Paco had eaten a stack of cakes soaked in butter and syrup, three scrambled eggs, and two orders of bacon. And he had downed them with two glasses of milk and a large glass of orange juice. I had a hard time reconciling the skinny kid with his appetite.

"Now what," he said, pushing back his plate.

"Let's go down to Stockton and see if we can find your house and school."

"Why?"

"To get the note that Cassie left for me."

"Oh, yeah."

"And we need to find a place where you can stay."

"I don't think there is one," he said.

TEN

We went back out to the Jeep where Spot waited, head out the window, panting. It looked like he was smiling again. Probably he was smiling because I'd brought a side order of pancakes in a doggie box.

"You want to feed Spot some pancake frisbees?" I asked.

Paco looked up at Spot's head. Spot's fangs were evident at the sides of his panting tongue. Paco took a step back and shook his head.

"Okay," I said. "Stand back."

Paco moved away as I pulled a pancake out and spun it toward Spot. Spot grabbed it out of the air with a click of teeth and a wag of his tail. Same for the second cake.

The third went high. Spot strained as it sailed over the top of the Jeep.

I fetched it from the parking lot, brought it back around.

"It's probably got sand on it," Paco said, frowning.

I held it up. It wasn't especially dirty, but it was soggy from landing on the wet asphalt.

"Good thing Spot ain't picky," I said.

Spot snatched it out of the air.

"Like Jerry Rice reaching over his shoulder as he makes a running leap into the end zone," I said.

Paco just frowned at me.

"Okay, so he didn't leap, but it was still a good catch." Spot kept looking at me. I could see his tail inside the Jeep, smacking back and forth between the front and back seat backs.

"Sorry, largeness. You want more to eat, you gotta settle for the sawdust chunks."

Spot's tail slowed.

We got in the Jeep and headed out of town. I periodically checked my rear-view mirror to watch for any possible tails.

Instead of driving down Highway 50 and the American River Canyon, I took the alternative route to the Stockton area by heading out of South Lake Tahoe on 50 and, before heading up Echo Summit, turning south on Highway 89, down Christmas Valley.

The rain clouds had dissipated somewhat, and patches of blue were visible here and there in the gray blanket that seemed to rest on the white mountaintops.

"At ten years of age, you'd be about fifth grade, right, Paco?"

"Fourth." Paco looked out the window, his face passive. "They held me back."

"Why?" I said.

"Because I'm dumb. I can't go to Middle School."

"You're not dumb. You probably know more about tomatoes and peppers and other vegetables than most people."

"Tomatoes and peppers are fruits," Paco said.

"You're kidding."

Paco shook his head. "Tomatoes hold the seeds. That makes them a fruit."

"But what about peppers? They have seeds."

"Fruit," Paco said. "You can ask a scientist."

"Well, that seems a stretch," I said, pleased that I'd found a subject that the reticent kid would talk about. "Squash and pumpkins are obviously vegetables, and they contain seeds."

Paco shook his head. "Fruit."

"Green beans?"

"Beans are called dry fruits. Like peas. Like corn and wheat and rice."

"Okay," I said. "If all of these are technically fruit, why do we have the word vegetable?"

"For vegetables."

"Give me an example of a vegetable that isn't technically a fruit."

Paco sighed. I was so tedious.

"Vegetables are like carrots and onions. Celery. Lettuce and spinach. The parts of plants you eat that don't hold the seeds."

"Got it," I said. "You want a vegetable, you eat the non-seed part of a plant."

Paco was quiet. Eventually he said, "You can't just eat any part of a plant. Tomato plants are poisonous. The leaves and stems. Potato plants, too."

"Really. But the fruit is okay," I said.

He nodded. "Unless it's not ripe. Then it can make you sick, too. And potatoes are vegetables."

"What would happen if you ate tomato leaves?" I said.

"Make you puke. Then paralyze you."

"Ah," I said. "Because the leaves of tomatoes and potatoes are both poisonous, are they related?"

"Yeah. They're called nightshade plants. Like peppers. And tobacco."

I was still marveling at Paco's sudden loquaciousness. "Why are they called nightshade plants?"

"'Cause they're like each other, I guess," he said.

I couldn't think of more questions.

We rode in silence.

We had climbed the incline at the south end of Christmas Valley, crested Luther Pass, and headed down toward the floor of Hope Valley, which sits at 7000 feet. We turned right at Pickett's Junction and climbed up toward Carson Pass at 8600 feet.

As we approached the crest, we drove above the snow level from the recent precipitation. The high forest already had a foot of snow, the beginning of what usually turns out to be a huge snowpack by the end of the season.

The plows had been busy, and the road, while slushy, was easily passable.

"Where do Europeans live?" Paco suddenly said.

"Europe. If you go east across this country, you get to the Atlantic Ocean. Europe is a bunch of countries on the other side of the Atlantic. Why do you ask?"

"Cassie says that tomatoes are the most popular fruit in the world. She says that Europeans made them popular. Spaghetti sauce and stuff."

"Makes sense," I said.

"But Europeans got tomatoes from the Indians," Paco said.

"You mean, our Indians? Our Native Americans?"

"Yeah."

"You know any Indians?"

"I have an Indian friend named Yoku. He's from the Miwok Tribe."

"He a tomato expert?"

Paco shook his head. "He knows all about acorns."

"And you know about tomatoes."

Paco nodded.

I added, "And you know lots about fruits and vegetables. That proves you're smart. You just know different stuff than what other people know."

Paco turned away and stared out the window. "Any farmer knows that stuff. I still can't read."

"You'll learn to read," I said.

Paco didn't react. He still faced the window glass, but I didn't think he was seeing anything outside.

"What do you do with the Field-To-Fridge deliveries?"

Paco was still staring out the side window. "I sort the bags and baskets. Then we take them inside. I count out the fruit for each client. Cassie makes the arrangements in the baskets. She says it's an art like with flowers. She says I can start doing arrangements when I'm older. But now she's shot. So I guess I won't be helping."

I didn't want him to focus on what happened to Cassie. "You help grow the tomatoes and peppers, too?"

"Yeah."

"Are the crops all done by the time school starts? Or does Cassie take over after you go back to school?"

"Hothouse crops go until Thanksgiving. I still have to do my chores. Before school. After school, too."

"So you have a lot of work to do while you're going to school," I said.

"Yeah."

"Must make it kinda hard to focus on learning to read," I

said, "when you've got all those chores to do."

Paco stared out the window. "Sometimes I skip school."

"To goof off with your friends? Or do the farm chores."

"Chores. That's how I make money."

From the top of Carson pass, we wound down past Caples Lake to Kirkwood Ski Resort, on out to Silver Lake, and then followed the long, high ridge down out of the snow to the foothills and the Gold Country town of Jackson. By the time we got to the Central Valley floor, what had seemed like low clouds were now high in the sky and made a general gray blanket far above us. The roads were moist, but the rain had stopped. The sun poked through in places and made the roads steam.

"What are your responsibilities in growing the tomatoes and peppers?"

It was a bit before he spoke. "Just all the planting stuff."

"Like?"

"I plant the seeds for the starter plants. In the hothouse. I set the timers on the grow lights."

"That all?" I said.

"I replant the starters in the spring. Usually, some of the drip lines break during winter. I have to fix them. I use Cassie's secret chart to fertilize the plants. I set the irrigation settings as the seedlings grow."

"Wait. What does that mean? Cassie's secret chart?"

"She says it's her secret weapon."

"How does it work?" I asked.

"The chart says how much water and grow lights to use based on weather. I measure the size of the starter plants. Then I use her chart to tell how many drops of her fertilizer to use. She calls it the secret sauce."

"Sounds like Cassie has lots of secrets," I said.

Paco nodded. "Our organic tomatoes are the best in the valley. Our Cassie's Amazements are the best of the best."

"Is that what Cassie says? Best of the best?"

"Yeah. It's true. And our Cassie's Vipers are the hottest peppers in the world."

"How do you know what pepper is hotter than another? Do

you just taste it?"

Paco shook his head. "They measure it. Scoville Units. They put the pepper stuff into sugar water. And tasters try to taste it. You can put ours with over a million times as much water, and you can still taste it."

"Ah," I said. "So you measure it by diluting it. The more dilution it can take, the hotter the pepper."

Paco shrugged.

We took 88 across the Central Valley. The two-lane highway crawled through dense orchards and fields of vegetables and vineyards and small farm towns. The world thinks of California as beaches and L.A., Disneyland and Hollywood, San Francisco and Silicon Valley. But it is also the most productive agricultural state, and this huge expanse of flat farmland is its quiet epicenter.

To pass the time, I put in a CD of Oscar Peterson's Night Train. As the evocative piano jazz came on, Paco sighed.

"What'sa matter?" I said. "You don't like jazz?"

"Ol' man music," Paco said.

I switched out the CD for Mozart's Oboe Concerto. As the opening lines began, I said, "Classical music has enchanted people for centuries. Hard not to like, right?"

"Ol' lady music," he said.

I hit eject and put on The Beatles Sgt. Pepper and hit random play. Lucy in the Sky with Diamonds started playing. "Not ol' man and not ol' lady," I said. "Just right, right?"

"Just old," Paco said.

I pointed at my CD box. "You're welcome to find something you like."

Paco ejected the CD, hit the radio button, and dialed a rap station. He turned it up loud, and we listened to a young man shout out a stream of angry words that were a mix of Marxist rage about the oppressor class and misogynist rants about 'emasculating bitches.' If there were a test for music like there is for peppers, it would be as hot as Cassie's Vipers. I had to roll down my window to dilute it with wind noise.

Paco didn't nod to the beat or show any other sign of connection to the music, but I could understand how a driving beat and angry lyrics could permeate a young boy's consciousness. It didn't seem like healthy inputs. But even as I had the thought, I realized that there was a time when adults fretted about all those long-haired groups that were polluting the minds of kids in the '60s, groups that are now the gold standards of classic rock.

After the rap rage was over, I turned down the radio and asked, "You get paid for your work on the farm?"

Paco nodded. "Cassie pays me eighty bucks a week if I do all my chores."

"What do you spend it on?"

"Cassie will only let me spend twenty-five bucks a week. I have to save the rest."

"So you're saving fifty-five bucks a week. That's over two hundred bucks a month which is, what, pushing three grand a year."

Paco shrugged.

"How long have you been working like this?"

"Since I started living with her. But she only paid me sixty-five a week back in the beginning."

"That means you've been getting merit raises. Good job. Your bank account must be pretty fat by now."

"I don't have a bank account. Cassie says banks aren't safe."

"Ah," I said. "Where do you put your money?"

"In a hiding place. You could never find it." Paco said it with pride.

Outside the Jeep window was a stretch of what seemed like endless orchards. Then came endless vineyards. I remembered the statistic that Napa, Sonoma, and other famous-appellation wines only made up a small percentage of California wines. The majority of the state's production came from the Central Valley.

"I've always wondered something about organic tomatoes," I said.

Paco didn't respond.

"How do you keep the bugs off of them when you don't use pesticides?"

"Beneficials," Paco said.

"What's that?"

"Cassie has books. When we find aphids and other bad stuff that eats the fruit, we look it up in her books. Once we know what it is, then we look up what beneficials eat them."

"Like what?"

"Like Lady beetles. Praying mantises eat caterpillars. But they're kind of scary. Sometimes they eat the Lady beetles, too."

"That's why you didn't want to go in Street's bug lab."

Paco nodded. "Once, Cassie got Assassin bugs 'cause they eat everything, just like Praying mantises. But they bite bad. I told her I won't do chores if she gets them again. At least, Praying mantises don't bite me. I still don't like them."

"I'm not much of a bug person myself."

"Cassie grinds up dried Viper peppers and sprinkles the powder in the hothouse. That keeps a lot of bugs away."

"And all this saves the tomatoes without using any chemicals."

"Yeah. It's in Cassie's book."

"How do you look stuff up in her books, if you don't read?"

Paco paused. "I can read those books. Lots of pictures," he said.

"Sounds to me like you can read when you want to earn money but not so much when you need to for school."

Paco didn't answer.

"Do the other kids in school know this stuff?"

"No."

"Doesn't that make you smart?"

"Tomato stuff isn't smart stuff. Other kids know smart stuff."

"Like what?"

"Computers and stuff."

When I got in the vicinity of St. Agatha's Elementary school, Paco suddenly sat up straight in his seat.

"This next turn to the right is my school," he said.

"Okay if we stop there?"

"I guess."

I turned.

We drove several blocks through a residential area. The small houses were painted turquoise and green and pink and red and yellow like a neighborhood in a small Mexican town. Pointy Cypress trees stabbed the sky. Mature oaks shaded dirt yards. Old cars in good condition – mostly Chevrolets and Fords – were parked in the tree-shade circles. An occasional California fan palm stood tall above the oaks, showing off its grand circular explosion of clacking palm fronds. The air was thick with aromas of fall flowers mixing with the smells of harvest in the fields.

"Turn left," Paco said.

I turned. One block down was a commercial district.

"That's the McDonald's," Paco said, pointing. "Turn right."

I followed his instructions.

Three blocks later, Paco pointed at a light-blue concrete block building, one-story, not much larger than the Chevron station across the street. Around it was a rough shape of green grass.

"That's Aggie's Green," he said.

I pulled into the school parking lot and parked.

"Let's go in," I said.

"I don't want to. My teachers will be mad that I missed school."

"Not to worry," I said, aware that I had no idea of what Paco was up against, missing school, believing that he was the dumb kid, maybe considered the dumb kid by the administration and teachers who held him back. "Come with me. I'll explain to them."

Paco held back. I had to open his door, take his scratchy little hand once again.

We left Spot in the Jeep and walked into the school.

ELEVEN

There was a small lobby area that led to a hallway with just one classroom on each side. On the left, through open, double doors, was a small group office crammed with several desks arranged back-to-back in pairs. Three people worked at the desks. A fourth was at a copy machine so old that the light gray plastic had discolored to a sickly greenish yellow. I left Paco in the lobby room and walked into the office.

"Excuse me, I'm looking for the principal's office," I said. "Is this the right place?"

A woman looked up from a desk. "Oh, hi. Yes, this is the principal's office. And the administration office. And the teachers' break room. And the PTA meeting room second Wednesdays of every month. Let's see, have I forgot anything?"

I pointed toward the counter at one side of the room where the coffee maker and microwave sat next to a mid-sized fridge. "Kitchen," I said.

"Yes! Of course. The most important activity that happens in this room."

The woman swiveled her chair and called toward the corner opposite the kitchen. "Pam! You have visitor," she said in a sing-song voice.

Through an open door into another office sat a woman at a desk, talking on the phone handset, which was wedged between her shoulder and head while she typed at a computer. Even at a distance I could see that she was better dressed than the others. She wore a navy pantsuit, and her black hair had been permed or otherwise treated so that not a single hair could be a renegade and get out of line. The woman looked ready to perform in a documentary about super-competent women.

The woman who called out turned back toward me.

"Pam is on the phone. She'll be with you in a..." she stopped as she stared past me. I turned to see Paco looking into the doorway behind me. The woman put a formal, almost stern look on her face.

"Mrs. Sagan, our principal, will be with you shortly. I'll tell her that you are here. Your name?"

"Owen McKenna. I'm here about Paco Ipar."

She nodded. "Yes, I see that. If you will just wait in the entry a moment."

I went back out to the lobby. Paco had moved over near a bulletin board that was plastered with pictures of smiling kids and adjacent printed pages that extolled their achievements. Some even had newspaper articles. I didn't look closely, but I didn't see any pictures of Paco in the display.

The woman in the navy pantsuit came out of the office, saw Paco and made a tight grin. "Hello, Mr. Ipar. We missed you yesterday. And you weren't here for roll call this morning, either." Despite smiling as she spoke, she had an edge in her voice.

Paco looked at the floor as she spoke. He didn't answer.

I reached out my hand. "Hi, I'm Owen McKenna, a private detective from Tahoe."

Her eyes widened. She glanced at Paco, then back to me.

She shook. "I'm Pam Sagan, detective. I hope that Paco hasn't gotten into more trouble." She looked again at Paco.

"May I speak to you alone?" I asked.

"Well, I suppose Paco can wait in the lobby while I talk to you. Paco, will you be good if we leave you alone for a few minutes?"

He made the smallest of nods.

I followed the woman through the group office into her small office at the rear corner. As she stepped behind her desk, I shut the door behind us.

She jerked her head at the sound of the door clicking closed, then sat down slowly, her hands tense on the arms of her chair. Her eyes flicked from me to the door as if she worried about the safety of being alone in a room with me and was judging her possible escape path. Of the two green metal chairs in front of the desk, I took the one that was farthest from the door and farthest from her, hoping it would help her relax.

Sagan was a trim woman who radiated grooming perfection. Her lipstick and mascara weren't directly observable but detectable through inference from her distinctive eyes and mouth. She had a gold brooch shaped like a miniature fountain pen on her lapel. It was angled exactly parallel to the cut of her jacket collar. She took a deep breath through her nose and shut her eyes for a second as she let her air out in a long exhalation.

I knew that whatever relaxation she'd achieved, I was about to destroy it.

"Mrs. Sagan, Paco's foster mother Cassie brought him to Tahoe early yesterday morning. He witnessed a shooting and was later trapped in the back of the shooter's pickup."

"Oh, my God! Where is Cassie?"

"We don't know. Paco believes that Cassie was the shooting victim."

"Cassie was shot?" she continued. "Oh, my God! The boy must be devastated!"

"He's holding up, but it can't be easy."

"You say that Paco believes the victim was Cassie. Haven't you found her body?"

"No." I tried to be brief as I explained what had happened, and how Paco had crawled into the covered bed of the pickup to hide, only to have them drive away. "We're looking for her van. Until we find it or her body, we won't know for certain."

"Was this some kind of random lunacy?" she asked. "Or do you think someone wanted to shoot Cassie?"

"I don't know. From Paco's description, it sounded like she was meeting someone in the mountains very early in the morning. Not the likeliest time for something random."

"But why would anyone shoot Cassie? She can't possibly have been involved in anything that would lead to violence."

"Paco told me that she raised tomatoes and peppers. Maybe she also raised some marijuana in with her regular produce. The money involved is so great that it has enticed many people and gotten them into trouble."

Pam Sagan shook her head vigorously. "No. Absolutely not. I don't know Cassie well, but I'm a good judge of people. Marijuana is not her style. Besides, I've been to her farm. I've even walked through her hothouse. Her entire focus is tomatoes and peppers. It's her identity. She's even named some of them after herself. A little weird, if you ask me, but more evidence that she's not growing pot."

Sagan looked out her window toward the Chevron station across the street. "That poor boy. He must have been scared to death. How did you rescue him?"

"He had Cassie's cell phone, found my number in its menu, and called me from the back of the pickup while the men were driving it away from the scene of the shooting."

"Paco did that?" She sounded incredulous.

"Yes. His resourcefulness was impressive. Later, when they stopped, he opened the topper lift gate and ran. He called me again as two men chased after him. I was able to get to his location before the men caught him."

"Why were the men chasing Paco if they didn't know he was hiding in the back of their pickup?"

"Presumably, they saw him run and realized that he may have witnessed the shooting."

"And if they had caught him...?" She raised her hand up to her face, her fingertips pressed against her lips, her nails manicured.

"They'd probably want to silence any witnesses."

"My lord, that's the most frightening thing for a child!" She looked again toward the door as if she were visualizing Paco in the school entry.

The woman's expression gradually shifted. I wasn't sure what it meant.

"You don't believe it," I said.

She gestured toward the closed office door. "If I hadn't seen Paco out there, I'd say you must be mistaken about which boy you saved. Paco has never... well, let's just say I'm surprised and impressed that he had that much initiative and leave it at that."

"Paco told me that Cassie doesn't have friends," I said.

"Well, I don't know about that. But I can say that Cassie is not real sociable. I've only seen her at the occasional meeting and once at her farm. She came to some school functions. She doesn't engage much with other people, but she's always tried to do right by Paco. She's a hard worker. I believe that her work is her first focus."

"I understand that she's an organic gardener," I said.

"Yes, although calling her a gardener makes it seem like a hobby. This woman must farm two acres with no big equipment and only the help of a little boy. Lots of varieties of tomatoes and peppers, I gather. She used to sell at farmers' markets all over. Now, she's been doing some kind of delivery service. I've heard that she's quite successful. Although, she also told me that she only gets to keep a portion of the produce. The rest goes to the landlord."

"Like a modern-day sharecropper?"

"Well, I don't know what term they use these days. But I suppose that's what it amounts to."

"Without even knowing the dollars involved, it seems like a steep price," I said.

"Yes. But she told me that the landlord set her up in the business, taught her how to do it all. She made a comment about how she was able to start the business with no money. The landlord provides the land she uses. She told me that without him staking her, so to speak, she would still be cleaning hotel rooms. So maybe it's reasonable. Who am I to judge? But when I gave Paco a ride home one day and saw the size of her operation, I thought she must be a juggernaut of farming and marketing to do it all."

"Do you know the name of the landlord?" I asked.

"No. Do you think he might know something about what happened up in Tahoe?"

"I have no idea," I said. "But I need to let him know about his tenants. I suppose that there isn't much tomato growing this late in the fall, but he may want to know that the crops are not currently being tended. Perhaps you would have an idea of where Paco can live until we find out what happened to Cassie?"

The woman frowned. "I'm trying to think of his friends in school. Most of them live in tiny rental houses with large families, so that wouldn't work. The only student his age who lives in a house with sufficient room has a father who is, shall we say, not the easiest person to get along with. That would not be a good possibility for Paco."

She reached forward and shifted the position of her desk phone a quarter inch, or maybe three-eighths of an inch. When it was just so, she said, "We have a problem on our hands. With Cassie missing, Paco is adrift and quite alone."

"Mrs. Sagan, now that Cassie has disappeared, it's possible that Paco won't have a home to go back to. As a foster child, Paco has some kind of a supervisor, correct?" I said.

"I should probably..." Sagan paused, then let it drop.

"You're not eager to call the state agency in charge," I said. "Do they have someone bad assigned to Paco's case?"

The woman put her fingertips on a nearby pencil, rotated it so that the printing on it faced directly up, then aligned the pencil next to the right edge of her desk blotter. She looked out the office window toward the larger room, then leaned sideways to get a more thorough view. She leaned forward, elbows on her desk, and spoke in a hushed voice.

"Mr. McKenna..." she hesitated again, thinking about how to proceed.

"Owen, please," I said.

"If you learned something that would put a person at risk of having the authorities come after them, even if they'd done nothing wrong, would you feel compelled to report them?"

"I already know that Paco is an illegal immigrant, if that's what you're wondering. I'm not about to call the border patrol. I know that he has no family."

"So I don't have to worry about you making trouble. Then there's something else you should know before you start calling the social service agencies."

"What's that?"

"Paco doesn't exist."

TWELVE

"Paco doesn't exist?" I repeated. "In what way?"

"In every way but the physical. He has never been in the data banks. The state doesn't know about him. While many local people know Paco, he doesn't officially exist in county records, either. He's a classic illegal immigrant, more invisible than most."

"So Cassie isn't really his foster mom."

"No, Cassie is most definitely his foster mom, in the truest and most important sense. She takes care of him and gives him a home and does it simply because it's the right thing to do."

"But she is not part of the state's program."

"Correct. She gets no money."

"Why doesn't she go through the normal channels? The state would help, correct?"

"My understanding is that it would be a possibility. But it is likely that the state would send out a case worker who would be required to report that Cassie is always working, that Paco is always working, which is clearly in violation of child labor laws, that Paco has no standard home life, that Paco has so little homework guidance that he hasn't even learned to read, that Paco barely passes some of his subjects and fails others, that Paco often comes home from school to an empty house, and that the house is substandard by any measure.

"That same case worker would note that in the spring and fall, Paco is mostly absent from school because Cassie works him harder on the farm than any child should work. And in the last several months, Paco has been busy helping her with the new delivery service that she's started. In fact, my sense is that Paco works harder than nearly any adult I know. In many ways, this is not the way a child should live. Yet, it works for Paco."

"What does that mean?" I asked. "You make it sound like Paco is a child slave."

Pam Sagan still had her elbows on the desk. She raised up her hands so that the knuckles of her index fingers were against her chin.

"Paco used to get in trouble," she said. "It started out as some simple vandalism. Throwing tomatoes against the school. At McDonald's. Then it escalated. He ran with some bad kids. One night they threw stones at a passing police car. The officer had been a track champion in high school. He ran after them and caught Paco and two others. Our local police chief knew that Paco was illegal. But he took mercy. He told Cassie that he would not cite Paco but only under the condition that she make certain that he never had idle time again."

Sagan took a breath, turned to look at a blank wall, then breathed out. She turned back to me.

"Paco has been in some other trouble as well. In my opinion, Cassie deserves credit for saving him. She made him a full-time worker in her business, taking him out of school as necessary. She made him work the production side of the business, the distribution side, and the retail side. And she paid him well. As I understand it, this boy has developed a good savings account. And, much as we'd like the boy to do better in school, he has turned himself around in many ways."

Pam Sagan gave me a hard look.

She continued, "I believe that if Cassie hadn't worked him so hard, he would have been pulled into the juvenile justice system. I don't think that Paco has a natural leaning toward a criminal mind like some kids. But he is a natural street kid. If he'd been left to hang out with other kids on the street, I have no doubt that he would have gotten into serious trouble. I know the type because I've seen it too many times. He's very young. But he was on track to something bad. He would eventually end up in custody and be deported.

"Of course, he's technically here illegally," she continued. "Many people would say a rule's a rule and that he should have been deported years ago."

Sagan looked down, moved her hands behind her desk in a way that seemed as if she were smoothing her pants on her thighs.

"I used to wonder about Cassie's focus on making Paco work," she said. "I don't think she's given him an ideal childhood this last year or so. But it's clear to me and others that Cassie saved him. She taught him the value of hard work, and she taught him valuable skills that he'll use for the rest of his life. Yes, she's been doing it outside of the legal system. For all I know, she could be accused of harboring an illegal alien. But she's done the right thing by the measure of something separate from the law. She deserves a medal, and the legislators who chant their slogans to get re-elected should have to answer to that separate thing."

She looked at me. "Does that make any sense to you? Or do you think I'm nuts?"

"It makes sense," I said. "Answer a hypothetical question, please. What if they didn't deport him? What if they simply registered him as a foster child or whatever it is that they do?"

"If Paco were officially put into the foster program, he would be taken from Cassie's care. She is not an official foster family. Because he is a willful child and not especially endearing, to say the least, it is unlikely they would find a new foster home for him. And even if they did, his foster parents would likely reject him after a time. He'd end up in an orphanage. It is not easy to find foster families for kids of any age and personality. But it is much harder for kids who aren't young and charming."

Sagan gave me a pleading look. I could see how much she cared.

"Paco has always lived here," she said. "This is his community. His home. He's not very likeable. In fact, he is one hardcase, tough kid. But he has some friends. His teachers and other community members look out for him. I try hard to insulate him from the forces out there in society that would look at him only as an illegal immigrant."

"You think the state would put him in an orphanage," I said. "Are you saying that he would also be deported?"

"It's hard to say anything definite other than that it's possible. Those of us who work with populations that have undocumented workers see how often somebody disappears. Sometimes we see it coming, witness a crime followed by an arrest, which is followed by the person being picked up by an Immigration Enforcement Agent. Next thing we know, they're gone."

"If Paco were deported, where would he end up?" I asked.

"Without a family in Mexico, he'd end up in a Mexican orphanage," Sagan said. "Or on the street."

"Paco told me he doesn't speak Spanish. Would they speak English in an orphanage?" I asked.

"Don't be naive. Maybe the odd worker would know some English. But Paco would basically be trapped in a world he doesn't know, where he can't communicate. It would be worse than prison."

"If I called the sheriff," I said, "or the local social service agency, or the local legislator – people who are knowledgeable about local, illegal immigrants – wouldn't they agree with you? Wouldn't they hesitate to do anything that might jerk Paco out of his hometown?"

Pam Sagan scoffed, shaking her head.

"All those elected or appointed officials will only speak on record, and they would tell you lies aimed at creating a sense that they are directed by compassion. The truth is that the U.S. routinely deports children to countries the children have never known, countries whose language is as foreign to the kids as Swahili probably is to you. And this country is deporting more people every year."

"What about the amnesty programs that we hear about? The so-called Dream Act? Surely, there must be a program that Paco could fit into. Something that would give him legal residency if not citizenship."

Sagan looked at me hard again. At that moment, I represented the enemy, those people who justify ripping apart kids' lives because there is a legal line drawn in the sand.

"As I said, Paco has been in trouble. Regardless of the platitudes you hear about the system having built-in safeguards designed to create a fair system for kids like him, those of us who work in the Central Valley can tell you otherwise. And kids who have been in trouble the way Paco has are likely to be deported if they get picked up by Immigration Enforcement Agents. Because these kids have no family and no advocates with any power, once they are sent to Mexico, no one ever hears about them again. They are the silent victims. The government doesn't tell their stories."

"How many people know about this, that Paco is not actually in the files of the state agencies?"

"Well, several of us at this school, of course. The women who've taken care of him over the years. Several other people in the community. The local dentist and doctor. No doubt the parents of his friends, some of whom themselves are illegal aliens. And you should know that Paco isn't the only kid in this situation. We have several in our school. I know other Central Valley educators who say that their schools have many undocumented kids."

"Can you tell me about Paco's history?" I said.

"We don't actually know it in detail. From what I've heard, his mother brought him over the border when he was a baby. She came with him alone, and she told people that her boyfriend, Paco's father, would be joining them soon. But the father never showed up. She worked in the vineyards picking grapes, carrying the baby in one of those back packs. But she died from some kind of infection.

"So the neighbor lady, who loved both Paco and Paco's mother, took in the baby and raised him. She knew of course that Paco was not legal, so she kept quiet about it. Unfortunately, that woman eventually started to suffer from Alzheimer's and had to go into a home. Fortunately, some other neighbor women who had a round-robin childcare for their kids put Paco into their rotation. He spent several years living at four different homes, switching among them as the schedules of the various families permitted.

"Eventually, the daycare circle dissolved, but one of those families took him in. They had a tumultuous home life, but at least Paco had a roof over his head. That family kept him until he began to get in trouble and became more withdrawn.

"This was around the time that Cassie got to know Paco. So she took him in shortly after he turned eight. She's had him for a year and about eight months. No one knows what motivated Cassie to step forward just as others were tiring of the boy. Some might say that she saw that she could combine doing the right thing by the boy with acquiring a source of cheap labor.

"Either way, Cassie was the best thing that ever happened to Paco. Warm and fuzzy, no. Playful and fun, no. Quirky in her opinions and even a little strange, yes. But steady as a supertanker in rough seas. She gave Paco the one thing he'd never had, a calm life that he could count on.

"Unfortunately, Paco hasn't been easy for her. Warm and fuzzy he's not, either. Inside, I think he's a good kid. But you've got to have a lot of faith to believe in him. He's as stubborn and resistant to the world as a granite boulder. You want to teach that kid something, good luck. Unless he sees it as something he needs, he simply won't pay attention. And, as you know, raising a child is very expensive. Cassie's work ethic has made it so she can provide for herself even though she came from a disadvantaged background herself. But it was a real sacrifice to take on the expenses of a child. She's a bit of a hero around here for not only taking Paco in, but doing it in violation of laws that show little favor for a child without citizenship in the very country where he grew up. And she has had to withstand some scorn, too."

"Why is that?" I asked.

"Even this community has some people who are hard-liners who say that Paco is a Mexican and that he should be deported."

"What about your school? How does that work without Paco having official records?"

"We just took him in the way the neighbor women did. He began to attend classes when he was six. We created some paperwork where it made sense, and kept him off the books where that seemed appropriate. Our guiding principle was to do whatever would give him some continuity. He had no memories of ever having a parent, nor had he ever experienced stability. So we wanted to keep him in our school and in our community. Until Cassie took him in, this little school and this town, poor and fragmented as it is, was the only community he's ever known. As with everyone else who has taken care of him, we wanted to avoid having some person with authority come in and uproot his life and put him in an institutional setting."

"An orphanage."

"Yes. In another community. Or another country. With another school. Where he would know no one."

Pam Sagan studied me, wondering, I thought, whether she could see any resolve in my face. Wondering if my resolve was in Paco's favor or disfavor.

"In your experience, if Paco remains under the radar, what is the chance that he will be caught, anyway?"

Sagan nodded. "There is absolutely a chance that he will be caught. If he is ticketed for any infraction or breaks any law, especially when he gets older, like driving without a license, that will set the gears of the deportation machine turning. And even if he isn't caught, as an illegal, he can't get a social security number, he can't get most jobs, he can't easily go to college, he can never borrow money or make use of the banking system. That means that he can't have a normal life."

"Wouldn't that be worse? Wouldn't he be given more latitude if he voluntarily comes forward as an underage illegal immigrant, brought here as an infant by his now-deceased mother?"

"Perhaps. But I think most of his teachers and other community members who know him would say, let's postpone that reckoning until he is older. When he's sixteen or seventeen, he might be able to cope with such an adverse situation. But at ten? It might destroy him."

She took a breath, then continued.

"I'm not an expert, but my experience suggests that finding some flexibility – or latitude, as you call it – in the agencies that deal with illegal immigration, is a very hit-or-miss prospect. Some people, in some situations, may exercise some discretion in his favor. But unfortunately, the government has rules, and bureaucrats have to go by them when they decide on which side of the line you fall. It's a brutal business, but the people making the choice don't have the opportunity to put a human face on that choice. Either you're in, or you're out, and once that decision is made, there is little you can do to change the outcome."

I said, "Paco told me that he has no siblings and no relatives that he knows of. Is that what you understand?"

Sagan made a little nod that seemed sad and resigned.

"He also told me that he's struggling in school," I said. "He said he's been held back for being dumb."

Pam Sagan frowned. "Well, he's certainly not dumb. He mostly has trouble reading. He's dyslexic. We would like to get him specialized help, but this school district has no money." She gestured at the building. "You can see by our facility that we have to make do with very little. Anyway, Paco will learn eventually. Holding him back actually gives him some advantages. He will have more confidence in future classes. One good thing is that he made new friends after he was held back."

I nodded. "You said that Cassie doesn't have many friends. But can you give me the names of anybody who might know her best?"

"Well, if Cassie has friends, they don't intersect with my circle. From the few times we've talked, I'd say that her entire life is about trying to raise Paco right and about earning a living as a farmer. I can testify that the first is the hardest job on the planet. And, as far as I can tell, farming is the second hardest job."

"Is Cassie close to Paco? I ask because he doesn't seem especially distressed by what happened. Don't get me wrong. It has been upsetting for him. I found him up in the night, crying. I know he's very held in, naturally reticent. But even so, I would think that he'd show more distress."

It took Sagan a moment to answer. "The thing is, Cassie never really took on the role of a mother. She was always more of a provider. Reliable but somewhat removed. She never had kids of her own. I think she felt that she wasn't mother material. But she's fair and she's dedicated to her role as provider. When it comes to making sure that Paco has decent clothes and decent meals, she's the equal of any mother out there. I also think that

Paco has been bounced around by life so much that he's not going to get invested in anything. Not his foster mom, not school, not any single interest. Paco is a survivor, not an engager. Also, Paco has only been with Cassie for two summer growing seasons and the intervening winter."

"Have you ever known of anyone who threatened Cassie or Paco? Has she had animosities with any people in the community?"

Sagan shook her head vigorously. Her hair stayed perfect, not a loose strand. "None that I know of. Cassie is not antagonistic in any way. She's not someone who has issues with other people. She's just focused on her work and trying to provide stability for Paco. As for Paco... Well, I guess I've already explained what I can about him."

The woman saw some speck on her desk and carefully wiped it off the edge of her desk into her other hand, then transferred it to the wastebasket.

She continued, "It sounds like you think that there might be something that one could learn about Cassie that would explain where she is or what happened to her."

"Sometimes the victim of violence is chosen by random," I said. "But usually the perpetrator knows the victim. And from what Paco told me about them driving up very early in the morning yesterday, it sounds like Cassie was meeting someone. The more I can learn about her, the more likely I am to find out something about the person or persons who assaulted her."

Sagan nodded, frowning, thoughtful. "If I think of anything or hear anything, I'll call you."

I stood, pulled out my card and handed it to her. She put it in the top drawer of her desk, then gave me one of hers.

"If Cassie remains missing," I said, "what is your thought on where Paco could live? You already said that the families of his friends don't have room. But he still needs a place to stay."

She shook her head. "I'm sorry to say that I can't think of anything. He's coming to that age where people are no longer eager to take a child in just because he needs a home. And I... Well, there's no way I could take him in. Same for our teachers. Only

Judy has the space and could have taken him in, but she's just been diagnosed with breast cancer, so that's out. Let's hope for a miracle. Maybe there has been some terrible confusion. Maybe Cassie is okay and turns up soon."

I nodded.

"I suppose Paco won't be back at school until you get things sorted out," she said.

"Right. I have to assume that as a witness to Cassie's assault, he is in danger. Until I am certain the danger is gone, he will have to stay in some kind of protective custody. After that, it seems clear that the best thing for him would be to come back to this community. His community." I stood and turned to leave.

"Owen," she said as I was walking out of her door.

I turned back to her.

She gave me an imploring look. "This protective custody you mention. I don't pretend to know you, but you seem like a decent man," she said. "That boy could really use a male role model. Maybe he could live with you for the time being."

THIRTEEN

Pam Sagan's last comment made my breath short as I walked back into the school lobby. Between Pam Sagan and Street, I felt like they were ganging up on me even though I knew they were just trying to think of what was best for Paco.

My breath got shorter when I saw that Paco was gone.

I pushed out through the doors, half running, but calmed when I saw Paco at the Jeep. Spot had his head out the rear window, panting in the sun that was struggling through the fall clouds. Paco was reaching up, carefully petting the side of Spot's neck. His hand looked tiny against Spot's neck and head.

Paco saw me coming, opened the passenger door, and climbed up into the Jeep.

I got in, started the engine, and looked at Paco. He must have known that the principal and I were talking about him, but he said nothing, asked no questions.

"Let's go to your house and get that note that Cassie wrote me," I said. "Where do I drive?"

"Go left," he said.

I pulled out of the school lot and turned left.

Paco directed me through three more turns, and then we headed out into the countryside on a narrow, paved road. We drove two miles, turned again, drove two more miles.

"It's that drive," he said, pointing at a craftsman-style bunga-low set back from the road and surrounded by an old cedar fence. The house was brown shingle with white window trim and white columns marking the edges of a wrap-around porch. It looked like it had been built at the turn of the 20th Century. The white paint was peeling off the columns in long strips. The front door was scratched as if from a dog that wanted in. One of the windows had a diagonal crack running through it.

Out front was a realtor's For Sale sign.

I pulled onto a circular drive of crushed white rock. Scraggly, brown weeds poked up through the rock. From up in the air, it would look a little like someone had sprinkled oregano onto a powdered-sugar doughnut. At the center of the doughnut drive grew a fan palm.

Off to the side was a rectangular parking area on which sat a Chevy pickup and a Corvette, both in much better condition than the house.

"Nice spread you got," I said.

"This is the landlord's house. We live in the house out back," Paco said. He pointed to a dirt drive that went through the fence, down the outside edge of the property.

"What's the landlord's name?"

"Kevin."

"Kevin what?" I said.

"Kevin Garnett."

"Like the NBA player?"

"Yeah," Paco said. "That's how I remember his name."

"But your landlord isn't that Kevin Garnett."

"No. He's white. And a lot shorter."

"How long has the landlord had the house for sale?" I asked.

"I don't know. Awhile."

I drove down the dirt drive and followed it 75 yards back. The dirt road was compacted smooth, but it went up and down in broad dips and crests. The Jeep bounced hard.

We came to a small house that made the landlord's house look like it belonged on the cover of Architectural Digest.

The wood siding was weathered into deep cracks. The roof leaned and had multiple missing shingles. Two of the three front steps up to the front porch were missing.

Behind the house was a large greenhouse made of wood frame and covered with plastic sheeting. It was probably 50 feet wide and stretched 100 feet long. Behind it was a larger field with planting rows shaped into the dirt by farm equipment. Whatever had grown in those beds over the summer had been trimmed away, no doubt to be replaced with new growth come spring.

"This is our house. The note is inside."

I parked. Paco jumped out, ran up to the porch, and jumped over the missing steps.

I let Spot out to run around, which he did with enthusiasm, nose to the ground, tail held high, the smells of a farm unusual and exciting.

Paco reached for the doorknob, jiggled it, then turned around and came toward me.

"The door's locked."

"Shouldn't it be?"

"It's never locked," he said.

"But when Cassie left with you in the middle of the night yesterday, didn't she lock it?"

Paco shook his head.

"Did you watch her shut the door and leave without locking it? Or are you just remembering times when she didn't lock it?"

"I didn't watch her, but she never locks it. The landlord uses one of the rooms to store stuff. He doesn't want the house locked."

We heard a noise and turned to see the pickup coming down the dirt drive. It was coming fast, its wheels bouncing on the uneven surface. Despite the recent rain, the sun had shined enough that a dust plume rose behind it like a giant bushy tail.

The pickup made a fast stop, wheels skidding a bit. A man jumped out wearing a hothead attitude front and center. It went with his silver-dollar belt buckle and silver-tipped cowboy boots.

"Private property," he said to me, his breath heavy with alcohol. I remembered that Paco had said that the landlord hit people when he'd been drinking. "You're trespassing," the man said.

The man wore jeans and a dirty T-shirt with the sleeves rolled up to show his biceps. His hair was greased back and to the side in an elaborate curl like a '50s caricature.

Everything about the man telegraphed an effort to look younger than his late-40s age.

Spot came running up to sniff the stranger. The man jumped

back, then looked embarrassed at his fear.

I took Spot's collar and pulled him back.

The man looked at Paco. "Paco, man, you're not allowed here anymore. You and your mom have been evicted."

"You make a nice homecoming, Garnett," I said.

The man turned to me, venom in his sneer. "You want to act like a smart ass, you can tell it to the cops." He pulled his cell phone out of his pocket.

"When did you evict them?" I asked.

He jerked his thumb toward Paco. "I served his old lady thirty days notice a month ago. She left yesterday, so the house is back in my possession. I'm selling the property, so I need the house vacant."

"Then we just have to pick up Paco's things, and we'll be out of your hair."

"You're not picking up anything." He stepped between me and the broken steps. "What's left behind is mine. I already changed the lock."

I turned to Paco. "Paco, did Cassie take all of her things when you left yesterday?"

He made the tiniest of head shakes.

"I guess they didn't move out," I said to the man. "They just left for a couple of days. Which means that in changing the locks you are guilty of trespass."

"It's been thirty days. I can file an unlawful detainer."

"You can file, but California law does not allow you to evict until your case is heard in court and the judge decides in your favor. Only then are you allowed to have the sheriff come and evict the tenants if they haven't moved out."

I pointed at his cell phone, which he still held in his hand. "Go ahead and dial. We'll see what the cops think. Meanwhile, we'll get our stuff. Please unlock the door."

"I won't. I have my rights. This is my house."

"If you don't, I'll have to let Paco in one way or another. It might cause some damage."

Garnett's ears were red with anger. He put his phone in his pocket and stepped in front of me. His eyes darted to Spot, came back to me.

"Touch my house, I'll break your nose. I'm within my rights to defend my property."

This guy seemed more bluster than real threat.

"Spot," I said, "stay."

I went to walk past the man.

He took a wild swing at my face. If he'd been sober, I might have been in trouble.

I grabbed his wrist and twisted his arm. I used his momentum to spin him around, levering his arm up hard behind him.

He grunted in pain, but otherwise didn't vocalize. Impressive control.

Spot had jumped forward and stood looking at me, then at the man, then back at me.

"Stay," I again said to Spot.

"Assault is a serious crime," I said from behind the man's ear. I marched him past Paco up to the house. Paco was staring at me as if I were an alien creature. I half lifted the guy up and over the broken steps.

"Unlock the door," I said.

"I can't with my arm behind my back."

"You don't want to try to sucker me again," I said. "I'm bigger than you. I have an attack dog."

"Just need to get my key."

I let go of his arm.

He slowly pulled it around to his front, testing his elbow movement. He inhaled with the pain. Then he turned as he hammered me in the ribs with his opposite elbow.

It wasn't a good move, but it was faster than I expected. It caught me off guard and sent stabbing pain through my chest. Pain can be incapacitating.

Anger can suppress pain.

I kneed him in the groin and pounded two quick punches into his gut.

He bent over, trying to suck air. I took hold of the back of his belt, walked him away from the front door, across the porch to the edge of the broken steps, then ran him into the door. I rotated him at the last moment so that he wouldn't break his neck. He hit shoulder first, and the door blew open, splintering the jamb. The man fell on the floor and curled into a fetal position.

I looked at Paco. His eyes were wide.

"Go get what you wanted to show me," I said.

Paco looked at the man on the floor, then said something in a small voice.

"I'm sorry, Paco, I didn't hear you." I bent down, my ribs screaming.

Paco spoke again, nearly a whisper. "I don't want to walk past him."

I reached under the man's shoulders, grabbed handfuls of shirt, and dragged him outside. His hips and feet bounced hard as we went over the two broken steps. As I dropped him in the dirt, he still couldn't breathe. If his diaphragm didn't loosen up soon, he'd start turning blue. I patted him down, rolling him on the ground. I went through his pockets, pulled out his phone, keys, and wallet, and walked over to his truck. The window was open. I set the pocket stuff on the dash.

I walked back over to the man and stopped near his head so that he could see my shoe near his face.

"You can go in, now," I said to Paco. "He won't touch you."

Paco took small, tentative steps, looking at the man, then he disappeared into the house.

The man wheezed, getting a spoonful of air into his lungs.

The principal's comment about being a role model for Paco came back to me. I'd just used a man's body to break down a door. It was the worst kind of example to set, resorting to physical violence to solve differences. I began to rationalize it by thinking that I wasn't used to having a small boy observe my actions. Then I realized the folly of that thought. The actions were questionable regardless of whether or not they were observed.

Spot had come closer, curious about what was going on. He sniffed the man in the dirt, put his nose on the man's face. The man stiffened.

Spot turned and trotted away. After a couple of minutes, the man was breathing a bit, sucking air in small, desperate gasps.

Paco was still in the house.

The landlord made a little jerk and swatted his hand at his head. He jerked again and reached down to scratch at the small of his back. Then, still unable to breathe well, he started writhing. He swatted at his legs, gasped a tiny breath, rolled over onto his stomach, did a feeble oxygen-starved pushup, his body jerking.

It was then that I saw the ants on his back. They were tiny and red and swarmed over him, their movement fast and frantic.

I lifted the man up by his belt, steadied him on his feet. He was bent at the waist, still struggling to breathe, swatting and doing a little dance step.

"Time to go, Garnett," I said. I gave him a push.

One of the ants bit my hand. Then another. It wasn't like getting stung by a wasp, but it was a sharp attention-getter.

I brushed ants off my sleeves and legs as the landlord stumbled toward his pickup, swatting as he went. He slowly got inside, grabbed his keys off the dash, and started the engine.

Through the reflection off the windshield, I saw a burning look of hatred on his face. He revved the engine, spun a fast circle, and shot back up the dirt path toward the house.

I went inside Paco's house. I heard soft noises back in one of the bedrooms. I went down a short hallway and looked into what must have been his room.

Paco's bedroom had generic boy stuff, a Transformers movie poster on the wall, an old skateboard lying upside down on the top of a green dresser. On top of the skateboard perched a dirty softball. The paint on the dresser had chipped in many places showing the previous coat of pink paint. Along one wall was a mattress on the floor. The bottom sheet was blue, the top sheet a print with Toy Story figures against a red background.

Paco had put a wooden toy box up on a chair. He had climbed up and was standing on the box. The ceiling was made with acoustic tiles. Paco had one tile bent back. He pulled out a small object, pushed the tile back in place, and climbed down.

Paco saw me, and handed me a bundle of copy paper, folded three times and taped shut.

"That's what Cassie told me to give you if she got in

trouble."

"She didn't tell you what it was about?"

He shook his head. "She said if I took off the tape, she'd find out, and I'd be in big trouble."

"What did she usually do when you were in 'big trouble'?"

Paco gave me a blank look.

"Did she ground you? Take away the TV?"

He shook his head. "She told me I'd have to skip my next meal. But she never made me do it."

"Is that why you're so focused on food?"

"I don't know."

"When you were younger, before you lived with Cassie, did you go hungry?"

"I don't remember anything before Cassie."

"The principal said you only lived with her since you were eight years old. You don't remember anything before that?"

He paused. "Not really."

I put the folded wad of paper in my pocket.

"How did Cassie know of me? Had she met me?"

"I don't know."

"What exactly did Cassie tell you?"

"She just said that if something happened, I was supposed to call you and give you that paper. She wrote down your name. She showed me your number in her phone."

Paco walked over to his dresser and pointed to a note that was taped to the side. My name and phone number were written in feminine cursive.

"Was she in some kind of trouble?"

"I don't know."

"It might be a bit before we get back here," I said. "Is there anything else you want to take?"

"Can't I stay here? You could stay here. Spot, too. If Cassie's alive, she will come back here."

"I'm sorry, but you saw how upset your landlord is. We need to go back to Tahoe and look for Cassie there. You should grab a change of clothes."

Paco looked dejected. "Can we get another cheeseburger?"

"Sure, Paco. Whatever you want."

Paco had obviously been through a lot in his young life and it had the ironic result of preparing him better for this situation. Take a happy kid out of a happy home, expose him to assault and maybe murder, then force him to stay with a stranger, and he'd probably suffer a meltdown. Take an orphaned kid who's lived his life in foster homes and expose him to the same thing, and he thinks that if he can get a good meal, life isn't so bad.

Paco found a paper grocery bag and put some clothes in it.

"Paco, remember how you said you had your money hidden?"

He nodded.

"Because we might be gone for awhile, you should get it."

He nodded, very serious. He carried the chair out of the bedroom and over to the front door. He came back and got the toy box, carried it out and set it on the chair. He climbed up onto the box, reached up and felt along the top edge of the door.

It was a good hiding place. Unlike most interior doors, front doors were usually solid core. And based on how resistant the door was when the landlord made his forced entry, this one was solid core, too. Yet somebody had modified it.

Paco felt something. Peeled off a strip of duct tape. Raised his hand and pulled out an out-of-round toilet paper tube. Climbed down off the chair. Handed me the cardboard tube. It was stuffed hard with rolled bills.

"If I roll the money real tight, I can still get it in the tube. But I can't get it out. I always have to tear the cardboard to add my new money. Then I put it in a new tube. When it gets too tight, Cassie gives me bigger number money. I give her five twenties and she gives me a hundred."

"It's your money," I said. "Maybe you want to carry it."

He shook his head. "I'm just a kid. Kids lose stuff."

"Good point. Okay if I take it out of the tube so it will fit in my pocket?"

Paco thought about it. "I guess so," he finally said.

I peeled the cardboard tube off, re-bent the bills so that they would lie a bit flatter, and slid them into my pocket.

"Anything else you want to pick up while we're here?" I asked.

He shook his head.

We went back outside. I sat on the broken front step and pulled out the folded paper.

"Let me look at this."

Paco nodded. He walked over to the Jeep, got in the passenger side, shut the door and slouched down against the back of the seat.

As I pulled out the note for Cassie, I faced the drive, watching in case the landlord returned.

FOURTEEN

The taped bundle of paper that Cassie had left in the ceiling consisted of several sheets folded twice. I unfolded them. The printing was 10-point type. Hard to read, but it was a long letter and the small font made for fewer sheets of paper.

Folded inside the letter was a check made out to McKenna Investigations in the amount of $5000.

Dear Mr. McKenna,
My name is Cassie Moreno.

I heard that you're a private investigator, so I looked you up. If my foster boy Paco gives this to you, then I'm probably in trouble. I'm not exactly sure what is going on, but something isn't right. I know of nothing bad that has happened. If I called the cops, I wouldn't be able to report any crime, and I couldn't even identify the person involved. But I've become concerned enough that I'm going to write down everything I can think of about my situation just in case. If things go bad, you can maybe make some sense out of it. The check is for your expenses.

The situation I'm in is in some way connected to my clients, although I don't know how. So first, I should tell you about my business.

I'm an organic gardener specializing in tomatoes and peppers that I used to sell at farmers' markets.

A year ago, one of my clients asked if I would deliver produce to his house in Tahoe. He is very focused on having a healthy diet full of fresh produce, but he didn't have time anymore to go to the farmers' market. He said he also travels constantly for business, and that when he comes home late after a hard trip, there's nothing better than a glass of wine and a stir fry dinner of fresh-picked produce. He said that he had tried sending his house-keeper to the farmers' market, but that she didn't have a good eye for produce. So he wondered if I could save my best produce and also buy the best from the vendors who sell other kinds of produce. He wanted me to deliver it to his house. He would pay top dollar for the privilege of having the freshest produce.

It worked out very well. Soon, I started getting calls from his Tahoe friends. They, too, wanted my delivery service. And the word kept spreading. I ended up quitting the farmers' markets, and instead I just focus on getting the best produce there is and delivering it to my clients up at the lake.

I called this new business Field To Fridge: Fresh Organic Produce, Hand-Picked and Hand-Delivered. It has gone very well.

Last winter, a time when I have no produce of my own, I started buying from distributors who fly in produce from countries like Chile to sell to restaurants. Because my customers are willing to pay extra, I pay the distributors a premium. As a result, they give me first pick of each day's air shipments.

My Field To Fridge business now runs year 'round, and I'm at a point where I can't take any more business unless I decide to hire an employee. (Of course, I have Paco's help, and he is a lifesaver.)

One day last spring, I got a call from a man who said his name was John Mitchell and he wanted to make me an offer. He said he would like to call me once a week. He said he knew a man who was one of my clients. If I could tell him when and where this customer traveled, he'd mail me two hundred dollars in cash.

I hung up on him because it just sounded wrong. I couldn't technically say what was wrong with it, but that's how I felt.

John Mitchell called each of the next three weeks and asked if I'd reconsidered his offer. I hung up on him each time.

The next week when I delivered to my client, the one that John Mitchell had asked about, the housekeeper told me that my client had left for San Diego the day before.

That evening, I got another phone call from John Mitchell. That time I didn't hang up. I thought, if the housekeeper is willing to tell me – a delivery woman – where my customer went, what would be so wrong with me telling the man on the phone?

So I did. It still felt wrong, but that's how I rationalized it.

(To be truthful, I was also influenced by some things that happened recently with Paco that cost a great deal of money. I'm not what you'd call well-capitalized. I'm just a hard-working woman. I used to clean hotel rooms and houses. Then I made the transition to organic farming. I've always put everything I made back into the business. But after Paco, let's just say that my back-up kitty was used up. I needed money pretty bad.)

The man asked for my mailing address, and two days later I got two one hundred dollar bills in the mail. The envelope was postmarked in Sacramento. No return address.

He's called each week since. Sometimes I have no information, other times I do.

I know you're thinking that I'm a bad person for doing this, and you're right. But the money from John Mitchell has really helped me.

Unfortunately, it gets worse. The man knows how to set the hook. After I'd received several payments from him, he asked me if I'd like to make many times more money. I asked how. He said that he would pay for the same travel information for some of my other clients as well. All I had to do was go through my client list and consider which ones I had enough contact with to learn about their travel plans. So I did. The next time he called I read him a list of client names. He said yes or no to each name. He ended up choosing nine names.

From that point on, when he called each week, I'd give him travel information on three or four clients. Two different weeks I had info on seven clients. One week, eight of the nine clients on the list were traveling, and I knew where they were all going. Now here's where it really gets dicey. The man raised what he pays me from two hundred to three hundred dollars per client per week. The week when I told him where eight different people were traveling, he mailed me $2400.

This money has changed my life, Mr. McKenna. I've been able to buy Paco anything he needs. I've been saving for a house.

To my knowledge, no one has gotten hurt from this. Of course, I still don't know what's going on, so I could be wrong. I have to assume that it involves some kind of financial graft. But since this all began, I've had lots of conversations with my clients, and not one has mentioned anything that would hint at any kind of problem.

However, as the money involved has escalated, I'm becoming increasingly worried. This anonymous man has paid me over $16,000 since spring. And he's starting to change. He'll say certain things that don't seem especially bad initially. But later, they start to bug me. He uses a condescending attitude. Like instead of saying, "If you want, you could do this for me," he'll say, "You'll want to do this for me, won't you?" And he does it in a controlling voice that has a bit of a threat in it. It's kind of a creepy change, like in a movie the way the psycho starts out seeming nice but then gets more and more crazy as he takes over the victim's life.

It's because of this that I decided to write this down. Please don't think I'm paranoid. I'm just very cautious. My life hasn't been trouble-free, so I've learned to be a little afraid.

Recently, John Mitchell has said some unusual things that I'm trying to figure out. But I've just noticed the time. I have to go. So I'll hide this note, and tell Paco where it is. Then, when I get more time, I'll finish what I have to say.

Putting this in print sounds like I'm sort of overboard with worry. But if anything happens to me and Paco contacts you, I guess that will prove that I wasn't too paranoid!

If you do ever end up getting this note, then I apologize for the hassle for you. I will be putting you in a situation where you don't get to decide beforehand if you want to be involved. Although I suppose you can just ignore all this. Either way, I'm hoping the check will be sufficient for the time being.

Cassie

I put her check in my wallet and folded her letter.

While Cassie had suspected that things might get worse, nothing she had written would logically lead to something like murder. There was no direct threat. No disagreement. No calamity that she was being blamed for. Just an unusual situation that made her uneasy. Uneasy could be a warning signal. But uneasy didn't usually mean murder.

I walked over to the Jeep where Paco was still sitting. He turned to look at me through the open window.

"If Cassie wanted to hide something the way you hid your money, can you think of where she would put it?"

He shook his head.

"Would she pick a hiding place inside? Or outside?"

"I don't know," he said.

"I'm going to do a quick search. Can you wait another ten minutes? Not go anywhere and stay with Spot?"

Paco nodded.

"Keep your eye on the drive. If you see the landlord coming, honk."

Another nod.

I left Spot outside with Paco, then walked back inside and went into Cassie's bedroom. It was neat, the bed made, clothes put away. On a bookshelf were a couple of dozen tattered paperback books. I leaned in to look. A dictionary, a thesaurus, a farmer's desk reference, a bunch of books on gardening and farming, an anthology of Greek tragedies, and some classic novels like *To Kill A Mockingbird* and *The Grapes Of Wrath*.

There was an old green, dented file cabinet. In the back of the top drawer was a hardbound book. I flipped through it. It listed customer names and addresses and had columns of numbers that showed Cassie's sales and delivery dates and the dates that she'd been paid. Each payment showed the check number or the Paypal invoice number. The sales journal was neat and thorough and indicated that she was an organized businesswoman. I set it aside.

I opened a few drawers, looked in the closet, went through a little writing desk that stood under the room's only window.

I found nothing revealing. Just the items that I imagine are common to most homes occupied by women and young boys. The only unusual items on the writing desk were catalogs for organic farmers.

Paco had said that Cassie didn't trust banks. I wondered if that was literally true. She had to have a bank account to deposit checks and get Paypal deposits.

But she didn't have to put all of her money in it. If she didn't really trust banks, she might have a good amount of cash hidden somewhere.

I made a quick search of the rest of the house. There were no bank statements or cash in any obvious place.

Unlike when people put a door key under the front mat, when people choose a hiding place for something very valuable, they avoid the usual places. Paco's money roll already demonstrated creativity. It didn't mean that I couldn't find another stash of money if I spent enough time at it. But a really good indoor hiding spot can take days to find. An outdoor hiding spot can be impossible to find. If I knew for certain that Cassie had squirreled away cash, I might put in the effort. But it wouldn't be long before the men who wanted Paco would show up at the house. I couldn't afford to take days.

I picked up Cassie's sales journal, went back outside, and looked around the house.

Out the back windows I had seen tarps wrapped over geometric shapes.

"What's under the tarps?" I asked Paco.

"Our stuff for the farmers market. Tables. And bins. Trays we put the fruit in. Cassie says we need a garage, but that would cost too much. But now we don't use that stuff. We just use baskets for our deliveries."

"How does that work, those deliveries? Do you just take the customers a full basket each time?"

"Yeah. Cassie arranges the fruit to look good. Then we take back the empty basket from the last delivery. And they're clients."

"What?"

"You called them customers. Cassie calls them clients."

"Ah," I said. "Will you show me the hothouse?" I said.

He nodded, got out of the Jeep, and walked around the back

of the house. Spot came running.

The hothouse looked flimsy enough that a serious storm might blow it away. But the plastic sheeting was lightweight. If the wind got strong enough, it would probably just rip off the plastic and leave the wood framework undamaged.

At one end of the structure was a large propane tank. Near the tank was a door made of one-by-twos. It too was covered in plastic. Paco opened the door, and he and Spot and I went in.

In the corner near the door was a hot-air furnace. Duct work stretched from the furnace down one side of the hothouse. The hothouse was arranged with raised-bed containers in long rows separated by narrow aisles. The beds held thick, lush tomato plants that were held up by wire racks. The plants were nearly six feet high, and they were heavy with tomatoes that were turning from green toward red.

Under the plants I could see thin, black, plastic irrigation tubing that arced from plant to plant. Just above the plants were rows of grow lights.

Paco pointed down toward a wall of plastic sheeting that divided the hothouse across the middle. There was another door in the plastic wall.

"That other end of the hothouse are all the Cassie's Vipers. Spot shouldn't go in there 'cause he might sniff them. We shouldn't touch them. You have to be careful."

"Got it," I said. "We stay in this side with the tomatoes. Looks like you've got several different kinds."

Paco nodded. He walked down one of the aisles, pointing. "These are Sungold. Over there are Better Boys and Early Girls. And at the end," he pointed, "are Cassie's Amazements. She says our future is going to be mostly Amazements."

"Why does she say your future is in that hybrid?"

"'Cause they don't need to be gas ripened," Paco said.

"What does that mean?"

"Store bought tomatoes are picked green and ripened with gas. Real tomatoes are picked ripe. If you put real tomatoes in a truck, the ones on the bottom squish down to sauce."

"But Cassie's Amazements are different," I said, getting a

sense of where Paco was going.

Paco nodded. "They can be picked green and tough."

"So they don't make tomato sauce in the trucks."

"Yeah. But they don't need gas to ripen. They ripen pretty good by themselves."

"Almost as good as vine ripened?" I said.

"Close," he said.

"Seems like a tomato like that would be in demand by the companies that ship tomatoes by truck."

"Yeah. A guy talked to Cassie about it."

"What guy?"

"A guy from a company," Paco said. "He keeps coming and trying to get her to sign a paper. He drives a red Audi quattro."

"What does he want?"

"He wants to sell Cassie's Amazements."

"Does he just want to sell them, or does he want the rights to her creation?"

"I don't know. The rights, I think," Paco said.

"This guy say his name or company?"

"Maybe. I don't know."

"He say anything else you can remember?"

"No."

I looked around at the hothouse. "You can grow all of these so late in the season?" I asked.

"We harvest until Thanksgiving. After that it's too cold and too dark."

"Even though you've got the furnace and the grow lights."

Paco nodded. He walked over to a shelf on which sat an old computer. He wiggled the mouse, and the old screen gradually came to life, making little static clicks. Paco clicked on an icon, and up came the National Weather Service website. Paco typed in his zip code and brought up the forecast. He hit print and took the sheet of paper as it came out of an old printer.

Paco looked at it for a bit, then carried it over to an electrical box on the wall. The box was up high, and Paco had to step up on a stool to reach it. He unlatched the cover door and swung it open.

Inside the box was a thin, red, metal wheel. On its outer rim were two little knurled knobs around the perimeter of the wheel. I watched as Paco consulted the paper with the forecast and then unscrewed one of the knobs to loosen it. He slid the knob a tiny bit, then tightened it. He looked again at the forecast, then moved the other knob.

"What's that do?" I asked.

"Changes the times the grow lights go on and off."

"Why do you change it?"

"'Cause the fruit needs more light when it's cloudy," he said. "We use the lights less on sunny days to save money on electricity."

"Sophisticated," I said.

"What's that mean?"

"Refined," I said. "Advanced."

He shook his head. "Cassie says it's stupid. She says she's going to get a professional system like the drip irrigation. It will be automatic."

"Based on her secret formulas, huh?" I said.

He nodded. "But it's expensive. She needs more money, first."

"How do you control the irrigation?" I asked.

Paco pointed to another box, this one modern and made of plastic. He pulled on the catch, and the lid snapped open. Inside was a digital readout and a keypad below it.

Paco shut the box, then walked down one of the aisles, squeezing a few of the reddest tomatoes.

"These will be ready to pick in two days," he said.

I didn't respond. I had no idea where Paco would be in a couple of days. If Cassie didn't miraculously reappear unharmed, the tomatoes would probably go to waste.

FIFTEEN

We got back in the Jeep.

"Sorry about that little disagreement with the landlord," I said.

"We are quick to flare up, we races of men on the earth," Paco said.

"What is that?" I asked, shocked at such words from Paco.

"Something Cassie always says."

"When did she say it?"

"When, like, people get mad at each other."

"Do you know where she heard it?"

Paco shook his head. "She gets books from the library. Maybe she read it in a book."

We drove to McDonald's. Paco got two cheeseburgers along with his large fries and Coke and chocolate shake. We sat at one of the outdoor tables, under the hot midday sun of a Central Valley November, one of the amazing things about California weather.

"When you were in the house," I said, "the landlord got bit by a bunch of little ants. Have you seen that before?"

Paco nodded as he chewed, his mouth as full as a mouth can get. If he stuffed in any more food, his cheeks would rip.

Eventually, he swallowed and said, "Fire ants. They don't bite, they sting."

"I thought fire ants were just in Central America or something," I said. "You have them in the Central Valley? Are they all over?"

"I don't think so. All I know is we have them." He stuffed fries into his mouth.

"Awful lot of them in the driveway," I said. "They were driving the landlord crazy."

"That's nothing. There's a real big nest at the corner behind the hothouse. Cassie says if you tripped and fell on it, you could die from the stings."

"Ouch," I said.

Paco kept eating like a starving prisoner let out to visit an all-you-can-eat buffet.

"Principal Sagan said you are smart," I said. "She said you'll be reading in no time."

Paco's mouth was stuffed full, chewing. He said nothing.

"You said that you didn't know computers, but you used that one in the hothouse," I said.

Paco drank Coke, then sucked on the straw in his shake.

"She doesn't like me," he said.

"Why do you think that?"

"'Cause I hurt her friend's kid."

"What do you mean?"

"Her friend is Mrs. Burns. Bobby Burns is a bully. He called me a wetback and jumped on me from behind. I fell down. But I turned and he hit first."

"How bad did he get hurt?"

"His head hit the ground, and his ear got split. It made a lot of blood. He started screaming about how I'd attacked him."

"But you didn't? He came after you first?" Paco had already stated that, but I wanted to press the point.

"He jumped me."

"Did Bobby Burns end up okay?" I asked.

"He had to go to the clinic to have stitches. But it all healed. Now you can't even see where his ear split."

"Did you get in trouble for this so-called attack on Bobby Burns?"

"Yeah. I had to go to the cop station."

"Why did that happen?"

"The teacher looked in my pack and found my harvesting knife, and she called the cops."

"What do you use the knife for?"

"For cutting the stems on tomatoes and peppers. Cassie got

it for me."

"Why did you keep it in your pack?"

"I keep all my harvest tools in my pack with my school stuff."

"What are your other tools?"

I could see Paco visualizing as he spoke. "My work gloves and my garden belt with my trowel, my knife, my snips, my wire roll, my wire cutter, and my pliers."

"Why do you bring this pack to school? Is it the only pack you have?"

"Yeah. I keep my tools with me because sometimes when I come home, Cassie is on the phone, and she doesn't like me to come in and make noise. She says I have to be quiet when she's calling a client. So I go straight to the hothouse to do my chores."

"Why not just leave your pack in the hothouse?"

"I used to. But it got stolen. Cassie said I lost a hundred dollars worth of tools and two hundred dollars worth of time 'cause we had to drive to two different farm stores to get new tools."

"So you bring your pack to school."

"It keeps my stuff safe," Paco said.

"Where's the pack now?"

"In the van."

"What happened at the cops?"

"They fingerprinted me and took my picture and locked me in a cell. Cassie had to come and let me out."

"Did they charge you?"

"What do you mean?"

"Did they accuse you of a crime?"

"They said I brought weapons to school. I had to go to court. I wanted to tell about how Bobby jumped me. But the judge said I couldn't tell about that. He told me that if I ever brought weapons to school again, I would be taken out of school and sent to a place." Paco stopped, looked up, frowned. "I can't remember what he called it. Cassie said it was a boy's prison. She said that after the boy's prison, I would be sent to Mexico."

Paco drank the last of his shake. "Then Cassie had to go to

court," he added.

"Why?"

"She said she got suited."

"You mean, sued?"

"I guess."

"Was it Bobby's parents who sued Cassie?"

Paco nodded. "They said I caused pain and suffering, and Cassie had to pay them a lot of money."

"Didn't her insurance cover it?"

"I don't know."

I drank my coffee. The lawsuit must have been the big expense that Cassie referred to in her note.

"Is Bobby Burns okay, now?" I asked.

Paco nodded as he stuffed more fries into his mouth. "He hasn't jumped me again."

"Do you like school at all?" I asked. "Is there anything about it that's fun?"

He chewed the last of his fries, and swallowed.

"Going to school is like putting on gray clothes," he said. "There's nothing exciting about it."

After lunch, we were walking out of the restaurant toward the Jeep when Paco spoke.

"Will you buy me something?"

"Depends on what it is," I said.

Paco glanced up toward the sun, his eyes squinting. "My sunglasses are in the van."

"You want new sunglasses," I said.

He nodded.

There was a gas station and food mart next door. It had two rotating racks of sunglasses, one by the magazine rack, and one behind the counter, safe from the customers. Even from a distance I could tell that they were the expensive ones.

Paco tried on every pair in the first rack, then looked at the rack behind the counter. The clerk said he could come under the flip gate and look.

Paco tried on every pair in the expensive rack. He finally chose a pair of gold reflective Oakleys.

"But these are fifty dollars," I said.

Paco gave me a serious look. "They'll protect my eyes."

As I paid for the glasses, I was pretty sure that I had never paid more than $20 for my own sunglasses.

Paco asked the clerk to cut off the little nylon cord. Then he went back to the mirror on the stand and slipped the sunglasses up on top of his head, the lenses nestling in his bristle-brush black hair. He angled them just so until he looked very cool, and we went back out to the car.

"I thought the glasses were to protect your eyes," I said.

"They are," he said.

We drove off.

Paco stared out the window. A very young kid was riding a bicycle on a side road. He wore a green helmet and matching green bicycle clothes, skin tight, like a famous racer. His mother rode behind him.

"Do you have kids?" Paco asked.

"No."

"Why not?" he said.

I wasn't sure how to answer him.

"Why not?" he said again.

"Never thought I was dad material," I said.

Paco's frown intensified.

I drove back to the school.

"Stay in the Jeep with Spot?" I said.

Paco nodded.

I went back in to talk with Pam Sagan.

"How come you didn't tell me that your friend's son got in a fight with Paco?"

Her face colored.

"I didn't see that it was germane to our conversation," she said.

"With somebody after Paco, anything that suggests animosity for Paco is germane." I watched her. She didn't react. "Did you talk to Cassie about it?" I asked.

"Yes. It was a painful subject around here."

"Paco said that Bobby Burns jumped him first," I said.

"That's what he said. Robert says otherwise."

"And you believe your friend's son."

"I didn't put stock in either boy's story. I just wanted to make it so our students get along."

"Did Cassie react?"

"Not in any significant way."

"You remained cordial," I said.

She nodded. "I appreciate that about Cassie. She always keeps a broad perspective. Neither of us would want to let our students' disagreements poison our relationship."

I nodded. Sagan's words sounded sincere, but her face revealed little.

"Tell me about when the cops took Paco in."

"I'm sorry, Mr. McKenna. I can hear the judgment in your tone. Like all schools, we have a zero-tolerance policy with weapons. If a student brings weapons to school, we must call the authorities. They took him down to the county office and held him until Cassie came to get him out. Later, he made an appearance at court."

"Paco said that they were harvest tools," I said. "And they were in his pack, not in his hands."

"I'm sorry, but it doesn't matter. In the eyes of the police, a knife is a knife."

"What was the court's decision?"

"I don't know the details. I think the judge sounded very stern to Paco, trying to scare him. But he let him go without any punishment as long as Paco didn't get into any further trouble. As I said earlier, our community has tried hard to keep Paco here, safe and out of trouble."

"The Burns' family's lawsuit punished Cassie," I said.

"It certainly did," Sagan said in a low voice. She looked around to make sure that no one was close to her office door even though I'd shut it as before. "If the Burns boy did in fact initiate the fight, then it was a serious miscarriage of justice. If not, then, well, I don't know. I can't say that I like that part of our legal system. Lawsuits against individual people seem so... so unfair sometimes. Either way," she said, lowering her voice further, "it looked like a money grab to me. I found it dis..." she stopped talking.

"Paco gave me a note that Cassie wrote me. It suggests that she thought she might be in trouble. Does that ring any bells for you?"

"You mean something separate from being sued?"

"Right."

Sagan shook her head.

"She also wrote that Paco was only to give me the note if something went very wrong."

Sagan raised her closed hand to her mouth, and her forehead wrinkled with worry. "That's terrible. Cassie must have been so afraid to write such a note. She must have been in bad trouble."

Sagan looked out the window. "I don't have any ideas about what to do with Paco, but I'll talk to his teachers and the parents of his friends. Perhaps we can come up with some ideas."

"Thanks. If Cassie had problems, with Paco or anyone else, who do you think she would talk to? Who would she confide in?"

"Well I don't know. To my knowledge she doesn't belong to any groups. She doesn't go to church. Maybe she would talk to Dr. Mendoza. He runs the town clinic. He is kind of stern when you first meet him, but underneath his facade, he can have a warm way about him. He's kind of a father figure to many in this town. I imagine that many people would confide in him."

I got the clinic's address from Sagan, thanked her, and left.

SIXTEEN

The Fan Palm Family Clinic was another old building made of concrete block, but with modern windows, a fresh coat of beige paint and generous flowers out front.

"You okay with staying in the Jeep again with Spot?"

"Yeah," Paco said.

I parked in the shade of a huge palm and got out.

"Don't open the door for anybody. I don't care what they say."

He nodded. His eyes were foggy with fatigue. He'd likely be asleep in minutes.

I cracked the windows a bit, locked the doors, and went inside the building.

The air was artificially cool and permeated with an antiseptic-meets-sickness smell. Behind the counter was a chubby woman wearing a tight baby-blue sweater and tight baby-blue pants. On the left side of her head was a baby-blue hair clip.

"Good afternoon, sir," she said in an enthusiastic, high-pitched voice. She appeared grateful that I'd interrupted whatever she'd been doing. "Do you have an appointment with Dr. Mendoza?"

"No. I'm calling on a different matter. I'm Detective Owen McKenna. I'm investigating a possible murder in Tahoe. Pam Sagan over at the school believes that Dr. Mendoza was the victim's family doctor. I'd like to ask the doctor a few questions."

The woman's cheerful demeanor changed to a mixture of horror and excitement. "Oh, wow, that's terrible! What is the victim's name?" She asked with a little too much eagerness in her voice.

"I should discuss that with the doctor. Is he available for a few minutes?"

"Oh, of course, that would be hush-hush information at this point, wouldn't it? I've seen that on TV. Let me look." The woman flipped open a baby-blue appointment book and scanned down the schedule which, from my angle of vision, looked to show only four names for the entire day. "I'm sure I'll have to ask him. Please wait." She pushed back her chair and hurried down a hallway that I couldn't see.

I heard a door open and shut. There was a murmuring of voices, the woman's high voice and a man's deep voice. I heard the same door open followed by heavy footsteps. A big man wearing a white doctor's smock came out into the reception area.

"I'm Dr. Mendoza. What can I do for you?" The doctor was hairy in the extreme. Except for his nose and forehead, every patch of visible skin on his big, round body and huge head was covered with fur. Most of it had been cut back, especially on his cheeks and ears, but it looked to be a daily job that would require an electric hedge trimmer.

"Owen McKenna," I said, shaking a paw that had more fur on it than any two of Spot's paws combined.

"Mindy said you have a murder victim who was one of my patients?"

"It appears that way. Can we go someplace private and talk for a few minutes?"

"I'm sorry, but I'm busy, and I can only answer the most basic questions, anyway. Doctor patient confidentiality, you know. Please ask me here and now. If I can be of help without violating patient trust, I will. Although I can't see what that would allow me to tell you." His voice was loud and gruff, and the level of garlic on his breath was sufficient to defoliate my nose hair.

"It sounds like I need more information than you are willing to give. I'll go to the D.A. first, and we'll come back with papers. Of course, the initial deposition will probably take several days. And if you need to appear in court, that would be additional. But I can see that taking time from your practice is preferable to spending a few minutes with me, talking off the record."

I turned to go.

"Just a minute," he said.

I turned back. The man's eyes were narrowed so much that his eyebrows almost joined with the upper crest of his beard.

"So you're going to play tough," he said.

I shook my head. "No. I'm the gentle type, easy to like. You want to chat? Great. Save us both a lot of time. If you don't, I still have to do my job."

He gave me one of those looks of antipathy that I'd seen doctors give lawyers in a courtroom.

"We'll talk in my office." He turned and went back down the hall. I followed.

Mendoza's office was a small cubicle with a single small window.

Every surface in the office was covered with disorganized piles of papers, books, and periodicals. The papers that I could see were filled with medical and scientific terms. The books were medical reference manuals. The magazines, scientific and medical journals.

There were no golf clubs in the corner, no travel magazines, no brandy snifters on the shelf. The man was one of the serious workers. I couldn't tell from his office detritus if his main focus was treating local patients or something else, but his dedication was obvious.

He sat down on his desk chair and uttered a large sigh.

"What law enforcement agency do you work for?"

"I used to be Homicide Inspector, San Francisco. Now I'm private."

His reaction was dramatic. "You mean to tell me that you have no official involvement with a law enforcement agency in this case?" He stood up. "You've deceived me. Get out."

"No deception at all," I said. "Everything I said still applies. I work with law enforcement in the county where your patient was assaulted. I currently have temporary custody of the victim's foster child. I can think of both civil and criminal procedures where the legal people involved will listen to my recommendations. In fact, those officials appreciate that my footwork doesn't come out of the county's budget."

The doctor sat back down. "So what do you want?" He made

the question sound like a command.

"Paco Ipar and Cassie Moreno are your patients, correct?"

The man nodded. Looked at his watch. Sighed again.

"At six-thirty yesterday morning, Paco Ipar called me using his foster mother's cell phone. Paco was near panic, claiming that he'd witnessed Cassie's shooting." I explained how Paco had ended up hiding in the shooter's pickup, how he'd escaped near Heavenly Ski Resort and run down the mountain to me. "We have verified some of the boy's story. I'm inclined to believe the rest."

"But you don't have a body," Mendoza said, seizing on it as if it were proof that I was wasting his time.

"Correct. The woman may not be dead. The FBI confirmed that they have been looking for two men who match the description of the shooters as described by Paco. These men are wanted in three separate murders."

Mendoza said, "What does this have to do with me?"

"Your local school principal, Pam Sagan, said that Cassie had no close friends. Sagan thought that if Cassie would confide in anyone, it would probably be her doctor. So my question is, did she ever say anything to you that would hint at why she became a victim of a violent attack?"

Mendoza made a single, exaggerated shake of his head. Left, then right. "No," he said.

"Did you prescribe any controlled substances that she could sell on the street for money?"

"No."

"Was Cassie healthy enough that she could live a normal life substantially unaffected by medical issues?"

"Yes."

"So nothing in your relationship with her gives you any idea of how or why she could end up driving to meet someone who planned to assault her."

"Correct."

I decided to switch the subject to Paco. "Cassie's foster child Paco Ipar... Are you aware that he is an illegal alien?"

"Of course. The entire town is aware, just as they are aware of all the other children who are illegal aliens. This is the Central Valley. Food basket of America. The economy of every town in this valley would collapse if we didn't have the Mexicans who do the work that American-born citizens refuse to do, because they think it is beneath them. Not to mention that the work is also brutal in its exertion and involves extreme high temperatures in the fields and orchards."

"So you wouldn't do anything to report Paco to the authorities or anyone else who might then target Cassie for harboring an illegal alien."

"Damnit, McKenna! I'm a doctor, sworn to heal, not to inflict misery! I leave my personal judgments about the law and our border problems at home. When I come to work, it's to make sick people better and keep healthy people from getting sick. Doctors do their work in all places. We work in prison and heal murderers. We work on the battlefield and heal soldiers and, if necessary, heal enemy soldiers. We are a force for good at the personal level. We try our damnedest to keep issues of government from coming into our exam rooms!"

"Sorry. I didn't mean to insult you. I have the boy outside in my Jeep. He has suddenly gone from a somewhat stable life to a life of uncertainty at best. He's witnessed traumatic events. I'm trying to find out what happened. Asking questions of people who've had contact with Cassie is my most likely source of information."

Mendoza looked at me, the disgust in his eyes softening a bit. "I don't even remember when the last time was that I saw Cassie. What I do remember is that she was healthy as an ox and stubborn as a mule. She wasn't the kind of woman who would generate warmth in most people. But anybody would respect her. Probably everybody did respect her."

He rubbed his eyes with the heels of his hands. "You think she's dead?" he asked.

"I don't know. The two suspects reportedly use a Taser to paralyze their victims, then use plastic-wrap around the victims' arms to immobilize them and around their heads to suffocate them."

"Christ," Mendoza said. "And you have no idea why she would be assaulted by these men."

"No."

"Why would they come after Paco?" he asked.

"He witnessed the assault. They would want to silence any witnesses."

Mendoza looked a little sick.

"I wonder if you can tell me something I've always wondered about," I said. "We all know the basic effects of a stun gun. But can you explain in medical terms just what happens when someone is shocked with a stun gun?"

Mendoza made a little jerk of surprise at the question.

"Well, I'm hardly the person to ask. I'm a family doctor working in a farming community. Violent crime here is when two guys drinking in a bar get into an argument and settle it with a fist fight outside in the parking lot. I wouldn't be surprised if no one has ever been Tasered in this county."

"But you could explain its effects," I said.

He took a deep breath.

"Okay, this is a very crude explanation. I'm a doctor not an electromedical researcher.

"Think of the body's nervous system as a set of electrical circuits that the brain uses to turn the muscles on and off. Of course, the reality is hugely more complicated, but the analogy will serve for your question.

"The electrical voltage that your brain sends to your muscles is very small, probably less than one hundred millivolts." He looked at me to see if I was processing.

"Less than a tenth of a volt," I said.

"Right. It doesn't take a lot of juice to make our muscle cells fire.

"A stun gun is simply two electrodes across which a large voltage is sent. The amperes, or the total current flow, is low, but the voltage is high. I've heard figures ranging from fifty thousand to over a million volts. I should back up and say that the amps are kept low because amps are what stop your heart and kill you.

"If you take a stun gun, put the two electrodes on your skin, and pull the trigger, you send this very high voltage into your body. When you put voltage into your muscles that is hundreds of thousands of times greater than what your muscles are used to, the result is total body chaos. Your muscles start contracting, and you lose all control. You fall to the ground in a seizure, unable to do anything about it.

"Even though the electrical shock is brief, it takes a long time for your body to recover. You want to stand up and make your legs and back and arms work, but the signals your brain sends out to make that happen are like candles against the Klieg lights of the stun gun."

"Do stun guns cause permanent damage?"

"They can. People have had heart seizures and died after being shocked. Other people have ongoing problems. But most people usually recover given enough time."

"Let me ask a different question, if I may."

Mendoza looked at his watch again.

"If in fact Cassie is dead," I said, "Paco will need a place to live. Do you have any ideas?"

"I run a medical clinic, not a bed and breakfast."

"I'm serious," I said. "Have you learned anything about the places that other illegal alien kids stay?"

"They stay with their families. Obviously, Paco isn't the only orphaned illegal, but he's the only one in our immediate town. I have no idea where he could stay."

"I'm wondering about trying to track down any relatives of his in Mexico, people who might take him in. Did Cassie ever say anything to you about that? Is is possible that she did any research about Paco's background?"

"If she did, I didn't hear about it."

"Is there any communication among doctors about these kinds of problems?"

"You mean, placing orphaned kids?" Mendoza said. "No. Not our business."

"So you have no ideas."

"No. Not unless you could get a response out of the Basque community."

"What do you mean?" I asked.

"The kid's Basque. The Basque in this country often stick together. Like orthodox Jews. Like Indian tribes. Like Puerto Ricans. They know each other. Maybe there are Basque people who take in Basque kids."

"How do you know he's Basque?"

"A little because of his looks. Eyes. Face shape. But mostly his name."

"Paco?" I said.

"No. Paco can be a first name for Native Americans or anyone of Spanish descent. And looking at Paco's skin color, I'd guess he's got some Native Central American in him, probably Maya.

"The reason I think he's Basque is that Ipar sounds Basque. Basque surnames are based on the family homestead. If I had to guess, I'd say that Ipar is short for Iparagirre. Which means, loosely, a house that faces the north wind, Ipar referring to north and agirre referring to a house exposed to the elements."

"How do you happen to know so much about the Basque?"

"We Mendozas are Basque. I grew up in a household that strongly identified with Basque culture."

"You say that Paco looks Basque, but you look nothing like Paco. How is that?"

"I know. I'm white and hirsute as a bear. Paco's brown, and he probably won't have much body hair. It's like the Black Irish and the Red Irish. Different colorations in a common people. Incidentally, it may be that the darker Irish people have some Basque in them."

"Forgive my ignorance," I said, "but are the Basque from Spain?"

"We call our land the Basque country, a semi-autonomous land on the border between Spain and France. Our people have been there for many thousands of years. In fact, we are the oldest continuous people in all of Europe. That is probably why we have such pride in being Basque."

"If I were to try to find a Basque family to take in Paco, where would you recommend that I start?"

"I'd contact the Center for Basque Studies at the University of Nevada in Reno. They might have an idea. You must be aware of the Basque presence in Tahoe."

"I've heard of it, but that's about all."

"Well, briefly, the Basque, like everyone else, came to the California foothills in significant numbers during the Gold Rush. After that died down, many Basque stayed on. Traditionally, the Basque excelled as sheepherders and they realized that they could earn their living the old-fashioned way, tending sheep throughout the foothills. Then they discovered that the high meadows in the mountains around Tahoe were excellent places to run sheep herds in the summer. Like the Washoe Indians, they moved down to Carson Valley in the winter, bringing their sheep with them. This is how Tahoe and Carson Valley both ended up with a substantial Basque population."

"Did you know Paco's birth mother?"

Mendoza shook his head. "Never met her. The first time I met Paco, he was about one year old. His mother had already been dead for many months."

"One more question and I'll let you get back to work. These patients that you see, many of them are no doubt poor. Is this pro bono work for you?"

"It used to be. Then a benefactor came along and offered to pay for all of the medical needs of the town's poor and uninsured. I bill out at a cheap rate compared to my colleagues in the city, but at least I'm now getting paid."

"What's the charity?"

"It's called the Medical Freedom Foundation. Their mission is to provide health care for poor neighborhoods. They try to raise awareness in the corporate world to help generate more funds. The ultimate goal is to ensure that no person in this country goes without medical care for lack of money."

"A good deal for all," I said.

"Yes. Spread the word if you know people who work for other foundations."

I thanked him for his time and went back out to the Jeep.

SEVENTEEN

Both Paco and Spot were sleeping, Paco stretched out across the front seat, and Spot across the back, comfortable in the shade of the palm fronds above.

I unlocked the Jeep and shook Paco to wake him up.

"What?" He sounded asleep.

"Where's the library?" I asked.

He frowned. "It's by the school."

I started the Jeep and drove to the school.

Paco pointed at a tiny building adjacent to the school. It too was made of concrete block and looked like a converted one-car garage. I parked and went inside the one-room library.

A cheerful woman in her seventies greeted me.

"Glad to see that budget cuts haven't closed you down," I said.

"Well, if we cost anything to speak of, they would have," she said, her eyes intense. "This facility is shared by the school and the community, so the idea was that half our funding would come from the county budget and half would come from the school district budget."

"Sounds like a good idea," I said.

"Ha!" she exploded. "Good idea, my ass. The county has decided that they have no money for libraries. Did you hear that number? None. And the school board has decided that what used to be the library budget should instead be spent on a football coach who goes around from school to school and teaches kids to butt heads and get concussions. Who needs a bunch of dumb books, anyway, when you can play football?"

"I'm sorry you don't have a strong opinion about it," I said and smiled. "How do you stay open?"

"Volunteers. We have a committee. Sixteen of us. We donate our time, and we pay the utilities. Fortunately, the mortgage on this gorgeous facility is paid for."

"At least it's too small to be turned into a football locker room," I said.

She squinted at me. "You look like you could play football," she said. "But can you read a book?"

"Am I allowed to move my lips?"

"You're a funny guy. I like that. What can I get for you? We have books from Dr. Seuss to James Joyce and very little in between. But an ex-math teacher willed her entire library to us when she died six months ago, so we have a great collection of volumes on geometry and trigonometry and calculus."

"Actually, I'm here because of bad news regarding Cassie Moreno." I gave the woman a quick explanation. The woman was shocked, but she handled it well.

"Although her boy witnessed the assault, and we've verified much of his story, we haven't found Cassie," I continued. "Anything I can learn about her may help in finding her."

"Whether she's alive or dead," the woman said.

"Right. I realize that a patron's borrowing records are private and you are obligated to protect Cassie's rights. But I'm hoping you'll balance what could be gained against what is lost with her loss of privacy."

"Who can vouch for you?" she said.

"You can call the sheriffs of any of the counties around Tahoe. You might also call Pam Sagan."

The woman picked up the phone and dialed a number.

"Pam?" she said after a half-minute. "Got a guy in here, says he's a detective working on an assault involving Cassie. You got a read on this guy? Is he legitimate?"

She watched me as she listened for a bit, then spoke, "'Course, if Cassie's dead, she's got no privacy rights. I read that in one of these moldy books." She listened a bit more. "Thanks," she said, and hung up.

"Pam thinks you're okay. Which means that I'll break the law to the extent of telling you about Cassie's book borrowing up to subject but not including title. You okay with that?"

"Yes. Thank you. What were the subjects of the books she borrowed?"

"In three words? Gardening, gardening, and gardening, which means she read all seven of our gardening books. She also borrowed books on farming, which amount to two titles. Let's see, she had a little thing for romance novels, which, if you knew Cassie, is a bit of an eye-opener. That's about it."

"Does 'about it' mean that was all she borrowed? I don't mean to be picky, but could you look in your records? Or do you have all of your patrons' activity memorized?"

"Well, you are thorough, aren't you? If you knew how many people come in here to borrow books, you would realize that I don't need to consult the check-out notebook. This is a small town library, emphasis on small. Make that, emphasis on tiny."

The woman walked down one wall, scanning the shelves, went across the back wall, came back up the third wall.

"Two more subjects come to mind," she said. "Our vast literary resources include a book on how to run a small business as well as a book on the Basque people."

"Both of which Cassie read," I said.

"Can't say that. Both of which Cassie checked out. There's a difference."

"Right. Tell me," I said. "Dr. Mendoza just mentioned that he thought Cassie's foster kid was Basque. Which makes me somewhat interested in the Basque people. I wonder if I might look at what you have on that subject?"

"Excuse me while I go search the stacks. It may take some time." She pulled her lips back in a tight half-smile. Without moving, she reached out and pulled a book off the shelf.

"Perhaps you'd be interested in this volume," she said.

I took it from her. It was a hard-bound book about the Basque country and general Basque information. As I flipped through it, nothing seemed applicable to Paco or California or killers who look like superheroes. I handed it back to her.

"I have a question that is a bit obscure, but you might be able to tell me where to look. There is a phrase that Cassie periodically says. It goes, 'We are quick to flare up, we races of men on the earth.' Does that mean anything to you?"

The woman made a quick grin. "Here's where I should give my lecture about the value of a liberal arts education, which, of course, all of us library committee members have. But the truth is that I know about that phrase only because Cassie said it to me once, and I asked her where it came from."

I waited.

"It's from 'The Odyssey,' Homer's epic poem."

"Heard of it," I said, "but that doesn't count for much. What's it about?"

"It tells the story of Odysseus, a Greek man who tries to find his way home after fighting in the Trojan War. One of those impressive feats of literature that pretty much no one other than Greek scholars ever reads. I looked through it once. Kind of rambles all over the place. But my strength is English Lit, so I shouldn't judge. Besides, Homer influenced my guys."

"Any idea why Cassie would quote it?"

She shook her head. "I think it's just a good line, that's all. But it shows that she has an ambitious intellect. She's not what you'd called an educated girl – she used to clean houses, after all – but she's real smart and has the mind for much more."

"Thank you very much for your time."

She nodded. "I hope you find that woman. Paco needs her."

I nodded and let myself out.

Back in the Jeep, I thought about how enigmatic Cassie seemed, a former house cleaner who quoted Homer.

I said to Paco, "That line, 'We are quick to flare up?'"

Paco looked at me.

"It comes from an ancient Greek writer name Homer. Did Cassie ever talk about Homer?"

Paco shook his head.

"She ever say other lines like that?"

"No." He shook his head. "Wait. Sometimes she says, 'The only thing that overcomes hard luck is hard work.'"

"Sounds like another quote. She say who originally said it?"

"No."

EIGHTEEN

It was dark before we made it back to Tahoe.

The rain had paused in the valley, but resumed a light drizzle as we climbed back up the Sierra. The temperature dropped more than the average 4 degrees per thousand feet of altitude gain. The light rain turned to snow flurries as we went by Kirkwood at 7800 feet. The snow grew more vigorous as we drove higher. By the time we crested Carson Pass at 8600 feet above the warm Central Valley, it had gone from a 79-degree Stockton afternoon to 32-degree twilight at 8600 feet.

Although my cabin above Tahoe is lower elevation than Carson pass, the temperature kept dropping with the onset of nighttime. When we parked in my drive, we stepped out into frosty air. Paco hugged himself and looked around at the dark as if something was wrong with a landscape that has never seen a warm evening.

As we walked to the door, a small rabbit ran across our path and dove into a hole that I didn't know existed. Spot ran after, sniffed the hole for a bit, then rejoined us at the door.

When we were inside my cabin, I said, "Now that you have some clean clothes, you should take another shower and put them on."

Paco gave me a look of resignation, then picked up the paper bag with his clothes and carried it into the bathroom. When he was finished showering and had changed, he came out of the bathroom. The sunglasses were back on his head.

I said, "I have to make some phone calls. You can sleep in my bed so that I don't wake you."

"I don't want to sleep in your bed," Paco said. "I'll sleep with Spot." He hugged himself and shivered. He seemed eager to get into the sleeping bag and absorb some of the excess warmth from the giant dog next to him.

"Your call," I said.

Paco pulled his sunglasses off his head, set them on the little table, and wriggled into the sleeping bag which was covering a good portion of Spot's bed. Spot walked over and stared at Paco. His head was down, jowls drooping, trying to figure out his next move. He finally stepped onto the small portion of his bed that wasn't covered by Paco and lowered his elbows until they touched the bed. With his butt still in the air, he looked at Paco who was instantly asleep. Then Spot lowered his rear, squatting on his haunches, looked at Paco again, and flopped over sideways, possibly crushing the boy's side.

Paco yelped, jerked his limbs out from under Spot, and scooted away from him. Paco rubbed his elbow vigorously. His permanent frown was even more pronounced than normal. "He just rolled on me!" Paco smacked Spot hard on his chest with an open palm.

Spot made a big sigh and went to sleep.

Paco jerked on his sleeping bag and turned the other way so that he was back-to-back with Spot. Paco breathed the quick, huffing pants of a snorting animal. After thirty seconds, his breathing calmed. In another half minute, he was out.

I got on the phone and called Diamond and Mallory to ask if either had any news of the missing Cassie or the van or the possible shooter. Diamond wasn't picking up, so I left a message. Mallory answered, but said that he had no news.

I opened up the sales journal I'd borrowed from Cassie's desk. She had 31 customers for her Field To Fridge delivery business. She'd written a tiny JM next to 9 of the names. Those must have been the names that the man named John Mitchell had picked, the ones for which he wanted travel information.

There was no evidence that suggested that the people on the list were connected to her disappearance and possible murder. But I knew that graft was involved in John Mitchell's travel-plans gig. It was a logical place to investigate.

I got out my laptop and began Googling the names, four of

which I'd heard of.

I got lots of hits on all of them.

I made notes so that I'd be prepared when I visited them. Three of the names on Cassie's list were people nearly everyone knew. One was a rock star. One, a late-night talk show host. Another, a famous baseball player. The less familiar names were successful people who were well known within their own circles. One was the CEO of a software powerhouse. One was a CEO of a national restaurant chain. One was a producer of documentaries. There was an owner of a medical stents manufacturer. There was an inventor who'd created several devices for NASA to use in the microgravity of earth orbit. The last person on the list, and the only woman, was a romance novelist.

My phone interrupted my research.

"You rang," Diamond said.

"I was in Stockton today. So I wanted to check in and ask if you had any news. You find a van or a body? That sort of thing."

"Nope on the van, nope on the body," he said.

"Then let me run an idea by you. Today Paco gave me a letter that Cassie had written to me. Turns out she suspected that she was involved in something uncomfortable if not illegal or dangerous."

I told Diamond about the man who called himself John Mitchell and his payment for travel information on Cassie's customers. I went down the list of customers.

"Tell me what you think of this," I said. "I've thought about how someone could make money using the travel plans of successful people who worked in disparate industries. The only possibility that comes to mind is playing the stock market. My idea is simple.

"Pretend that one of Cassie's customers is a major software CEO, and he flies to a medium-smallish city. This John Mitchell guy finds out about it from Cassie. Mitchell does some research and discovers that the smallish city has a fast-growing company that produces software. Further research shows that the small company's product might be useful to the large company.

"So Mitchell figures that the big company might be looking into buying the small company. Mitchell immediately buys a bunch of the small company's stock. If Mitchell's hunch is true, the small company's stock will soon surge, and Mitchell will make a lot of money. Better yet, no one can accuse Mitchell of insider trading. He knows next to nothing about either company. He is insulated from the executives of both."

"This woman has a bunch of CEOs among her customers?" Diamond said.

"As far as I can tell, about half of Cassie's Field To Fridge customers live on the lake. The rest are in expensive neighborhoods like Glenbrook and Incline Village. They are super successful in a wide range of businesses. Simple stock investing based on my scenario might work."

"Yeah, it might," Diamond said. "But it might not. John Mitchell could buy and lose big time."

"Sure. But consider what the averages would be. Most successful people work in successful businesses. Tahoe people are more highly represented in the software business, for example, than in horse buggy manufacturing. Even if you invest blindly in successful fields, you are likely to do better than if you simply invested evenly across the economy. Two of the guys on Cassie's list are billionaires. Any little thing they do can move the stock price of their companies."

I paused.

"You done?" Diamond said.

"No. I'm just pausing so the full effect of my brilliance can sink in."

"Be a little scary," Diamond said, "investing in something based on your notion. What if your CEO is traveling to this little city not to pick up software business assets but to take a cooking class or buy a new boat or visit his aunt?"

"Then John Mitchell's investment doesn't jump, but just rides the market. That's where Cassie's range of customers makes the difference and spreads the risk. If John Mitchell is playing the market nine different ways, sure, some of his calls are going to be duds. But some of his investments might benefit. And maybe one goes through the roof. Either way, at the minimum, it would probably beat the averages. And consider what would happen if Mitchell figures out a big corporate acquisition? Mitchell might bet his farm and make a killing."

"I get your point," Diamond said with a tone I'd heard before.

"You sound dismissive."

"Nah. Just wondering how a romance novelist fits into your scenario."

"That's a hard one," I said. "Unless you're J.K. Rowling, no publisher's stock is going to jump on news of signing an author. So maybe this romance novelist owns controlling interest in a company on the side. Maybe she's an aggressive business woman. Her travel could indicate plans for her own business, plans that would bump its stock price."

"That sounds better," Diamond said. "Could be the ball player, the rock star, and the talk show host are business owners, too. "If you look at it with that in mind, maybe your idea makes sense."

Before we hung up, Diamond asked, "You drop off the boy down in the valley?"

"Couldn't find anyone to take him."

"So where is he?"

"Sleeping on Spot's bed as we speak."

There was a pause before Diamond spoke. "Where is Spot?" he asked.

"Sleeping next to him."

Another pause. "Like you've suddenly got a regular family almost," Diamond said.

"I'm hanging up now," I said and hung up.

I turned off the computer and went to bed.

NINETEEN

I awoke to a noise. I stopped breathing and listened to the night. Spot wasn't growling out in the living room, so it was probably nothing. But dogs can be in a deep sleep, too. I'd witnessed Spot sleeping through a noise, twitching his ears as he incorporated the sound into his dreams.

I lay motionless and listened. From within the thick log walls of my cabin, my room seemed as devoid of sound as it was of light. I heard the low, dull hum of the fridge in the kitchen nook. Then came the rattle/snore of Spot. The snore trailed off and then restarted. There was nothing else. I kept listening.

The focus of careful listening is fatiguing. I got drowsy. Started to nod off.

Another noise.

I sat up. Turned my head back and forth like a dog.

Nothing. Until I cupped my ears while I was facing the outer wall.

Some creature was crying. It sounded like what I'd expect if a bunny rabbit had been picked up by a Great Horned Owl.

The squeaking sound repeated over and over. As I listened, the sound got louder.

I generally accepted this aspect of the forest. For a small creature, the natural world is a harsh place, and owls, if that's what it was, are among the most effective predators on the planet. But I'd also seen predators who picked up prey and didn't show them the mercy of a quick kill. Add to that the fact that I couldn't sleep while some little animal was being tormented. Maybe I could scare the owl off.

I slipped out from under my covers. Pulled on my jeans and shirt and running shoes.

Spot was now awake as I walked into the living room. He was dimly lit by the light of the readout on the microwave. Paco's arm was over him as before. Spot was still lying down, reluctant to leave Paco's embrace, but his head was up listening.

I walked to the front door. Spot jumped up. Paco's arm fell to the sleeping bag, but Paco didn't wake.

"No, Spot," I whispered. "You stay with Paco."

I put my hand on the doorknob, turned it quietly. As I opened the door, Paco suddenly spoke, his voice groggy.

"Where are you..."

I turned. "I'm just checking a sound," I said. "Spot will..." But as I began to say that Spot would stay with him, Spot shouldered past me and trotted out the door.

"Stay here. I'll be right back," I said.

I flipped on the outdoor flood, shut the door behind me, and took fast steps out into the night.

"Spot, come," I said. I didn't want him to mess with any unknown animal. No matter how gentle he was, if he contacted a Great Horned Owl, he would likely hurt it.

I went around the corner of the cabin and saw Spot walking slowly toward an object on the ground. It wasn't directly lit by the floodlight, but it looked light in color. About the size of a baby bunny rabbit. It squeaked incessantly.

A small noise came from behind me. I spun. A dark shape moved in the night. A popping sound. A stabbing burn on my left kidney.

My left leg collapsed as my entire body lit up with electricity. I went down. Fell to the ground.

Pain shot through me, burning my insides like a fireball. The origin was my back, but the pain was everywhere. I had no control. Every muscle was in spasm. My brain short-circuited. No thoughts but pain. No movement except uncontrolled contraction of every muscle in my body.

At some root level I realized that I'd been punched with a stun gun, with 100,000 volts or more of incapacitating juice. I was more helpless than if I'd been shot with a bullet, and the pain was much greater than that of a mere projectile piercing through flesh.

I struggled to fight it, but I was impotent against the flow of electrons. My entire body was in seizure. I had no control.

After an exhausting interval, unable to even breathe, I became aware that the current was off. I still couldn't move, but I could begin to think. After many long seconds, I was able to turn my head. Spot was still over where he'd gone to investigate the sound. He was sitting up but his head drooped down. He was moving, but I couldn't see what was wrong.

I focused on making my paralyzed muscles move. Turn the legs. Push with the arms. Get up onto my hands and knees. Raise one knee. Foot to the ground. I braced my hands on the knee. Push. Straighten. Stand. I was wobbly, but upright.

"GO!" someone shouted from the darkness. A deep, booming voice.

I heard movements, running footsteps, charging close, then receding. I tried to turn on my pins-and-needles legs, lost my balance, fell into the dirt.

I limped over toward Spot.

As I got closer, I could see in the glow from the distant light that he was okay. Trapped by a fishnet of some kind, but okay.

Spot pawed at the net that draped him, getting nowhere.

More running footsteps went by. Heavy. A big guy. And whimpering sounds. A car door slammed shut over in the dark forest. Engine roared. Wheels spun.

I reached Spot, pulled at the fishnet. The cords of the net were hooked on his claws and elbows. One of his ears poked through a small opening, his ear stud flashing in the night. He was chewing on the cords, but it was clear that he wasn't going anywhere until I cut him free. But my pocket knife was on my night stand with my other pocket stuff.

I grabbed at the net over Spot and tried to tear it. The cords cut into my skin. They were much too strong to rip apart.

Spot would have to wait.

I put my hand on him. "I'll be back, largeness. You be good."

I stumbled toward the cabin, my legs still barely working. The front door was standing open. I went in, turned on the light.

Paco was gone.

I dialed Street.

She answered on the second ring.

"Listen carefully, sweetheart." The words came broken. The Taser had affected my vocal cords just like the rest of my muscles. "Men broke in and took Paco. They are coming down the mountain. If you are very fast, you could turn up my road and..."

"And park sideways at the narrow place near the giant boulder," she finished. "I'll do my best." She hung up.

Street was fast, nimble, and most important, she was quite functional within a moment of waking up.

I struggled back outside, limping, dragging my left foot which was still most affected by the shock. I got into the Jeep and drove down the mountain. At the second curve I saw their headlights three switchbacks below. Driving fast. They might get through the narrow point before Street could block it. Worse, Street might block it as they were approaching. She could get rammed. Her little VW Beetle would collapse when hit by their truck. She could get killed.

I tried to focus on driving.

I've driven the twisty, private mountain drive that I share with my neighbors thousands of times. I'm not a professional driver, and my Jeep is not designed for fast cornering. But I can get down the mountain faster than most. I had a hope that I could catch them.

At the big curve below the switch backs, there is an overlook of sorts. Visible in the distance, but closer than before, was the headlight glow of the other vehicle. It was still upstream from the narrow place that Street was heading for. I saw brake lights flash bright red in the night just as I came to another curve and lost my view. Maybe that meant that Street had already gotten there.

I pushed it harder. I careened around the next two curves and accelerated down the straight before the narrow spot. Up ahead were distant red lights. I turned off my headlights. The red lights up ahead turned white.

A vehicle moving in reverse. Coming up toward me.

Brake lights flashed again, and the white lights went out. They'd shifted into drive.

They turned left off the paved road. I knew where they were going. There is an old trail, easy to see, easy to navigate. It looks like a good way through the woods. But in the interest of preventing erosion and soil compaction, the Forest Service blocked it with boulders. It gave me an idea.

I continued to drive my road by starlight and by feel. I raced past the place where they'd turned off. I stopped before I came to the narrow place where Street's car would be parked. I couldn't see their lights through the forest, so I hoped that they couldn't see my brake lights.

I jumped out and did a wobbly, limping jog into the forest.

I headed for a walking path where I remembered a little raised section that crossed a miniature ravine. To help hold the dirt fill in place, the Forest Service had put down a log on each side. If my memory was correct, the logs were just the right size for what I wanted. More important, I remembered that the logs were just fitted into the dirt and hadn't been staked in place. When I got there, I knelt in the dirt and felt for one of the logs. It was about the size I remembered, eight inches in diameter and ten or twelve feet long. And while I didn't feel any stakes, it was completely packed into the dirt. I couldn't get my fingers around it to lift it up.

I stumbled two steps away from the trail and felt a nearby tree for low, dead branches, found one, and broke it off. The sound was loud. The men probably heard it.

By gouging the broken end of the branch into the dirt around the edges of the log, I was able to excavate a trench in the hard-packed dirt. I worked fast. I knew I was nearly out of time. I dug and stabbed and scraped with my little stick. When I had enough dirt removed to get my fingers under the log, I tried to lift. It didn't budge. I squatted down and put my forearms across my thighs for support.

At first, it didn't work. Then I shifted position and tried again at the very end of the log. It shifted, then came free. I lifted the end up until the log was vertical, then lowered it back down at an angle so that the middle of the log rested on my shoulder. The log teeter-tottered on my shoulder. I shifted it a bit for balance, then jogged away toward the vehicle that contained Paco.

The log was a good hundred pounds, heavy to carry while jogging, but perfect for my needs. I cut through the woods toward the old trail. The vehicle's taillights appeared in the distance. I tried to speed up.

As I got closer I could see a figure in front of the vehicle, illuminated by the vehicle's headlight. I couldn't see well through the trees, but he appeared to be a very big guy. Maybe a huge guy. Big enough to move boulders. Like a bad superhero. He was bent down, rolling one of the boulders that blocked the trail. Another boulder had already been moved. As soon as he got it out of the way, the trail would be clear.

I ran faster, huffing so loud that I was worried I'd give myself away. But their engine was loud. I hoped it would provide sound cover.

I didn't know for certain if the man rolling the boulders was alone or had a partner. As I got closer, I angled my course to let the illuminated scene be visible through the vehicle's front and rear windows.

Silhouetted against the light was the shape of another man in the driver's seat. Another big guy.

I couldn't see Paco's shape. Maybe he was too short. Maybe he was down on the floor.

I angled into the woods, moving slower, trying not to hit anything that would make noise and alert the men.

Up ahead was a pickup. The woods were so dark that I couldn't see the color or make.

I circled through the woods until I was about twenty yards straight out from the driver's door.

The man moving the boulders had the second one out of the way. He straightened up. "Okay," he shouted. "You can come on through."

I was too late. I started running toward the pickup. If the driver drove away, I was out of luck.

"C'mon!" the boulder guy shouted, gesturing.

As I got closer in the dark, I saw the driver gesturing, waving the boulder guy to the pickup.

Maybe the driver sensed me coming at the last moment. He started to turn. Lifted his arm.

My log crashed through the driver's window, hit the driver on the tip of his shoulder, then glanced off and struck his head, snapping it sideways.

I pulled the log out and leaned it against the truck. I jerked open his door and grabbed him by the same arm that took the blow from the log. He yelled in pain, reached his hand over to his injured shoulder.

He was as advertised, superhero-sized, with the body weight to fit. I had to pull hard to dump him out on the ground where he writhed and moaned.

In my peripheral vision, I sensed the other man running toward me through the headlights. He would get to me before I could escape with Paco.

I picked up the log, held it at my side as a battering ram, and made another, stumbling run, hoping he was blinded by the headlights.

His running was jerky. I came out of the dark and into the light from the headlights just as he approached the front corner of the pickup. The headlights caught his face. The guy had a feral look, like a bull who wants to gore his tormentor. His eyes were small and close-set.

When I burst into the light beam, he tried to dodge.

The log caught him on the side of his abdomen. He went down and curled up and howled. I raised the log high and dropped it onto his body. He yelled.

I ran to the passenger door and opened it.

"Paco, where are you?" I reached in. Felt the seat. Waved my arm through the space just above the floor. He wasn't there.

TWENTY

"Paco!" I yelled.

"I'm here," came a small voice from the darkness of the woods.

I turned.

Paco stepped out from behind a tree.

I picked him up and ran with him through the black forest, putting distance between us and the men. I kept going until I got to the drive up to my cabin, then turned and trotted to where I'd parked the Jeep.

Street was waiting there in the dark.

"Thank God you found him!" she said.

I set Paco down. Street hugged him.

"You okay, Paco?" I asked. "They didn't hurt you?" I figured that the greatest hurt was his fear, but I wanted him to focus on something better.

He nodded.

"Are those the guys who chased you before?"

He nodded.

"Okay, let's get Street's car, and she can come up and help Spot."

"Is Spot hurt?" Street sounded horrified.

"No. He's just tied up."

I took Street forward to her car. She got in and followed us up the mountain. I parked at an angle so my headlights would shine toward Spot.

Street ran over and pet Spot. "He's trapped in a fishnet!"

"I walked right into it," I said. "I heard a noise and walked out. Spot pushed out past me. They dropped the net on him and hit me with a stun gun."

"That's why you're walking strange!" Street sounded horrified.

"Let's get inside." I took Paco by the hand, and we ran into the cabin. "Call Diamond," I shouted while I fetched my pocketknife from the bedroom.

"I already called Diamond after I blocked the road," Street said. "Lucky for us, he's working graveyard. He's on his way."

"Lock this door behind me." I ran outside.

Spot hadn't moved. He was still chewing on the cord. Unlike some people, dogs don't give up until they have exhausted themselves.

I was careful with the knife, working away from Spot, careful not to cut him. I had him freed in a minute.

He immediately ran toward where the men had parked their pickup, then he trotted toward the cabin, following their scent trail. I went with Spot up the short steps onto my deck and peered down the mountain. I saw the flashing lights of two patrol units as they turned up the private drive 1000 feet below. There were no other vehicle lights. Maybe the men were hiding in the woods, lights off. More likely, they had gotten away.

Still without my keys, I had to knock on the front door to get Street to let me in. She opened the door. Her hand was locked hard onto Paco's as if she wasn't going to let go no matter who tried to take him.

We sat down, me on the rocker, Street and Paco next to each other on the little couch.

Paco's eyes were wide and worried underneath an intense frown. He still held Street's hand, but he kept some distance between them. Street probably wanted to pull him into her lap, but she was a good judge of these things. Give the boy time and space. Be there, but don't push.

"Maybe Diamond's boys can pull some prints," Street said.

I looked around the cabin. The men hadn't ruined anything except maybe Paco's psyche. Paco seemed fine, but no kid can be fine after what he'd been through.

There was a knock on the door. Spot didn't bark, so it was okay. I opened it to see Diamond. Two Douglas County vehicles were in the road. I stepped outside and gave Diamond the whole story while his crew collected evidence, took photos, filled out forms.

"Both of the kidnappers are wounded in some degree," I said. "And I broke the left front window of their pickup. But I'm sure they are gone."

Diamond walked over to my deck and looked down the mountain. There were no vehicle lights in the forest.

"Sergeant," one of the deputies said. "Something here."

We walked over. The deputy shined his flashlight on the fishnet, then moved it so the beam traced the edges of the net.

"This was carefully set up," he said. "The net was rigged with a line that laced through the perimeter of the net. See how these cords are all gathered together? It looks like they held the net up loose and tossed it over McKenna's dog. Then they pulled on this cord, and it snugged the net up, kind of like a drawstring on a mesh bag. The cord goes to this slip knot so you can tighten it, but it won't loosen."

"Good work, Denny," Diamond said. "You find any sign of what made the squeaking noise?"

"Yeah. Real simple, but kind of brilliant, too, if you know what I mean." He shined his light on the ground near the middle of the net, right about where I'd cut Spot free. "Simple rubber-duckie squeeze toy," he said. We could see it in his flashlight beam. "I figure one guy steps on the duckie. Spot runs up. Maybe he couldn't see the guy in the dark, but he probably smelled him when he got close. But by then it was too late, and the guy tossed the net over him. Meanwhile, the other guy hits McKenna with the Taser."

"Why didn't they just Tase Spot?" Diamond asked.

"I could only guess," I said. "Could be they only had one Taser. Could be they didn't know if a Taser would work on a dog."

"You think they could be that dumb?" Diamond said.

I shrugged. "It wasn't the kind that shoots out wires. It was the hand-held type. You have to stick it against your victim, then pull the trigger. Maybe they thought that Spot could get his teeth on them if they came that close."

Diamond nodded in the dark. "Like a cartoon, dropping a net on him. But I guess it worked well enough." He lowered his voice. "If these guys want to kill the boy so he can't testify to the shooting he witnessed, why didn't they just pop him and you both in your cabin?"

"All I've got are guesses. My road is long and there's only one way out. If one of my neighbors were here and heard a gunshot, they might call it in, and a cop like yourself might come up the road before they could get away. Or maybe I'd stay alive long enough to call it in. Or maybe a gunshot would rile my dog so much that he would chew through chain-mail to get to the shooter. But probably the most obvious reason of all is that even idiots know that if you shoot a cop or ex-cop, you bring the wrath of all cops down on you. Right or wrong, we often put more focus on the killer who takes out one of our own."

Diamond turned to Denny. "Let me know if you need any help getting that net unstuck and gathered up. Maybe there'll be a tag on it that will tell us the manufacturer. If we could track it through to a point of sale somewhere, somebody might remember who bought it."

"Probably stolen," Denny said.

"Of course," Diamond said.

"Right," Denny said. "Like you always say, police work is about being thorough."

Diamond turned to me. "Any idea what kind of pickup?"

"It was dark and I was kind of busy," I said.

Diamond nodded. "Fishnet is creative," he said. "These guys look like fishermen?"

I smiled. "Hard to tell what they looked like. The one moving the boulders was big and white. The one driving the pickup was big and black. Both were bald."

"Total bald, like shaved? Or part bald like natural?"

"Total."

"Anything else?"

"They're not athletes and they're not fighters."

"Why do you think that?" Diamond asked.

"Way they moved. Clunky. Way they dealt with pain."

"How did they deal with pain?"

"Yell and scream."

Diamond nodded. "But muscles."

"Lots," I said.

"You think these guys are show girls? Or do you think they are dangerous?"

"Worst kind of dangerous. The way the one guy looked when he ran toward me, he telegraphed mean and amoral."

"You guess these guys are hired killers like Agent Ramos thinks? Or are they personally involved in this?"

"I'd guess hired. They didn't radiate any vibe of emotional involvement."

"I don't like the hired killer thing."

"No one does," I said.

"What's your next move?"

"Haven't figured that out, yet. C'mon inside, I'll make you a copy of the letter Cassie wrote me."

We went in, and I put the letter through my copy machine. I found the sales journal pages with Cassie's entire customer list and made copies of those as well. I handed them to Diamond. We went back outside to talk away from Paco.

"I wonder if selling travel info is legal," Diamond said.

"Probably. But ethical? Borderline. Technically, anyone could conceivably get travel info on executives. But it's not like studying a company for its assets and technologies and innovations and then investing on that basis. It's coloring outside of the lines. Either way, short of finding Cassie's body and evidence related to her death or bringing in the men who took Paco, these cash payments this JM guy made to Cassie seem like the most productive place to start looking."

"Makes sense to me," Diamond said. He folded the pages, put them in his pocket. "I'll see if I can find anything on these names."

Diamond looked around at the dark forest. "You know that those boys will be back," he said.

"Yeah."

"Where you gonna stay?"

"I'm hoping that Street's okay with us crashing at her place for the rest of tonight. Tomorrow, who knows. But it looks like I better keep Paco moving."

"Maria is coming over tomorrow night, but it's okay if you want to put my place on your itinerary after that."

"Glad to know you're still seeing her. She's a good influence on you."

"Actually, Maria's pulled back a little. We still have dinner now and then. She still likes me. But it's been a long time since any sleep-over. Kind of miss that."

I nodded. "I'll call you tomorrow. Let you know if our lodging plans bring us your way."

"Those guys know your wheels," Diamond said. "I've still got the old pickup, if you want to borrow it. Be tight, though, with your hound in the same seat as you and the boy."

"Tight and still alive is a good thing," I said. "The trick will be getting to your place unseen. Take a careful driver."

"Who better than you?" Diamond said.

"Good point," I said.

TWENTY-ONE

Street was okay with us staying at her condo, but none of us slept much. Although I was confident that Salt and Pepper wouldn't be back the same night, I'd parked the Jeep at the far end of the condo lot so it wouldn't be so obvious.

A few hours later we were eating toast and jam and bananas for breakfast. Paco skipped the banana. He put enough butter on his toast to make it soggy.

"We could force feed him spinach," Street said with a wink. "Try to get some nutrition into him."

Paco didn't comment.

There was a knock at the door. Spot wagged.

I looked out of the peephole and opened the door for Diamond and another officer.

"We went back up to your cabin after dawn to see what we could find," he said.

"Don't you ever sleep?"

"We didn't find anything," he said, ignoring me. "Some chunks of seaweed in the fishnet they threw over Spot, and that's all."

Spot wagged at the sound of his name, stuck his nose in Diamond's abdomen. Diamond pet him.

"Any tag on the net? Something that might indicate where it came from?"

Diamond shook his head. "They probably found it washed up on a coastal beach somewhere. Or stole it out of a fishing boat. Not likely it will give us a lead. But we'll let you know if anything comes of it."

"Thanks. We still on to crash at your place tomorrow night?"

"You come without a tail, yes."

"See you then."

He left.

Street poured more coffee, and we went out on her small deck. The deck boards were wet from the previous night's drizzle, but the sun was stabbing through the clouds, and things were starting to warm and dry.

Street brought out a towel to dry off the deck chairs, and we sat in the sun.

I told Street I had to make a call and asked her to keep Spot with her and Paco. I stood outside where I could see Street and Paco but far enough from the building that I had a little privacy.

I called my old friend Conan Reynolds, the full-time hiker, biker, skier who puts in a few part-time hours as a lawyer.

He was in, we traded chitchat, and I asked him if he knew anything about immigration law.

"A divorce guy like me? Are you kidding? But I know a guy in Sac who does some immigration stuff. Name's Kyle Bolen. Let me find his number and call him on the other line."

I waited five minutes. Conan came back on the line. "Bolen is willing to give you five minutes, professional courtesy to me."

"Wow, you've got some pull, huh?" I said.

"No. I just reminded him about the last round we played at Edgewood. I told him that I'm still keeping it a secret. So he wanted to return the favor." Conan read me Kyle Bolen's number.

"Thanks, Conan."

I dialed Kyle Bolen, and his secretary put me through to him.

I introduced myself, explained that I had temporary charge of a young undocumented immigrant, and asked if he could give me any information on whether or not the boy might be allowed to stay in the country if he came out of the closet.

"Hey, McKenna," Bolen said, "I don't want to put you off, but you're talking about opening a real can of worms, here. A big can. Big worms."

"Can you describe this can a bit?"

"Let me just say that the government tells a story that they've created for public consumption, and the story is that they don't search out and deport undocumented workers who don't cause trouble, especially undocumented children who've been in this country for some time. But the underground reports are different. And the voices of those who get picked up and put into the deportation machine have no forum. They post their tales of misery on little-known websites. The general public never hears about them."

"What does the law actually say about deporting illegal immigrants?"

"Oh, bud, you don't want the actual legalese. It's a bunch of unreadable lawyer-speak. But in essence, the Illegal Immigration Reform and Immigrant Responsibility Act in nineteen ninety-six did in fact cut back on habeas corpus rights for illegal immigrants. Congress wanted to make it easier to deport undocumented immigrants. It sounded good in principle. But the INS interpreted the new law as giving their agency a broad increase in their power. Many legal scholars question that interpretation."

"Are you saying that the government is abusing their power?" I said. "Or are you saying that the law is bad?"

"Both answers depend on your point of view," he said. "If you are an undocumented worker, doing your job and staying out of trouble, then yes, the new law would seem over-reaching.

"But if you are a victim of crime committed by an illegal alien, or if you are an environmentalist or a hiker confronting the countless tons of trash that illegal immigrants leave in the desert during their three-day walk across the border, or if your house or land have burned up in a wildfire that was started by illegal immigrants not putting out their campfire, then you will think the law is good. Although, even then one might argue that deportation doesn't prevent the trash and fires. Only stopping illegal immigration in the first place would solve that problem."

He paused. "Why don't you tell me about this kid."

"He's ten years old, born in Mexico, brought here illegally. He was a baby when his mother carried him over the border."

"I'm hoping you're going to tell me that the kid speaks

Spanish," Bolen said.

"Nope. The kid's mother died soon after they came over the border. The kid was taken in by the neighbor lady. Then she got dementia. At that point the kid was rotated into a round-robin daycare in the neighborhood. He stayed in different houses and apartments for several days at a time, always moving."

"No state foster care?" Bolen said.

"No. Apparently, the people in the small town thought that engaging the authorities would come with the risk that the child might be yanked out of the little bit of stability they'd made for him after his mother's death. They worried that he would be put in a state-sponsored orphanage and possibly even deported. I didn't get the impression that they thought the boy's life in the town was ideal. But they reasoned that it was better than having him sent to a country he doesn't know and a language he can't speak."

"Of course, his school must be complicit in giving him cover." It was a statement, not a question.

"Yeah. The principle and teachers have taken the same approach as his caregivers. They have tried to do what's best for the kid rather than what the law demands. I understand that they've had to make appropriate adjustments here and there. Paperwork and such."

"As with all illegal kids," Bolen said. He took a deep breath. "I'm afraid I don't have very good news for you, assuming you'd like this kid to stay in this country. Immigration law is a mix of good law, stupid law, and everything you can imagine in between. Further, many of the laws have conflicting components. Some state and federal laws don't mix well and that includes California law. And nearly all of the laws have unintended consequences."

"Like most laws," I said.

"Yeah, but Immigration law has the extra difficulty of being an area that inflames passions. People get almost as worked up about immigration as they do about abortion. The result is that our laws are rarely judged with calm remove."

"All this suggests that this kid I'm talking about may get deported."

"There's a chance of it, yes. Hold on a sec." I heard what sounded like the click of a cigarette lighter, then a long exhalation.

"The basic position of the government," he said, "is that anyone who is here illegally, regardless of the reason, has to leave and apply through the normal channels. Even if they aren't caught and deported, even if they leave voluntarily, they have to wait ten years after leaving before they can apply for entry.

"For many illegals who've raised families and built small businesses, it can be like a death sentence. There are mothers whose children were born here and hence are legal. But the mothers get deported and possibly never see their children again."

"We always hear about illegal immigrants who were picked up because they committed a crime," I said.

"Powerful reasons to deport them," Bolen said. "And some illegal immigrants, just like some legal citizens, commit crimes. And some of those crimes are horrific. But the association often adds to the rhetoric even as it subtracts from common sense. When a news story describes a criminal suspect who's an illegal alien, they almost always sensationalize it, giving the impression that illegal immigrants are naturally bad people."

"Do illegal immigrants commit more crimes as a percentage than legal citizens?" I asked.

"I don't know how the groups compare. But I do know that some anti-immigration people get pretty loose with statistics. Sometimes you'll hear or read comments about how many millions of illegal immigrants are criminals, when they are leaving out the fact that for many of them, the only crime they have committed is coming over the border illegally. The statistic gets used to paint a picture that is clearly a mis-characterization. It's a black-and-white view of something that has a lot of gray area.

"The mother of the boy you are talking about broke the very serious law of coming to this country without papers. She probably did it to find work and make a better life for herself and her baby. According to the law, she should have been punished, fined and/or deported had she not died.

"People often stand behind a law without asking if it's a good law. But how bad was the woman's illegal entry? Maybe she'd already been deported and then re-entered illegally. If so, that second entry is a felony offense. Yet would she be bad like other felons? Should she be characterized like someone who robs or rapes or murders?"

"Congressmen have a lot of reasons why they pass laws," I said.

"Yeah, but you don't want to hear my take on legislators. I should also point out, however, that most deportations are administrative and aren't attached to any criminal prosecution. They simply pick up people, make a decision, and deport them. They call these cases removals."

I could hear more breathing on the line. It sounded like Bolen's cigarette wasn't going to last long.

"I think," Bolen said, "that the root of the worry over illegal immigration is that they will take our jobs, overload our social services and suck the taxpayer dry. And there's no doubt that some illegals absorb costly healthcare services, and send their children to public schools, paid for by our taxes.

"But the studies don't support the job question, and a good portion of illegals have their taxes deducted from their paychecks just like the rest of us."

It sounded like Bolen was getting lathered up.

He said, "If you ask hotel managers and farmers and restaurant owners and landscape companies if they could find American citizens to clean the rooms, pick the produce, fry the eggs, run the lawn mowers, and build rock gardens should illegals all be deported, they almost universally tell you no. Most Americans who were born here won't do that work. Even if you find an uneducated American looking for a job and you offer him work cutting up chicken meat or cleaning the bathrooms in your factory, many if not most will say they're going to keep looking.

"Does that make coming here illegally right? Of course not." He paused to breathe and no doubt suck down more smoke.

"Is there a way to plead this boy's case that ups his odds of staying?" I asked.

"If you were to hire a good immigration lawyer like me, and if you're willing to spend some money, we may find a way through the thicket of fine print that is stacked against him. But I make no promises."

"It sounds like you're saying that if this kid wants to stay in the country, he should stay undercover."

"Hard to say," Bolen said. "Undercover, he could get picked up. He breaks any law, jaywalks, rides his bicycle through a red light, could be a cop stops him. Next thing you know the kid might be taken away to a detention center. A lawyer can sometimes intervene. And while the system is full of exceptions – and this kid's situation may fit one of those holes – the system is also inflexible. You've got some bureaucrat filling in the form boxes on a computer screen. She's been doing it all day, and she's got to do a hundred more before she can go home. Your kid's form gets filled in the wrong way for him, next thing you know, he's on a plane to Mexico and there's nothing anyone can do about it."

"Let me tell you one more thing about this kid," I said. "He's been in trouble."

"What kind?"

"He got in a scuffle, and when the teachers checked his pack, they found his harvest tools, including his tomato knife. He was hauled in for bringing a weapon to school."

I heard an exhalation.

"Christ, McKenna, if you'd told me that up front, you could've saved us both several minutes worth of my hot air. No way is any agency gonna let him stay. He's toast. You better start teaching him Español."

I thanked him and walked back over to Street's. She and Paco and Spot were still sitting outside enjoying the November sun.

I sat down and looked up as a small plane whined above on a path from Squaw Valley. It headed toward the mountain behind us, roughly near where my cabin perches. The plane continued on, heading toward Carson Valley down below the back side of the mountain. It gave me an idea.

"You ever been in a plane?" I said to Paco.

Judging by Paco's look, I might as well have asked if he'd ever flown to Paris for dinner at Maxim's.

"No."

I looked up at the clearing sky. "Good day for flying," I said. "Want to come?"

He compressed his lips. "Where would we go?"

"I want to look for your van."

Paco looked doubtful. "I don't think you could."

"Why?"

"My friend Rafael went on a plane when his father died. He said it went real high. He couldn't see anything on the ground."

"I'm not talking about a jet airliner. I'm talking about a little plane." I pointed at the one that had gone above us. "See that little plane flying over the mountain?"

Paco squinted against the bright sky. He put his hand up to shade his eyes against the morning sun but never touched his sunglasses on the top of his head.

"That kind of plane," I said. "Small. Flies at low altitude."

Paco shrugged, the indeterminate version.

"Is that a yes?"

He shrugged again.

The absence of any emotional response from Paco was difficult to deal with.

I turned to Street. "You want to come?"

"And ride in a plane with you driving?" She was no doubt remembering my crash landing the last time I flew in a rush to save Jennifer Salazar from a killer who had her out on a boat in the middle of Lake Tahoe.

"The last time was in a blizzard," I said, avoiding further explanation in front of Paco. I looked up at the cloudy sky. "It looks like it will be calm for several hours at least."

Street gave me one of her beautiful, enigmatic smiles. "Thanks, but I have bugs to identify, bugs to count, bugs to put through my pheromone merry-go-round."

So Paco and Spot and I got in the Jeep. As usual, Spot was overjoyed to go for a ride, and he held his head out the open rear window, an endless appetite for the sights and smells and sounds. Paco stared through the glass, zero appetite for the sights and smells and sounds. I wondered if it had diminished since the shooting.

We headed south down the East Shore. I kept my attention on the rear view mirror as much as in front of us. I saw no pickups.

At a few minutes before 10:30 a.m., we pulled into the South Lake Tahoe airport and parked in the lot. I left the windows open enough that Spot could see his view of choice. I told him to be good, grabbed his head, and shook it fast enough to make his jowls flap. He wagged.

Paco and I headed over to a small hanger building between the tarmac and the parking lot.

Across the top of the door was a painted plywood sign that said Tahoe Valley Wings. I tried the door. Locked. There was a little piece of paper taped to the window pane.

In red ballpoint pen it said, "Giving a lesson. Back at 11:00." There was a rough, crude, line drawing of an airplane and an arrow that pointed up.

I stepped away from the building, looked up, and scanned the sky. Nothing but cobalt blue.

Fifteen minutes later, Paco pointed at the sky. A white Cessna 152 came into view out of the north, taking a straight-in approach to runway 18. It dropped down on final, lowering to just eight or ten feet above the landing strip. Then it slowed to the speed of a car going through town before it flared and made a soft landing in front of us. It taxied across the tarmac and stopped twenty yards away.

After the prop stopped, a skinny young man got out of the right seat, stepped to the ground, trotted around to the left door and opened it for a trim woman, younger than he. Been a long time since I'd seen a young guy open a door for a girl. He nodded at me. "Be with you in a few minutes," he said as they went into the hanger office.

They emerged five minutes later.

"You're ready for your first solo next week," he said to her.

"No way," she said, beaming.

"You greased that last touchdown. Next week solo, next month your license, eventually your instrument rating."

"No way," she said again.

"You got the chops, girl. Go for it."

They said goodbye, and the instructor turned toward me and introduced himself.

"Hi, I'm Ben Rashid."

We shook. I told him my name.

Ben Rashid looked Pakistani and talked Brooklyn, New York. "You want to rent a plane?"

"Please. I'd like to go up for an hour or two. Maybe more. But I'm not current. Can you take me up for a check ride?"

"Sure, man." He waved his arm toward the Cessna. "We've got this One-Fifty-Two, or, if you want some speed, we have a newer One-Seventy-Two Skyhawk."

"I'm doing an aerial search," I said. "Slow is good." I looked at the smaller plane. "But we'd probably have a weight issue on the One Fifty-Two."

Ben looked at the plane, then smiled. "You obviously know your stuff." He pointed at the plane. "Gross payload on this sweetheart is five hundred pounds. Subtract off full fuel tanks and we're down to three forty-four. What do you weigh?"

"Two fifteen."

"I'm only one-forty, but just the two of us puts us over her limit. So we need to trade up. Our Skyhawk has a payload after fuel of a bit over four forty. What's your boy weigh?"

I turned to Paco.

"Sixty-four and a half when they weighed me at school," Paco said.

Ben wrote on his clipboard, added the numbers. "So we three are about four nineteen. And after I get out of the plane, you'll have lots of room to spare. What are you searching for? Do you need to bring along any equipment?"

"No. We're looking for signs of a missing woman," I said.

He raised his eyebrows. "Oh. So sorry to hear that. I'm certainly happy to help."

Paco wanted to wait outside while I made arrangements. I considered the risks and decided he could stay outside only if he remained in front of the big window where I could see him.

"Keep your eye on the parking lot. You see Salt and Pepper, you come inside fast, right?"

He nodded.

Ben and I went into the hanger office, filled out several pieces of paper.

I kept turning around to check that Paco was still standing in front of the window.

Ben asked me the basics and made notes while I gave him my particulars from my hours in the cockpit to showing him my last medical paperwork, a copy of which I keep in the Jeep. Then he gave me the oral exam, smiling at my answers.

He stood up and handed me the ignition key.

Outside, doing the preflight inspection, I made a show of being extra thorough while I checked everything, engine components to propeller to wheels to aircraft surfaces, wings and tail, to sampling the wing tank fuel sumps.

When we were done, I showed Paco the rear seat. He climbed in and immediately reached for the seat belts.

"I thought you didn't like seat belts because they trap you inside. If something happened, you wanted to be thrown free."

"Not in a plane," he said.

I checked Paco's belts, then we climbed inside, me in the left seat, Ben in the right.

I continued the preflight routine, going step-by-step through the long list. Then I started the engine and checked the instruments, oil pressure, fuel pump, fuel mixture. I turned on the radio, the transponder, checked the flaps. I taxied to runway 18 and did my engine run-up, checking magnetos, suction gauge, engine instruments, and ammeter.

When the radio chatter made it clear that there was no nearby traffic, I announced our takeoff, pushed the throttle all the way and released the brakes. The prop turned into a blur, and the plane gained speed like an ungainly little insect with its wings extended. The buzz-saw whine rose in pitch as the Cessna gathered speed. At 60 knots, I eased the yoke back, and we lifted off. By turning the yoke to the right just a touch, I crabbed into the west wind as we rose above the tarmac, knowing that Ben would notice that, despite the cross wind, our position stayed directly above the runway as we climbed into the sky.

Ben put me through some basic maneuvers, then had me do two touch-and-goes before he asked me to land and drop him off.

"It's like you fly every day," he said as he got out of the plane.

"In my dreams," I said.

"Good luck with your search." He made a little wave.

We helped Paco move from the rear seat to the right front. Then I taxied back out to the runway, and took off once again.

TWENTY-TWO

I kept the plane at the best angle of climb for our altitude, which held the airspeed to 66 knots despite full throttle. As I approached the south end of the Tahoe Basin, I was up to 7000 feet of altitude, 700 feet above the ground. I turned the yoke, pulled it back, and put the plane into a climbing turn to the left.

The Cessna creaked over the wind noise as the ailerons grabbed at the air and banked the plane, but the plane dutifully executed my commands. I came around in a big sweeping turn in front of Trimmer Peak 3000 feet above. Behind it, another thousand feet up, was Freel Peak.

Paco was curiously indifferent. He looked out, but he had no reaction. No exclamations about his first plane ride, no remarks about how things looked from up in the air, no comments about the tiny cars. The kid was shut down. I didn't think that his emotions were stunted and undeveloped. They just seemed locked in a vault.

I kept up a running commentary in an effort to get him to loosen up. I pointed out the lake, the mountains, and other landmarks. I showed him the cliff road coming down from Echo Summit, a road he'd traveled on many times.

When he still expressed no interest, I turned my attention to my search task.

It made sense that on the morning that Paco's foster mother was assaulted, she had driven at least some distance past the farmers' market, enough that Paco had fallen back asleep. Although Paco had said that she'd parked near a cliff, no particular cliff came to mind. I thought I'd head out from the center of town and see if I noticed any remote areas that were accessible by car and had a cliff or two nearby.

I leveled off 1000 feet up, what's officially called Above Ground Level, and I brought the Cessna toward the center of town. The landing approach to the airport comes out of the north, over the lake and across the center of town. At 1000 feet AGL, I would possibly be in the way of aircraft approaching from the north, so I stayed to the east side of town.

The weather was clear, with visibility in the high mountain air nearly unlimited. The lake stretched out 22 miles to the north, an improbable blue, an improbable size, and, for a giant lake, an improbable elevation.

I pointed down. "See that main road? That's Lake Tahoe Boulevard. And see the lumber yard with the big piles of lumber? Across the road and down a bit is the parking lot where you used to sell your produce at the farmers' market."

Paco looked, but he didn't react.

I didn't have a flight plan other than to check out areas northeast from the farmers' market in the center of South Lake Tahoe. Paco had said he'd fallen asleep after seeing the farmers' market. A kid can fall dead asleep in a minute and wake up five minutes later, not having a clue about how long he'd been asleep. So it could be that the location I was looking for was as close as five minutes from the center of town.

I could estimate the other end of the time range. Paco had said that they'd driven up from the Central Valley and that they'd left at 3 a.m. A little arithmetic could give me a time range.

The drive from Stockton up the west slope of the Sierra takes roughly three hours, getting them to the South Shore at approximately 6 a.m. So Paco had seen the farmers' market area at about that time. Then he called me at 6:30. Which left approximately 30 minutes during which Cassie drove someplace while Paco fell back asleep. Paco woke up and witnessed her assault, and the men drove off in their pickup with Paco hiding in the back.

If the assault took ten minutes, the place where Paco's foster mother was assaulted was somewhere within a 20-minute drive from the center of South Lake Tahoe. Because they were going northeast past the farmers' market when Paco saw it, the likelihood was that Cassie drove someplace up off Kingsbury Grade, or possibly up the East Shore, maybe as far as Cave Rock.

When Paco escaped the pickup, he came running down the gondola lift line. So the pickup had probably been in the nearby neighborhood. But it could have driven from anywhere. When Paco called, he said the pickup was going fast. There were only a few places in Tahoe where you can drive over 40, but it indicated that Cassie could have been shot in a wide range of places. The only hope was to look for cliffs and/or the van.

I wanted to fly low above the ground. But Tahoe has many tall rocky outcroppings that can be dangerous in a low-altitude search, so I decided to come down from the slope above. It is easier to suddenly pull up above an obstruction when you're gliding down slope than when you're angling up and already using most of your engine power.

I put the Cessna into a climb. When I got up to 8500 feet, I began my search in the area surrounding Daggett Pass at the top of Kingsbury.

The Cessna was about 30 years old, with a sun-bleached instrument panel and cracked, ripped fabric seat covers. The cockpit glazing was abraded and slightly fogged. It was hard to see clearly as I reached altitude and once again approached the mountains. But the low stall speed allowed me to glide down at a comfortable 65 knots.

I did a zig-zag search pattern, always heading down at a gentle angle like a skier traversing back and forth to descend a mountain. I watched for cliff faces and a dark-colored van as well as for a dark pickup with a light topper. I stayed within a perimeter that seemed the maximum distance from the center of town that someone could drive in twenty minutes.

Paco kept his face turned to the window. He said nothing.

After an hour, we'd covered all of the areas adjacent to Kingsbury Grade. I even followed some dirt trails that looked like they'd be accessible by a van. But there were only a few cliff areas that fit what Paco described, and none of them had a van nearby. I also saw four different pickups with toppers over the beds, but in each case, the toppers were dark in color.

I wanted to begin a new search above the East Shore, taking the same approach, gliding down from above. I pushed the throttle all the way forward and pulled back on the yoke. The engine roared like an old VW Beetle with the accelerator floored. Although the plane's rate of climb was not fast, it ran smoothly. I stayed away from the mountains as I gained altitude.

I started above the highest roads surrounding Zephyr Heights, flew back and forth, looking for cliffs, following obscure trails out into the forest.

Gradually, I moved north toward Cave Rock and on toward Glenbrook, scanning all of the areas one could reach by van. When I was certain that I was more than a half hour drive out of South Lake Tahoe, I banked around down slope, checking out every obscure corner, trying to think like a thug who planned to meet and shoot a woman farmer.

My search was fruitless. Either Paco had given me information that wasn't accurate, or I'd made an error in judgment. Or, possibly, the men who'd shot Cassie had come back and moved or hidden the van and the shooting victim.

As I flew, I reconsidered the possibilities for where she could have driven her van. The vast majority of the Tahoe Basin is roadless wilderness. A high-clearance, 4-wheel-drive vehicle could access many of the old logging trails. But it was unlikely that the van fell into that category. It would be limited to normal roads, which made my search area relatively small. I felt confident that I'd done a thorough search, but I hadn't seen anything.

Frustrated, I brought the Cessna back around and headed back south. I could take a shortcut across the lake, but I stayed over the shore, scouting the mountains, looking for any spots I'd missed. I was approaching the Stateline hotels when I saw a Dodge Ram pickup, dark brown, with a white topper.

I throttled back and got Diamond on my cell.

"What's all that noise?" he shouted.

"Paco and I are doing an aerial search, looking for Cassie's van. Where are you?"

"Coming down Kingsbury, lake side."

"I'm the Cessna above the hotels."

We shouted over the roar of wind. I told him about the pickup.

"It's traveling southwest on Highway Fifty, just passing the Kingsbury Grade turnoff."

"I'll be there in a minute," he said. "Can you watch him? Fly circles or something?"

"Will do," I said as I put the plane into a tight bank to the left. I watched over my shoulder as the plane turned away. Then I caught a view of the pickup on the other side as we came all the way around.

"Turning into the Mont Bleu parking lot," I shouted into my cell.

"Got it," Diamond said.

"The truck is parking on the open lot, near the ramp."

"I'm just now turning from Kingsbury onto Fifty," Diamond said.

I was still circling counter-clockwise. With the pickup now stationary, I kept it at the center of my circle. I pushed in the yoke a bit to lose some altitude. When I was down to 500 feet AGL, I leveled off. I glanced to the northeast, saw Diamond's patrol unit approaching.

"The driver's door of the pickup is open," I shouted. "A person is getting out. Wearing a black jacket, blue jeans. Looks like a woman. It looks like she's carrying a bundle of flowers. She's walking toward the hotel."

As I completed my next revolution, I saw Diamond pulling into the parking lot. He parked behind the pickup and got out.

The woman opened the door of Mont Bleu and walked inside.

Diamond looked into the pickup's windshield, then walked around back. He peered into one of the small dark windows of the topper, holding his hands next to his face. Then he reached for the handle of the topper gate. It was unlocked. Diamond lifted it up and looked inside.

Not exactly by the book. But I would have looked inside, too.

Diamond shut the topper gate.

I saw him raise his cell phone to his mouth.

"It's from one of the local flower shops," he shouted. "The back is filled with enough flowers for a wedding. There are flowers on the front seat. She's obviously making deliveries."

"Roger," I said. "I'll keep searching."

I continued to fly a search pattern until I felt I'd covered all possible areas Cassie could have driven to with the boy.

It was a good time to head back to the airport as the clouds coming in over the Sierra crest were getting thicker and darker.

I was on a flight path that would allow me to slip into the landing pattern on the final leg when I noticed some rock outcroppings close to town near the base of Heavenly Resort. They were just around the side of the mountain from The Face and Gunbarrel ski runs. It was the same area where the young autistic girl had fled a year before, lost in the dark until Spot found her.

I banked the Cessna and came around by the outcroppings. From the air they didn't look like much, rocky projections only 50 or 60 feet tall. They wouldn't be notable unless you were on the prairie. But from the perspective of a Central Valley kid looking out a van window at night, they might look like cliffs.

I pointed. "See those rocks, Paco? They kind of sit at a right angle from each other. Remember how you said that Cassie parked in front of cliffs? What do you think? Could those be the cliffs?"

Paco just stared down at them. He didn't speak. I couldn't tell if it was just another instance of his engagement being dialed down to the lowest setting. Or was he revisiting that early morning and the trauma of the shooting?

"I don't know," he finally said.

The rocks weren't on a paved road, but they were near Pioneer Trail, and the nearby ground was grus, a kind of coarse granite sand. It looked packed as if high school kids regularly drove off-road to party in the shelter of the rocks.

I took a pass over the outcroppings, banked around 180 degrees, then came back again. The rocks were on a slope. I flew across the slope. I saw no sign of a van or anything else unusual.

It looked like there was a trail that went around the back,

upper side of the rocks. If the woman had driven the van behind the rocks, I wouldn't be able to see it from the air unless I flew very close to the trees above the rocks.

My flight had so far been calm. But even on calm days, there can be thermals and downdrafts in the mountains, especially with increasing clouds. Nevertheless, I thought I could get in closer without too much risk.

I lined up the Cessna so that I could again find a line that was like skiing a traverse, heading across the mountain at a slight downward angle.

My pass over the rocky projection revealed nothing, but I was still too far up and out to see clearly behind the rocks.

From Paco's description, his foster mom was shot not far from the van. There was no van nearby, but it may have been moved. And if someone dumped a body, they would likely leave it where it would be difficult to see from an air search.

I banked in a large circle and came back around, close to my original track but picking a course that was much closer to the trees above the rocky outcropping.

"There," Paco said, pointing. It was the first voluntary word he'd said since we took off.

I tried to look where he pointed. Maybe there was a bit of something in the trees. Something light-colored. Maybe not.

"What did you see? I didn't see anything."

"A shoe," he said. "It's Cassie's."

If only I could go slower.

"How do you know it's hers?"

"She has Nikes with a red swoosh."

I made another circle and came back for another flyby.

I edged the throttle back a bit, slowing the plane a touch. Too slow would be dangerous if we hit a down draft or wind shear. But Ben Rashid had told me that the Skyhawk's stall speed was 54 knots. I still had some margin for error.

I came in just above the treetops.

As I approached the rocks, I studied the forest below. I scanned back and forth, looking into the rocky crags.

There were trees and rocks and dirt.

Paco pointed again. This time I saw it. A white athletic shoe with red stripe, lit by a lucky beam of sunlight shining through an opening in the forest canopy.

I turned away from the mountain, throttled up and circled around, climbing like a soaring raptor. I went around twice, climbing back to 500 feet Above Ground Level, scanning the ground below continuously.

I saw no van.

Paco was still facing the window, but I don't think he was seeing anything outside.

Pioneer Trail was the closest paved road, but it was unclear from my position where the dirt trail turned off.

I circled again, climbing up to 1000 AGL. From that altitude I could see the turnoff in relation to other streets I knew.

Then I headed back to the airport, entered the pattern on final, and landed. After I settled up with Ben Rashid, Paco and I rejoined Spot in the Jeep, turned left out of the airport, took Elks Club over to Pioneer Trail, and drove toward the part of the forest where we'd seen the lost shoe.

TWENTY-THREE

The dirt turnoff from Pioneer Trail was unmarked and faint enough that the Forest Service hadn't erected their standard barrier of boulders and logs to prevent unauthorized driving in the woods. Respecting their desire to prevent unnecessary soil compaction, I left the Jeep at the side of Pioneer Trail, and we hiked in.

After being cooped up in the Jeep at the airport, Spot ran around, excited, sniffing out the mysteries of squirrels, bears, and coyotes, and the less common Tahoe residents like mountain lions.

The trail wound back through a Jeffrey pine forest that the Forest Service had recently thinned. Hundreds of cut tree stumps showed a laudable effort to reduce the disastrous fuel buildup that was the result of 100 years of misdirected fire suppression. If they could multiply that thinning by ten thousand times, they might make the Tahoe Basin relatively fire safe. But no amount of mechanical thinning can bring the forest back to its natural condition where small, regular lightning-caused fires not only clear out the underbrush but open the cones of fire-dependent pines and let the seeds out to germinate in fire-cleared soil. Instead, the Forest Service burns the slash of the thinned-out trees, and hand-plants new trees, an ironic effort to restore some semblance of nature to a forest that managed itself for eons before Smoky Bear's arrival.

At occasional intervals, I saw tire tracks on the trail. The varying marks appeared to have been made by multiple vehicles. The only information I could infer came from the softness of the marks. There were no skid marks and no areas with dirt thrown up. It appeared that all recent vehicles had been driven at a slow crawl, by drivers who were calm.

I paused now and then to keep Paco from falling too far behind. His face was toward the ground.

A quarter mile in, where the land began to rise up toward Heavenly Ski Resort, I saw rock projecting up above the forest canopy.

When I approached the rock, I tried to visualize where the shoe would be, based on what we'd seen from the air. I only knew that it was toward the back side of the rocks.

I turned around. Paco looked at me. Spot was not in sight.

"Spot!" He appeared in the woods to the side, loping toward us.

The trail with tire tracks went up a gentle slope toward the rock outcropping.

"Are you coming up this slope with me?" I asked Paco.

He shook his head.

"Then stay there where I can see you?"

He nodded.

I hiked up the slope. Spot bounded past me. The woods became thicker, but I could still look down and see Paco and the open woods around him. No one could approach him without being obvious.

I scanned for the shoe that we'd seen from the air. This was an area the Forest Service had not thinned, and the forest was so dense that I could see very little distance up into the trees.

Spot ran ahead. Near the outcropping, he made a sudden turn, trotted to the side and stopped.

As I approached, I saw him sniffing a shoe.

It was a Nike athletic shoe, left foot, nearly new, with a red swoosh.

I picked it up by the laces to minimize damaging any evidence. It was large for a women's shoe, and it had a number 9 printed inside of the tongue. Assuming it belonged to Paco's foster mother, Cassie was a good-sized woman.

I turned, studying the woods for any other signs. As I'd already seen from the air, there was no van or anything else of interest.

In a few places were marks that may have been made by boots or shoes, but they were inconclusive. The ground was dry, and the granitic grus, with its lack of cohesiveness, was among the worst materials for picking up tracks. It took only the vaguest of impressions.

Without walking on the tire tracks, I stood in several places trying to reconcile the tire marks with the description Paco had given me. He said he looked out the van's windows to see a pickup against a cliff. Then he ran from the van to the pickup, saw no escape around the rocks, and hid inside of the pickup.

It took some imagination to make the rocks before me seem like a cliff around which there was no escape.

I walked down to Paco, held up the shoe.

"Does this look like Cassie's?"

He nodded. I couldn't quite read the look on his face. Not so much sadness as significant fatigue. Like pictures I'd seen of the faces of starving children.

I pointed at the rocks. "Could these rocks be the cliffs you saw in the dark?"

Paco looked up at the outcropping. He shrugged.

Spot walked over to me. He sniffed the shoe. Then he lifted his head, turned a bit, raised his head farther, his snout pointing toward the forest.

Air scenting.

"Spot, sniff the shoe, again," I said. "Do you have the scent?"

I grabbed his chest and gave him a little shake, the sign that indicates he has a job to do.

"Find the victim, Spot! Find the victim."

I gave him a smack on his rear.

He trotted off between some trees, stopped, sniffed the ground. Spot made a single paw-swipe at the dirt, sniffed again, then lifted his head and looked at me.

"Find the victim, boy!" I said again. "Find the victim!"

Spot swung his head around to look out through the forest. But he didn't move.

"C'mon, Spot," I said. I walked through the trees toward a

clearing. Spot followed. In the open space, the breeze was more prominent.

Spot suddenly lifted his head.

He walked directly upwind. It was a low-grade alert. He had a scent, but he wasn't excited about it. His tail was down. Paco and I followed behind, not distracting him. Thirty yards down the trail, there was a rise, and the trail turned. Spot went straight. Off the trail. Walking upwind.

He didn't trot like an eager dog. But he went relatively straight, which told me his intent. An ambling dog looking for a scent leaves a track that goes this way and that and circles back. A purposeful dog with an air scent follows the scent as long as it's clear.

I followed, keeping back, not wanting to distract him. Paco followed behind me.

Spot went around a boulder and came to a clearing. He stopped, did a kind of a point, holding his snout forward in a steady position. But his tail was down. It was an alert of the worst kind.

Then he lay down.

I walked past Spot. Five yards ahead of him was an area of dirt that bulged up just a bit. The dirt was mostly sand, which, after you pile it, dries fast and looks just like the ground nearby.

Had Spot not found it and reacted with sadness, I wouldn't have noticed it. It didn't stand out in any significant way. But his reaction made it clear that we had found a grave.

TWENTY-FOUR

I took Paco's hand and put it on Spot's collar. We walked back toward the Jeep. The sky had gotten darker. Rain began to fall. I saw Paco turn back and look for a moment toward the area where we'd found the grave.

I checked my cell phone. There was one bar of reception. I dialed the South Lake Tahoe PD, asked for Commander Mallory, was put on hold, transferred, and put on hold again.

"McKenna, here," I said when he answered. "Got a probable murder victim that is probably in your jurisdiction."

"Probable and probably aren't very concrete words," he said. "You got a body?"

"Not yet. But Spot found a grave. I'm thinking that your boys might have a shovel." I explained to Mallory where I was and what had happened.

"You say it may be in my jurisdiction. We've got enough problems in our city. Why don't you call the county. Get Sergeant Bains to take care of it."

"It's probably yours," I said.

I heard him breathing over the phone.

"Come down Pioneer Trail," I said. "You'll see my Jeep on the east side of the road. Bring a rain jacket."

"On my way," he finally said and hung up.

Paco and Spot and I were waiting in my Jeep, out of the rain, when Mallory showed up in his unmarked, followed by a patrol unit.

We got out. I pulled my spare rain jacket out of the back and draped it over Paco's shoulders. It came down to the ground.

"I don't want it," Paco said, shrugging it off. "It looks like a dress."

"No it doesn't," I said, putting it firmly back on him. "It looks like a cape. Makes you look like a superhero. Especially with those shades on the top of your head."

Paco gritted his teeth, but left the jacket on his shoulders.

"You want to leave your sunglasses in the Jeep? It's raining."

He shook his head.

Mallory got out, Coke can in his hand. His frown wrinkles were deep enough to hold nickels.

Two cops got out of the other vehicle. The one I'd met, Sergeant Tibbs, nodded at me, but I didn't know the other. Mallory didn't introduce us.

Mallory looked at Paco, then back at me. "I heard about a brief kidnapping at your place last night. Is this young man the subject of interest?"

"Yeah. Meet Paco. Paco, meet Commander Mallory."

It was probably a pointless introduction. Paco and Mallory appeared to ignore each other.

Mallory spoke to me. "Diamond said that you foiled the perpetrators."

"With the help of Street blocking the road. I also was lucky to find a handy battering ram nearby. Used it to momentarily subdue the kidnappers."

"You think the men who took this boy are the ones who perpetrated this grave you're talking about?"

"Yeah."

"I heard from Diamond that these guys are bruisers," he said.

"Paco says they look like superheroes."

Paco flashed me a look of anger.

"And I thought superheroes were good guys," Mallory said. "What's your guess on why they took the kid?" He talked like Paco wasn't standing right next to him.

I tried to think of how best to phrase it considering that Paco was listening. "He was a witness to a shooting."

Mallory nodded. "Got it. So you're sitting on the kid?"

Paco looked up at him.

I shrugged, using Paco's affirmative version.

"I guess you're pretty good protection," Mallory said, "in spite of the kidnapping."

"You want to volunteer?" I said. "We could take turns."

"Well, I'm not..." Mallory glanced down toward Paco, then looked back to me. "My schedule's real busy," Mallory said. He held my eyes for emphasis.

"Right," I said.

"Show me what you got?"

We started walking.

"Your dog found the grave?" Mallory said.

"Probable grave, yeah."

"How'd he do that? He's just in the habit of looking for graves?"

"He sniffed the shoe. Paco saw it from the air. He believes it belongs to Cassie Moreno, his foster mom. The shoe's in the Jeep. You can take it when you leave."

"You did an air search?"

"Nice day for a plane ride, so we went up looking for signs of the woman's van or the cliffs that Paco described. Paco saw this shoe. We drove over here and found it. I scented Spot on the shoe, and he walked over to the grave."

"Just like that, huh?" Mallory glanced at Spot, then muttered under his breath, "I'm glad I don't have a nose like that. I'd hate to go around being able to smell dead people in graves." Mallory gave Spot a longer stare. "Why's he acting so depressed?"

"He doesn't like smelling dead people, either. Makes him sad."

"Likes to find them alive, huh?"

"Yeah. That makes him happy." I knew that I could set up a live find to turn Spot's funk around, but it would have to wait until I was done.

Sergeant Tibbs and the other cop carried shovels. We walked through the trees. The sky got darker, the rain harder. When we got to the dense trees, I pointed toward the gentle mound of dirt.

Mallory pulled up on the creases of his pants, squatted down and looked at the sandy mound. "How you figure it went down?" he asked.

"I didn't see any tire tracks around here, but I did back at the rocky cliffs. I think that the shooting that Paco witnessed happened over there. After that, Paco hid in the back of the pickup and said it didn't move for a time. So my guess is that the killers picked up the body, carried it here, and buried it."

Mallory nodded. "I don't see any marks," he said. "Someone shoots somebody over there by those cliffs, then carries the body all the way over here, there would be marks."

I saw a branch on the ground. It had recently broken off from a tree, so it still had green needles. I walked over and picked it up. Then I walked backward, using the branch like a broom to rub the grus cover and erase my footprints as I backed up.

"You learn that working Homicide at SFPD?" Mallory said.

"Westerns," I said. "John Wayne. Or maybe it was Eastwood."

Mallory turned to the other cops.

"Go ahead and dig this mound up. But go gentle. I don't want you contaminating a corpse with your shovels."

"Like we want to stick a shovel blade into a corpse," one of the cops said.

I winced at the words, stole a glance at Paco.

"Let's go over to those trees," I said. "Get out of the rain."

Mallory walked with us. He said, "You think your hound could find shell casings like he finds bodies?"

"If you find one to scent him on, he might be able to find others. But Agent Ramos said these superhero guys match the description of some dirtballs known as the Collectors. They go by Salt and Pepper. Their M.O. is to Taser their victims, then suffocate them with heavy plastic wrap."

Mallory looked at me. "The stuff that holds boxes on pallets?"

"Yeah."

Mallory nodded, thinking. He looked over at Paco who was sitting on a rock under a big Red fir.

"When this kid first called you, how did he happen to have

your number?" Mallory asked.

"My name was in his foster mom's cell phone."

"Why you think he didn't just call nine, one, one? That would be faster."

"Paco knows that nine, one, one goes to the cops. He said that his foster mom had told him never to call the cops. I've since learned that the boy is an illegal immigrant."

"Didn't he think you were a cop?"

"He said her cell phone listed me as 'Private Cop.' Apparently, she'd told him the difference."

"Christ, these Mex workers think we got nothing better to do than send them back over the border. They work hard, we leave them alone. Without them we'd be screwed, anyway. No one else will pick crops in the hot sun."

"People still get deported."

"True, but most of the time it's just the crooks."

"So the authorities say. Not what I heard from a Central Valley school principal."

Mallory frowned at me harder than before. He turned his attention to his boys digging. They inserted their shovels into the ground as carefully as if they were digging up an unexploded landmine.

"You got a take on this whole gig?" he asked me.

"No. Unusual for a woman to leave the Central Valley in the middle of the night and drive up to Tahoe to meet someone who then assaults her. What kind of threat could she possibly represent to someone that they set her up to kill her for it? If, in fact she is dead."

"We'll know more in a few minutes." Mallory sipped his Coke. It was empty. He turned the can upside down and shook out the remaining drops. "How could they get her to drive up from Stockton in the middle of the night without her suspecting something?"

"She had switched from selling at farmers' markets to doing a custom delivery service. They come up here almost every day. Maybe she was planning to meet a client. But it could have been something else. Turns out a guy named John Mitchell called her on the phone and arranged to pay her cash for information about the travel plans of her business clients. She knew it was a funky thing to do even if it is technically legal. So she wrote me a note about it and told Paco to contact me if anything bad happened."

Mallory made one of those big, ah-ha nods. "So she did suspect that something bad was going to happen. I still think that her warning lights would go off when someone wanted her to meet her at such an hour. Most people would either refuse such a meeting or take along someone else for safety."

"I agree," I said. "But Paco says they always leave really early to make their deliveries. Once Cassie agreed to meet someone, it was probably her who chose the time."

I turned to look for Paco. He was still sitting on the rock.

I called out to him. "Paco, you said you were sleeping in the van, then you woke up. Did Cassie say anything to you before she got out of the van, before she was shot?"

"She told me to stay down. Not to let them see me."

"Did she sound like it was just a normal meeting? Or did she sound like she was frightened?"

"Like she was scared," Paco said.

I turned to Mallory. "So she went to a meeting that she thought would probably be safe. Then she saw something that made her concerned."

"But she didn't drive away," Mallory said.

"No. She wasn't that worried. Just concerned enough that she wanted Paco to stay down."

Mallory nodded.

"Got something," one of the cops said.

Mallory looked at Paco. "The kid going to be okay with this?"

I said, "Hey, Paco. Looks like there is something in this grave. You want to take a walk someplace? You want to go do something with Spot?"

He shook his head.

"You gonna be okay about this?" It was too big a judgment to expect a ten-year-old kid to make, but he'd been dealing with big stuff for the last three days.

He nodded, but he didn't get up. If he wondered about the grave, he wasn't curious enough to walk over and look up close.

The men were down on their knees, scooping loose dirt with their hands. It didn't take them long to get the corpse uncovered.

The victim was female, lying face down in the grave, wearing jeans and a flannel shirt and one Nike shoe with a red swoosh. The plastic around the body's arms and head was several layers thick. Although the body smelled bad, the decomposition was not as advanced as it might have been in a warmer climate. Tahoe's cool ground and cold nights had slowed the natural processes. I'd also learned from Street that when a body is buried, blowflies can't get to it to lay their eggs. So there was no maggot mass trying to make fast work of her flesh.

The men carefully cut the plastic sheeting from the victim's head.

When her face was revealed, it was dark with pooled blood, but it wasn't yet bloated with decay.

Mallory walked away, faced the woods, took several deep breaths. After a minute, he came back. He didn't look at the corpse and instead spoke softly. "You think this kid can ID her without falling apart?"

"Yeah." I went over to Paco and sat next to him.

"Paco, there is a body in the grave. It could be Cassie, or it could be someone else. A dead body looks pretty bad. You could maybe identify the body for us. But it might make you sick or very angry. You don't have to do it if you don't want to."

"I've seen bodies on TV," he said.

"Bodies on TV are fake. This is real. It's quite a bit worse than seeing one on TV. If you want, we can take a picture and show that to you."

"I'll do it," he said. He stood up, walked over, and took a look.

"It's her," he said.

"You're sure the body is Cassie?" I said just to be certain.

"Yeah." Paco walked back and sat back down on the rock.

His face didn't seem to change, but I thought I could see a hint of weary old man in Paco's young face. The boy looked toward the forest, his face impassive. He stared at the trees, but he was no doubt seeing something much different, something that young kids should never have to see.

"This might be a good time to get a statement from the boy," Mallory said. "You think he would be up to it?"

"Yeah. Probably be good for him, too," I said. "It'll focus him on the idea that you cops can help find the guys who put that woman in the grave."

Mallory nodded. He went back to his car to get his tape recorder.

I went over and squatted down in front of Paco. "Commander Mallory wants to ask you about what happened, what you saw. You don't need to worry about this. Nothing you tell him will cause any problem for you. It will just help him catch the killers. He will ask you to tell him what you saw. He'll ask you to describe as best you can what these guys looked like, what they did, what they said. What Cassie said, too."

Paco glanced at me, then looked away.

"You okay with this?"

He nodded.

"Good," I said. I reached out and held his shoulders. "You're a tough kid," I said. "I like that about you."

Paco didn't respond.

Mallory came over, and I left them alone.

Later, I told Mallory to call if he had questions, and Paco, Spot, and I left.

As we walked back to the Jeep, I tried to imagine Cassie coming up from Stockton to Tahoe, planning to meet someone. It obviously seemed innocent enough that she felt fine bringing Paco. But she'd told him to stay down. It was as if she pulled up and then realized that the men at the pickup were not the men she was planning to meet.

Yet something kept her from driving away. Maybe she thought they'd chase her. Or maybe she thought that the person she was planning to meet was there in the dark, and she just couldn't see him.

A third possibility was that the man who paid for executive travel plans arranged to meet Cassie, maybe to finally pay her in person. Although she didn't know what he looked like, when she saw Salt or Pepper, she might not believe that either of them could possibly be the man who called himself John Mitchell.

In Cassie's note to me, she'd written that she was a cautious woman. So whomever enticed her to the meeting must have seemed benign because she willingly went. And it got her killed.

We got in the Jeep, and I turned the heat on high to dry us out.

Paco stared out the side window. The clouds had gotten thicker, the rain harder, the sky darker.

I put my hand on his knee. "Sorry you had to see all that back there," I said.

He kept facing out the window. He said, "Rafael and his sister got to put up a string of Christmas lights in their bedroom. They have lights in their life. All year long."

TWENTY-FIVE

As we drove away, my insides were twisting into knots. In all of the difficult moments of a difficult career, I'd never been in this situation. I didn't know what to do, what to say, how to behave. I had a kid in my car who could well be on the verge of coming apart. Instead of making his life better, it seemed that everything I did pulled the string that was slowly unraveling Paco's life.

Desperate for a change of scene, I called FBI Agent Ramos and explained that I was with Paco. I suggested that Ramos might want to get an update from Mallory, hoping that Ramos would understand my reluctance to talk about what we'd found. Then I asked if we could stop by the FBI's Tahoe office.

"It would just be a short visit," I said, hoping he would realize that I wanted Paco to see that lots of law enforcement personnel were working on the case.

"I understand," he said. "Come on by."

We parked outside the nice-but-plain building, and left Spot in the Jeep. I took Paco with me to the security door, pressed the button. Someone spoke through a speaker while a camera stared at us from behind glass.

"Owen McKenna here to talk to Agent Ramos," I said.

The door buzzed. We walked through a metal detector into a glass-walled entrance room where we could be seen and appraised. Another door buzzed and we walked into the office.

Ramos was on the phone.

The other agent who shared the office pointed at his watch, then held up three fingers.

We waited. Paco stared at the FBI insignia on the wall. I watched the clock. Ramos got off three minutes and three seconds later.

Ramos stood up from his desk and came over. He looked ready to attend the opera. His suit was freshly-pressed, his hair perfectly combed, and his pencil mustache was trimmed with such precision that he must have used a drafting ruler.

Paco looked at Ramos's shiny shoes.

I introduced Ramos and Paco. Ramos nodded at the boy. Paco stood silent and rigid and looked at the floor. Ramos gave no indication that he recognized the skin-color-match in the room. The other agent and I shared the pale skin of Irish brothers, while Ramos and Paco both had the rich brown coloring of Central American Indian-Spanish mix. They could have been uncle and nephew.

"So this is the boy who hid in the pickup bed," Ramos said. "Brave kid."

"Yeah," I said. "Why I came by. I wanted you to meet the bravest kid in Tahoe."

No reaction from Paco.

"Mallory is fast," Ramos said. "He's got some kind of new transcription software. He ran the recording of Paco's statement into his computer and just emailed it to me. I also heard from Diamond about the kidnapping of this boy last night."

Ramos tapped Paco on his shoulder.

Paco looked up at him, his frown mixed with concern. The sunglasses in his hair reflected a vivid gold in the fluorescent office light.

"It took real courage to hold it together during that," Ramos said to Paco. "I'm impressed."

Paco didn't respond other than to pinch his lips together. He looked back down at the floor.

Ramos looked at me. "You think the murder of the woman and the boy's kidnapping are connected." It wasn't a question.

"Paco said it was the same guys in both cases," I said. "The kidnap attempt shows that they're persistent."

"More dangerous than a lot of their colleagues, too," Ramos said. "Not because they're smart – they're not. But because they don't know their limitations, and they have no governor. They think they're some kind of underworld superheroes. They like to do unnecessary, grandstanding stuff just to get press and puff up their rep."

I looked at Paco, wondered if he noticed that an FBI man saw the same superhero motif as he did.

Ramos continued, squinting at me. "Like Tasing you and dropping the fishnet on your hound. Diamond told me about it. What a ridiculous move. The only reason to do that is to get press. The media has already picked up the fishnet story. It's not just another kidnapping, it's The Fishnet Kidnapping by The Collectors. There are kids out there who will idolize these guys. Like famous gangsters. Like superheroes. Salt and Pepper might be stupid, but they have an instinct for press, and they're building a legend."

"Paco also said they looked like superheroes," I said. I rubbed Paco's shoulders. "How do you think these guys have evaded the law?" I asked Ramos.

"Mostly luck, a lot of bluster, and a vehicle disguise."

I raised my eyebrows.

"There's a man in – let's say Detroit – who makes a clever device that shuffles up to six license plates. Works just like a fifties jukebox pulling records up and out of the stack. The whole contraption is only two inches deep, so it can be installed in most vehicles without any outward sign. We leaned on this guy, and he told us that the Collector boys purchased front and back units from him some months back and had him install them in their pickup.

"He also said that Salt and Pepper boasted to him about their pickup topper. They got it from a sometime-military contractor that deals in techy material. Custom fabrics that can be mounted on most surfaces. Solar fabrics that generate electricity, bullet-proof Kevlar fabrics, fabrics that glow in the dark. It turns out, these boys had their topper laminated with a fabric that looks like a different color depending on what kind of light shines on it. It looks like white at night when it's illuminated by man-made light. But under sunlight, the same fabric looks dark. Amazing stuff."

"Paco said the pickup topper looked white," I said. "But that was at night. So we should be looking for a dark topper during the day."

Ramos nodded. He looked at Paco, then gave me a questioning look as if he was wondering whether or not I understood the seriousness of the danger to the boy. "From what our informant says, it sounds like Salt and Pepper act without hesitation. No moral code to get in the way. Doesn't matter who the victim is."

"Message received," I said. "They ever work for themselves? Or do they only hire out?"

"Hire out, from what we've heard."

"So, in addition to Salt and Pepper, we're looking for someone else."

Ramos nodded. "About whom we have no clue," he said.

"There is one thing," I said. I told him about the man named John Mitchell who paid Cassie for information about the travel plans of her clients. We talked about it for a few minutes, I thanked Ramos for his time, and we turned to leave.

Ramos reached out and rubbed Paco's head. Paco's sunglasses slipped sideways and caught on his ear. Paco grabbed them and shot Ramos an intense frown. He put the glasses back on.

"Sorry, Paco," Ramos said. "Just want you to know that we're glad you're helping us put the finger on these bad guys."

Paco looked away, and we left.

I was trying to think of something to say to lift Paco's spirits. After we'd driven some distance, I said, "Now you've met a county Sergeant, a city Commander, and an FBI guy. They're all trying to help catch Salt and Pepper."

Paco shrugged like it was no big deal. "Seen 'em on TV," he said, his face to the window.

"TV cops and FBI agents aren't real. They're just actors pretending. These guys are the real thing."

A minute later, Paco said. "They got nice clothes."

I nodded.

"They carry guns?" Paco asked.

"Probably," I said.

"Cops have them on their belt," he said. "Like Diamond."

"Some cops have concealed-carry holsters," I said. "Under their arms. Or in the arch of their backs. Could be, that's what Commanders and FBI agents do."

"Like undercover cops," Paco said.

"Yeah."

"Do you carry a gun?" he asked.

"No."

"Why not?"

It was always a difficult question. "Because a gun makes it easy to get yourself into a situation that you can never get out of."

Paco didn't say anything.

TWENTY-SIX

I didn't dare go back to the cabin. It was too easy for Salt and Pepper to watch. They could sit at any of a dozen points in the forest and see vehicles coming and going on the drive up the mountain. I thought about going across the grade to Street's lab, but my Jeep was easy to spot, and I didn't want it sitting outside her workspace.

Instead, I called her.

I told Street about our day. "Diamond said we could stay at his place starting tomorrow night. We shouldn't repeat at your place, so I'm thinking of a back street motel."

"They could be watching for your Jeep," she said. "You should rent a car."

"I tried that once, but when the rental agent saw Spot, she said they were out of stock."

"Then you should take mine."

"They may know your car from when you blocked my road," I said.

"Still better than the Jeep," Street said. "Besides, I watched them as they came down the road. They turned off the road onto that trail a long way back. I doubt they could have noticed the make and color of my car. Where shall we meet?" Street said it as if the decision was made.

"I'll park behind Harrah's, and we'll walk through the passageway by Embassy Suites. You can pull up on the main boulevard, and we'll get into your car. If Salt and Pepper are following me, they'll watch my Jeep, waiting for us to come back. By the time they figure out what happened, it will be too late to do anything about it. We can drop you at your condo."

"I've got work to do. You can drop me at my lab and I'll take a cab home. Or do a lab sleep-over."

"Okay. Give us ten minutes."

"Make it twenty?" she said. "I've got another call coming in."

"You're the best," I said and hung up.

We drove over to the hotels and parked in the far back lot at Harrah's. I was vigilant, but I saw no pickups following us.

We had some extra time before Street would arrive, so I called information and got the number of the Sacramento Bee. When the receptionist answered, I asked to be put through to a reporter who covered the farm economy in the Central Valley.

"Well, that would be any of several," she said, "but they're all out except for Kirk Chamone. Would you like me to connect you?"

"Please."

"Kirk Chamone," a man answered.

"Detective Owen McKenna calling with a quick research question, please. We're working on a case that may connect to Central Valley tomatoes."

There was a pause. "You mean, regular tomatoes? Like the vegetable?"

"Yeah. My question is about the potential value of a new kind of tomato. If someone created a tomato that was substantially better than what is currently available, would the value be enough to motivate potential theft or worse?"

"First, let me ask," Chamone said. "If this turns into a human interest story with an agricultural component, will you give me the details first?"

"Promise," I said.

"Okay. Let me describe what I know about tomatoes," the man said, "and you can draw your own conclusion. I'm no expert, so take everything I say as coming from a layman.

"If you look at the three main types of tomatoes, the large, the cherry, and the Roma-plum type, you've got uncountable varieties of tomatoes out there. But I'd guess that the commercial growers get most of their sales from maybe two dozen varieties.

You come up with any single variety that has some big advantages over what's currently popular, and you could have a very large number of growers eager to put your new tomato into their production. So yes, there could be motivation to pirate your tomato."

"How much could a single type of tomato be worth?" I asked.

"Good question to which I don't know the answer. But the tomato market in the United States is around two billion dollars a year. Let's say your tomato had the potential to claim five percent of that. One hundred million a year sounds like a motivating number to me."

"Me, too," I said.

"And you'll remember to call me if a story comes out of this?"

"Will do."

It was time to meet Street. Paco held Spot's collar while we walked. As we went by the Embassy Suites, we had to stop for a bit so two women could pet Spot and exclaim and gush and hug him. But we were out in front of the hotel when Street pulled up. It was not easy to fit the four of us into her VW. Spot took up the entire back seat. So I jumped in the driver's seat, while Paco grudgingly sat on Street's lap in the passenger seat.

We dropped her at her lab.

"Even when we're not with you," I said to Street, "you are still at risk."

"Don't worry. I'll keep the lights down and the blinds closed. Even if they know about my lab, my car won't be here. They'll think I'm out."

"Merci very much," I said, kissed her, and we left.

We headed into town.

"You like Chinese takeout?" I asked Paco.

He shrugged.

I had the restaurant put the food into three sets of boxes so we didn't need plates. The restaurant parking area was well blocked from the main boulevard by trees and buildings, so we ate outside in the lot, balancing our food on the curved hood of Street's Beetle. Spot ate his rice and chicken on the ground. He made a mess of it, but was meticulous about cleaning up after himself, licking every grain of rice off the pavement.

We'd forgotten to bring supplies when we left my cabin, so we stopped and bought a change of clothes and toothbrushes for each of us, then checked into a motel where Salt and Pepper would be unlikely to find us even if they knew the make of Street's car. I parked the car on the opposite end from our room.

The room was small but had a king-sized bed.

"Where do you sleep?" Paco asked.

I pointed to left side of the bed.

"Where do I sleep?" he asked.

I pointed to the right side.

"Where does Spot sleep?"

I kept my finger pointing to the right side.

He shrugged. Affirmative.

We were in bed early.

TWENTY-SEVEN

The next morning we began our route. The rain had stopped, but the forecast said that more precipitation was to come. I didn't mind because they said the snow level would be at 7500 feet, the best situation for this time of year. I love snow, but it was too early in the season to get excited about shoveling. If the forecasters were right, the ski resorts could start building their base, while I'd only get rain at my cabin. Only the few people who lived above me would get snow.

In my pocket, I had my list of the Field To Fridge clients from Cassie's sales journal. I'd put them in counterclockwise order around the lake. Paco could probably tell me how to drive to all of their customers, but the addresses would be good backup.

The first person was the inventor for NASA, a guy named Rob Tentor. He lived on the lake in Skyland. The house was easy to find, because as soon as I turned through the Skyland entrance, Paco said, "This is the guy who likes persimmons."

"Let me guess. A fruit, not a vegetable."

"Yeah. Go down to the lake." Paco pointed, showed me where to turn at the end, pointed out the house.

I pulled into the drive and parked. "You should come with me to the door," I said.

"Why?"

"Because you're my credibility. They know you, right?"

"Not really," Paco said.

"But they've seen you."

"Yeah."

"Then they'll be more likely to talk to me. Your presence will give them comfort."

Paco thought about it, then opened his door and got out. We

left Spot crammed in the back seat and walked to the front door.
I rang the bell. Chimes sounded far off.

Paco pointed at the lock. "Cassie has a key. We just go into
the kitchen."

I nodded.

The door opened. A woman wearing a smock and holding a
rag and bottle of Windex said, "May I help you?" Then she saw
Paco.

"Paco! What are you doing here?"

"Hi, my name is Owen McKenna. I'm a local investigator."
I handed her my card. "I'm here with Paco because we have bad
news. I'm sorry to tell you that Cassie Moreno, your Field To
Fridge woman, was murdered three days ago."

The woman immediately paled, hugged herself, and looked
horrified. "Paco! I'm so sorry!" She bent down and hugged him.
He didn't move as he was engulfed by her embrace.

The woman looked at me. She stuttered, "Wh... Wh... What
can I do to help?"

"You work for Rob Tentor?"

"Yes, I'm his hou...housekeeper. Bridgett Jordan."

"Is Mr. Tentor home?"

"No, he's in Spain. He won't be back for two weeks." As she
said it, I understood how easily Cassie was enticed into forward-
ing travel information that people gave freely.

"When did Mr. Tentor leave here?" I asked.

"A week ago last Tuesday."

"We believe that Cassie's murder may have something to do
with her Field To Fridge business."

The woman's look turned to fear. "I... I... I can't believe that.
We all love her. She's a dear friend. She feeds us."

"Were Cassie's arrangements with Mr. Tentor primarily handled by him? Or did you make the arrangements?"

"Well, Mr. Tentor first called her after Mrs. Swanson told
him about Cassie. But after the first visit, I was the one who dealt
with Cassie."

"What was involved in your dealings?"

"Nn...Nn...Not a lot. Mr. Tentor was on her 'Just The Basics' plan. Every week she showed up with tomatoes and peppers and persimmons, broccoli, asparagus and spinach. The fruit was usually bananas, apples, and oranges. Now and then she would add other produce. She used her judgment on what was tastiest in any given season."

"Did Mr. Tentor get along well with Cassie?"

"Oh, he loved her. I mean, he loved her service. He rarely ever saw her. But he was very taken with the whole concept. I loved what she did, too."

"Any disagreements or tension?"

The woman shook her head.

"What about her as a person? Did you and Mr. Tentor find her to be as personally agreeable as her business service was?"

Bridgett frowned. "Well, I'm not sure I understand what you mean."

"Did you like Cassie?"

"Y... Y... Yes. Ab... Ab... Absolutely. She maybe wasn't super chatty and friendly. Just real business-like. She did a great job."

"How often did you talk to her?"

"Once a week when she came. That's all."

"Did Mr. Tentor see her each week?"

"N... Not most weeks. Cassie comes early. Mr. Tentor is usually still in bed."

"Who paid Cassie's bill?"

"I did. Every four weeks, she would bring an invoice, and I'd write her a check out of the household account."

"Was Cassie's weekly visit your only contact with her?"

"Of course. She lived down in the Central Valley. Where else would I have contact with her?"

"Where do you live?"

"Carson City," she said.

"Did you ever tell Cassie about Rob Tentor's travel plans?"

She frowned. "No. Why would I do that?"

"Maybe she just asked you casually. Something like, 'So where is Mr. Tentor these days?' Like that."

"I c... can't ever think of any time we talked about such a thing."

"You're sure."

"Of course, I'm sure," she said in an irritated voice.

"Tell me," I paused, "did you consider the amount that Cassie charged a fair price for her product and service?"

"W... Well, I d... don't know that I could judge that."

"Why not? You buy fruits and vegetables in the store, right? If you add a delivery fee, and add for Cassie's time, did the result seem appropriate to you?"

Bridgett Jordan paused. "I may just as well tell you the truth, Mr. McKenna. Cassie's p... produce was probably the most expensive in the world. Many times I've wondered why I didn't think of such a business. I mean, how hard can it be? You go and buy some nice veggies and deliver them in a nice-looking basket. Then you charge ten times what they cost. It was a real racket, this business of Cassie's." Bridgett stopped abruptly as she realized that her voice had gotten an edge to it.

"Don't get me wrong," she continued, her voice softer. "Mr. Tentor loves the service. He'll be d... dismayed to hear that Cassie is gone."

"And you?" I said. "Are you dismayed?" It was a pointed question to which I expected an angry, defensive response.

Instead, Bridgett said, "Yes," her voice quiet. "I'm very dismayed."

I pointed at the card in her hand. "If you hear of anything that might be useful in our investigation, please give me a call."

She nodded, and began to close the door. Then she opened it and spoke to Paco. "I'm s... so sorry, Paco." She gave him another hug.

We left.

Back in Street's Beetle, I started a new list.

1) Rob Tentor – Nasa inventor – Out of town. Housekeeper Bridgett Jordan was Cassie's main contact. Envious of Cassie's business success. No travel discussed.

The next person up the East Shore was romance novelist Jayleen Swanson, the Mrs. Swanson who Bridgett said first told

Tentor about Cassie's business.

Jayleen Swanson lived in Uppaway, the exclusive gated community just south of Glenbrook. I pulled up to the gate, punched Swanson onto the keypad and the machine dialed her phone. After five rings, her answering machine picked up.

At the tone, I said, "Hi, my name is Detective Owen McKenna. I have important information about Cassie Moreno, the owner of Field To Fridge. Please give me a call at your convenience." I left my number and was about to push the disconnect button when I stopped. I added, "If you prefer, you can call Commander Mallory of the South Lake Tahoe Police Department. Thank you for your time."

As before, Paco said, "Cassie knows the code. We just go in."

"No doubt," I said.

I updated my list.

2) Jayleen Swanson – Romance novelist – Unavailable.

The third person on my counter-clockwise trip around the lake was the ball player for the Oakland As. He lived in Glenbrook, just north of the Uppaway entrance. I drove to the Glenbrook gatehouse. The woman on gate duty gave me a stern look. With a Great Dane stuffed into the back of a little Beetle, I was clearly not someone she recognized. She probably spent a good part of every day asking house gawkers to turn around and leave.

I pulled close to her open window and gave her the name of the ball player and explained who I was.

"He's a famous ball player," she said. "Not like he's sitting around at home waiting for visitors."

"Can you try him, please?"

She frowned, reached for the phone, and punched in a speed-dial code.

After what couldn't have been more than two rings, she hung up and said, "I'm sorry, he doesn't appear to be home." Then she noticed Paco sitting beside me. She leaned forward to get a better look at him. It was obvious that she recognized him.

"Are you sure you let it ring enough?" I said. "Maybe he's in the shower."

She hesitated, thinking. "He's got it set on auto. So I know he's gone."

Maybe it was true. And if not, there wasn't much I could do.

"Can I leave him a message? Even a famous ballplayer will think it's important."

"If it's important, you should email him. That way you know he'll get it." She made a flat, little grin, no doubt knowing that I didn't have his email.

I thanked her and turned around. I stopped before pulling back onto the highway.

3) Ball Player – Unavailable.

As we drove away I said, "She just lets Cassie drive right in?" Paco nodded.

Our next three on the list were all in Incline Village, on Lakeshore Boulevard, vacation home central for Bay Area tycoons.

We drove up the East Shore and turned off on the grand route that on more than one occasion has been written up in the Wall Street Journal for having the most expensive home for sale in the country.

The first was the rock star, front man for a group that had sold 90 million albums in the last ten years.

Paco showed me which drive to pull into. I stopped at a huge gate. Behind the gate, the drive made a gentle S-curve through the trees and went out of sight. The lakeshore house was not visible from the entrance.

To the left side of the gate stood a stone post with a doorbell at the right height to push from a tall SUV.

I looked at Paco. "How did Cassie get in?"

"She pushes the button. When the machine starts talking, she says, 'it's Cassie,' and the gate opens."

"You mean, it's got voice-recognition software and it's programmed to know her voice?"

Paco nodded.

I pushed the button.

"Hello," came a pleasant robotic voice that had been programmed to sound very snooty, upper-crust British. "Thank you for calling. Unfortunately, the master is out, so please have your agent call our agent, and perhaps we can set up a meeting."

Just before it could say 'Goodbye,' I spoke in a high voice, "It's Cassie."

But the 'Goodbye' came, and the gate didn't open.

4) Rock Star – Unavailable.

TWENTY-EIGHT

The fifth person on Cassie's list was Mike Kalili, the producer of documentaries. Because the name Kalili sounded Hawaiian, I had an unreasonable picture in my mind of a beautiful tropical beach with a sprawling spread of thatched-roofed buildings.

Paco showed me the drive three blocks down. This house was not on the lake, or what Hawaiians call the makai or ocean side of the road, but was instead on the mountain side of Lakeshore Boulevard, the mauka side of the road. Instead of a tropical design, the Kalili residence was a simple unfenced, timber-frame cabin of maybe 8000 square feet. We pulled in under the portico. As Paco and I walked up to the five-foot-wide door, it occurred to me that no mere documentary filmmaker would earn enough for such a crash pad. There must be something else adding to the income stream.

Another woman answered the door, this one dressed in a suit and looking very trim for her sixty years. "Paco!" she said, clearly glad to see him. "What a surprise. This isn't your delivery day, and," she turned to me, "this isn't Cassie."

I gave her the same introduction and the same explanation of Cassie's death that I'd given Bridgett. The woman in the doorway gave me the same reaction that Bridgett had given me but without the stutter.

"I'm so sorry! I'm Mrs. Kalili, Mike's mother. Mike is busy right now."

I asked some of my questions about Cassie and her business. The woman had no useful information.

"Were there times when Mike was gone and you saw Cassie during her delivery?"

"Yes, a few. I remember having some conversations with her."

"What did you talk about?"

"I have no idea. Vegetables, I suppose," she said.

"Cassie was involved in a travel project," I said. "Those times when Mike was gone, do you recall ever talking with Cassie about Mike's travel plans?"

"Again, I don't remember. But it's not like he was protective of information about his whereabouts. With Mike, everything is pretty much public. Not that I approve. Things that I think should be private, he puts on his website. And on his Facebook page. So there's not much that I could reveal about Mike that he doesn't reveal himself."

"You said that Mike is busy, but would you consider asking him if he will see me?"

"Mike is in his editing room. I normally hate to interrupt him, but let me go ask. Please give me a minute."

She left us standing in the large entry. Paco sat down on a long leather seat that was built into one wall.

"You've met Mike Kalili?" I said.

Paco nodded. He pointed over toward the dining room. "That's one of our baskets."

On the dining table was a large basket filled with gorgeous red tomatoes and green peppers and orange peppers and yellow apples. The colors were so intense, they shimmered. I walked over to admire it.

"That looks great, Paco. You do good work."

I took a few steps toward the living room to admire the monster cut-stone fireplace with a photo portrait of a man above. Framed in a modern, pewter frame moulding, the portrait showed an intense, homely, middle-aged man with substantial eye-bags.

"Admiring Luis Buñuel, are we?" a man said.

I turned to face an imposing man with a big grin and happy eyes. His head was shaved, an unfortunate cosmetic affectation given the thick, meaty shape of his head and neck and his pale, puffy skin. He was dressed as if for a photo shoot to advertise something casually elegant. Thin-soled, pointy leather shoes, linen pants and matching linen jacket that draped a silk shirt.

"I don't know Luis Buñuel," I said, shaking the man's hand. "I'm Owen McKenna."

"Mike Kalili." He pointed at the portrait. "Famous Spanish-Mexican surrealist filmmaker. All film buffs are, of course, aware of his profound influence. But even you may know of his films. El Gran Calavera, Nazarin, El angel exterminador." His tone was condescending.

"Sorry," I said. "My taste in film runs to Spielberg, Eastwood, Scorsese, Allen. I've always thought they were pretty good, but perhaps the surrealists like Bunnell go another step beyond."

"Buñuel," Kalili corrected me, irritation pulling his mouth into a hint of sneer. "And, yes indeed, those boys you mention do a good job of keeping the film economy going with pedestrian fare while real auteurs make real art."

"I'm sorry that I haven't seen your films," I said. "Or maybe I did but didn't take time to notice the director credit."

"No problem," he said again. "I'm not familiar with your work, either." Kalili made a loud laugh at his joke and smacked me lightly on the shoulder.

"So," he continued, putting his hands on his hips. "Mom says that you have bad news about the veggie lady."

"Yes." I reiterated what had happened.

"That's too bad," he said in a cheerful tone. "Hate to lose my veggie delivery. What can I help you with?" He looked at his watch.

"Just a few questions, if you can spare the time."

"Of course. Let's sit." He gestured toward a group of over-sized leather furniture arranged in front of the fireplace. We sat. Then he saw Paco. "Your boy doesn't have to stay in the entry." He raised his voice. "Hey, sport, you can come sit with us, if you like."

Paco didn't move.

"He's Cassie's boy. Name is Paco," I said. "You've met him during the Field To Fridge deliveries."

"Really?" Kalili squinted over at Paco. "Oh, sure, I remember now. The little brown-skinned boy. Mexican, no doubt."

"Like Luis Bunnel," I said.

"Buñuel," Kalili corrected me again. "And yes, I get your intimation. Mexicans are often good at many careers. Even that boy might grow up to be good at something. So what are your questions?"

"How well did you know Cassie Moreno?"

"Not at all. She was the veggie lady. What's there to know?"

"How did you learn of her Field To Fridge service?"

"Let me think. I have a documentarist's memory. It's like a photographic memory, only in three-D, both spatially and timewise." He closed his eyes and put his fingertips to his forehead. Then he raised his head and looked at me. "Yes, I recall. With documentary precision, I should add. It was my neighbor from two doors down. Robert Whitehall. He told me I should sign up, so I did. The lady makes good veggies, by the way."

"Have you ever seen her other than when she made her deliveries?"

"No."

"Have you ever had any other kind of written or phone contact with her?"

He shook his head. "Can't imagine why I would. She wasn't my type."

"If she was?" I said, trying to be flip.

He must have thought I was serious. "I usually start with a chat over coffee," he said. "When women discover the depth of my artistic vision, it is quite the aphrodisiac." He winked at me then glanced at Paco.

"I bet," I said.

"These things usually progress according to my plan. By the time they see my round bed, they've begun to sense what a gift the coming experience is about to be."

Despite the impulse to throw Kalili through the window, I managed to keep control.

"Other than your neighbor Whitehall," I said, "has anyone else ever mentioned her?"

Another head shake.

"Did you know that Cassie was selling information about her

clients' travel plans?"

Kalili frowned. "What for?"

"Money. Somebody had apparently figured out a way to make money based on where movers and shakers like you travel. That person paid Cassie quite well for it."

"Oh, I get it," Kalili said. "Stock market fluctuations based on potential business plans by big companies, plans revealed or at least hinted at by executive travel. Good idea! Should have thought of that one myself! But I don't see how I would fit into it. Certainly, people consider me influential in the world of film making. But how would you monetize it? Learn my screening schedule and be the first one to bring your hotdog stand to the theater?"

"Some variation, perhaps," I said. "Any thoughts on why someone might target Cassie for violence?"

Kalili paused. "Maybe she developed a new strain of veggie, and someone else wants to use it in their business. It would be like stealing any artist's production. Of course, the significance of my work was recognized from the beginning, but the truth is that really creative people often produce fabulous work and no one else knows about it for centuries, if ever. So if the creator is dead, and someone steals and markets the product, there is no one to come after the thief."

Kalili looked pleased with himself. He continued, "I bet there'd be a lot of money in tomatoes if you could develop one for the trade that had the same luscious taste and color of home-grown. What do you think? If I didn't have the vision of a documentarist, I could be tomato visionary."

"I think you may have a good idea. I appreciate it."

He grinned so big that the sides of his puffy shaved head stuck out. "I get such ideas because of the creative way I think. It's a mark of my work as a..."

"A documentarist," I interrupted, standing. "What was it? Three-D, spatially and time-wise. Impressive."

Mike Kalili stood, pleased as a kid who's just won the spelling bee. Like many self-absorbed narcissists who have no capacity for self-critique, he didn't hear even a hint of sarcasm in my words.

I thanked him, and Paco and I left.

5) Mike Kalili – Documentarist jerk – Probably a trust fund baby or has additional income from something other than filming documentaries.

TWENTY-NINE

Next on my list was Kalili's neighbor, Robert Whitehall, just two doors down. Whitehall was the owner
of the medical stent manufacturing company. Whitehall's modern manse was no bigger than Kalili's, but because it was on the
makai-lake side of the boulevard, he'd probably spent another
few million for it.

The big gate swung open as we turned in. I cruised past two
cameras at the gate and another one mounted on a tree thirty
yards in. More cameras were visible around the sprawling low-
slung, glass-and-concrete affair that looked like it had been
plucked from the desert near Palm Springs.

A gentleman in his seventies emerged from the double glass
doors as we pulled up. He was wearing a French blue cardigan
sweater over a blue shirt, blue slacks, and blue slippers.

I parked.

"Can I stay in the car?" Paco asked.

He sounded weary and depressed. Maybe if I gave him a
focus.

"Nope, you can't stay in the car," I said as I looked through
the windshield at the man who stood in his entry looking at us.
"Duty calls. You're my six o'clock."

"What's that mean?"

"Noon on the clock is what's in front of me. Six o'clock is
what's behind me. I need you to cover my back, be my eyes and
ears, keep me safe."

Paco made a slow nod and got out of the Beetle.

I jumped out, walked over to the man, and introduced myself and Paco.

He shook my hand and nodded at Paco. "I'm Robert

Whitehall. I knew you might be coming because my neighbor Mike Kalili just called me and said that a man asking about Cassie's Field To Fridge might be about to drop in." Whitehall's voice was soft and gentle and a bit tentative. The opposite of the brash Kalili. Whitehall's eyes went to the back of Street's Beetle where Spot was attempting to turn around.

"My, my," he said. "You have a large, spotted animal in the back of your car."

"That's Spot," I said.

"Ah," he said. "Please come in. Is it okay not to invite Spot in?"

"Yes. It takes the two of us to shoe-horn him into the back seat, and our success rate is iffy. So once he's inside, we're reluctant to ever let him out."

Whitehall nodded.

We walked into the concrete-and-glass box. The floors were polished concrete, stained in beautiful, muted, swirling blues. The lake side of the house was all glass, and there were no trees so that the blues of the swimming pool and the lake and sky would accentuate the blues of the floor.

At one end of the room was a simple fireplace, a rectangular opening in the gray concrete wall, lined above and below with a blue concrete hearth and mantle.

The large room had one group of four chairs facing each other with a low table between them, and another group with two chairs flanking a couch that faced the fireplace. All the seating was a 1950's-modern design with orange upholstery and stainless steel legs. No frills. No patterns. The lamps were also the same modern design, made of the same steel. On the floor were several woven rugs, all orange.

I'd read about complimentary colors in one of my art books. It said that if you put blue next to orange, it would make your eyes flash. I wondered if Paco and I should worry if Whitehall sat his blue form down on one of the orange seats.

Above the mantle hung a large framed print of a painting that I'd seen in several books. Whitehall must have noticed me looking at it.

"Do you know the painting Guernica?" he said, his comment mirroring Kalili's comment about the portrait of the film director above Kalili's fireplace.

"I know that it is a famous Picasso, but not much else."

"Yes, it is a Picasso. Although it is only a print. I could never afford an original. Most of the major Picassos are now over one hundred million. You obviously know a lot about art." He left it at that. No boasting. No beating his chest about his exemplary mental skills and photographic 3-D Picasso memory.

"Please sit down," he said.

I sat on the couch, facing the Guernica print. Whitehall took a chair. I expected Paco to take the other chair. Instead, he sat alone on a chair behind me.

He had my six o'clock.

I looked at Whitehall. He looked pretty cool against all that hot orange. But my eyes didn't flash, so maybe the art book was wrong.

Whitehall said, "My neighbor Mike told me that the reason for your visit is that the proprietor of Field To Fridge died. I'm very sad to hear that."

"Did you know Cassie Moreno outside of her delivery service?"

"I'm sorry to say that I've never even met her. But my tenant Andrew Garcia sung her praises. He referred to Cassie as a tribute to the profession of farming."

"Your tenant was the one who saw her each week?"

"Actually, Cassie let herself in most weeks. I set up the schedule over the phone. Cassie came to this end of the lake on Tuesdays, and Andrew is often gone on Tuesdays. His son has a medical condition that puts them in Reno every Tuesday. So he didn't see Cassie much, either."

"So Cassie was alone most of the times she came."

"That is correct."

"Did you ever wonder about security? Giving the keys to the house to a stranger?"

Whitehall made a little smile. "I have a security system, of course. Cameras. Monitoring by a competent firm." He glanced over at Paco. "I never had the pleasure of meeting Paco in person before today, but I know from the security reports that he accompanied Ms. Moreno on her rounds. I've seen from the video that this young man is always a big help to Ms. Moreno, carrying baskets of vegetables. Sorry, I guess I should say 'was.'" He turned to face Paco. "Young man, I'm very sorry for your loss. If there's anything I can do..." he trailed off. His eyes looked misty.

I proceeded to ask Robert Whitehall the same questions that I'd asked the others. He gave me the same answers that the others had.

Five minutes later, I'd learned nothing. I stood to go. I saw movement outside the windows. Whitehall turned. On the far side of the swimming pool, an older man was pushing a younger man in a wheelchair.

"Oh, here come Andrew and Martin. Please come outside and I'll introduce you."

Whitehall pushed open one of the huge glass doors in the glass wall, and we went out into the crisp air of fall in Tahoe.

The man pushing the wheelchair looked to be approaching seventy. In the chair was a younger man. They came around the end of the pool and over to us. As they got close, I saw that the older man's snug, patterned outfit was an athletic uniform, a skin-tight, shimmery stretch fabric emblazoned with bright graphics and a large number 67 on the front. The man was thin and muscular.

"Andrew and Martin, I want to introduce Owen McKenna and Paco. This is Dr. Andrew Garcia and his son Martin."

Andrew and I shook hands. He said hello in a pleasant but quiet voice. I went to shake Martin's hand, but as I got close I could see that his smile was more of a painful grimace, and he wasn't moving his arms. He nodded but said nothing.

"As you can guess from his clothing, Andrew is a marathon runner, and he is in constant training. What was it that you said your current schedule is?"

"Ten and ten," he said with a bit of embarrassment.

"Oh, yes, that's right." Whitehall turned to me. "He runs ten miles every morning and ten every evening. Can you believe it?"

I said to Andrew Garcia, "Yes, I believe it. But I can't imagine running like that myself."

"You look pretty fit to me," he said.

"Andrew and Martin live in my guesthouse," Whitehall said. He pointed toward what I thought was the neighbor's cabin. It was maybe the last of the original cabins on the lake shore of Incline Village. Most of the others had been torn down and replaced with mansions.

"Andrew and Martin are vegetarians," Whitehall said. "We had Cassie make a single delivery of her wonderful vegetables for both of us, and we split it each week." He turned back to Andrew and Martin.

"Andrew and Martin," Whitehall said, "Mr. McKenna is an investigator, and he has very sad news. It turns out that Cassie has died."

Andrew Garcia looked shocked. "My Lord," he said. He turned to Paco. "Paco, I'm so sorry."

"Mr. McKenna is asking if we have heard or seen anything unusual about her recently."

"Are you implying that Cassie didn't die a natural death?" Garcia asked.

"She was murdered," I said.

"My God!" Garcia's face contorted with stress. He began to tremble. He looked down at Paco.

"That is such terrible news," he said. His eyes got red and moist.

"Tell me about your contact with Cassie Moreno when she made her deliveries?" I asked.

Andrew Garcia nodded. He rubbed his eyes. "I don't really know what to say. She was dedicated to her business. Her vegetables were the best. And she was so kind. Of course, if you know Cassie, you know that she was all about being efficient and businesslike. But she was also kind."

"As Mr. Whitehall commented," I said, "I'm wondering if you ever heard Cassie say anything that might reflect on her death."

Andrew Garcia paused, then shook his head.

"Have you heard anybody else make any reference to her or

her business?"

"No," he said. "It was very exclusive, from what I understood. Just a small list of clients who can afford the best in fresh produce."

"Did you ever see Cassie outside of her role of delivering produce?"

Garcia shook his head again.

"But you talked to her during some of her deliveries?"

"Yes, especially one time. I mean, we barely knew each other. But I'm... Well, it's embarrassing to admit, but I don't get out much, and Martin and I don't have time for socializing. So once when Cassie came, I rather talked her ear off. But it turned out that we had a connection of sorts. I'm a retired veterinarian, and Cassie told me that when she was a little girl, she always wanted to be a vet."

"Interesting," I said. "From what I've learned, Cassie was such a dedicated organic farmer that I assumed that had always been her long-term dream."

"She told me that she used to earn her living as a house cleaner," Garcia said, "and that she had no way to finance an education. But she was able to get into farming on a crop-share basis with no upfront expense. Strange as it may sound, there is a kind of base-level similarity in what we did. As I understood it, Cassie pursued the scientific side of farming, developing new types of tomatoes. And of course, veterinary work has a science foundation. So we both worked in and around biology."

"I'm looking for anything she may have said that indicated that she was in trouble. Does that ring a bell for either of you?"

Both Whitehall and Garcia shook their heads.

Garcia looked at his watch. "I'm sorry, we must leave. We have a doctor's appointment in Reno, and I still have to change."

Garcia looked down at Paco. "Again, Paco, I'm so sorry." Garcia reached into a little pocket on the back of Martin's wheelchair and pulled out his business card. He handed it to me.

Dr. Andrew Garcia
Veterinarian, ret.

At the bottom of the card was his email address.

"If you think of any questions that I can help with, please contact me."

I handed him my card. "Call if you think of anything."

"I will." He gave Paco a gentle pat on his shoulder, then wheeled Martin away.

After they left, I asked Whitehall, "Where did Garcia practice?"

Whitehall frowned. "It slips my mind. I'm at that age where I can't trust that any memory will be there when I want it. I know that I've heard him refer to doing work in both Tahoe and Reno, but I can't recall where his practice was."

"If I may ask, what is Martin's disability?"

"As I understand it, he's got stage four cancer of some kind," Whitehall said. "He's in pain, and he has to take quite a regimen of drugs. The drugs keep him from being very lucid. I get the sense that it's very serious, but Andrew's not the type to give up the fight. He's a sweet man. I hate to see what's happening. The cancer is devouring him just as surely as it's devouring his son."

I nodded. "What about you? Are you retired?"

"God, no," Whitehall said, his eyes wide. "I have many colleagues who made good money and then sold their businesses. They thought the money was what made life exciting. Why work after you have it, right? But after retirement, they quickly discovered that the excitement was gone, and now they're stuck with nothing to do but play golf and walk on the beach and fly to Hawaii in the winter. They learn the hard way that an easy life is not a rewarding life.

"Fortunately for me, they had set the example before it came time for me to do the same. I'm not even married, so I would have little to do were I to quit. Running my business is what I find interesting and rewarding. My foundation is even more rewarding to me. So I will keep at it as long as my brain functions."

"You run your business from home?"

"Yes. My company makes medical devices. Our plant is in the Bay Area. Not far from downtown Hayward. My job can be done from any place with phone, email and teleconferencing ability." He pointed to a corner of the house. It had the same concrete-and-glass walls as the rest of the building.

"It suits me to have my office there." Then he turned and pointed at the lake and the mountains in the distance. "From inside my office, I look out at that view. And if I want to lunch with some of my colleagues, there are several of them who have houses on this same beach."

"Smart decision," I said.

"I think so."

"Someone was mailing Cassie cash every week in return for travel information about her clients. Do you have any thoughts about that?"

Whitehall looked very concerned. "I don't understand. Are you saying that this woman was profiting from providing information about my movements?"

"Your movements along with those of her other clients."

"How would that work?"

"I don't know. My only guess is stock market fluctuations. Perhaps you traveled someplace relative to your business. Whatever you did or whomever you saw could possibly correlate with a subsequent bump or dip in your company's stock price. Or another company's price. Does that seem possible?"

"Yes, of course. But if someone traded on that information, that would be illegal insider trading."

"Maybe, maybe not. If your travel information could be found out by anyone doing basic research, then it's public information. Perfectly legal."

Whitehall stared off at the lake. "I was down in Tucson a few months ago. We were looking at acquiring a publicly-traded manufacturing facility. Its stock has risen thirty percent since word got out that we are interested. If someone had been confident about that possibility, they could have made a fortune."

"Can you think of any way that Cassie might have found out your travel plans for Tucson?"

He shook his head. "As I said, I never met her. She came and went by herself with Paco and only spoke to Andrew now and then."

"Maybe you left something out that she could see. A hotel

brochure. A Post-it note. Maybe you told Andrew, and he mentioned it to Cassie."

He made a slow nod. "Yes, maybe I did do one of those things."

I thanked Whitehall for his time, and we left.

"You had my back," I said to Paco when we were back in the car. "Thanks."

Paco frowned, not understanding.

"My six o'clock," I said.

Paco nodded.

"Do you have any thoughts on these people?" I asked him.

"What do you mean?"

"I'm looking for some connection, some information that would give us a clue about why Salt and Pepper are after you. Has anything any of these people said seemed unusual to you?"

Paco paused, then shook his head.

I wrote on my list.

6) Robert Whitehall – Medical devices – and tenants Andrew and Martin Garcia – retired vet and son with cancer. Andrew knew Cassie some, they shared interest in biology.

THIRTY

We had just three more names on our list. One was Anthony Vittori, CEO of a major software company. He lived on the lake out on Dollar Point. Paco showed me where to turn. I was surprised that a billionaire didn't have a fenced estate. But the house was no less grand for it. Video cameras watched as we stood at the door and rang the bell. No one answered.

7) Anthony Vittori – Software exec – Unavailable.

We continued on through Tahoe City and turned left on 89. The road goes immediately over Fanny Bridge where people line up to bend over and watch the trout just below the dam that holds in the top six feet of Lake Tahoe and regulates it like a reservoir.

Michael Schue lived in a townhouse development a few miles south. He was the founder and chairman of a national restaurant chain of which no franchises were located in the Tahoe Basin. I wondered if that was why he chose to live here. My research had also discovered that Schue owned a sister company to the restaurant business, a produce distribution company.

I followed the instructions on the keypad at the entrance but got no answer from the auto-dialer. I could wait until another resident drove up and then follow them in through the gate. But once inside, I would probably find the condo vacant.

They had a little turn-around for people like me. I pulled back onto the highway.

A red Audi came toward us. Paco spun in his seat as it went by.

"That's him," he said.

"Michael Schue?" I slowed and pulled over.

"No. The guy who came over to the hothouse and wanted to buy Cassie's Amazements."

I was about to pull a U-turn, but a truck was coming. It went past. I turned a fast U and hit the gas.

The Audi was pulling through the townhouse gate. I cranked the wheel and pulled into the entrance, but the gate was already closing. We came to another stop.

"You know that guy's name?"

Paco shook his head.

"Kind of a coincidence that he pulls into the place where Michael Schue lives. Did he ever say anything that made it seem like he was connected to Michael Schue?"

Another head shake.

"When you delivered to Michael Schue, did you ever see that guy?"

"No."

I pondered that while we waited. While it was entirely possible that the guy who wanted to buy the rights to Cassie's tomatoes just happened to live in the same development as one of Cassie's customers, my instinct said they were connected. My hope was that the guy in the Audi was going to Michael Schue's townhouse.

We pulled off the road and waited fifteen minutes just in case the Audi-tomato guy was meeting Schue at Schue's place. I drove back up to the gate and once again dialed Schue's number on the gate keypad. Still no answer.

The keypad had a scroll feature that showed the residents' first initials and last names.

"I'm going to read off the names of the people who live here," I said. "It only shows the first initial, so it won't sound normal. But I want you to listen anyway and tell me if any of them sound familiar."

Paco nodded.

I started reading the names aloud. A furniture delivery truck pulled in behind me. I kept reading. There were a lot of names.

The truck honked. Paco turned around to look.

"Try to ignore the truck," I said.

Paco faced forward again.

I kept reading. The truck honked again. I made finger motions at the keypad like I had found the combination. Soon, I was done reading.

"You didn't recognize any name?" I said.

Paco shook his head.

I jockeyed Street's Beetle back and forth, got it turned around and out of the truck's way. The truck driver pushed a code on the keypad. The gate opened. I pulled behind the truck and followed it into the townhouse development.

There were several buildings, each with its own underground garage. All the garage doors were shut.

"How did Cassie and you get in to make your delivery?"

"Garage door opener," Paco said.

I drove around and looked at the outdoor parking areas. No Audis.

It didn't leave me many options. I could dial everybody's phone from the gate keypad. That would take a day or two. I could stake out the front gate and wait for the Audi to drive back out. But it could be hours. Or days. Or next spring.

We left.

8) Michael Schue – Restaurant business – Unavailable. Audi-driving tomato hustler at same residential complex. Maybe connected. Maybe not.

Further south down the West Shore, Paco directed me to turn into a long drive, marked only by No Trespassing signs. The drive wound through thick forest as it crawled toward the lake. It brought us to a wrought-iron fence with pointed spikes along the top. In the distance, we could glimpse the sprawling home of the comedian-turned-TV talk show host, known to all Americans and watched by millions.

There was no bell at the gate, no keypad, and no house number. Just cameras. Lots of them. On the fence and in the trees.

"Cassie have a transmitter for this gate, too?"

Paco nodded.

"When you got to the house, did the transmitter open the door to let you inside?"

"No. The butler let us in the house."

I nodded. I waved at the cameras, backed up, turned around and left.

9) TV talk show host – Unavailable.

THIRTY-ONE

"**W**e need to get some food and find a place where Spot can run," I said.

Paco nodded.

"You okay with a deli sandwich in place of a burger?"

"Yeah."

I went north. Before we got to Tahoe City, I turned into the Tahoe House Gourmet Bakery and got some custom deli sandwiches. Then we headed around the north end of the lake to the Mt. Rose Highway and turned up the mountain.

We cruised up the mountain, past the jaw-drop views at the vista overlook and climbed on up to the Mt. Rose meadows at close to 9000 feet. Clouds cloaked the summit of Mt. Rose, but the sun was out on the meadow.

I found a place to park, and we let Spot out of his back seat prison.

He showed his enthusiasm by running off into the snowy meadow. Paco and I ate another meal on the hood of Street's car. When Spot smelled us opening our sandwiches, he came running and joined us.

When Paco was done, he got back in the Beetle, reclined his seat back and went to sleep. When Spot was done with his sandwich, he went back into the meadow.

I looked again at my notes about Cassie's customers whose travel information she'd sold to the anonymous John Mitchell.

1) Rob Tentor – Nasa inventor – Out of town. Housekeeper Bridgett Jordan was Cassie's main contact. Envious of Cassie's business success. No travel discussed.

2) Jayleen Swanson – Romance novelist – Unavailable.

3) Ball Player – Unavailable.

4) Rock Star – Unavailable.

5) Mike Kalili – Documentarist jerk – Probably a trust fund baby or has additional income from something other than filming documentaries.

6) Robert Whitehall – Medical devices – and tenants Andrew and Martin Garcia – retired vet and son with cancer. Andrew knew Cassie some, they shared interest in biology.

7) Anthony Vittori – Software exec – Unavailable.

8) Michael Schue – Restaurant business – Unavailable. Audidriving tomato hustler at same residential complex. Maybe connected. Maybe not.

9) TV talk show host – Unavailable.

Other than the red Audi, no information came up that gave me a clue about where I should look next.

But I still had possession of a kid who had no home. The doctor near Paco's school suggested that I contact people in the Basque community.

I looked at my cell and saw that I had reception.

I called Information for The Center for Basque Studies at the University of Nevada in Reno, the organization that Dr. Mendoza had mentioned as a good resource for all things Basque. They connected me, and I told the young woman who answered that I was looking for general information that might help me find some family connections for a young orphan who is Basque.

"Well," the woman said, thinking, "none of our professors is available. But you might want to speak to Marko. Sorry, but I can't pronounce his last name, but it starts with a V so that's what I call him. Marko V. He's a student working on his doctorate in Basque linguistics. He just stepped out, but he's due back shortly. I could have him call you."

"Thanks," I said. I gave her my cell number.

Paco was still sleeping when Marko V called twenty minutes later. I paced along the shoulder of the highway while I talked.

Marko V gave me his full name, but I also found the last name difficult to understand. Despite the unusual Basque name, Marko V spoke like he grew up in Long Beach.

After a quick introduction, I told him I wanted a quick education in those things Basque that might help me place an orphan boy who might be Basque and who had no family that I knew of.

"What's the boy's name?"

"First name Paco. He's not sure of his full last name. He goes by Ipar. A Basque doctor near Stockton told me he thought Ipar was short for Iparagirre."

"That sounds likely. Tell you what. I'm teaching a class in ten minutes. Then I have to run downtown. Could you meet me at the Nevada Art Museum in, let's say, an hour and a half?"

"I'll be there."

"How will I know you?"

"Tall guy with a baseball cap." I pulled if off to see which one I was wearing. "Red," I said.

THIRTY-TWO

I woke Paco and helped him raise his seat back, then called Spot in from the meadow. Paco helped me coax Spot into the back of Street's little car.

We drove into the clouds as we crested the Mt. Rose Summit, the highest year-'round pass in the Sierra. Then we popped back out of the gray soup and wound down ten twisty, switch-backy miles as we dropped 4500 vertical feet to the sunny desert in the valley that Reno and Sparks residents call The Truckee Meadows. As always, I kept my eyes on the rear-view mirror. I didn't see any dark pickups.

We drove into a patch of sunshine. It got warm, and Paco had rolled down his window. Spot leaned forward to put his head out the window, testing how much air pressure he could take in his nose and ears. I'm always amazed at how dogs are unique among all other animals. If you took any other creature, from guppies to rhinoceroses, and held them out a car window at high speed, they would probably think it terrifying. Yet dogs think it's the greatest thing since steak.

Paco hadn't said a word in an hour.

Although humans and dogs are very different species, the comparisons between Paco and Spot were unavoidable. Quiet and shut down compared to loud and enthusiastic. Placid and without expression versus boisterous and expressive to a fault. Paco gave new definition to introverted. Spot was the essence of gregarious extrovert. If Paco had any dramatic personality qualities, they would be hard to discover. Whereas Spot was all drama, and his personality quirks and characteristics were inescapable. He imprinted himself on you even if you tried to ignore him.

At the desert floor, we turned north on the 395 freeway and

took it up to downtown Reno. I got off 395 onto Mill and headed west to downtown, found a parking place near the Nevada Art Museum, and got out.

"C'mon, Paco. Time for a dose of art."

He got out and stood, shoulders slumped, still lethargic after his lunch and nap.

I let Spot out and put Paco's left hand on Spot's collar.

"You've got hound duty, kid. Don't let go of Spot. Remember how he heels? This is more practice." As I said it, I worried that Spot might see something exciting and take off running. At 170 pounds to Paco's 64, the result would be like a cowboy being dragged by a runaway horse.

We headed across the street and down the block. I walked on the other side of Spot. When we got near the museum, I saw a cop parked nearby, filling out what looked like a long form. She might be there awhile. Handy in case Salt and Pepper had managed to follow us.

We walked into the museum. They probably had a rule prohibiting dogs, but I didn't see any sign.

I brought Paco over to a corner where we were out of sight from some of the windows.

Spot sat down, then slid his front paws forward, lowering himself to the ground. Paco was still holding onto his collar. He sank down to his knees as Spot lowered. Paco sat on the floor, then shifted a bit so that he could lean against Spot, his arm reaching sideways so that he could keep his grip on Spot's collar.

A woman rushed up, scowling at me.

"Sir, I'm sorry but we don't allow dogs in the museum."

I gave her my best smile. "He's a service dog. The law allows service dogs everywhere."

She shook her head. "Service dogs have to wear the official bib. I know because my friend is blind, and she has a dog."

"We forgot the bib. We had a meeting here with Marko V from UNR. I'm sure you know him. Anyway, we were half way down from Tahoe before we realized it. If I'd taken time to go back, we would have been late for our meeting, and Marko V would be annoyed.

The woman looked doubtful. "I don't know any Marko V. What kind of a name is that, V? Anyway, my friend also told me that her service dog trainer says that service dogs are always from the medium size breeds so they can fit in elevators and such."

"Usually, that's true. But this dog was apparently so attentive to his job that the training school made an exception."

As I said it, Spot rolled over onto his side, jerking his collar from Paco's grip. Spot's panting tongue flopped out onto the floor, the size and shape and look of a Kokanee salmon fresh-caught during spawning season when they turn bright red. He appeared to immediately go to sleep.

"You obviously don't need a dog," the woman said. "The dog serves the boy?"

I nodded. I tried to look solemn. "Yeah. Poor little William. Born deaf. And we haven't had much success with sign language. But he's smart. Trust me, I can tell these things. It's only been a couple of days since William got the dog. But already they're inseparable."

The woman looked doubtful. "William can't hear?" she said loudly, carefully watching Paco to see if he turned at the name. Paco didn't show any reaction. He just stared at the floor.

I shook my head.

The woman's reaction went from disbelief to sympathy. "We have a woman working here who signs. I'll have her come out and work with William while you have your meeting."

"Uh, no thanks. The boy is very shy. And he's got, ah, a condition..."

"I don't understand."

"It's an unusual situation. The doctor says he should refrain from social interaction with strangers. It could really set him back."

Behind the woman came a man in a suit.

"Tall guy. Red baseball cap," the man called out as he raised up his index finger. "Gotta be Owen McKenna."

"Marko," I said, stepping past the woman to shake his hand. "Thank you for meeting me."

The woman looked Marko over carefully, then raised her

hand toward me in a little wave and left.

The man bent down in front of Paco. His shoes were black and freshly polished. "So your name is Paco Ipar."

The boy wouldn't meet Marko's eyes. He looked vaguely at the floor.

I said, "As I mentioned on the phone, Dr. Mendoza, a doctor near Paco's hometown, thought that Paco's last name, Ipar, might be short for Iparagirre. He said that name refers to a house that faces the north wind."

Marko nodded. "It is common for the Basque to name their houses like that. And in some cases, when a Basque family home is sold to new residents, the new residents will take the name of the residence as their new family name. Tell me, Paco," Marko said. "Do you think that Iparagirre is a possibility for your last name?"

Paco shrugged. Affirmative version.

Marko straightened up and smiled. "If Iparagirre is Paco's last name, this boy's ancestors are certainly Basque. Many of the Basque, when they came west from the east coast of the U.S., headed to this part of the world, from Idaho down to Mexico City. They also went in significant numbers to Chile."

I turned to Paco. "Has anyone ever said anything to you about being Basque?"

Paco made a nearly-imperceptible shake of his head.

I said to Marko V, "Paco was born in Mexico, orphaned in this country as a baby. We have no knowledge of any relatives. But we could look for other Iparagirres."

"I've learned that some of the Basque in Tahoe eventually relocated to Mexico because their high-elevation range lands are great for raising sheep, and they don't have the downside of heavy winters. So it's possible that Paco is completing the circle. His lineage may include Tahoe. You could take him hiking up on the meadows of the East Shore mountains and show him the arborglyphs."

"What are those?"

"The Basque have always been artistic. The sheepherders carved drawings into the bark of Aspen trees. One of our UNR professors has documented them in a beautiful book. It's an ephemeral art form. Every year we lose the oldest drawings as the trees die off, which makes those that remain more precious as time goes on."

"What did they carve?"

"You name it. Names, dates, poems, landscapes, pictures of their girlfriends. Those sheepherders may have lived quiet lives as loners up on the mountains, but they certainly were boisterous as artists. Some of the arborglyphs are X-rated. If you take all of the arborglyphs as a body of work, it is an amazing record of the lives of the Basque sheepherders. Could be that Paco has some artistic ability in his genes."

"It sounds like sheepherding was sort of the national occupation," I said.

"It was important," Marko said, "but as with all groups, the Basque pursued a wide range of occupations. Baseball player Ted Williams was part Basque. As was Olympic skier Jimmie Huega. And John Ascuaga, the guy who owns the Nugget."

"The giant hotel in Sparks."

"Yeah. And back in the late nineteen sixties, Paul Laxalt was governor of Nevada, and, in the seventies, he became a senator from Nevada."

I remembered the name. "Senator Laxalt is Basque?"

"Along with his brother, Robert, who wrote a bunch of books and started the University of Nevada Press."

"Tell me," I said, wanting to ask a question as much for Paco as for me. "The little I've heard about Basque people, it always sounds like they're a big deal. If I hear something about the Scottish, Irish, and Welsh – my ancestors, for example – it's no big deal. But it seems different with the Basque. What's that about?"

"It's probably because of our uniqueness. We have very little connection to the other people of Europe or anywhere else. It shouldn't be that way because our land is on the border of Spain and France, on the Bay of Biscay. So we are proximate to most of Europe."

"Proximate," I repeated.

"Yeah. It would make sense that we would have many similarities to people in nearby countries. But we don't."

He continued, "We are linguistically and culturally distinct. To a substantial degree, we are even genetically distinct. Our DNA contains components not found elsewhere. Our blood type is like no other group of people on earth. We have dramatically more O negative blood than any other people, and we have almost no B type.

"The Basque language, Euskara, has no clear relation to any other language, European or otherwise. Our history is a mystery. The best guess seems to be that we were some of the earliest Europeans. The other early European inhabitants were overrun by subsequent waves of migrations from all directions. Celts, Romans, Goths. But somehow the Basque survived centuries of onslaught," Marko said. The man was obviously proud of his heritage.

I noticed Paco shifting his position on the floor, always draping his arm over Spot's prostrate form.

"Tough people, huh?" I said.

"Some say," Marko V said, "that the reason the Basque country has been so durable is the nature of Basque government. President John Adams even commented. He went there in the late eighteenth century and was impressed that, while the rest of Europe had succumbed to the rule of kings, the Basque had resisted any kind of overlords.

"But I have yet another theory about how the Basque have remained cohesive," Marko continued. "And it is part of my dissertation."

"What's that?" I said.

"You probably know about the Spanish Civil War," he said.

"No, I'm sorry to say that I'm ignorant about that."

"Well, very briefly, during the Depression, Spain's right wing became more alarmist and disenchanted with the democratically-elected Republican government. So General Franco, who was a fascist, staged a coup and took over the government and put his Nationalist Party in charge. They executed tens of thousands of suspected leftists, especially Jewish leftists. The resulting civil war pitted the Republicans across the country against the fascist Nationalists."

"And because the Basque were in Spain," I said, "they must have got caught up in the war. Which side were they on?"

"As they have always done throughout history, the Basque fought against tyrannical leaders. They were against Franco and the Nationalists. They wanted to be left alone. But Franco wanted to appoint himself king and rule everything. He knew from Basque history that the Basque would never submit. So he engineered one of the worst massacres in history."

"Killed the Basque?" I said, wincing at the thought.

"Yes, and in the most vile way. He talked Hitler and Mussolini into using their warplanes to bomb the Basque country."

"This was before the start of World War Two," I said.

"Right. Nineteen thirty-seven. It was one of the worst terrorist attacks in history, like an evil World War Two training run for Hitler and Mussolini. They unleashed the German Luftwaffe and the Italian Aviazione Legionaria onto a defenseless Basque town where there hadn't even been any fighting.

"The Basque men were all off fighting Franco's forces on other fronts, so when the bombers came in to blow up the Basque country, they mostly killed women and children. It was a ferocious, surprise attack on the most innocent of people. Thousands of mothers and their kids."

"Hard for a people to forget that," I said.

"Yes. The Basque were peaceful sheepherders. That massacre still sears in family memories. Many writers and composers and painters have commemorated the atrocity."

"The Basque men must have been outraged."

"Yeah, some of those peaceful sheepherders turned out to have as much appetite for vengeance as anyone. There were reports of them slaying some Nationalist sympathizers." Marko gritted his teeth. "War is an ugly thing."

I was silent for a moment as I contemplated what he said. I walked a short distance away from Paco. Marko followed.

Marko turned to me so that his words wouldn't be heard by Paco. "You said the boy is an orphan?"

"Yeah. And his foster mom died recently."

"The foster system can't find a new home?"

"Not quite," I said. "Turns out that Paco is an undocumented kid. His foster mothers have been neighbor women in the town where he lived when his real mom died. We could prevail upon the state of California to try to find a home for him, but he's been in trouble, and they would likely deport him to Mexico, a country he doesn't know."

Marko looked over at Paco who was still sitting on the floor, half-draped over Spot.

"Do you know about the Basque clubs?" Marko V asked.

"Haven't heard of them."

"There are about four dozen of them spread across the country. Their purpose is to give people of Basque ethnicity a way to connect with each other."

"And keep the culture alive," I said.

"Exactly."

"You think I should contact the clubs? See if they know anyone who would take in a Basque child?"

"Might be worth trying."

"You have a list?" I asked.

"I can email it to you," he said.

I pulled out my card and handed it to him.

I thanked Marko for his time and the information about the Basque clubs. We all left.

THIRTY-THREE

When we were back in the car, Paco said, "Why did you tell that woman that my name is William and that I was born deaf?"

"You were listening?"

"I always listen," he said.

I realized that I would have to be much more careful in the future. Paco was not as unobservant as I thought.

"The woman wanted us to take Spot back outside. I'd already made an appointment with the Basque expert Marko V. So I told a white lie so we could stay inside the museum and meet him. I didn't want us to wait outside where it would be easier for Salt and Pepper to see us."

"What's a white lie?"

"A white lie is what you tell when you have good intentions," I said, thinking that there was probably a better way to phrase it.

"So it's good to tell white lies," Paco said.

"No. It's probably bad. Most of the time, anyway. It's just not as bad as telling other lies."

"Does everybody lie?"

Now I regretted saying anything to the woman. I should have just left the museum and met Marko V outside. "Probably most people lie sometimes," I said. "Especially white lies."

"Like breaking the law," Paco said.

"How do you mean?"

"Some laws are bad to break. Some are not so bad. And everybody breaks some laws."

"Yeah," I said, "like not wearing seat belts."

"Why do they make some laws if everybody breaks them?"

The simplest questions were often the most difficult to answer. Yet I was glad that Paco was talking.

"An optimist would say that we make laws with the best of intentions and that those laws are good even if somewhat unworkable."

"What's an optimist?" Paco asked.

"Someone who thinks things will probably work out for the best."

"That's why they make stupid laws?" Paco said.

"A cynic would say that people make stupid laws because people have a natural desire to make rules for other people to live by."

"What's a cynic?"

"Someone who thinks that people often have bad reasons for doing things." Another answer that didn't feel quite right.

"Then I'm a cynic," Paco said.

"I think you have reason to be a cynic. Some bad men killed your foster mother and chased after you. Meanwhile, some kids have nice families and nice homes and don't have to worry about the authorities sending them to a country they don't know. From your perspective, life isn't very fair. It looks like lots of people have bad motivations.

"But you also have reason to be an optimist," I added, trying to think fast. "Even though your mother died when you were a baby, other people took you in. They gave you food and clothes and a place to sleep and no one paid them to do it.

"I spent twenty years as a cop. I've seen first hand that there are a lot of very bad people out there, enough to fuel the thoughts of endless cynics. But I've also met lots of really good people. People who would take in a kid like you."

Paco turned away and looked out the window. I realized that while I'd talked about good people who had taken him in during the past, I couldn't find any now.

I called Street, got her voicemail, left a message about meeting up to return her car.

I called Diamond. "Checking in to see if your bed and breakfast offer is still good," I said when he answered.

"Sí."

"Gracias. We're currently in Reno in Street's car, so I need to get it back to her, then figure a way down to your homestead in Minden to borrow your old truck."

"Why don't I pick you up at Street's lab or condo? Bring you down myself."

"Muy gracias," I said.

"Not quite right, but I get the idea," Diamond said. "Which will it be, lab or condo?"

"I've got a message in to Street. Okay if I let you know in an hour or two?"

"Sí."

THIRTY-FOUR

We drove south to Carson City, then turned west on 50. We were coming over Spooner Summit, back up into the clouds above Tahoe, when Paco said, "That's the pickup." He pointed up the highway.

A dark blue pickup was turning across the highway, coming from the southwest, heading north on 28 toward Incline Village.

I turned to follow it and sped up, closing the distance between us.

"When I saw the pickup after the men grabbed you at my cabin," I said, "it was too dark for me to tell the color. But you said you thought the pickup was dark gray with a white topper. We've since learned that the topper might look dark in daylight. This topper is dark, so that fits. But it and the truck are dark blue. That's not what you thought before."

Paco stared at the truck as we drew near. I stopped accelerating when we were eight or ten car-lengths back. If the pickup belonged to Salt and Pepper, I didn't want them to realize who was behind them. They might remember Street's Beetle from when she used it to block their escape path from my cabin.

"Which do you think it is?" I asked. "This blue pickup, or another one?"

"This one," Paco said.

"You sound so sure. How do you know?"

"I can tell. The shape of the topper. And the way the bumper sticks out. That's the bumper I climbed on."

"Paco, when you first saw the pickup, it was dark, and you were under serious stress. I can understand that your impressions of what the pickup looked like might have been wrong. But why would you think differently now?"

"I saw the pickup again when I got out and ran away down the mountain. It was daylight."

"Ah, that's right. What color was the pickup when you saw it then?"

"Blue." Again, he sounded certain.

"Well, it makes sense that your daytime sense of color would be more accurate than your nighttime sense."

We followed the pickup north, past Sand Harbor. I dropped farther back and pulled over to let two cars get in front of me.

"The handle on the topper door," Paco said. "It was kind of broken. Like it flopped a little. We could check that."

"Good idea," I said, thinking that I'd seen multiple broken topper door handles over the years. But despite the often faulty design, if the one in front of us was broken, that would be a good reinforcement of Paco's belief that this pickup was the one in which he'd ridden.

"How was it broken? Was the door just hanging loose?"

"It was like this." Paco held his hand up, fingers out.

"I don't understand."

"It was at an angle. And kind of floppy loose."

"So you still had to turn it to open the door, but it didn't sit out straight?"

"Yeah," Paco said.

I reached under the driver's seat and pulled out the binoculars that Street keeps for birdwatching. I handed them to Paco.

"You could look at the pickup and see if the topper handle is at an angle. You know how to focus them?

"Yeah."

He didn't sound convincing.

I said, "There's a little knob on the top and another on the right eyepiece."

"I spin it, right?"

"First, you shut your right eye and look with your left. You use the top knob."

Paco held up the glasses and worked the focus knob.

After a bit, I said, "After your left eye is focused, you look only through your right eye and use the right knob."

He pointed. "This one."

"Yeah."

Paco looked through the glasses, adjusted the knobs.

"The picture jumps around."

"That's the problem with binoculars. You magnify the image eight times, and that's great. But you also magnify the vibrations of your hands eight times."

Paco kept looking through the glasses, adjusted the top knob again. He leaned forward and put his elbows on the dash, steadying the glasses. Held the position longer than I would have thought possible for a ten-year-old.

He lowered the glasses to his lap. "The handle's broken. It's at an angle."

"You're sure."

"Yeah. That's the truck."

"Can you see how many people are in the truck?"

"No. It's got smoked windows."

"Be ready with the glasses in case they turn off the road. You might get a glance at who's inside the cab." I thought about when I ran the battering ram log through the pickup. "If they turn to the left, you can see if the driver's window is broken."

I varied my distance from the pickup, generally keeping two or three vehicles between us. We were just coming into Incline Village when the truck's brake lights flashed.

"They're going to turn," I said. "Look through the glasses."

Paco propped his elbows on the dash, put the glasses to his eyes. Big rain drops began to splatter on the windshield, obscuring the view. I turned on the wipers, but they left streaks on the windshield. Paco kept watching through the glasses.

The pickup made a right turn onto Country Club. I got the briefest glimpse of the passenger side window before the pickup disappeared into the trees.

"It's the guy," Paco said.

"Which guy?" I sped up, got to the turnoff and pulled in after them.

"One of the superhero guys. The black guy."

"Pepper."

"Yeah."

"You're sure," I said.

"Yeah."

The pickup followed a winding road through the forested neighborhood of modest vacation homes.

"Was Pepper in the passenger seat? Or was he driving?"

"Next to the window. The passenger seat."

"Could you see who was driving?"

"No."

I tried to stay as far back as possible and still keep the pickup in sight. If we'd been spotted, the driver stayed cool about it.

His brake lights flashed again.

"He's turning again," I said.

Paco kept the glasses up. The pickup turned right again.

"See anything?"

"Just the same guy."

The pickup turned into a driveway. I stopped well back and watched as the pickup moved through the trees. Its brake lights went on, and it pulled into the garage of a house that was tucked back against the slope. The garage door closed.

I pulled forward just enough to see the house better through the trees.

"Watch through the windows," I said. "See if you see anyone moving."

Paco held the binoculars steady.

"No," he said. "You can't see. The windows all have curtains."

I wanted to take the binoculars and look for myself, but it seemed there would be little to gain. Better for Paco to feel useful.

"What's the little blue sign above the garage door?"

Paco looked, then handed me the binoculars.

I adjusted their focus.

The sign said,

VACATION RENTAL
TAHOE TURF RENTAL AGENCY

Underneath was the phone number. To the right of the sign was the house number.

I dialed.

A woman answered, "Tahoe Turf Agency, giving you your piece of Tahoe when and where you want it."

"Hi, I'm calling from Tahoe Gold Pizza. I've got a Deep Delish Extra Large to deliver, but when I got to the house up here at five six two three Forest Glen Circle in Incline, it's all dark and no one answers the door. It's got your rental sign. So I'm looking at the ticket, but Terry, who's got, like, the worst writing in the world, totally scrawled the name. Now I'm wondering if I've got the right house. Can you tell me who's staying in five six two three? Maybe I could recognize the name."

"I'm sorry. We're not allowed to divulge that information. If you gave me a name, I could confirm or deny, but that's all."

"Well I asked the neighbor and she said it was two guys. Can you confirm that? 'Cause if you could, then at least I could decide what to do with this pizza."

"I'm sorry, I can't help you with that." She hung up.

Salt and Pepper could be in for the night. I didn't want to risk knocking, so I drove away, changing my route from the way we'd come in, watching the rear-view mirror. When I got back down to the lake, I pulled over and called Mallory.

"Calling with an update," I said when he answered.

"Yeah?"

"We saw a pickup that Paco thinks is the one that belongs to the suspects in Cassie Moreno's murder."

"You make a positive ID on the Collector boys?"

"No. They pulled into a garage on a vacation rental in Incline. I called the agency. The lady is playing it by the book. No help at all."

"You knock on the door?" Mallory asked.

"No. I assume they'll lie low and not answer."

"No ID, no crime, no way to go in after them," Mallory said. "At least you identified the pickup."

"Not really. Problem is, it's blue with a blue topper."

"You're kidding me," Mallory said. "A couple of days ago, one of our officers called in about a pickup that was loitering near the "Y" in South Lake Tahoe. Had two big guys in it. He ran the plate, but got no hits. We had no reason to push because it was a blue over blue instead of the white over dark gray like the boy told us about."

"The officer didn't stop them?"

"No. He let them drive off when their plate came up clean."

"Sorry about the confusion," I said.

"When the boy gave me his statement, he was certain about his description. How certain is he now?"

I glanced at Paco who had his head against the window.

"Pretty certain," I said.

"Pretty certain," Mallory repeated. "Those of us in law enforcement love terms like that. Simple descriptions that sing with clarity."

"You're a poet," I said.

"I'll amend our description to include blue," Mallory said.

"Thanks."

THIRTY-FIVE

I called Street.

"Any luck today?" she said when she answered.

"Not much. I'm still at the stage where I've got a pile of jig-saw puzzle pieces but no sense of the picture I'm trying to build. Figured you could use your car back. Diamond's going to take us down to his house for the next night or two. Are you at your lab or condo?"

"Lab. You can bring my car here."

"See you in an hour or so."

I called Diamond.

"I thought I should pick up dinner and Pacifico," I said.

"You want me to make dinner, all you gotta do is ask," Diamond said. He paused. "'Course, I've got standards. What were you planning to bring?"

"Burrito fixings?"

"I eat burritos all the time."

"You want me to bring some non-Mex food? Lutefisk or something?"

"Mex food is usually best, don't you think?" Diamond said.

"Tacos?"

"Sounds good. Where should I pick you up?"

"Street's lab, please. An hour or whatever works for you," I said.

I drove back down the East Shore. Paco was quiet as always. Spot snored in the back seat. I thought about the case.

I maybe knew where Salt and Pepper were staying. But I wasn't sure. I could stake out their street, but the road layout was very risky. Any of the places from which I could see them were highly visible.

They'd already failed in their first attack on Paco. The next time they would be bolder. And they would be doubly careful to get both Spot and me with a Taser or a more serious weapon.

If I staked them out and they spotted me as I spotted them, it was almost a certainty that they would try not to let me out of their sight. At the first good opportunity to act, they would make their move.

Spot and I were pretty good bodyguards, but we wouldn't have much chance of preventing them from taking Paco or killing him along with us.

The men had many advantages over us. Weapons, surprise of timing. Choice of technique. Twice as many men, both of whom were much bigger than me. The only advantage I had was Spot, a huge asset in some situations, but a liability in others.

I had to take control. But I had no idea how.

Paco and I picked up supplies at the Safeway in Round Hill. I put the beer in the back with Spot, but I didn't want Spot to be tempted by food, so I handed the grocery bags to Paco.

"Maybe you could set these on the floor?"

He said nothing, but put them next to his feet.

Street was cheery for Paco's benefit and maybe for mine, too, but I could see the worry on her face. She showed Paco how to look at bugs with her microscope, then turned up the music a bit to help cover our voices. We moved over to her desk and spoke in quiet tones while we waited for Diamond.

I told her about our day, meeting some of Cassie's clients, talking to the Basque expert in Reno about finding a home for Paco, followed by Paco seeing what he believed was the pickup with Salt and Pepper and following them to the vacation rental.

"What can you do? Can you get the cops to go in and find them?"

"We'd need a search warrant, but we don't have probable cause. I have no evidence. All I've got is Paco's belief that he saw one of the two heavies in a pickup that went into the house."

"But Paco's attempted kidnapping proves that these men

exist."

"Sure. But the pickup doesn't match Paco's earlier description."

Street was silent for a long moment.

"So you've got nothing," she said, "except your belief that Paco is correct about the man's identity."

"Right," I said, glancing at Paco who was still looking into Street's microscope.

"The Basque expert in Reno," Street said. "Did he have any ideas about finding a family for Paco?"

"Not really. He's going to email me about Basque clubs, groups of people across the country who try to keep Basque culture alive."

"That sounds unusual."

"Apparently, the Basque are a distinct people culturally and physically. Unique language, history, even DNA. And they've been persecuted, so that motivates them to maintain some cohesiveness."

Street reached up and hooked a loose button on my shirt.

"You don't want to take him in yourself?" she said in a soft voice.

"You're kidding," I said, even softer.

"No, I'm not." Her look was unwavering.

"It's not like taking in a stray dog," I said. "Even if I could provide, he needs some kind of a family life."

Street said nothing, waited.

"You know how often I'm gone. You know that a kid should have a home that is more than a one-bedroom cabin with no central heat and no TV. Other than you and possibly Diamond, I have no other friends who would provide any significant support. I'm ill-equipped and ill-trained in the ways of kids. But mostly, I have a dangerous job."

Street looked at me some more. "Why does it sound like you're marshaling evidence to support your desire to live without children?"

"Because it's true, I suppose. But that doesn't alter the fact that no kid should be in an environment where the only adult sometimes gets shot at and stabbed and chased and otherwise assaulted. Paco should have a home that is reliably free from those stresses. And all kids should have a parent or two who are at least somewhat enthusiastic about the day-to-day minutiae of children. A kid should have kid activities. I would not be good at kid activities."

"How much of that is reality, and how much is your fear of the notion?" Street asked.

"I don't know. What would I do with a kid? For many years I've been thoughtful about not having kids because I didn't want that responsibility. Is it fear? Certainly. Is it sensible? That, too. I do have one of the world's worst jobs if one wanted to be a parent. Maybe it's mostly simple preference. I like my quiet life, coming home to drink a Sierra Nevada Pale Ale while I walk Spot, visiting you when you're available, paging through my art books in front of the fire, gazing out at the world's most beautiful view without the distractions of kid-stuff." I touched Street's cheek. "Making love in front of the woodstove at any time of the day without planning it in advance is nice, too."

"Especially that," Street said.

"Okay. Especially that. But remember also that I've never had the desire to be a parent, whether that desire is fueled by the infatuation of a new baby, or the sense of guiding the growth and maturation of another human, or the joy of watching a new generation produce grandkids. All good stuff. All not for me."

Street had her hands on my forearms. She squeezed.

"I understand. More than any woman I know, I understand."

THIRTY-SIX

Diamond picked up Paco and Spot and me in his patrol unit. I again handed Paco the groceries and directed him to sit in the front seat with Diamond so that he could see all the cop gear up close.

I sat in back behind the safety screen with Spot. Spot did the bounce thing on the seat, excited because he'd never ridden in the back seat with me. I had to repeatedly push him off my lap.

"Seat belt?" Diamond said, looking at Paco.

"He doesn't believe in them," I said.

While Diamond gives his opinion freely, he's not the kind of guy to press his opinions on others even if it is the simple activity of an adult trying to teach a child. Especially when the child is under severe duress. Diamond started the SUV and drove off.

"We're getting a free ride in a vehicle paid for by taxpayers," I said.

Diamond pointed at the dashboard clock. "My shift's over. Anyway, I gotta get these wheels back down to the valley. If anyone asks, I'm helping to keep the riff-raff off the roads of our beautiful county."

We drove up and over Kingsbury Grade. Another weather front was pushing through the basin, and variegated autumn clouds swirled around the trees near the top of the grade, light gray tendrils snaking through dark gray masses. Drizzle coated the windshield. The micro drops were so small that you couldn't actually see them strike the glass, and the slowest intermittent wiper speed was too fast. But the windshield gradually shifted from transparent to translucent, and the world became an impressionist mix of blurred colors until Diamond ran the wipers and brought everything back to a wet clarity.

At the top of the grade, the cold, clammy, pale ghosts wrapped the Douglas County SUV as if to pull us away into the coming winter. In a short rise of highway, we drove into the cloud blanket, a fog that was so thick that Diamond had to slow to a crawl.

"Hey sergeant, maybe you could roll down this locked window. Make Spot happy."

"It's raining."

"Spot loves the rain."

Diamond hit the button.

Although the damp, high-altitude air was chilling, Spot stuck his head far out the rear window, his huge panting tongue flopping and looking very pink in the gray fog.

We crested Daggett Pass, pitched down toward Carson Valley, and popped back out of the clouds. Our view expanded from 20 feet in front of us to the mist-muted far side of the valley 15 miles away. The irrigated pasture land of the valley floor 3000 feet below us still showed green late into fall.

Carson Valley is a desert according to rainfall definition. But it stays relatively green because it sits below mountains that poke almost 11,000 feet up into the regular winter storms that charge off the Pacific. The heavy annual snowfall melts all year long creating a stable water source for people who are glad they don't have to shovel the way Tahoe's residents do.

Paco ignored the patrol computer and radio and other gear, and stared out the window, his face impassive and unchanging. His right elbow was on the door's armrest, and his chin sat in his palm, the side of his forehead touching the side window. The sudden change from no vision in the clouds to the long view below them didn't appear to register to him. He was so stoppered down that he probably wouldn't react if he saw mermaids swimming through the foggy sky. Sometimes he seemed more like a statue of a kid than a real kid.

I watched him from the back seat. Paco had skin the color of teak and thick black hair that showed his Mestizo ancestry, but he apparently had no knowledge of his country of birth. I'd watched him study Diamond the night at my cabin. Paco had noticed Diamond's gun, his uniform, his radio, and his shoes. But I also saw Paco making surreptitious glances at Diamond's face, and later, Agent Ramos's face, no doubt because he saw in them the skin color they shared with him.

I wondered if Paco realized that because Diamond had two languages, he had two countries, while Paco had just one language and, by some of the measures we care about, no country. Did Paco know that people were born into widely diverging circumstances? If Paco remembered Diamond in future years, would he realize the huge advantages given to Diamond by having had a continuous and attentive mother over the course of his childhood? Would Paco understand the folly of self-aggrandizing people who claim credit for all of their bootstrap success even though that success almost always arises from an environment that included at least one caring parent on board? Diamond had worked very hard to find success in a new country and with a new language, and he deserved credit for making what he did out of what he had. But Diamond, like me, might have floundered if his family roots were as shallow as Paco's.

I also wondered if Paco was beginning to notice the dichotomy between people with an education versus those without. Diamond and Ramos looked like Paco, and they may have even been born in the same place as Paco, but they had good careers and good paychecks, and they owned their own houses, and they controlled their own futures. By contrast, the field workers in Paco's community were trapped by circumstance. But some of them, and more of their children, would climb up and out of the fields and into Diamond's and Ramos's world. And the single, universal climbing technique was a focus on education.

Paco couldn't read.

But he knew organic farming. He knew tomatoes and peppers. He knew many of the most important components of running a small business.

If there were some way to get him to understand that his knowledge was a significant type of education itself, perhaps that would give him the confidence to open up, be more outgoing, and segue into a more formal educational environment.

We were silent as we wound down the east side of the grade. As we got lower, the sensation was very much like bringing a small plane in on a glide path to a landing. One of the straight valley roads below even stretched out in front of us like a runway.

At the valley floor we headed east and crossed 88 with its steady stream of ranching pickups mixed with the all-wheel-drive cars and SUVs of the local residents. Despite the fall weather, many of the fields were lush and dewy green. Regal, grazing horses mixed with chunky grazing cattle, all looking like they belonged in ads for Marlboro country.

Spot never pulled his head inside, always willing to put up with cold wet ears in return for the plethora of intriguing ranch smells.

We took the back roads across the valley toward Minden and Gardnerville, two adjacent and charming little ranching towns that were gradually gentrifying as the population shifted from ranch workers to young families employed in service industries and retirees enjoying the high-desert climate with spectacular views.

Diamond's house sits just off the Minden town square. It's a restored bungalow that stretches back on a narrow lot with a skinny drive that squeezes between the house and the fence and ends in a back yard with a big cottonwood tree. The tree drapes over a single garage just big enough for Diamond's Green Flame, the Karmann Ghia a woman bought to replace his Orange Flame when it was destroyed in an explosion.

Diamond parked the SUV on the street out front. I let Spot out and grabbed the 12-pack of beer. Once again, Paco stayed sitting inside.

I opened his door. "C'mon, Paco. This is Diamond's home. We're staying here tonight."

He stared at me, his eyes showing a touch of alarm.

"For your safety," I said. "So Salt and Pepper don't know where to find you."

"I don't like staying in strange places."

"It's not strange. You've already met Diamond. So you're just staying at a friend's house."

Paco looked at me.

Diamond had come around the vehicle and called out to Paco from behind me, "Hola, mi amigo. You got some sustenance for me, por favor?"

"He's asking you to hand him the groceries," I said.

Paco lifted one bag up and handed it to Diamond. Diamond took it and walked over to unlock his front door.

Spot came running across the lawn and did a quick stop in front of Diamond's front step. Bits of turf flew from his claws. Spot spun around and stuck his nose into Diamond's abdomen. Diamond pet him without enthusiasm, holding the grocery bag in his other hand.

"Your hound just tore a bunch of holes in my lawn," Diamond said.

"Aeration service at no charge," I said.

Diamond unlocked the door. We walked into the house. I put the 12-pack in the fridge. Diamond set down his bag, then turned back toward the open front door to see Paco standing there with the other grocery bag.

Diamond reached out, took Paco's grocery bag in one hand, put his other hand around the boy's shoulders, and walked him into the house.

"Mi casa, su casa," Diamond said to Paco as they came down the short hallway.

"I'll go change," Diamond said.

I started laying out the food we'd purchased.

Diamond came back wearing jeans and a sweat shirt.

Paco looked at him. It seemed that his permanent frown deepened as he studied Diamond's clothes.

"Hey, I could use some help," he said to Paco. "Paco, you know how to cook?"

Paco shook his head, looked at the floor.

"Can you use a knife without cutting off your fingertips?" Diamond asked.

Paco nodded without looking up.

"Okay," Diamond said. He pulled out a large knife that I

wouldn't even have in the same room with a ten-year-old. He set out a cutting board, hung a vegetable wash basket over the sink, and pushed the tomatoes and peppers toward Paco. "You can wash these vegetables and slice them up," he said.

"They're fruit, not vegetables," Paco said.

"Tomatoes and peppers?" Diamond said.

"Fruit," Paco said again.

"Mr. O over there said you grow them."

Paco nodded.

"Okay, you're the expert. Do these tomato fruits, dude. Por favor."

"Those aren't real tomatoes," Paco said.

Diamond picked up a tomato and turned it around. "Looks like a tomato."

Paco shook his head. "Store bought. Stores don't sell real tomatoes."

Diamond nodded. "Good to know." He set the tomato down. "Tell you what. I'm gonna switch us over to the recipe that calls for pretend tomatoes. So maybe you could slice them into wedges just like you would if they were real. Let's use just one pepper, and cut it into little pieces."

Paco went to work. I almost couldn't watch. Diamond had no more experience with kids than I did, and his request to Paco to wield the giant knife seemed as inappropriate as asking him to load his gun.

But Paco was surprisingly coordinated with the knife. And he was careful and deliberate, good qualities for preserving fingers.

Diamond got out a fry pan, put it on the stovetop to warm up.

When Paco was done chopping, Diamond said, "Lemme show you some cooking tricks. Take this olive oil, pour some in the pan."

Paco looked at him, skepticism on his face.

Diamond thrust the olive oil toward him.

Paco took it, looked at Diamond again to see if he was serious, then poured some in the pan.

"Perfect," Diamond said. "Now, we cut up some garlic and

some chicken." This time Diamond did the cutting. He moved fast. In a few moments, he'd minced three cloves of garlic and turned two chicken breasts into small pieces.

I was sitting at the kitchen table watching. Spot was sitting on the floor next to me, his head above the table. Also watching.

"We saute it like this." Diamond put the chicken and the garlic in the pan. It sizzled. "Take this spoon." He handed a wooden spoon to Paco. "Move it around. Good. Maybe we need more heat. Keep moving."

In a couple of minutes, Diamond said, "Okay, take this salsa and pour some into the pan."

Paco did it carefully.

Diamond handed him another bottle. "Put in a few drops of hot sauce."

Paco started shaking the bottle.

"Whoa! Dude!" Diamond said, grabbing the bottle.

Paco looked worried.

"Don't worry, kid," Diamond said. "You did the perfect amount."

In another two minutes, Diamond said, "You can turn down the heat under the pan to low."

Paco looked at the knobs, figured out which one to turn.

"Now put in the pepper."

While Paco brushed the pepper off the cutting board into the fry pan, Diamond opened a can of black beans and rinsed them.

He handed it to Paco. "Time to add these, then stir this stuff around."

Paco did so with care and precision. Only one bean flopped out of the pan.

"Let's set the oven for three-fifty."

Paco looked at him, a question on his face.

"Yeah, you. You're head chef."

Paco looked at the oven controls. Diamond pointed to the knob. Paco set it.

Diamond set a bowl on the counter and handed the bag of

shredded cheddar to Paco. "You can open the cheese and dump it into the bowl."

When Paco was done, Diamond said, "Now it's time to put the taco shells in the oven." He handed Paco the box. Paco got it open without breaking any shells, a trick I rarely manage. He opened the oven door.

"You can drape the shells over the wires on the rack," Diamond said, "but don't touch anything in the oven, or you'll burn your patooties off."

"Patooties?" I said.

"A funny word I've heard Norteamericanos say," Diamond said. "Thought I'd try that one, see how it sounds."

"I'm pretty sure that patootie refers to another part of the body."

Diamond pointed at Paco, who was carefully reaching the shells into the oven. Paco got all twelve shells over the wires and shut the oven door.

"Looks like Paco knew what I meant," Diamond said. "Owen, why am I even helping cook? Kid's a pro chef. Like he grew up in the back of a Mexican restaurant. You and I could just park, drink a brew, and let the chef do it all."

I watched Paco. Not even the smallest of grins.

Diamond said to Paco. "Let's set the table." Diamond pulled out some plates, napkins, and silverware and handed them to Paco. Paco carefully rolled the forks up into the napkins and put them out on the table.

"There's four plates and three sets of silverware," Paco said.

Diamond pointed at Spot. "His largeness don't use silverware," Diamond said.

Diamond continued to work with Paco, and a few minutes later they served up four plates of tacos piled high with chicken and salsa and pepper and black beans and shredded cheese and fresh tomato and lettuce.

Spot, from much experience, knew to hang back and be miserably envious while we ate. He sat there, his butt down, his head above the table. Without making any perceptible movements, he nevertheless slowly inched forward, moving like a glacier. Periodically, I held the back of my hand to his nose and eased his head back.

Spot kept licking his chops and swallowing. After some time studying us, he stopped looking at Diamond and me, having decided that Paco held the most opportunity for dropped food. He watched as Paco finished first, and Diamond and I tied for second.

"You must like pretend tomatoes," Diamond said to Paco when he was done.

Paco didn't respond.

After we were finished, we took the fourth plate outside and fed it to Spot, who ate it like he was on fast-forward. Paco watched Spot's instant vacuum technique, but didn't react.

Diamond opened two more beers and pushed one across the table toward me.

Paco looked at the beer, looked at Diamond, looked back at the beer.

"Why the concerned face?" Diamond said. "You expecting me to offer you one?"

Paco didn't respond, so I answered for him. "Paco's landlord smacks people around when he drinks. Paco's witnessed it. Makes for a poor association with brew."

Diamond turned to Paco. "Always remember that drink doesn't cause good, non-violent people to become violent. But drink makes it easier for not-so-good, insecure people with violent tendencies to lash out. You want, like, a post-prandial tea or something?"

Paco stared at the table.

"I shoulda got hot chocolate or ice cream," Diamond said.

"My fault," I said.

Paco didn't answer.

"Wait," Diamond said. "I've got some chocolate I take hiking. We could use it to make a chocolate soda."

Paco looked at him. Interested.

"Isn't that semi-sweet?" I said. Paco looked at me.

"Good point," Diamond said. "Better yet, I've got chocolate Joe Joe cookies from Trader Joe's."

With Paco's help, he put chocolate cookies and milk and ice cubes in the blender, and ran them into a froth. He poured it into a tall glass, then added club soda.

"Taste it, see if we need to make an adjustment."

Paco sipped it.

"Is it good?"

Paco made a little nod.

"I'm sorry, I didn't hear you," Diamond said.

"It's good," Paco said.

Diamond looked at me.

"You got a plan?" he said.

"I've been working on a concept. Paco and I need to keep moving to stay safe. But if we just keep hiding, if Salt and Pepper are persistent, they will eventually find us. So it may be that the best way to get these guys off Paco's back is to go after them."

Diamond nodded, drank Pacifico.

"Any idea how to find them?"

"Paco saw their pickup today. He looked through binoculars and made a positive ID on one of them. They're staying in a vacation rental in Incline Village. Also, it turns out that their pickup is dark blue with a dark blue topper."

Diamond looked at Paco. "I thought he said it was dark with a white topper."

Paco kept sipping his chocolate soda.

"Paco had a mistaken impression from when the shooting happened. It was dark. Same for when I saw the pickup in the woods. I couldn't really see it because it was so dark out. According to Ramos, these guys got a topper that's laminated with a fabric that looks light by night and dark by day. Today, Paco remembered that he also saw the pickup when he got out and ran down under Heavenly's gondola. He remembers that it was blue. That was daytime."

"And this second memory was triggered by the sighting today."

"Yeah."

Diamond looked doubtful.

"This ID is based on Paco's identification from looking in

the binoculars." Diamond glanced at Paco. Diamond's words had skepticism in them, but his look didn't.

"Enough of an ID in your mind to constitute probable cause?" Diamond said. "Can the Washoe County sheriff get a warrant?"

"No. But Paco's belief that he saw Pepper is enough for me to act on it in some way," I said.

"Be a big risk for you," Diamond said, "you get caught in a breaking and entering."

"If I go in, I'm likely to get killed. I'm thinking of something more like getting them to come out of the house. Maybe I could do something at their house. Something that doesn't need a warrant."

"Like..." Diamond said.

"Like maybe we can catch them. Maybe we can set a trap."

THIRTY-SEVEN

"How you gonna set a trap?" Diamond asked. "Or even get them out of their vacation rental?"

"Don't know," I said. "What if they get a nice roaring fire going in the fireplace and I accidentally plug up their chimney?"

"You just happen to be up on their roof, carrying a sandbag, and you trip, and it falls into the chimney," Diamond said.

"Yeah. I was trying to save a lost bird or something. And I had this accident."

"And the smoke drives them out. They'd study your brilliance at Harvard Law for years to come."

"No doubt," I said. "I wonder how many laws I'd break."

"Take awhile to count," Diamond said.

Paco was watching Diamond. He was still sipping the soda, trying to make it last. A first.

"So the smoke drives them out of the house," Diamond said. "Then what are you gonna do?"

"Help someone arrest them. That's Washoe County. I could tip them off, get them to do the honors."

"What would the arrest be for?"

"Maybe they will run out carrying contraband. But then the defense attorney would probably be able to get any case against them thrown out because my illegal activities caused them to run out."

"What if," Diamond said, "they were to commit a new crime after they ran out of the house?"

"So even if the D.A. can't prosecute their previous crimes because I corrupted the case with my actions, he could put them away on a new crime."

"Assuming they commit a new crime."

"I could entice them to commit a new crime."

"How?" Diamond asked.

"I don't know. Get in their face. Call them names. I'm pretty good at getting bad guys to take a swing at me."

"What if instead of swinging, they just pull out a gun and shoot you full of holes?"

"Good point. I'll think of something. In the meantime, I still have to get them out of the house."

"You sound serious," Diamond said. He looked at Paco as if he could see that I was already influencing him with my bad intentions.

"If I could get Paco and me into a controlled environment, maybe I could entice them to come after us."

"Where you could get the jump on them," Diamond said.

"Yeah. Trap them," I said.

"That's a better idea. Then we have a reason to arrest them. Even if we stop them before they commit assault, we still get them for busting into your place. The controlled environment."

"Got to find one."

Diamond raised his finger. "I just had a good thought. You know Doc Lee's friend Celeste Redack?"

"I don't think so."

"You must. She's as tight with him as a woman can get. They even go shopping together. Ob/Gyn, I think."

"Oh, you mean Doctor Redack," I said. I remembered a tall, skinny redhead that I'd met at a party held by Doc Lee.

Diamond nodded. "She bought a tear-down house on the West Shore, not too far from Chambers Landing."

"Nice area. I didn't think there were any tear-downs near there."

"Not many. But the foundation is sinking or leaning or something. She basically paid for the location, the view and the sewer/water hookup. It'll cost a peso to build a new spread, but it'll be worth the result."

"It's vacant?"

"Yeah. The county condemned it. Doc Lee was talking about it because the local fire department is interested in using it for a practice burn. Redack was asking Lee his opinion. It could be perfect for you."

"If I could hide up there with Paco, we could make arrangements to protect Paco's safety, yet make a few thoughtful mistakes that Salt and Pepper can use to track us. Once they find out where we're hiding, I bet they'll come in after us." I glanced at Paco. He'd finished his soda and was petting Spot and didn't appear to be listening.

"Yeah," Diamond said. "And if you're ready, you could trap them. Pull the fishnet trick on them."

"The idea is kind of out there. Maybe we should call Doctor Redack and see if it is even a possibility."

Diamond handed me the phone book for Tahoe while he turned on his laptop. I flipped through the pages.

"No Redack," I said.

"Give me a minute, here," Diamond said. I couldn't see his screen. Maybe he was doing a basic Google search. Maybe there was a new secret website that cops use to find doctors. We waited. Spot walked into the living room and lay down on the rug. Paco joined him, sat on the rug and leaned against Spot's body. Spot started snoring in less than 30 seconds. Diamond clicked keys, waited, clicked some more. Paco yawned.

Diamond picked up a pen and wrote on the back of an envelope. He shut his computer and handed me the envelope.

"Doctor Redack's home number."

"I can't believe you found it online. Doctors always keep their private numbers private."

"I texted Doc Lee. He texted me back her number."

"Ah." I dialed.

"Hello?" a woman's voice answered. A slow, I'm-trying-to-sleep voice.

"Hi, this is Owen McKenna calling for Celeste Redack, please."

"Speaking," she said, even though I could tell she was still sleeping. "You're the detective I read about. Out on the hijacked boat. Doc Lee's friend."

"Yeah." I tried to be brief as I explained what my situation was and how her tear-down might serve the cause of justice.

"Sure," she said.

"Sure, we can use your house?"

"Sure."

"Great. How would I get the key?"

"I'll... Lemme think. Can you come by the hospital? I'll leave the key with Doc Lee in Emergency. The address is on the little paper fob."

I thanked her profusely, hung up, and looked at Diamond and Paco.

"Now the question is how to trap them once they break into the house," I said.

"Always looks easy in the movies," Diamond said.

"Pepper spray," Paco suddenly said from the living room.

We turned and looked at him. "Now there's a hypothetical," I said. I got up, walked in, and sat down on one of Diamond's big chairs. Diamond followed.

Paco was looking at the living room wall. His brow was furrowed with the normal frown and something else. The look of a kid solving a puzzle. The sunglasses on his head reflected the living room lamp and looked like giant bug eyes.

"Pepper spray comes in small containers," I said. "Good for shooting into a person's eyes if they attack you. But a house is a big space. We probably wouldn't know in advance if they were coming in through a door or a window. Or maybe through the attic. Now if we had tear gas canisters, then we could fill the building and possibly trap them."

Diamond was shaking his head. "Tear gas is hard to get. You have to be a qualified official from a law enforcement agency."

"I thought tear gas was like pepper spray," Paco said.

"Kind of," I said. "They both make your eyes burn. You can't see or breathe. The big difference is volume. You need a lot of gas to fill a building."

"We could make a lot of pepper spray," Paco said.

"Make it? How?"

"Our Cassie's Viper peppers are over a million Scoville units. If you touch them, you can't touch your eyes, or you're in big trouble."

"You have enough of them to make a lot of spray?"

"One whole end of the hothouse is Vipers."

"You got an idea of how to turn peppers into pepper spray?" Diamond asked.

Paco shrugged. "I don't know." He looked back toward the kitchen and the counter where they'd made the chocolate soda. "Pro'bly put them in the blender or something."

Diamond raised his eyebrows. He looked at me. "Kid's maybe got something."

"Yeah. Maybe you'll be a chemist when you grow up," I said to Paco.

"What's a chemist?" Paco asked.

I had to think about how to answer that. I looked at Diamond.

"A chemist is a person who understands the chemical properties of materials," he said. "Things called atoms and molecules. A chemist knows how to put them together and take them apart. A chemist can make completely new chemicals using that knowledge."

"Like making a chocolate soda out of cookies and ice cubes," Paco said.

"Yeah," Diamond said, "but what's cool about chemists is that the atoms and molecules they use are super small. So small, in fact, that you could put many thousands of them on the point of a needle."

Paco made the smallest of head shakes. "You couldn't even see them," he said.

"No, not with your eyes."

Paco's disbelief was obvious.

"Okay," I interrupted, "we use a blender to grind up lots of Cassie's Viper peppers," I said. "And we figure out how to make spray. Our plan is to get Salt and Pepper to break into this house to get you, Paco. Not a simple setup, but doable. Once they break in, how do we use pepper spray to trap them in the house?"

"I don't know. I'm just the chemist," Paco said. "But if it gets in their eyes, they couldn't see to get out." He narrowed his eyes, thinking. Then, in a sudden outburst, he almost shouted, "We could use fire ants, too."

"Are you thinking of ants instead of pepper spray? Or are you thinking we could use both fire ants and pepper spray?"

"If we did use both," Paco said, "the superheroes would have to do whatever we wanted."

"Which would be worse to get hit with?" Diamond asked. "Pepper spray or fire ants?"

Paco thought about it "They'd both be bad," he said.

"Does pepper spray hurt fire ants?" I asked.

Paco shook his head. "Nothing hurts fire ants. They're superhero bugs."

"We can get fire ants at your farm, right?" I said.

"There's a bunch of nests in the field behind the hothouse. Cassie tried to kill them."

"Didn't work?"

Paco shook his head. "You can't kill fire ants. All you can do is run away when they come after you."

"How would you collect the ants?" I asked.

"I don't know. Shovel and bucket. But you'd have to cover your skin. They can chew through anything and then sting you to death."

"Really," I said. "Let's see if we can get some details from the bug expert." I picked up the phone and called Street.

"Doctor," I said when she answered.

"You only say that when you want to use my expertise," she said.

"I'm not calling about sex," I said. I glanced at Paco when I realized what I'd said. He showed no reaction.

"Funny guy," Street said.

"I'm calling about your second major expertise. Insects. Specifically fire ants." I hesitated. "Or are they one of those bugs that aren't technically insects?"

Street laughed. "Oh, yes," she said with emphasis. "When entomologists say that insects will inherit the earth, we are often specifically thinking about creatures like the social insects. And of those, fire ants are by some measures at the apex."

"Of course," I said. "Apex insects."

"Toughest bugs there are," Street said.

"You mean that collectively? Or individually?" I said.

"Both. If you were proportionally as strong as a fire ant, you could crawl up a vertical wall at fifty miles an hour. You could pick up your cabin and toss it into the lake. You could jump from any height without getting hurt. Plus, fire ants can eat almost any organic material, animal or vegetable. Practically everything is food to them. And they communicate with pheromones. Which, with the social organization, is what makes them such pests. Dangerous, even."

"Because they sting? Paco said that fire ants could kill you."

"Well, a single fire ant sting is only one-point-two on the Schmidt Sting Pain Index. When one or two or three fire ants sting you, it hurts, but you'll survive. But if you trip and fall into a nest, that disturbance will cause the ants to send up a phero-mone-style fire alarm klaxon. If you're very quick, you can get up and out with only a few dozen or a few hundred stings. But if you've bumped your head and are dazed and hesitate, you could be in serious trouble."

"Some people are allergic to their stings, right?" I said. I saw Paco looking at me.

"Yes," Street said. "But fire ants are dangerous even if you're not allergic. When an entire nest mobilizes to attack you, they swarm over you. It's often worse than having a nest of hornets come after you because there are such great numbers. You could end up with ten thousand stings. Fifty thousand stings. That's enough to kill a cow."

I paused. "So obtaining fire ants to use in subduing people might not be very practical."

"What!" Street sounded appalled.

"Paco had a fantastic idea. Remember the two heavies who took Paco? Salt and Pepper? We're thinking about making a trap for them. Doc Lee has a colleague who bought a tear-down that we can use. We get Salt and Pepper to think that Paco is hiding out in the house. Our hope would be that they would break in, attempting to get Paco, and we would take them down with pepper spray and fire ants."

"Owen, that could be really dangerous," she said. "Both because of the men and because of the ants and spray."

"But it could work, right?"

"I suppose. You'd have to be very careful."

"Paco was already telling me the same. So I wondered what I should know about fire ants before I try this."

"I've never thought of ants as weapons. But fire ants would certainly be a good species to use. We refer to them as RIFA, Red Imported Fire Ants. They were accidentally introduced into this country during the nineteen thirties in Mobile, Alabama by ships coming from Brazil. Since then, they've spread across the southwest and up into California. They get a lot of attention from people because of their poisonous stings and their aggressiveness."

"Can they actually kill people?"

"They have. They kill lots of smaller animals. And they make life really difficult for ranchers and farmers."

"Because they kill farm animals?" It sounded unbelievable.

"Healthy livestock run away," Street said. "But when a cow gives birth, if the calf lands close to a nest, the ants can kill it. We've developed a few techniques for destroying individual nests, but we've had no luck with large-scale eradication."

"How would you recommend that I dig up and transport a nest of fire ants?" I asked.

"I've never thought about such a ridiculous thing. The main thing to remember is that fire ants don't run away from you like other ants. They run toward you in mass attack mode. They will swarm up your shovel the moment you stick it in the ground, so you're going to need something like a hazmat suit. Booties over your shoes, sealed at your pant cuffs, heavy jeans, gloves sealed at your sleeves, hood, goggles, all taped and sealed."

"You don't think I could just shovel fast?"

She paused. "There are probably many people who have under-estimated the risks of fire ants. You could end up thinking that the fire ants are worse than those men who are after Paco."

"Got it. Any idea how big a fire ant colony is? Would it fit into a five-gallon bucket?"

"There's a lot of variability. Large nests can go six feet deep in the ground and contain millions of individual ants. But if you could get a concentrated portion in a bucket, you'd probably have tens of thousands of ants. They're quite small compared to carpenter ants. The problem is getting them into the bucket. As soon as you shovel them in, they're going to swarm back out, trying to get to you."

"I'll shovel twice as fast."

"I don't think you understand how fast fire ants move."

"I saw some at Paco's house. They were running, but it didn't seem like a big deal."

"Have you seen a nest?"

"Paco's going to show me where to find some."

"When you see it, you'll know what I mean. Fire ants are frenetic. Frantic. Like they're in constant panic mode. They run so fast it's as if they're dancing on a vibrating platform. The moment you touch them, you'll get an explosion of movement. Transferring any significant number of ants into a bucket will be a real trick."

"I was thinking that I could just scoop with a bucket and then pop the lid on."

"Then you'll crush them," Street said.

"I thought they were super tough."

"They are, but if you dump enough dirt on top of ants, you'll immobilize them just like burying a human. They move around underground through their tunnels. Without tunnels, they'd be trapped and eventually die. At least the ones that don't figure out how to get into your underwear."

"Lovely picture."

"And when you get ants in a bucket, you can't just put the lid on, either. They'd suffocate."

"Ants need air?" I said.

"Of course," she said.

"I could wrap screen over the top instead of a lid."

"Not just the top. They need air down in their dirt. If you had some kind of a miniature lattice network to dump them into, then they'd have air and they wouldn't get buried with too much weight on them."

"Right."

There was a pause on the phone. "As a scientist, I should also let you know about the risks of introducing new species into an environment that hasn't previously seen them."

I'd heard about that problem. "Like the bird-eating snakes in Guam?"

"Yeah. But as I think about it, I don't think you'd be creating an ecological catastrophe. Fire ants are very temperature sensitive. As soon as they experience a single cold fall night in Tahoe, they will mostly die. The rest will succumb soon after."

"Hey, hon?"

"What?" Street said.

"You're a dream."

"Because of my expertise?"

"Yeah," I said. "All kinds."

"Thanks."

We said goodbye, and I told Diamond and Paco what she'd said. I didn't expect Paco to respond, but I thought it was probably good that he have the experience of an adult running ideas past him.

"Once you get ants," Diamond said, "you'll have to be ready to move fast. Even if they're superhero bugs, they won't survive long in a bucket."

"Which brings up the same point about pepper spray," I said. "Let's say we grind up a bunch of peppers. It could be that the potency of the chemical wouldn't last long. Whatever method we devise for spraying it would have to be ready to go."

Diamond finished his last swallow of beer and stood up. "A problem that will be easier to solve after we get some sleep."

"Still okay if we use your truck to move around? Salt and Pepper know my Jeep. Your truck would be a good disguise."

"Of course," Diamond said. "Just remember that it barely runs. You might want to put alternative transportation in the back. Bicycles. Or Roller Blades."

"We'll take our chances."

"It's got so many rusted holes it's like built-in air conditioning."

"One of its many attractions," I said.

"Be my guest. The key is under the mat."

"It won't fall out one of the holes in the floor?" I said.

"Not while it's just sitting still in my drive. Unless you bump the truck hard when you get inside."

Diamond fetched two sleeping bags from his camping closet, and he showed us which towels to use in the bathroom. Paco, Spot, and I climbed the steep stairs to the attic bunk room where, a year ago the previous summer, Spot and I had grappled with the killers who came onto Diamond's roof.

Diamond's second floor is one of those classic, fun spaces with an angled ceiling following the roof's contours, the kind of place where kids naturally like to play. But Paco didn't even seem to notice.

There were two bunks, narrow beds tucked under the sloping roof on either side of the room.

"Which bunk do you want?" I asked Paco.

He looked around. "Where is Spot sleeping?"

I pointed to the narrow four-foot area between the beds. "Here, probably."

Paco studied it. Realized that the center aisle was equally close to the beds.

"I'll sleep on the floor with Spot," he said. "Then he can use the edge of my sleeping bag. It would make him happy."

"Kind of hard, that thin carpet. But as you wish."

I helped spread Paco's sleeping bag on the floor. Spot saw his opportunity to lie on human bedding, and he immediately sprawled across the entire expanse. I had to push him toward the side to make a small area for Paco to lie next to him.

Paco got down, snuggled close to Spot.

We lay in the dark for a time. By Paco's breathing, I could tell that he wasn't sleeping.

"Whatcha thinking?" I said.

"Nothing," Paco said.

"You still think trying to catch these superhero guys is a good idea?"

He was quiet for a bit. "Yeah," he finally said. "If we don't catch them, they'll catch me. Then I'll have no future."

"What do you want for your future?" I asked.

More silence. "Maybe just to work and make money and buy some good things."•

"What would you like to buy?"

"I don't know. A place where I could stay."

"Is that what you wish for? A place of your own?"

"It doesn't have to be mine. I just want a place where I don't have to leave if I don't want to."

THIRTY-EIGHT

The next day Diamond was already gone when we got up.

While we ate breakfast, I turned on Diamond's computer and Googled the other aphorism that Paco told me about, the line that Cassie sometimes said.

'The only thing that overcomes hard luck is hard work.'

It turned out that it was a quote from Harry Golden, a guy who was convicted of mail fraud when he was young. After he was released from prison, he became a writer and through dogged determination became very successful.

I wondered if Cassie's prison was housecleaning and if her success at tomatoes was like Harry's writing. Probably lots of people could grow good tomatoes and experiment with making them better. But Cassie was driven far beyond ordinary gardeners.

After breakfast, Paco and Spot and I took Diamond's old pickup and headed out to acquire supplies. We picked up three empty 5-gallon paint buckets and lids at the paint store. The closest thing to a hazmat suit was a painter's jumpsuit. The store had an extra large, which wasn't long enough. But I planned to augment it with heavy plastic garbage bags and packing tape. At the hardware store, we got a roll of window screen, aluminum dryer vent pipe, duct tape, flexible dryer vent tubing, a short roll of aluminum flashing, some utility lights, extension cords, and power strips.

The store also had safety goggles, but they had vent openings and wouldn't protect our eyes from pepper spray. So we went to a sporting goods store where we got two pair of swim goggles.

"My harvest tools are in the van," Paco said. "We'll need stuff to pick the peppers."

"Got it." I drove to the farm store and followed Paco as he walked down the aisles picking out knives and snips and gloves.

Back in Diamond's tiny garage, which he'd set up as a workshop, I handed Paco a shears and showed him how to cut and bend the screen. While he worked the shears, I put a fine-tooth blade in Diamond's saber saw and cut multiple window openings in the sides of two of the paint buckets. I also cut a larger circle in the lids.

I took a short section of aluminum vent pipe and made cuts in one end to create tabs. After bending them out 90 degrees, I inserted the pipe through the underside of the paint bucket lid so that the tabs rested up against the plastic. With duct tape on the metal tabs, I secured the pipe in place. I now had a bucket lid with a vent pipe coming out of it like a smokestack coming out of a flat-roofed building. Next, I rolled a sheet of flashing to make a large funnel, the small end of which I duct-taped into the smokestack.

I also duct-taped pieces of window screen onto the inside of my window openings.

"How you doing on the screen?" I said to Paco.

He shrugged and handed me a lumpy, round chunk of shiny screen. It was a mangled, knobby contraption about 10 inches long by 14 inches in diameter. It looked vaguely like an asteroid model for a low-budget sci-fi movie.

"Perfect. You got two of them?"

Paco handed me another.

I positioned them both inside the buckets.

"What's it for?" Paco asked.

I pointed to the mini-asteroids. "These will provide air spaces in the dirt so the fire ants can breathe. And these windows let in fresh air. The bucket lids snap on top. I shovel ants and dirt into the funnels. They fall into the bucket. They'll try to climb out, of course, but it won't be easy to go up the bucket sides, across the lid, down the protruding funnel, around the edge and out."

"They will," Paco said. "Fire ants can go anywhere. Fast."

"Because they're superhero bugs," I said.

Paco nodded, solemn as always.

"How are we gonna get the ants out of the bucket and into the house?" he asked.

"Same way we get the pepper spray out of the third bucket. Venturi effect," I said.

"What's that?"

"If you blow across the top of a straw, it reduces the air pressure over the straw, which means the air pressure in and below the straw will push up whatever material is in the straw. Probably, the person who figured it out was named Venturi."

"It doesn't make sense," Paco made a slow head shake.

"You ever used a pesticide sprayer?" I said. "You put the stuff in the sprayer jar and screw on a lid that's attached to a hose?"

"Oh, yeah," Paco said. "And it's got a tube that sticks down into the liquid."

"Right. That's the straw. Turn on the hose, and the Venturi effect draws the pesticide up and mixes it with the water spray."

"I don't think we should mix pepper spray with water," Paco said. "It would make it... not so burny."

"Right. We don't want to dilute it. So we won't use water to spray it. We'll use air." I picked up the lid with the vent pipe coming out of it. "But I have to figure out some way to get a high pressure air hose to blow air across the top of this smokestack. Except that a typical air compressor doesn't put out very much volume. We'd never be able to inject enough pepper spray and ants into a house to drive people out of it."

I looked at the bucket lids. "Paco, my plan may have a major flaw. I need more air. I need something that..." I paused.

"Leaf blower," Paco interrupted.

"My God, Paco! That's brilliant!"

No smile. Not even a hint of a grin.

"I can use this other piece of dryer vent," I said. "I'll cut a hole in the middle and attach that to the smokestack pipe. We'll put a flexible dryer hose on one end of the vent pipe, and on the other end we'll put the leaf blower. The blower will blow high-powered air across the top of the smokestack."

I spent an hour cutting and bending flashing and vent piping. When I was done, I had a T-shaped pipe that protruded from the lid. I set the lid on the bucket and showed it to Paco.

"The leaf blower goes on this end. The flexible hose goes from the other end. The ants come out the flex hose. Will it work?"

Paco looked into the T-shaped pipe and hose.

"I think the leaf blower is going to blow the ants into the bucket instead of sucking them out," he said.

I looked where he looked. "I think you're right. I need to create a baffle to direct the blower air over the top of the smokestack and out the flex hose. Then the Venturi effect will work."

It took another hour of cutting and bending and taping. Paco watched me the entire time. Periodically, I found ways that he could help. Hold a strip of flashing while I cut it. Crimp a bend with the pliers. Tear some duct tape. Paco was able to put his entire hand inside of the vent pipe, securing the baffle with tape. When we were done, we had two lids with T-shaped vent pipes ready to put onto buckets with ants.

We still had to have a way to blow homemade pepper spray.

I took the third bucket lid, cut a much smaller opening, and fit a section of hose through it. The hose went down to the bottom of the bucket.

"Like a superhero bug sprayer," Paco said.

"Yeah. I'll drill a couple of vent holes in the top to let air in to replace the pepper spray as it gets sucked out." We cut a small opening in another piece of vent pipe and inserted the hose into it. With Paco's small hands, we once again created a baffle inside the vent pipe, hoping that it would aid in sucking the pepper spray out, rather than forcing air down into the pepper spray.

When we were done, I did a kind of a talk-through dress rehearsal. As I spoke, the plan sounded crazier than ever. But I wanted to stay with it because it just might work and because the pepper spray and ants were Paco's ideas. It would be good for him to witness the power of his thoughts.

"What do you think?" I asked him when I was done recapping our plan. "You think it will work?"

Paco shrugged. Affirmative style.

THIRTY-NINE

We left before dawn the next morning. I worried that a departure in the morning darkness would bring bad associations to Paco, but, like always, he showed no emotion.

Diamond's pickup was ridiculously tight with Spot, Paco, and me all in one seat. I didn't think that Salt and Pepper would have set up a continuous stakeout at Harrah's rear parking lot, so I pulled Diamond's pickup into the space next to my Jeep, and we transferred to the Jeep so that Spot could have his own seat.

We arrived at Cassie and Paco's house at 7:30 a.m. I was relieved to see that the landlord's pickup was gone. We turned through the fence opening and drove down the long dirt road that followed the outside of the fence. Paco's house stood dark and seemingly untouched since our last visit days before.

"You want anything in the house?"

Paco shook his head. It was hard to see a kid who appeared to have no more connection to his own home than a homeless man has for his last curb-side sleeping spot. Either Cassie failed to provide a psychological sense of home, or Paco was a world-record hard case. But when I looked at Paco's face, rigid and tense, I realized that neither interpretation was correct. He didn't want to go in because it was too painful. Everything that he'd ever become attached to had been taken away. This house was just one more set of disappointments.

We parked and got out. Spot ran around, excited to be back in farm smells.

"Let's get the peppers first," I said. I grabbed two of the big plastic garbage bags.

Paco picked up the bag with the new harvest tools. He led the way around the house to the hothouse. He opened the flimsy door and walked inside. Spot and I followed.

Spot trotted up and down the aisles, sniffing the planters.

Paco walked over to the inner door that separated the tomatoes from the peppers. He opened the door and pointed.

"All the Cassie's Vipers are in here. Spot can't come in. Too dangerous."

I looked in through the door. Within this side of the hothouse were many peppers. But unlike the large, rounded bell peppers that I bought at the store, these were narrow, bent, squashed, and mostly colored orange or red.

We stepped inside and shut the door behind us. Spot sniffed from the other side of the screen.

I got out the garbage bags. "Any trick to picking them?" I asked.

Paco pulled gloves out of the bag and handed me the larger pair. Then he handed me a snips. He put on his gloves.

"Like this," he said. He held onto the plant and cut the pepper off so that it retained a short stem. "That's the best way for the plant," he said.

I pulled on gloves, and we started picking.

"Don't rub your eyes," Paco said.

"Got it," I said.

"And don't, you know..."

"Don't what?" I said.

Paco looked down, embarrassed.

"What, Paco?"

"If you have to pee, you can't touch yourself with your gloves. Otherwise, you'll be doing the hot chili dance." He looked up at me. "It really burns," he said, almost pleading.

"Lesson received," I said.

Ten minutes later, we'd filled two garbage bags. They were heavy enough that I worried that they would rip apart. I cradled the bottoms as I carried them back to the Jeep. We put our pepper gloves in the Jeep.

"Ready for ants?" I said.

Paco nodded.

I grabbed my other gloves, my jumpsuit, goggles and other

gear, picked up the two customized paint buckets and said, "We'll follow you."

I held onto Spot's collar. I didn't want him running into a fire ant nest.

This time Paco went behind the hothouse and walked toward the far corner. Then he turned and walked diagonally away from the building. He moved slower with each step, eventually stopping and staring out toward the field.

Paco took very slow tip-toe steps as if he were sneaking up on a sleeping tiger.

After three steps, he turned and came back to me.

"Right out there," he said pointing.

I wasn't sure, but I thought his voice had a touch of tremolo in it.

"Okay, you hold Spot's collar while I suit up. Don't let go of him."

Paco took Spot's collar, nodding.

"Spot, you stay with Paco. You understand?" I said. I knew that the words were pointless, but I hoped that my tone would give Spot a sense that he should not run.

I pulled on my jumpsuit, stepped each foot into a plastic bag and taped it up around my pant legs. I tore a small opening in another bag and pulled the bag over my head, positioning the opening around my eyes. I taped that bag around my shoulders and chest and had Paco add tape where the plastic came down my back. I tore a smaller opening at my mouth, stretched a dust mask over my head, and taped the edges of the mask to the plastic bag on my head.

My swim goggles covered my eyes. I taped them in place.

Last, I put bags over my gloves and had Paco tape the edges around my sleeves.

"Do I look like the creature from the black lagoon?" I said through the dust mask.

Paco stared at me just as he would if he saw me playing the monster in the movie he'd never heard of. But he didn't react.

"Remember not to let go of this hound's collar?"

He nodded.

"I don't know how long this is going to take me, so be patient. And even if I slip and fall, don't decide to come and help me, okay?"

He nodded again.

I picked up the buckets and lids and shovel, and turned and walked toward where Paco had pointed.

The first nest didn't look like much as I approached. Just a mound of dirt with a reddish coating. But when I got closer, the mound seemed much bigger, maybe 12 inches high, and the reddish coating turned out to be swarming ants.

Street was right. These ants were crazed with frantic movement. These were ants on steroids. They all seemed to be in a mad rush, racing around and over each other and in and out of many tunnels leading into the dirt mound.

I set the buckets down nearby, checked that the funnel was still properly positioned in the first one, and got my shovel ready. Nothing I could possibly do with the shovel could accelerate their already-panicked movement.

I was wrong.

I plunged the shovel into the soft ground, levered it, and tried to raise up a pile of ants and dirt. I wanted to lift it up and dump it into the bucket funnel in one smooth movement. But I jerked, and the shovel came free in a jerk. The pile of ants and dirt flipped up into the air and showered down on me.

My goggles allowed for only limited vision. I had to point my head at something to see it. I bent my neck and looked down at my jumpsuit. What I saw was no big deal, probably fewer than a hundred ants racing over the fabric. But their intensity was disturbing.

I looked back down at the nest. The pheromones were obviously working. The ants had exploded in movement. If any of them had gone into safety mode and retreated underground, I would never know. All I saw were thousands of ants moving at a sprint. They came up my shovel, swarmed over my plastic baggie-booties and up my pant legs. I remembered what Paco had said. Fire ants can chew through anything. My skin was already twitching in anticipation of the coming assault.

I ignored that thought and began shoveling.

I got a scoop of ants and dirt into the funnel. Then another.

I'd barely gotten any down the funnel, and already ants were rushing back out.

I kept shoveling. Ants were rushing out of the nest. It was like watching the world's biggest army sprinting toward a naive and ill-equipped invader. There were so many that the hundreds, or thousands, of ants already crawling up me seemed like a minor event. But when I again looked down at my legs, it was frightening to see the hoards preparing to breach my jumpsuit fabric, ready to plunge on through the openings they were no doubt chewing, and devour me.

I tried to brush some of them off, then stuck the shovel back into the earth, and dumped another scoopful into the funnel. It looked like it was all dirt and no ants. Yet ants kept crawling back out of the funnel. I stopped thinking about the proportion of dirt to ants. Either I'd get a bunch of ants or not.

I felt the first sting on my back. There wasn't even any opening in the back of the jumpsuit. So either they'd chewed through, or they could sting through the fabric. I hadn't thought about that.

Another sting on my back. Then a sting on my right thigh.

I shoveled faster. Ants and dirt flew.

Somebody shoved a burning needle into the top of my leg at the underwear line. The ants were going to get me where it would really hurt.

I took a moment and rubbed the fabric over the sting, back and forth hard. The ant or ants were inside my pants, but maybe I could squish them from the outside.

I kept shoveling dirt into the funnel.

The next time I dug the shovel into the ground, I hit the mother lode. My shovel plunged into a soft spot, and when I brought it up, it was as if I had scooped into solid ants and no dirt.

I was ecstatic even as I was repulsed. The shovel was alive, a softball-sized scoop of solid, swarming, angry ants. I plopped them down the funnel and went back for more.

Another sting burned into my neck near my adam's apple. I ignored it. And dug another, even larger, scoop of raging ants.

Two more stings as I dumped the ants into the funnel. Hot needles in my stomach and butt. The ants had put out the word that they didn't need to get inside my suit. Just fire their poison darts through the fabric. Another sting higher up on my groin. I started doing a dance of sorts. Jumping up and down, trying to shake off the ants.

Kept shoveling. Dumped them into the funnel. Jumped up and landed hard to jerk the ants off me. Shoveled again. Jumped and landed.

The bucket was nearly full. Mostly dirt. But a lot of ants.

I dropped the shovel. Picked up the bucket and banged it on the ground to shake the ants off the funnel and down into their new, temporary home.

I peeled off the duct tape that held the funnel in place, and pulled it out of the smokestack vent pipe that protruded from the bucket lid. Ants swarmed up my arms. I wrapped pieces of screen over the vent pipe opening and taped it in place. Then I put the funnel into the second bucket and continued shoveling.

The ants were endless. The stings more frequent.

A hot needle stabbed me in the side of the neck, just below my ear. I swatted at the pain. Ants flew off my plastic-bag mitt and landed on my goggles. I saw them crawl across my field of vision. But I didn't care. I had my treasure, and I was still alive.

I continued shoveling until the second bucket was full, and I repeated my process of removing the funnel and taping screen over the pipe opening.

I held up the buckets to see if the little window screens were succeeding at keeping the ants inside. Ants swarmed over the outside of the buckets, but it seemed that none of them was emerging through the screens.

I took the shovel and buckets and ran away from the nest. Stopped and banged the bucket and shovel on the ground to try to leave excess ants behind.

Another hot needle into the back of the knee. It was the worst sting, yet. Like a soldering iron going through the skin into the joint itself. I grabbed at the area and rubbed it. The pain intensified. Maybe I'd gotten a bunch of stings at once. I bent the leg, straightened the leg, shook the leg. It felt like I had a wound into which someone had poured boiling sulfuric acid. I'd have to have the leg amputated at the nearest clinic. No time to even go to the city hospital.

I did some vigorous jumping jacks, then sprinted down the plant rows, away from Paco and Spot.

It was a mistake. Spot got excited and pulled free from Paco.

When I saw him come running, I set the buckets down, then dove onto the ground and rolled over to try to rub off ants.

Just as fast, I was back on my feet and running farther away when Spot caught up to me.

He jumped onto me in play as I knew he would. I only hoped that the ants were mostly gone so that he wouldn't be attacked.

I began jerking off my wraps. Plastic bags and duct tape, goggles and jumpsuit.

Eventually, I was down to my ordinary clothes, my other gear scattered among the plants.

Spot had that demonic look I'd come to know well. He stood with his body lowered a bit, front legs splayed out, watching me, wagging. He was waiting for my first hint of movement so that he could anticipate which way I was about to run. Then he'd launch himself onto me, knock me down so that we could roll in the dirt and get seriously muddy.

Spot suddenly lowered his head and began chewing at his right front paw. Then he bit at the outside of his elbow.

"Sorry, dude. Collateral damage from hanging around me." I reached down and rubbed his foot, then saw two crazed ants running up his leg. I wiped all his legs down.

"Let's move, largeness. We'll do the wrestling match later. We have an ant assault to plan and execute."

I pulled an unused garbage bag from my pocket and bagged up the jumpsuit and my torn bags and tape.

Now largely ant free, I called out to Paco as we walked back toward the hothouse.

"Mission accomplished," I said. "We've got a lot of ants."

Paco stared at the buckets as I approached, his trepidation obvious. Behind the little screen windows, ants swarmed. When I got close, he stepped away. He couldn't have had a more dramatic reaction if I were carrying a bucket of rattle snakes.

At the Jeep, I took two of the extra large lawn-and-leaf bags and set the buckets inside of them. I figured that if I enclosed enough air with the buckets, the ants wouldn't suffocate during the ride back to Tahoe. If any ants got out through the screen-covered bucket windows, the bags would help contain them. I was scratching at my stings as I put the bagged buckets into the Jeep.

By the time we were all loaded into the Jeep, we hadn't seen a loose fire ant in thirty seconds or so.

"You get stung?" Paco asked as we drove out the long dirt road.

"Me. Not at all. Did you?"

"No." Paco said. Gradually he relaxed as we headed back up into the Sierra.

FORTY

Back in Tahoe, we drove over to the Harrah's parking lot and transferred our precious weaponry into the back of Diamond's old pickup. As Spot and Paco once again squeezed into the front, I hoped that Salt and Pepper hadn't seen us drive the Jeep into the basin and followed us to Harrah's.

I drove over Kingsbury Grade and down to Carson Valley, watching the rear view mirror the entire time. I saw no blue pickups. But that was no guarantee that we were safe.

Before we drove to Diamond's house, we went back to the hardware store and got a few sundries we'd forgotten including two electric leaf blowers that claimed to produce 240 mile-per-hour air streams.

Back at Diamond's I called Street.

"We've got ants and peppers," I said.

"And you're still alive," she said. "Always a good sign."

"Now we want to brew up some pepper spray, and I wondered if you could give me some tips."

"I study bugs, remember? What would I know about pepper spray?"

"I don't know. But you're a scientist and a smart person. I wouldn't know how to begin. You might. Got any helpful ideas?"

"Well, all I know about peppers is that the hot ones, the chili peppers, all have a chemical called 'capsaysen.' It's spelled C-A-P-S-A-I-C-I-N."

"Paco made sure we were well protected when we worked around them," I said. "Even so, just having them close makes your eyes and nose sting. Quite amazing to think that a plant can be so potent."

"Capsaicin is a serious irritant for lots of animals, so the presumption is that the chili peppers evolved this chemical adaptation so they were less likely to be eaten by animals."

"You mean bugs," I said.

"Yeah. Bugs and larger animals. Although, I seem to remember reading that birds aren't affected by chili peppers. Most animals having grinding teeth and they chew seeds up, destroying them. So it makes sense that capsaicin would be off-putting to animals. But birds can't chew, so many seeds go through them without being ruined. And, appropriately, capsaicin was an evolutionary adaptation that didn't bother birds."

"Ah," I said. "The bottom line is that whatever traits help a pepper to produce and disseminate seeds are traits that carry on to future generations."

"See?" Street said. "You could be a scientist."

"I couldn't stand the tedium of focused study. Unless I could make a science of studying your attractiveness."

"You're talking about sex again," Street said.

"Why would you jump to that conclusion?" I said. "I'm talking about the science of your romantic aura. The beauty of your line and form. The poetry of your cadences."

"Like I said, sex."

"If you insist," I said.

"Anyway," Street said. "Commercial pepper spray manufacturers have perfected the techniques of how to collect and concentrate capsaicin. Maybe they've even synthesized it. Homemade spray would no doubt be much less potent. But you could probably make something effective. The trick will be keeping the capsaicin in solution."

"How would you do it?" I asked.

"I would probably just grind up the peppers, strain out the juice, and mix the juice with an emulsifier."

"What's that?"

"Something that holds it in solution. Think of how oil and water don't mix. An emulsifier like detergent will suspend grease and oil in water and allow it to wash away."

"You think I should mix ground-up peppers with

detergent?"

"Possibly. But detergent is such a good emulsifier that it might lessen the effectiveness of capsaicin when it hits someone's eyes or nose. You don't want a person's tears to wash it away. Let me grab one of my books."

I heard the phone being set down. The thud of heavy book. Rustling of pages.

"Here we are. Let me scan down this. A hygroscopic, miscible... I'll save you the details. It looks like propylene glycol would be the ticket. Problem is getting it.

"Is it a hazardous material?"

"No. It's found in cosmetics and food and moisturizers. But you won't find it on the shelf at the store. You'd have to order it from a chemical company. How soon do you want to do this?"

"Yesterday," I said.

"Then let's skip that idea. You could probably use denatured alcohol. Rubbing alcohol."

"Then I'd have a fire hazard. I don't want that."

"Good point," Street said. "Let's go back to detergent."

"Which would lessen the effectiveness?"

"Yeah. But if you used a small amount, just a few drops, it might work well."

"How would you decide how much to use?" I asked.

"I'd probably add a drop or two of detergent to some water, mix that up and then pour it into the pepper juice. Once you mix that up, you would be able to see if your juice settles out into layers or not. If it stays mixed, then you have enough detergent. You can tell how hot the liquid is by touching a tiny drop to your tongue."

"Hot sauce with a hint of detergent."

"Maybe you should just buy hot sauce."

"Sure. But like pepper spray, they are in little containers. I want a lot."

"Just be careful," Street said. "You're doing this with a little boy."

"You think I'm corrupting his innocent mind?" I looked at Paco. His face was passive.

"Yeah," she said.

"I'm also showing him how old-fashioned American ingenuity works."

"You are indeed."

I thanked Street, and we hung up.

Spot poked around Diamond's fenced back yard while Paco and I went to work. I opened the single window in Diamond's garage and fit Diamond's window fan into it to vent the fumes. Paco found a couple of pieces of wood and used them to prop the garage's passage door open about ten inches. It was enough to allow for ventilation but not so much that neighbors could look over the fence and see what we were doing inside the garage.

There was a light breeze, sufficient, I hoped, for any chili pepper aroma to disperse.

I fetched Diamond's blender from his kitchen and brought it, water, and detergent into the garage. We put on gloves and goggles and loaded the first batch of peppers into the blender.

"Stand back," I said. Paco moved to the other side of the garage, demonstrating a respect of peppers that came from past experience. I took a firm grip on the lid of the blender to be sure it wouldn't fly off, and hit the button.

It whirred, and the peppers turned to a blurry orange slurry.

I stopped the machine and took a careful look inside. It looked like a fibrous fruit slurpee. Paco came over to look, too.

"What do you think?" I said. "Will that take down a super-hero?"

"Over a million Scoville Units," he said.

Careful not to splash, I poured the orange slurpee through a strainer and into a clear glass. As we looked at the glass, the juice started to separate just a bit, with the top layer getting a little clearer and the bottom layer a bit denser. I visualized all the capsaicin sitting on the bottom, unable to go through a sprayer.

"Looks like it's separating," I said. "Street said we should add some detergent to a little water and mix it up. Can you do it?"

Paco nodded. He picked up a water bottle, poured some into a cup, then picked up the detergent.

"Smallest drop possible," I said.

Paco tipped the bottle just past horizontal, held it without squeezing. A tiny drop began to form. Paco kept it steady. The drop eventually separated and fell into the cup. He stirred until the water got sudsy.

"Now add the water detergent mix," I said.

Paco carefully tipped the cup and poured the mix into the glass. I stirred until it was frothy. We watched again. The bubbles all rose to the top, but the mix didn't separate. We repeated the process a couple of times, straining the slurpee into the 5-gallon bucket. When it came time to mix in the detergent/water mix, I handed Paco the portable cake mixer.

Paco was like a surgeon in his precision as he ran the mixer on slow speed, then increased the speed one notch. The juice turned into orange foam. Satisfied, he turned off the mixer and lifted it out.

Paco continued to stare through his goggles at the orange foam as if he expected a creature to emerge.

"Looks good," I said.

I found a matchstick on Diamond's workbench. I dipped the wooden end into the pepper sauce in the five gallon bucket.

"How hot will this taste if I touch it to my tongue?" I asked.

Paco's eyes got wide. "Real hot," he said.

I stuck out my tongue and gently touched the matchstick.

At first it just tasted hot. Like hot sauce from the supermarket. Then the hotness grew and spread through my mouth. In twenty seconds my mouth was on fire. My nose burned. My eyes were watering enough to send tears down my cheeks.

"Stay here," I said. I rushed out of the garage. Spot came running, excited at my fast movement. I ran into Diamond's kitchen, bent down and stuck my mouth under the kitchen faucet. Spot had come in with me, and he stuck his nose over the sink, sniffing at my head.

The cold water took the edge off. I rinsed thoroughly. When I was done, the hotness came back, searing my tongue.

I re-rinsed. And again.

As I went back out to the garage, I saw an elderly man

frowning at me from the upstairs window of the neighboring house. I gave him a little wave. He didn't wave back.

When I came back to the garage, Paco looked at me.

"Was it hot?" he asked.

"Pretty much," I said.

"Your eyes are red," he said.

"Over one million Scoville Units," I said.

We reloaded the blender and repeated the process.

I had blender and strainer duty. Paco had mixer duty. We stopped adding detergent. The growing volume of juice still seemed to stay mixed.

When we'd gone through the entire stock of chili peppers, we had about a gallon of juice in the bucket.

I took the bucket lid and snapped it on.

I wanted to attach the leaf blowers and test our setup. But I thought of the neighbor man. Leaf blowers make a huge amount of noise. Would the man ignore the sound of a jet plane or two taking off inside of Diamond's garage? Or would he call the cops to check us out? I couldn't take the risk. It would be hard to explain why we had such quantities of pepper spray and fire ants. It was risky, but we'd have to wait and test our gear at the tear-down house.

"We now have two formidable weapons," I said to Paco, my eyes still watering. "Fire Ants and pepper spray. Ain't no super-hero could stand up to those, huh?"

Paco shook his head.

FORTY-ONE

We loaded Diamond's old pickup with the Cassie's Viper pepper juice and the fire ants, our extra vent pipe supplies, and several tools. I took care not to drop them. We drove into a cold rain as we climbed Kingsbury Grade back into the Tahoe Basin.

We stopped at Street's lab.

"On our way to set the trap," I said. "Wondered if we can leave Spot to help with your entomological studies."

"Sure."

"Also wondered if you have some dark construction paper and packing tape."

She shook her head. "The closest thing to that would be paper grocery bags. Would that work?"

"Yeah." I told her what I wanted. She helped me cut up some bags, taped them together into large, stiff sheets, then cut shapes out of them as I explained my idea.

"It sounds kind of crazy," Street said, "but it just might work."

When we were done, Paco and I left. The pickup was much roomier without Spot.

We stopped at the hospital and got Celeste Redack's house key from Doc Lee.

As we drove out to the West Shore and around Emerald Bay, I talked to Paco about our plan to entice Salt and Pepper into breaking into a house where they would think Paco was staying.

"We're going to set a trap," I said. "And..."

"And I'm the bait," he finished.

"Yeah. The premise is simple. But pulling it off is complicated. I don't want you to go into this without understanding that there are risks."

Paco was quiet.

I stopped talking. I wanted him to sit on the idea. Let it steep. Paco was only ten, and he might not grasp the seriousness of the situation. But I could still remember when I was a kid, and I chafed at adults who didn't tell me the truth all because they thought I was just a kid and wouldn't understand. Maybe I didn't understand important things as fully as an adult did, but I grew up feeling that it was a mistake for adults not to inform kids about serious stuff that affected them.

"They could take me again," Paco finally said.

"Yeah, that's exactly what I'm thinking. We'll try very hard to keep that from happening. I can't guarantee that you'll be safe. But I'll do everything possible to keep you safe."

"You promise?"

It was a question that radiated back through my past to my own childhood. I'd asked the same question when adults had made serious claims to me.

"I can't promise I can keep you safe. But I promise I'll try."

On the north side of Emerald Bay, we drove past D.L. Bliss State Park and then Sugar Pine Point State Park. I told Paco what I had in mind.

"When I picked up the key," I said to Paco, "Doc Lee told me that this old house is two stories tall. My idea is to trick Salt and Pepper into thinking that you and Spot and I are upstairs in bed when we will, in fact, barricade ourselves downstairs. We're going to be like Oz in the Wizard of Oz. Have you seen that movie?"

"No."

"Oh. Well, you'll see what I mean when we get to the house. When these thugs break in, we can hit them with the pepper spray and the ants."

I glanced over at Paco. He was staring ahead, frowning.

"After we set up our trap, we'll take the Jeep so that Salt and Pepper will recognize us. We'll stake out the vacation house where they're staying.

"Hopefully, they'll come out at some point and see us. We'll make like we're trying to escape them, but we won't do a good job of it. As they follow us, we'll stay in populated areas so they don't dare try to jump us. They'll follow us to the trap. I'm hoping that when they see the situation, they'll decide to wait until night to make their move."

The turn-off to Doctor Redack's tear-down was as Doc Lee described, not far from Chamber's Landing, on the mountain side of the highway.

The house was in a quaint neighborhood of old cabins. To get to Redack's house, we drove two blocks in from the highway, turned north and went three more blocks. We parked and walked up carrying our supplies in black plastic lawn-and-leaf bags. If anybody saw us, I hoped they would think that we were simply doing fall cleanup work.

Redack's tear-down was reminiscent of a Halloween Haunted House, a two-story affair that looked out of place in Tahoe. The clapboard siding had lost most of its paint long ago. It leaned to the north a foot or more.

We moved fast, not wanting to attract attention from any neighbors, most of whom, I hoped, were vacation-home owners who wouldn't be in the area until the ski resorts started up their chairlifts in another few weeks.

The house had a ground-floor porch. Near the front door was a yellow Condemned Property sign. The porch steps were rickety, and a floorboard to the left of the door was missing, a long dark opening waiting to break someone's ankle.

The key the doctor had given me worked in the front door lock, and we were inside in seconds.

Because my cargo was precious and dangerous, I moved with care, setting them one at a time in the kitchen. I opened the plastic bags so the ants would have plenty of air.

I brought the leaf blowers inside and set them on the kitchen counter.

Looking at the layout, we plotted our strategy. How the men would likely break in, and what and how and where and when our response should be. I included Paco in my deliberations. Partly, to make him feel included. Mostly because he'd already demonstrated with the pepper spray and fire ant concepts that he had valuable ideas.

I explained my thought that while Salt and Pepper might first try the windows, they were the kind of guys who were inclined to kick in the door and storm us with a Blitzkrieg assault.

Paco asked what a Blitzkrieg assault was. When I started talking about Hitler and World War II, his eyes glazed over. I may as well have been talking about the Trojan War and Homer's postwar Odyssey where Cassie got her quote about how quick men are to flare up.

I segued to a discussion of how Paco and I intended to outsurprise Salt and Pepper with our own shocking counterattack.

I looked around for a way to disguise our dryer-vent, flexible hose through which we wanted to deliver our goods. The house relied on a simple wall-mounted furnace on the outside wall of the living room, so there was no duct work system to tap into.

The living room took up the front of the house. Behind the living room was the dining room on the left and the kitchen on the right. As was common in older houses, the kitchen was separated from the dining room by a door.

I looked in the kitchen. There was no obvious way to get our ants and home-brew pepper spray from the kitchen into the living room.

Back in the living room, I studied the wall for hints about the best way to punch a hole big enough for dryer vent flex-hose. The wall was made of old wood paneling. It was too dark to see the tiny nail holes that would tell me where the studs were located. And I didn't have a saw. A determined person can go through sheet rock with a sturdy butter knife. But even flimsy wood paneling resists such tools. I'd have to find a different approach. I was about to leave when I saw the light switch.

I made a rough measurement with my arms and hands. Walked back to the kitchen. Measured. It made sense that the kitchen switch was near the living room switch so the wires could be routed through the wall together.

My pocketknife has a small slotted screwdriver.

Unlike the living room, the kitchen wall was sheetrock. I

took off the kitchen switch plate.

Fortunately, the electrical box had been nailed to the studs with short roofing nails. By sticking my pocketknife driver into the opening at an angle, I was able to get the shaft of the driver above and below the box and lever the nails out of the wood. The box was now loose but roughly held in place by the Romex wire that went both up and down from the box. By wiggling the box, I could see that the wires going up went directly into another box, which faced the opposite direction.

The living room switch.

I went around, removed the living room switch plate and levered out the nails that held that electrical box in place. The two boxes were now much looser, and I could push them sideways, away from the stud.

Back in the kitchen, I used my pocketknife to cut away the sheet rock above the opening, moving up behind the box that faced the living room. In ten minutes, I had an elongated opening in the kitchen, the upper portion of which lined up with the living room switch opening.

I was able to push the two linked boxes away from the stud, compress the flex hose into an oval shape, and insert it through the opening.

Paco tore off pieces of duct tape. I positioned the hose to point out toward the main part of the living room where someone would walk if they came in through the front door or windows and headed toward the stairs. I ran the pieces of duct tape from the inside of the flex hose onto the edges of the wall opening.

In the light, it was very obvious. But at night, with the lights out, it wouldn't be the first thing that attackers noticed. Even if they shined flashlights around right after they broke in, it would be too late for them.

I plugged one of the leaf blowers into an outlet above the kitchen counter and the other into an extension cord that I ran around the corner into the bathroom. My hope was that the two rooms were on different circuits so we could run both blowers at once without blowing the circuit breakers.

I realized that I could only fit one vent pipe through the wall.

Fortunately, we had enough extra vent pipe to make a Y intersection.

I took the new Y vent pipe and taped it to the flex tube that went through the wall. Then I attached both leaf blowers to the Y. With both air streams narrowing to one tube, the pressure might be too much. I didn't want it to explode.

"Paco, let's test these babies. Make sure they work and that the outlets have power. You hold this one."

He looked at me, a little concern on his face.

"Let it rest on the counter. Just hold it tight so that it doesn't take off."

He took hold of the handles.

"Put a little weight on it and put your thumb on the switch. I'll do the same with the other one. On the count of three, we'll turn them both on. Then we'll turn them off. A short blast should prevent the entire neighborhood from getting worried. These things make quite the noise, so be prepared. Ready?"

He nodded.

"Okay, ready, set, go!"

We both hit the switches. In the enclosed space of the kitchen, the sudden roar was like a Space Shuttle at blastoff. The tube on my blower immediately came undone. The blast of air went across the counter and peeled a large piece of wallpaper off the wall. We shut them off, and the blowers wound down. The ensuing silence was dramatic after the crush of sound.

Paco's eyes were wide.

"Kinda loud, huh?"

He nodded.

"I guess I didn't get mine taped well enough. Help me hook them up to the bucket lids?"

Paco tore off more duct tape and handed me pieces while I secured the blowers to the counter and fit the blower nozzles into the vent pipes that were already attached to the bucket lids. Paco's blower attached to the lid from the pepper spray. My blower attached to the lid from the ant bucket. Then both of them plugged into the Y, which gathered ants and pepper spray together to shoot through the wall into the living room.

When it came time to use our weapon, we only had to switch the current lids on the buckets for the custom lids with the Venturi pipes that would suck out the pepper juice and the ants.

Next, we rigged some lights, downstairs and up. We strung extension cords from the kitchen, out the kitchen window, up the outside of the house, and back in through the upstairs bedroom windows.

We covered the upstairs windows with newspaper sheets. It would look like someone had simply arranged for the cheapest kind of temporary window covering.

The next task was the tour de force of our project.

Street had helped me cut and tape Kraft paper bags into two-foot-long shapes that resembled a tall man and a boy and a Great Dane. Upstairs in the house, I had Paco hold the cutouts while I suspended them from light nylon line. I put some screw-eyes in the ceiling, then ran the line up through the screw-eyes and across to a window at the back of the house.

I used one set of cutouts in one room, and another set – cut in a different shape – in another room. The nylon lines went out the window.

Back outside, I pulled the lines down to a screw eye just outside the kitchen window. We labeled the extension cords and the lines by attaching pieces of masking tape. Cord number one had one piece of tape. Cord number two, two pieces, etc. That way we could tell which was which in relative darkness.

I went outside and talked through the window to Paco in the kitchen. As I directed him, Paco worked the extension cords. Then he worked the nylon lines as if they were the strings on marionettes. Paco called out which number cord or line he was pulling on. I made notes.

Lights came on upstairs. Paper cutouts moved across the room. Because the cutouts were close to the lights, the shadows were projected much larger on the newsprint window coverings. Although it was still daytime, the house was well-shaded by big fir trees. I could make out the faint shadow of a man moving across the newsprint window covering. Then came a boy. Then a giant dog.

The man moved back. The light went out. Another light turned on in a different room. The man went in. He was lit from a different angle. It looked like he was carrying something. Bedclothes, maybe. The boy joined him. They appeared to talk. Then they moved back from the window. It looked like the boy lay down on a bed. The light went out.

It was a crude but powerful illusion. If the nylon cords didn't get tangled, and if the lights didn't malfunction, it would be a convincing suggestion of Paco and Spot and me going to bed.

I had Paco run through the process again. We developed a choreography. Then Paco went outside, staying where I could see him through the window. I gave him the show, then called him in.

"You think it will work?" I asked.

Paco nodded. Serious.

Next, we covered the inside of the kitchen windows with black garbage bags, leaving loose corners out of which we could peek. If someone came during the day, it would look suspicious. But I hoped Salt and Pepper would come under cover of night.

The kitchen windows had old-fashioned shutters that were still functional. I shut them, and used Diamond's portable driver to buzz multiple screws around the perimeter of the shutters to screw them shut. The wood was old and split in a few places, but the shutters seemed strong.

On the inside of the kitchen door, I screwed large brackets into both sides of the door frame, then dropped a two-by-four into the brackets. It would withstand a substantial assault.

To discourage entry to the kitchen, we dragged a downed tree branch over near the back door of the house. In a vacant, neighboring lot, we found two more large branches that had broken off in a storm. We arranged them so that they looked like they'd fallen in place. But they also provided a bit of a barrier to the kitchen door and windows.

"After we immobilize the men," I said, "we'll pull this two-by-four out of the brackets and go out the kitchen door. We'll have to jump over these branches. Will you remember that?"

Paco nodded.

FORTY-TWO

When all was ready, we drove around the lake to Street's lab. It was getting dark. The rain increased.

Spot pushed forward when Street let us in, not to see me, but to see Paco, his new sleeping companion.

Paco pet him. Spot banged his tail against Street's closet.

I told Street about our preparations.

"We'll sleep at Diamond's again tonight. Then tomorrow we'll use the Jeep to stake out Salt and Pepper, and when they see us, lead them to the trap."

Street was tense. She took me aside, held my hands, looked up at me, her eyes searching mine.

"Are you sure you want to go through with this?"

I knew that she could see my self-doubt.

"I've wrestled with this for hours," I said. "I wake up at night, struggling with the danger. There's no clear best approach."

"You are putting a boy at substantial risk. It's one thing for you to walk into the fire, but taking an innocent child..."

"I know. But he's already at great risk. I think this will give us a decent chance of catching these men. Yes, this increases the risk now, but my best sense is that the potential benefit is worth it."

"What if it goes bad, Owen? What then?" Street's eyes moistened, the prospect of disaster bringing tears. "Isn't there a way you can do this without Paco being there?"

"I've thought about it, and I think it will only work if Salt and Pepper see him going into the house. I don't have a good alternative. Wherever he is, he's at risk. I've talked this over with him. But let's ask him again."

"He's just a kid. He won't have a full grasp of the situation."

"Nevertheless," I said, "I think it's fair to get his input, don't you? If you were in his situation, you'd want to be consulted."

Street paused. "Yes, I suppose you're right."

We sat down on her work chairs. Spot sat next to Paco.

"Paco, I want to ask you again about this thing we're doing."

He glanced at me for the briefest moment, then pet Spot.

"This trap we're planning? Getting these bad guys to come after you so we can catch them?"

Paco didn't respond.

"You and I already talked about it," I said, "but I'm wondering if you've reconsidered. As I already mentioned, there is substantial risk involved. Things could go bad. It could backfire, and we might only succeed at making Salt and Pepper very mad."

Paco kept petting Spot.

"It's even possible that they could get the upper hand. They could hurt me and Spot, and they could take you away."

Paco kept his eyes down.

"It's a serious risk, Paco. If you are still sure it's a good idea, we'll continue. But if you have doubts, we'll cancel. We can keep you in hiding while we try to catch these men another way."

I felt stupid putting it into words. I was asking a ten-year-old to pass judgment on something that he was ill-prepared to answer. It was a cop-out on my part. But I didn't see a better solution to his ultimate safety other than giving him a new, secret name and sneaking him off to live with a new family in a different part of the country. A family willing to take in an illegal alien. A family I didn't have a clue how to find.

"They already kidnapped me," Paco said. "I was trapped in the back of their truck. They chased me down the mountain. Then they grabbed me at your cabin. I thought I was going to die like Cassie."

"If this doesn't work out, it may happen again."

Paco looked up at us. "If we don't spray them with pepper spray and fire ants now, they might find me in a year and take me then. I will always be scared. I'd rather try to get them now. Maybe it won't work. But I think it's worth it."

I looked at Street. Her eyes were wet.

I kissed her. "I'll do my best, hon. You know that."

"Yes, I know you will. Good luck. I love you." She went over and sat down next to Paco. "Paco, I want you to concentrate on what Owen says to do. Don't get distracted. Okay?"

Paco nodded.

Street gave him a long hug. Paco didn't hug her back. But he didn't pull away, either.

We said goodbye, took Spot with us, and left.

With Spot rejoining us, it was a tight fit in Diamond's pickup. This time Spot sat his hindquarters on the floor where Paco's feet would normally be, and Spot's front legs were up on the seat.

We headed over the mountain and down into Carson Valley to stay once more at Diamond's and return his pickup.

After dinner and another chocolate soda for Paco, Diamond, Paco, and I sat at Diamond's kitchen table. Spot sat in the fourth place and rested his chin on the table. His head was still, but his eyes moved back and forth, depending on who was speaking.

"Instead of going into the lion's lair," Diamond said, "you're luring them to come into your trap."

Diamond looked at Paco as he gestured toward me. "This guy explain what you're up against, Paco?"

Paco nodded. "We're going to bring down the superheroes," he said. He had enough confidence in his voice that it sounded more like an announcement than a statement of tentative possibility.

Diamond looked at me. "Kid's a philosopher."

"Fire ants and pepper spray against two bad guys," Paco said.

"You think these superhero dudes are tough enough to stand up to ants and pepper spray?" Diamond asked.

"No one's as tough as fire ants," Paco said. "And our Cassie's Vipers are over a million Scoville Units."

"So I recall," Diamond said.

"You're a tough kid, Paco," I said. "I'm rooting for you."

I made a fist and held it out toward Paco.

Paco made a fist and bumped knuckles with me, and then he smiled, a small half-smile, but the first one I'd ever seen on him.

FORTY-THREE

The next morning as we packed bag lunches, Diamond said, "Redack's tear-down is in Placer County. You want me to call the Sheriff's Office and alert them to your plan? They could set up surveillance and help catch Salt and Pepper."

"No thanks. I'd be afraid that any undercover cops could be spotted and give us away. Assuming our trap works, I'm confident that Salt and Pepper will be incapacitated. I'll secure them and call it in myself."

Diamond nodded, but he didn't look convinced. A short while later, Diamond drove Paco, Spot and me up to the lake in his Douglas County patrol unit. We went to Harrah's parking lot and transferred back to the Jeep.

We headed north up the East Shore to Incline Village and parked in sight of the vacation rental house where we'd seen the men that Paco thought were Salt and Pepper.

My plan was to wait until one or both of the big men drove out of the garage or came back from someplace else and headed toward the garage. Because of our position, Salt and Pepper wouldn't see us until I pulled out.

Whether they were coming or going, I planned to pull out in time that they could see us.

They would probably follow at a distance to see where I was going. If they tried to force us off the road, I'd call 911 dispatch and hope that a cop could intercept us before Salt and Pepper succeeded in catching us.

I hoped that they would have enough sense to avoid jumping us during the day and instead follow us and wait until night. Judging by their reputations, these guys were serious criminals. As such, they would realize that their best strategy was to hang back and see where we holed up for the night.

Spot slept, and Paco and I played games while we waited. I taught him some timeless road-trip diversions – Rock-Paper-Scissors, Squares, Tick-Tack-Toe, and such, all of which he didn't know, and all of which he no doubt thought were hopelessly old-fashioned because they weren't played on an electronic device.

His willing participation made me grateful. After a couple of hours we ate our lunches. Paco once again devoured his turkey, lettuce, and pretend tomato as if he were starving.

The afternoon ground on, seeming very long. Paco went to sleep, leaning against the car door. It was late afternoon and approaching twilight when I saw the blue pickup with the blue topper coming up the road. I didn't have a clear view through the trees, but I thought I saw two men in it.

I waited until they got a bit closer, then I shot out of my parking spot, turned down the road and raced toward the lake. My objective wasn't about speeding so much as to make an impression. I wanted them to notice us. But I also wanted them to think that we were trying to escape. It was important that they never suspect that we were leading them to our trap.

If they tried to figure out what we were doing in the woods, I hoped that they would think that I was staking them out, then got cold feet when I saw them and decided to flee.

I slowed as I got down to Tahoe Blvd. I turned west toward Tahoe City, then turned off in another block. It was a simple trick. Make them think that we were trying to lose them, but do such a lame job of it that they found it easy to follow us at a distance. I made an elaborate series of turns. Left and right, right and left, four rights in a row going all the way around the block. Assuming they were following us, they would think I was trying hard to evade them.

After a long charade, I turned back onto Tahoe Blvd., cruised over to Tahoe City, then turned south on 89 and went down the West Shore. I couldn't see a pickup following me, but I assumed they were back there.

"Time to pull on your sweatshirt and gloves and tape your cuffs," I said as we drove. "Ankle cuffs, too. In case someone sees us up close, we'll wait before we pull on our goggles."

We arrived at our haunted house just as twilight was making it hard to see. Perfect.

I pulled up onto the yard to the side of the house and drove forward under a large fir tree, pushing against the branches, which squeaked as they scratched the Jeep's paint. I got out, lifted some branches that were jammed against the windshield and pulled them up over the roof. Back in the Jeep, I drove forward another couple of feet, and we got out.

As with my driving, it looked like I'd tried to hide the Jeep but had done a lousy job. Anyone who looked carefully would see it tucked under the tree.

We got out and walked up to the front porch carrying a bag of groceries and two bulky sleeping bags, looking very much like we were coming here to crash for the night. Spot ran around, investigating haunted smells. He leaped up on the porch, clearing the steps without touching them. We all went inside, and I shut the door behind us. Then we went directly toward the back of the dark house, through the dining room into the kitchen. I called Spot in a whisper, and he trotted in, his nails clicking on the linoleum floor. I shut the kitchen door behind us.

I plugged in two of the dimmest, miniature flat-panel night lights we could find. With the kitchen windows covered in black plastic, it was a good bet that no one on the outside could detect our presence in the kitchen.

"Okay, Paco," I whispered. "Time for the light at the base of the stairs."

Paco had arranged the extension cords and power strip in an order that made no sense to me. He picked up an extension cord and plugged it into the power strip.

I saw light appear under the door to the dining room.

"Time to put on our goggles," I whispered. He pulled his over his eyes. As I picked up mine, Spot stuck his nose on the lenses, smearing them. I wiped them on my pants and pulled them on. If the world was blurry, it was too dark in the kitchen to tell.

Paco already had his gloves on. I pulled on mine. It was too late to tape my cuffs. The tape dispenser noise would warn anyone outside that we were doing something unusual.

"I'm opening up our ammo, Paco," I whispered. "Hold Spot back by his collar. Careful not to bump the buckets."

I knew that Paco's past experience with both peppers and ants would make him respectful of the danger.

I loosened the tabs on the lid of the pepper juice bucket, removed it carefully, and replaced it with the lid that had the Venturi exhaust pipe.

"I'll hold Spot. You do the light at the top of the stairs."

Paco plugged in another cord and then took Spot's collar again.

I moved to the ant bucket, hoping that the darkness would keep them mellow until our man-made tornado whipped them toward Salt and Pepper. I pried off the lid and quickly replaced it with the Venturi lid. It was too dark to see escaping ants. I carried the ant-proof lid over to a corner and set it down. Whatever ants were on it would have to come across the floor to get us. I felt a sting on my neck. I swatted at it. How did an ant already get up there? Were they crawling all over me? I said nothing about it.

The buckets were now ready, attached to the blower pipes on one side, and exhausted into the living room on the other.

"You can let go of Spot," I said, hoping he wouldn't go sniff the bucket lid I'd removed. "Downstairs light off."

Paco pulled out the first cord. I could see him in the dim blue glow from the night lights. In his goggles and hood, he looked like a cartoon character, which seemed fitting considering our cartoon plot to capture two super anti-heroes.

"Light in the upper left bedroom."

He plugged in a third cord.

I pulled on one of the nylon lines to move my paper cutout.

The man's shadow that was hopefully appearing on the newsprint window shades on the floor above was invisible to me in the blacked-out kitchen, but I imagined how it would move. I closed my eyes, thinking more like a music conductor than a trapper drawing in his prey.

I pulled another line, visualizing the dog and then the boy walking over to the man.

"Light in the right bedroom," I said.

Paco plugged in another cord.

I pulled the lines that would make the characters appear to move into the other room.

Paco and I worked smoothly together. If our show was as effective as I imagined, we could have gotten special-effects jobs at a theater.

We continued the performance for another couple of minutes.

"Okay, lights out," I whispered.

Paco unplugged the cords, our pretend characters now in bed.

I whispered to Paco. "Get ready with your blower."

We both put our hands on the handles, thumbs on the switches.

"When it comes time to turn these on, hang on tight and keep it going until I say stop."

We waited.

We heard small sounds in the night. They could have been from mice or raccoons or neighborhood cats. Or maybe from Salt and Pepper. The assault at my cabin was preceded by scratching outside my cabin wall. But that was them luring me. This time, they would know that I wouldn't fall for it.

Based on the appearance that Paco and I were using the house as a hideaway, they would probably assume that I didn't have backup. But having Tased me before, they would also assume that I would arm myself with a gun or more.

Paco coughed.

My impulse was to say something critical, but I realized it would make no difference except to make Paco tense. He knew as well as I did the importance of silence.

The wait grew long. Even five minutes is very long when you're waiting in the silent dark. A kind of psychological deprivation sets in. Maintaining ten minutes of no movement is difficult. Twenty minutes becomes excruciating.

I thought about whether I should have tried to convince the Placer County Sheriff to stake out this location, but I still had no evidence. We were putting on this operation based on the word of a kid.

"Ouch," Paco said. He took one of his hands off the blower, swatted at his leg, then scratched. He put that hand back, removed his other hand from the blower, stretched. When he grasped again at the blower, he hit something that sounded like a screwdriver as it clattered to the floor and rolled a bit.

I heard him wince.

"How will they come in?" Paco finally asked, his voice too loud to be called a whisper.

"They'll probably try to break open a window lock," I whispered, much quieter. "These guys are too big for the smaller windows, and the biggest windows are in the living room. We should be very quiet and listen carefully. Don't turn on your blower until I say so. If we hear a noise it may be them outside the house. It's absolutely critical that they are inside the house before we hit them with our ammo."

Paco went silent.

Ten more minutes passed. I heard Spot turn circles, nails clicking, and lie down. He sighed. I'd never realized how loud his sighs were. Assuming Salt and Pepper were out there, they were probably waiting until they were sure that we were in a deep sleep.

A sudden explosion came from the living room. Someone had kicked in the door. Spot jumped up barking.

I whispered in Paco's ear, "Not yet!"

More noise. Thudding kicks. The sound of breaking, splintering wood. Spot's barking was loud, but I hoped they would think that his barks were coming from upstairs.

More kicks. Wood being pried.

"Hurry!" Deep, booming voice.

"Upstairs!" A second voice, higher. "Don't let them get out the window."

"Now!" I whispered to Paco.

I hit my blower switch, and Paco hit his. Two blowers roared. It was like a freight train thundering at high speed through the kitchen.

I didn't know what to expect.

In a moment, over the roar, came shouted words.

"Oh, Jesus! Oh, God!"

The other voice screamed, "My eyes are on fire! Can't breathe! My skin's burning. It's acid. He's shooting us with acid!" The words trailed off below the volume of the blowers.

We kept the blowers running. I reached down with one hand and lifted on the pepper juice bucket. It was noticeably lighter. I shook it, hoping to keep the juice mixed for potency. I also shook the ant bucket. It was very light. I popped the lid on the second ant bucket and switched the Venturi lid over to it, the leaf blower still roaring.

The men screamed as if they'd been lit on fire.

More staccato screams. Someone falling to the floor. A crash of glass. More thuds that I couldn't make out over the blower volume.

After the second ant bucket felt empty, I spoke in Paco's ear.

"Okay, Paco, let's turn them off."

We hit the switches. The motors ran down.

With the roar gone, the screams from the living room were much louder.

I flipped on the kitchen light. The floor had many ants rushing around, but a quick glance through the screen window in the side of the ant bucket showed that most of them were gone.

Burning pepper mist began to fill the kitchen.

I lifted the brace out of the door brackets. Opened the door for Paco.

"Paco, take Spot out the kitchen door. Wait for me outside. I don't want you to get the pepper juice or the ants on you."

Coughing, he went out with Spot, into the night.

I took a deep breath of air at the outside door, then opened the door into the dining room and living room and flipped on the living room light.

The room was drenched and vibrating with the movement of countless tiny specks.

The front door was broken into splinters. A window on the side wall was smashed, shards of glass sparkling on the floor.

Salt and Pepper were writhing and jerking on the floor, screaming. Their eyes were clenched shut, their faces contorted with pain. I saw ants on their clothes and skin, but it appeared that the major debilitating weapon had come from the magic of Cassie's Vipers.

I was amazed to see that our crazy scheme had worked.

I stepped back to the outside kitchen door to get away from the pepper juice miasma and breathed five quick, deep breaths. Then I went back into the living room.

The white man was on his back on the floor, bawling like a child. Near him was a Taser. Using my foot, I forcibly rolled him over onto his side. I grabbed his belt at the back and lifted him up onto his hands and knees. He didn't really hold himself up, but he took enough of his own weight to lessen the load on me. Ants crawled from him up my arm, but I didn't care.

"Outside, dude," I said. "Fresh air."

He sort of helped me, crawling across the ant-covered floor, slick with pepper juice, as I walked him out the broken door. I sped him up and then lifted him as we got to the porch steps. He made a blind, flying belly flop onto the dirt in front of the house, where he collapsed in a heap, still crying, still jerking from ant stings.

Spot stood nearby, licking his chops, sniffing the air, keeping his distance. He snorted and shook his head.

I thought of telling Spot to watch the man, but it was obvious that the guy wouldn't go anywhere until the worst of the pepper juice and ants was past.

I took more fast breaths to clear my lungs, then went back inside for the other guy. Spot stayed outside.

Pepper wasn't crying like Salt, but he looked to be in more pain. He was choking and gagging. Ants swarmed him.

In thirty seconds, I had him outside, on the dirt next to Salt.

I held my breath and went back inside to the kitchen to grab the duct tape.

It was the heavy-duty variety, and it only took two turns each to do Salt and Pepper's hands behind their backs, their feet, and their knees. They both choked and gagged and cried like children. I heard a car not too far away and wondered if the driver would come to investigate the bawling sounds from the men. If so, the scene would be awkward to describe.

I lifted each of them up to a standing position and walked them up face first against Jeffrey pine trees. With their faces turned sideways, cheek-to-bark, I ran tape around their necks and the tree trunks. I didn't want to suffocate them, but I wrapped the tape tight enough that their molars would get re-aligned from the bark pressing through their cheeks. Then I wrapped tape around their feet and the trunks. When I was done, they were immobilized against the trees.

Through it all, they continued to gasp and sputter, and the stinging fire ants made them twitch and jerk. I was glad I'd kept my goggles on. There was no antidote for pepper spray. All you could do was wait an hour or two for the burning, blinding chemical to soften its grip on your skin and eyes and lungs.

Despite my gloves and goggles and holding my breath, a bit of the pepper had gotten into my lungs, and it burned as if I were inhaling fire. I couldn't imagine what a full dose would do to a person.

Spot had disappeared back around the house.

I left the men against the trees, sagging down, their bulk held up by their tree-tape necklaces as much as by their own legs.

In the light that spilled out from the broken front door, I saw Spot come running back from behind the house. I held my gloved hands up in the air so that Spot wouldn't touch them.

"Okay, Paco, it's safe to come around the house," I called out. "Just stay back from these miserable jerks. I don't want any of the pepper juice to get on you."

Spot ran back behind the house, nose to ground.

"Paco, c'mon out," I called.

No response.

My gut clenched.

I sprinted back to the rear of the house. Spot ran with me.

"PACO!" I shouted.

He wasn't there.

FORTY-FOUR

I ran up to the kitchen door and shouted.
   "PACO!"
I circled the house. Held my breath and ran back inside. Up the stairs. The bedrooms were empty.

"Spot," I said when I was back outside. "Where's Paco?" I said.

Spot's brow was furrowed.

I pounded down the stairs. There was a trail of sorts behind the house. Cars probably used it like an alley. I'd gone out the front of the house just seconds after Paco and Spot had gone out the back. Paco must have gone toward the alley.

I ran out and looked both ways.

Nothing. It was a dark path into the night with no sign of vehicle lights.

I'd been so stupid! I'd focused on Salt and Pepper. When Spot came running to see what I was doing in the front yard, a third comrade ran off with Paco.

If Paco had cried out, Spot would have run back to intervene. But if Paco knew the person, he might not have been suspicious.

Even if the person was a stranger, he might have muffled Paco's mouth and got him into a car before Spot noticed.

It must have been the car I'd heard while I was taping Salt and Pepper.

I ran back to the front of the house. "WHERE'S PACO?!" I shouted at the closest man, Pepper.

He was still sagged down as if his weight was hanging from the tape around his neck, wheezing, struggling to breathe, his bronchial tubes inflamed from the pepper spray. He wouldn't be able to speak for a long time.

I went over to Salt. Asked him the same question.

He could breathe, but he said nothing.

I stepped behind him and jerked up on his taped wrists, stressing his elbows and shoulders.

He yelled.

"WHERE'S PACO?" I shouted again.

"I dunno," he grunted. "I thought he was with you."

"Tell me what you do know!"

"I dunno anything."

Another jerk on his arms. Harder. He screamed louder. Ripping apart a shoulder or elbow is a pain near the top of the scale.

"Who do you work for?"

"I dunno."

I bent down, got my shoulder under his bound wrists and began to straighten up. I heard squeaks coming from his joint tissues.

He screamed like he was being torn in half by a lion.

I backed off just a touch.

"You don't answer my questions, I'm going to take apart both of your shoulders and elbows. It's tough to repair that kind of injury. And when your shoulder pops in that position, sometimes it rips the brachial artery. You'll bleed out in a couple of minutes. At least then you'll get some relief from the pain."

"Once more," I said. "Who do you work for?"

"Just a guy that sent an email. A referral thing." He stopped to breathe. Gasping breaths. "My arms..."

I let off the upward pressure.

"The guy said he'd pay us our fee for two jobs. Thirty thousand each. Fifty percent down."

"You were paid to kill both the woman and the boy?"

"We were only to kill the woman. Kidnap the boy. We had orders. Make sure the kid ain't hurt." The man's eyes were still shut tight. Tears flowed out from between red, clenched eyelids.

A million Scoville units, Paco had said. It was Paco's brilliant idea that brought these two men down. It was my incredible stupidity that let a third man take Paco while I'd been focused on these men.

"Why would he kidnap the boy?" I asked. "There's no money to ransom."

"We jus' sell our services. Someone pays our money, we don't ask why."

"What'd the guy look like?"

"Never saw him." The man's words were hard to understand. He coughed and wheezed.

"How'd he pay the deposit?"

"Mail. He mailed it to us."

"He mailed you thirty thousand dollars cash?"

"Yeah. In a Flat-rate box. Hunnerd dollar bills."

"And now he has the kid?" It was a reasonable assumption. But so far I'd been wrong about a lot.

"I 'spose," the man said, his voice rattling with mucous. "Musta followed us. We do the work, and he snatches the kid out from under us. We'll still get the money."

"How were you supposed to deliver the kid?"

"Gonna email the guy. Then he'd give us instructions."

"What's his email address?"

"I dunno. It's in my computer."

"Where's your computer?"

"In my truck. Down the block."

I looked through the dark. Didn't see any vehicle in either direction.

"You believed he'd pay you the balance even though you don't know his identity?" I said.

The man coughed. "We have a rep. He stiffs us, we track 'im down and make 'im pay. We always get paid."

"Not this time," I said.

"I can't breathe," he said. "You gotta take this tape off my neck, or I'll choke to death."

I ignored him.

By his bulging jaw muscles, I could tell that he wouldn't hesitate to use his debt-collection techniques on me if he could.

"If I let you go, where would you go to look for this guy? Or the boy?"

"There's a college kid in Vegas. Knows how to hack computers. He can track email."

"Why'd the guy hire you to kill Cassie?"

"I dunno. Maybe the bitch screwed him over."

I gave him the hardest jerk, yet. Something snapped loud and crisp in my ear.

He cried out in an ear-ripping shriek, ragged with terror, followed by a long moan. He sagged, knees bending, tape pulling tight around his neck. His breath was fast, short panting gasps, tense with desperation. Drops of sweat mixed with pepper juice on his forehead. The man turned a deep red, visible in the dim light spilling out from the house.

"You wrecked my arm. I'm gonna kill you for that."

"Your other arm is next. Why'd he want you to kill Cassie?"

"I dunno."

"Why did Cassie drive to meet you?" I asked.

"I don't know! Guy who hired us set it up. He'd made some deal with her. She thought she was meeting him. All so we could do her and grab the boy. Then the little shit hid and ran. Kid runs like an animal or something. At least we got the woman. She was one tough bitch. Tried to fight when Pep pulled his piece. Guess she's sorry now."

He said it as a boast. I lost control. I bent my arm and put a hard elbow punch to his temple. With his head against the tree, it could not bounce away to lessen the blow. He went limp like I'd flipped a switch. He'd live, but he'd have a hell of a headache when he came to. I didn't think I broke his skull, but thought he might end up with enough brain bruising and swelling to cause permanent damage. The possibility didn't bother me.

I ran to the Jeep, ripped away the branches. Spot was at my side. I let him into the back, then jumped in, threw the shift into reverse, and backed the Jeep out from under the tree.

I grabbed my phone and dialed 911 as I raced down the road. When the dispatcher answered, I said, "Owen McKenna calling. There are two killers who are known as Salt and Pepper. They are wanted for three murders in Vegas. One of them just confessed

to the murder of Cassie Moreno as well as the attempted kidnapping of her foster son Paco Iparagirre. Paco has now been taken
by a third, unknown party.

"You will find the men tied to trees in front of a condemned
house on the West Shore, not far from Chambers Landing." I
gave her the address. "Tell the officers to be careful. There's pepper spray on the men and inside the house." I hung up.

I called Diamond and got his voicemail. I explained what
had happened. It was out of his jurisdiction, but I knew he'd
want to know. Then I dialed Street. In crisis, phone home to your
soul mate. She'll have an idea.

I got her voicemail, too. I stumbled through a description of
who, what, where, and when, but didn't have the why.

When I hung up, I stared at my phone, trying to think of
what to do next. After ten seconds, the phone lights went off. I
felt like my world had just gone from dark to black.

I drove around the block, looking for Salt and Pepper's pickup, but saw nothing. I circled the next block, and the next still.
Still nothing. Maybe they'd hidden it. Or maybe they'd come
with a third person, someone other than the guy who hired them,
and that person took Paco and left in the pickup.

I thought about all the people who I'd talked to and the ones I
hadn't. Although I'd learned that Cassie didn't have many friends,
a lot of people knew her because they wanted her produce. They
wanted Cassie's Amazements.

Which made me think of the man Paco had mentioned, the
guy who drove the red Audi. The guy who'd come to Cassie's
farm several times to talk to her about her hybrid.

The Jeep fishtailed as I pushed it on a curve, shot past Chambers Landing, and headed up through Homewood. A bit farther,
I turned into the townhouse project where Michael Schue the
owner of the restaurant chain and produce distribution company
lived. He wasn't in when Paco and I had stopped by before. Maybe he was in now. Maybe he'd know the owner of the red Audi,
the man who'd turned into the same complex the day Paco and I
had tried to visit.

FORTY-FIVE

I found Schue's code on the keypad readout at the gate. His phone rang. This time he answered.

It took all of my control not to yell.

"Mr. Schue, my name is Owen McKenna. I'm a private investigator looking into the murder of Cassie Moreno, the owner of Field To Fridge. She delivers your fresh vegetables every week."

"Yes, I heard about her death," Schue said. "Very sad."

"I need to talk to you about it. I'm at the condo gate."

"Oh?" he said. "Well, perhaps we can set up a time if you send an email to my secretary. You can find it on the contact page of my company's website. I..."

"Mr. Schue, I must speak to you now."

"I'm sorry, I don't allow unscheduled visits. So I'll have to hang..."

"Michael Schue, if you hang up, I will have the Placer County Sheriff's Office get a warrant, and a small army of deputies will be back to take apart your townhouse so thoroughly you won't recognize it when they're done. Not that you'll care from your jail cell."

There was static from the keypad speaker.

"What are you saying?" Schue finally said.

"You let me in now and answer a few questions, maybe we can avoid a warrant and a search, and future depositions and court appearances. If you don't, maybe we get eager in our search, find something we think suspicious. Have you ever spent a night in jail while you're waiting for your lawyer to call back from Grand Cayman?" I knew that few wealthy men like Schue had ever spent a night in jail. The idea would scare him.

More static.

Eventually, he said, "I'm in the Blue Lake building. I have the top floor. The garage code is 'Beauty'."

The gate began to open.

I found the Blue Lake building, typed 'Beauty' into the garage keypad, and drove down the ramp as the door rose up. The garage held a dozen cars. One was a red Audi quattro. There was an elevator at one end. I left Spot in the Jeep and rode to the top floor.

The door opened on a room with a window overlooking the beach and dark lake beyond. There was a small seating arrangement, a table and lamp, and copies of financial magazines. Opposite, was a grand door. I crossed to the door and pushed the button.

The door opened, letting out soft classical music. Violins and cellos stepping in a stately procession down a series of chords. Baroque, maybe. A man stood in front of me wearing leather slippers and burgundy pajamas underneath a dark green robe.

I showed him my ID.

He sniffed, wrinkled his nose at the pepper smell emanating from me.

"I'm Michael Schue. Come in." I followed him to a semi-darkened living room with a grand view of the dark lake with its perimeter of twinkling lights. The only room light came from canned ceiling spots turned down to their lowest dimmer setting and three large candles on a low table. Near the candles was a bottle of wine and two half-full glasses.

Behind the table was another man lounging on a couch. He, too, wore night clothes, and he held a pipe that looked to be packed with unlit tobacco.

"Mr. McKenna, this is my friend Albert Zimmer," Schue said.

Albert nodded and gestured with his pipe.

"Please sit," Schue said as he joined Albert on the couch.

I took one of the big over-stuffed chairs that faced the couch. I took a couple of deep breaths, trying to calm myself, then gave a brief explanation about Cassie's death, her foster son Paco, and his kidnapping a few minutes ago.

"That's terrible!" Schue said.

"I'm here for two reasons. One is because you, Michael, were a client of Cassie's. The other reason is that Cassie was periodically approached by a man at her organic farm down near Stockton. The man wanted to acquire an interest of some kind in her hybrid tomatoes. Among other things, Paco noticed that the man drove a red Audi quattro.

"Recently, Paco and I went around the lake visiting Cassie's clients. When we came here to see you, there was no response to my keypad call from the gate. Yet, as we left, we saw a red Audi quattro pulling in. Paco got a look at the driver and said that it was the man who came calling at the farm and wanted to buy tomato rights.

"Naturally, it seemed too much of a coincidence to have two such connections to Cassie at this townhouse development, especially considering that your restaurant chain also owns a produce distribution company. So my question is, do you know who the man in the red Audi is?"

"Yes," Schue said. He gestured at the man next to him. "Albert is the man you are looking for. The red Audi is his. Although I'm sorry to say that this knowledge won't be the breakthrough you are looking for."

Albert spoke up, "Michael and I have been partners for many years, and we have worked side-by-side on several business projects. I'm a part owner of our company, California Produce Growers and Distributors. I heard about Cassie from Michael. Then, when I tasted her hybrid tomatoes and realized that they were delicious, I made some inquiries. I found out that she was simply selling them herself. She called them Cassie's Amazements. So I visited her and explained that this new strain she'd developed could be marketed worldwide. But when I told her that this tomato could make her rich, she declined.

"I was, frankly, very surprised. I was willing to hand her a fortune, and she responded with a kind of a speech about small business and hard work and how she was suspicious of big agribusiness.

"I'm a salesman at heart, which means I'm persistent. So I

came back a few weeks later and repeated my offer and explained that compared to the really big companies, our produce company was closer in size to hers. She was more amenable, but she still said no. When I told her that she wasn't being practical and that eventually someone was going to get her secret and she'd lose her rights, she started talking about Kant and the moral imperative of an organic farmer. I didn't even understand what she was getting at. So I decided to leave and let her calm down. I thought I'd go back in a year."

I talked to them some more, but when it was obvious that they had nothing to offer me, I left and went back down to my Jeep where Spot waited.

FORTY-SIX

I drove out of the garage, out through the fancy gate and headed up the West Shore, my speed increasing until I was going 60.

The blackness closed in on me like tunnel vision until I could no longer see anything but the rushing, dotted line on the highway.

Someplace out there was an orphaned boy whose last hope was me. But through the folly of a reckless plan, I'd let him be taken in the night. I'd made the worst decision a man can make, and as a result, Paco was in the possession of a killer whose identity and motivation and location I didn't know.

I was racing through the blackness without even knowing where I was going. I slowed, and where the highway passes next to the public beach, I stood on the brake and slid to a stop, gravel flying and dust clouding around the Jeep.

I got out, let Spot out. The early winter rain was coming back, soft drops, but colder than before. I walked to the water, pounding my fist into my palm, talking to myself, shouting out loud about my idiocy. I struggled with outrage over how little I knew. And what I didn't know was nearly everything important.

I didn't know why Paco was kidnapped. Without potential ransom money, it made no sense. Babies and toddlers were often kidnapped by people who were desperate to obtain a kid for themselves. Girls of all ages and sometimes boys were often kidnapped for unspeakable reasons. But who would want Paco enough to pay $30,000 for him? It was too much money for sex slavery. It was too much money for nearly anything. He had no valuable secrets. Many people wouldn't even think him particularly likeable.

Did he alone know Cassie's trade secret about tomatoes that a corporation could use to make millions? That was a more reasonable notion, but still far-fetched. If someone wanted to steal Cassie's tomato secret, they would break into her house and steal her notes, or break into her hothouse and steal the actual tomatoes. They wouldn't take the kid.

He had no villainous characteristics that would make him a target for any revenge. No one I'd met other than Paco's landlord had any animosity for Paco at all. No matter how I thought it through, I couldn't believe that Paco's landlord had anything to do with it.

Nothing made sense. Paco was just an unwanted kid, in the country illegally, with no value to anyone. Yet, a $30,000 price on his head meant he was hugely valuable to someone. Why? I tried to consider any possibility, no matter how outlandish.

Did he have a piece of costume jewelry that was in fact made of diamonds? Had he learned incriminating evidence in some crime? In either case, he'd be targeted for murder, not kidnapping.

I got out my wallet and pulled out the card Principal Sagan had given me, dialed the number.

The message was long and detailed. At the end her voice said, "If this is an emergency, please dial the following two numbers." She recited both home and cell.

I dialed the first one.

"Pam Sagan," she answered.

"Owen McKenna calling. I'm the guy who..."

"Is helping Paco Ipar," she interrupted. "Are you having any luck?"

"No. I have a question. What could Paco possibly know that would be very valuable?"

"I don't understand."

"I've learned that there was a thirty thousand dollar price on him. Now he's been kidnapped by the person who hired Cassie murdered."

"What?!" she shouted in my ear. "Someone kidnapped him?!"

"Yeah. But I can't figure out why."

"That poor boy! Oh, no!" I could hear her crying.

"Can you think of a reason why someone would pay money to kidnap him?"

"No! Absolutely not! People kidnap for ransom money, right?" she said in a near shout. "There isn't anybody who knows Paco who would have ransom money. This is a poor community."

"There must be something remarkable about Paco," I said. "Some secret that he knows."

"I'm sorry to say it, but there is nothing remarkable about Paco. I think he has a good heart. I know he works very hard. But special, no. He's like any other kid except for two things. One, he's an illegal immigrant."

"What's the other thing?"

"I shouldn't even say it. Other people wouldn't think it is remarkable. And it certainly isn't worth any money. But he is Basque."

"Why is that remarkable?"

"I don't really know. If you knew the Basque people, you'd understand. They are special. They have a heritage that is unique. They are Europe's oldest people. And even the ones who've been on this continent for generations, it... I don't know. It shows in their manner. I've seen it in our local doctor. He's Basque, and he... Wait, you met him, right? Dr. Mendoza. Not only is he Basque, but he's quite an expert on Basque people."

"Yes, he told me that Paco was Basque," I said. "Do you think he would know anything else about Paco? Would he pay ransom money for Paco?"

"I don't know," Sagan said. "You could call him."

"It's late. He won't be at the office. Do you have an emergency number for him?"

"Yes," Sagan said. "Let me look it up." She read it off. "That's his home number. He's probably there at this hour."

I thanked her, hung up, and got Mendoza on the phone.

I told him what had happened. I heard an intake of breath, but he didn't exclaim.

"Did you ever tell anyone anything about Paco?" I asked

when he answered.

"No," Mendoza said. "I would never do that. I have complete respect for the privacy of my patients."

"The foundation that paid the medical bills for your poor patients, did you tell them anything that could be used to identify Paco?"

"No. All I did was give them the medical reports for their researchers' epidemiology study. It's totally anonymous with regard to my patients."

"What does an epidemiology study do?"

"It's a standard approach to judging what is needed with regard to public health. Understanding the etiologies of disease, or the causation, if you will, is central to making policy to improve health everywhere. So, in return for the funding for medical service for the poor people in our community, we gave them standard medical reports."

"What is in those reports?"

"I'm not sure how to answer that," Mendoza said. "There are many complicated components to health analyses, and they tell us many things about the patient's physiology, any current diseases, biochemical imbalances, certain genetic information, drug use, and so on. We can also make predictions about heart disease, diabetes, and a host of other conditions based on aggregated community medical information. Great breakthroughs in health treatment worldwide have come as a result of these kinds of studies."

"I asked Pam Sagan what was so special about Paco, and she said nothing except that he is an illegal immigrant and he is Basque. When I asked her why being Basque is special, she said I should call you. So I ask you, what is so special about being Basque?"

"Certainly nothing that would make someone kidnap a boy. What is special about being Basque is largely a matter of pride, of our history."

"How?" I said. "You must be able to describe it."

"I guess it's about enduring. When all of Europe's earliest inhabitants succumbed to invading forces, the Basque people survived. Even when Hitler and Mussolini committed the unforgivable atrocity of bombing a peaceful people, they still survived. Their endurance has been celebrated, and they..."

"Wait," I interrupted. "What you just said. What do you mean that their endurance has been celebrated?"

"Just the whole brutal bombing. It was disgusting. Hitler's men bombed Basque women and children, more than a thousand of them. It was even commemorated in a famous painting by Picasso."

"The painting. Do you know the name of it?"

"Of course. It was named for the town that was bombed. It's one of the most famous paintings in the world. It's called Guernica."

My heart beat hard enough that I felt it bang in my chest. Guernica was the painting that I saw hanging above the mantle in Robert Whitehall's house.

"Doctor, the foundation that pays those medical bills. Tell me again, what was the name of it?"

"The Medical Freedom Foundation."

"Who runs it?"

"A philanthropist up at Lake Tahoe. A man by the name of Robert Whitehall."

"Thanks, doctor." I hung up.

FORTY-SEVEN

I pulled up outside of Whitehall's gate. I could try to crash through, but maybe I didn't have to. I dialed his number. It rang five times. A machine picked up.

I didn't want to accuse Whitehall of kidnapping Paco. If I did and he was guilty, he would flee. Maybe I could make him think that I just needed information.

At the tone, I said, "Mr. Whitehall, this is Owen McKenna. I'm parked outside of your gate. Cassie Moreno's boy Paco has been kidnapped. You are connected to it in some way. Maybe you know that, maybe you don't. I need to talk to you immediately. If you're home, please open the gate. I need to find..."

"I'm here, I'm here," Whitehall's voice said on the phone. "I was in the bathroom. I could only hear some of your words. What is this about?"

"Cassie's boy Paco has been kidnapped."

"Hold on while I open the gate."

I hung up. The gate opened. I drove in. The front door opened. I let Spot out of the Jeep. He trotted inside Whitehall's house while I flattened myself against the outside wall of the house. If Whitehall was armed, maybe Spot would sense it and do something that would clue me in.

Nothing happened. Spot came back out the door. He looked at me, his tail on intermittent wag.

I went inside. Whitehall was over by the fireplace, pacing.

"You said Paco's been kidnapped. Why would he be kidnapped? I don't understand. Is this connected to Cassie's murder?"

I pointed to a chair. "Sit," I said.

He sat on the edge of the chair, back straight, feet and knees together like a school girl. Spot sat, too, probably thinking that I was talking to him. Spot looked at me, then at Whitehall.

"What do you know about Paco?" I said.

"Nothing. He is Cassie's son. Or stepson, or something like that. I believe she referred to him as her son. He helps with the vegetables. I never met him until you brought him by the other day."

I stood opposite Whitehall.

"Paco and I set up a trap in a house on the West Shore. We succeeded in catching the two hired killers who murdered Cassie. But I was suckered. The person who hired them must have been there in the shadows as I worked my trap. When the commotion was over, Paco was gone."

Whitehall paled. "Why would someone kidnap Paco?" His voice was small. Frightened.

"That's what I want to know. It might have something to do with his being Basque."

"Paco is Basque?" Whitehall said. "He looks Mexican. Mestizo."

"I've learned that many Basque emigrated to Mexico. They married Mexicans the same way that the Basque who came here married Americans."

"What would being Basque have to do with Paco getting kidnapped?" Whitehall frowned. His concern seemed genuine.

"I don't know," I said. "But every time I learn something more about Paco, I hear something more about his Basque background. There are too many Basque connections for it to be a coincidence."

Whitehall's frown deepened. "Speaking of which, the painting behind you." He pointed toward the fireplace.

I looked at the famous painting we'd discussed the last time I was in Whitehall's house.

"Picasso's Guernica," I said. "That's why I'm here."

"It was a terrible attack," Whitehall said. "You can see all the symbols of agony in the painting. The women and children and even the horses that were blown to bits."

I sat down. Put my fingertips to my temples. Pushed as if to force understanding into my brain.

"What is your connection to the Basque?" I said, unable to keep anger out of my voice.

"None," Whitehall said. His fright had turned his face nearly white. He shook his head.

"Then why do you have the painting? You just happen to love a painting that portrays the horror of an atrocity committed against the Basque?"

"The painting pays honor to the victims and what they went through."

"I don't buy it, Whitehall." I was shouting. "A young Basque boy is kidnapped, and it turns out that you've been funding medical care in his community. I spoke to Dr. Mendoza. He says that one of the conditions of the medical funding was that he turn in medical reports on his patients. The school principal thinks that Paco's Basque heritage is involved. You have on your wall a painting about the Basque."

Whitehall was sputtering, suddenly seeming old. He struggled to get the words out. "But it's not even my painting. It belongs to my tenants. When they moved into the guest house, there was no wall large enough to hang the painting, so I said it could hang here for the time being."

"It belongs to your tenants? The retired vet and his son who has cancer," I said.

Whitehall nodded. "Yes, Dr. Andrew Garcia and his son Martin. You must remember meeting them. Andrew was wearing the running suit, and his son Martin was in the wheelchair. I never see the reports that Mendoza sends the foundation. I turn them over to Dr. Garcia. He gives them to medical researchers. In fact, it was Garcia's idea that my foundation fund the medical services for poor communities. He's a vet, but he's deeply involved in medical charity for people. Now that I think of it, it was Andrew Garcia who first learned about Cassie and her business. He first met her at the farmers' market."

"Was that before or after he directed you to fund medical services?"

"After."

"So Garcia may have learned about Paco from the medical reports, then had you sign up for Field To Fridge just so he could get to know Cassie and Paco better. Is Garcia home?"

"No. Andrew left with Martin that day you and Paco came by. Andrew said they'd be out of town for several days."

I pulled out my cell phone. Dialed Dr. Mendoza one more time.

"McKenna again," I said. "I'm at Robert Whitehall's house. Do you know a retired veterinarian named Dr. Andrew Garcia?"

"No. Why?"

"I'm wondering if he has any connection to the Basque."

"Well, I don't know anything about him. But Garcia is one of the most common Basque names, if that makes any difference."

"It does, yes. Can you think of a reason that a person of Basque heritage would kidnap a Basque boy?"

"No, of course, not. From my perspective, there is nothing about Paco that would attract a kidnapper."

"What about a medical reason?"

Mendoza was silent for a moment. "Well, I hate to think it because it is so horrible, but yes, there is a medical reason, and that would be to use Paco as an organ donor. I don't have Paco's blood work in front of me. But as a Basque boy, there is a good chance that he has type O negative blood. If so, that makes him what we call a universal donor because his tissues would be less likely to be rejected than donors with other blood types."

"Is forced organ donation something you've heard much about?"

"Mostly, doctors hear about it the same way the general public does, in stories, in movies."

"Yet, you believe it happens?" I asked.

"Absolutely. But it's very uncommon because stealing an organ doesn't do a thief any good unless it is a close tissue match to the recipient. The idea of someone kidnapping someone for the purpose of taking their organs is highly impractical for that reason. Even if the person is type O negative, there are many other factors that are necessary for an ideal match."

"Dr. Garcia had access to the medical reports you sent the

medical foundation. You said that the reports didn't have names attached. But is there other information that could be used to figure out a person's identity?"

Mendoza inhaled. "Yes, if one is determined. The reports include patient age, gender, and race."

"Garcia has a son who has some kind of stage four cancer. Paco is an undocumented, illegal immigrant who wouldn't be missed by many."

"You are scaring me, McKenna. You are tearing out my heart. What can I do?"

"Does a typical cancer victim have use for organ donation?"

"It depends on what kind of cancer and how far it has progressed."

"Hold on." I turned to Whitehall. "Do you know what kind of cancer Martin Garcia has?"

"No." He shook his head hard as if to throw off demons.

I repeated the answer to Mendoza.

"Well, even without knowing the cancer, I can make a generalization. Most cancers are treated with chemo. The chemo that best kills cancer cells also kills certain healthy cells that are more vulnerable than others. Bone marrow is one of those types of cells. Often, doctors will find a bone marrow donor whose tissues match the recipient. Then they'll give the cancer victim an especially high dose of chemo knowing that, while it kills the cancer, it also kills all the bone marrow. Once that is done, the only hope for the victim to survive is to have the matching donor ready to replace the bone marrow."

"Can a bone marrow donor be a kid?"

"It's not common, but yes, they can."

"What is the risk to a kid who donates bone marrow?"

"If it is done correctly, the risk is there but not great." He paused. "Unless..."

"Unless what?" I said.

"Unless they take other organs."

"Such as?"

"Well, cancers often destroy organs, and doctors often transplant replacement organs from brain-dead donors at the same time they transplant bone marrow."

"But organs from donors who aren't brain dead would work just as well, right?"

"Yes, of course."

"Where can a doctor do a transplant?"

"You mean, which hospitals? Most, probably. It's like any other major surgery."

"Could human organ transplants be done by a veterinarian?"

"Well, we always use specialists for such delicate operations. But having said that, I've heard of vets doing transplants on pets."

"Are pet organs and pet operations hugely different from people? Or would the skills transfer?"

"They would transfer. In fact, in most ways, doing a transplant on a human isn't much different from doing a transplant on a dog. Most veterinarians don't have a lot of staff as we've come to expect in hospitals for people. But they manage. The risk would be greater, but the operation could still be done."

"And a veterinarian could presumably do a human transplant in the same place as he does pet surgery, right? In an animal hospital?"

"Yes. It is certainly possible."

"Thanks." I hung up.

FORTY-EIGHT

I looked at Whitehall. He looked stunned. Spot lay on the floor, his head up, watching Whitehall.

"Are you sure you don't know where Andrew Garcia practiced veterinary medicine?" I asked.

"No, I don't. I'm sorry. I should've paid more attention."

"You don't know where Garcia and his son Martin went?"

Whitehall shook his head. His eyes were watery with distress. "No. If only I could help, but I don't know what to do."

"I need to see their house."

Whitehall didn't hesitate. "Okay, let me get the key."

As Whitehall stood, Spot jumped up.

I followed Whitehall into his office. He opened a drawer in his desk. I stepped close just in case he tried to surprise me. He reached into the drawer and pulled out a key.

We went out the front door and walked to where a narrow connecting path led to the neighbor's house, the cabin that Whitehall rented to the Garcias. Spot trotted ahead.

The drive of the rental house was just wide enough to accommodate two vehicles. On one side was a brown Hyundai. The other space was vacant.

"How does Garcia transport Martin?" I asked.

"A white Ford van with a wheelchair lift gate."

Whitehall walked up a shallow wheelchair ramp that had been built over the one-step threshold and let us in.

It was a four-room cabin, not much bigger than mine. The kitchen and living room were on the east side, the two bedrooms on the west side with a bathroom separating the bedrooms.

I searched the desk in one bedroom, looked through kitchen drawers, checked over the bookcase, and found nothing of note except a key for a Ford. I slipped it into my pocket.

"Did Garcia have any vet friends?"

"I don't know any of his friends," Whitehall said. "His entire focus in life seems to be taking care of his son."

"You said that you don't know where he practiced. But did he ever say anything about other places, places of familiarity?"

"No. I have always had the sense that he was local, although I can't say precisely why."

"May I use your computer?"

"Yes, of course."

We went back to Whitehall's big house and into his office.

I used his computer to search for Dr. Andrew Garcia, but got nothing. Either his name was false or he'd worked for someone else or he'd retired before the internet became comprehensive. I also looked up all the local animal hospitals from Reno to Placerville including all of the ones in the Tahoe Basin. I copied and pasted their addresses into a list, then logged onto my email and sent the list to all of the local law enforcement agencies along with a short note explaining that I believed Paco to have been kidnapped by Dr. Andrew Garcia for the purpose of harvesting his bone marrow and other organs for his cancer-stricken son Martin. I notated which animal hospitals I would investigate.

I mentioned Garcia's white Ford van and suggested that, regardless of what might sound like a far-fetched suspicion, they put out an Amber Alert.

I added Whitehall as a contact for information, logged off, and told Whitehall to stay put in case any law enforcement had more questions.

Spot and I got into the Jeep and drove out through the gate.

It took me two hours to drive by all of the Tahoe animal hospitals from the north half of the lake to Truckee. I knocked and looked in windows and listened at back doors and studied the parking lots looking for Garcia's van with the wheelchair access gate. I satisfied myself that none of those hospitals was occupied at this late hour.

While I drove, I received phone call progress reports from Diamond at Douglas County and Sergeant Bains at El Dorado

County. Sergeant Santiago at Placer County called and said that they'd picked up Salt and Pepper, but they'd found no sign of the kid or anyone else at Placer County animal hospitals.

Then I remembered something that Mallory had said. I got him on the phone.

He explained that they'd checked all the veterinary clinics on the South Shore, but found nothing.

"I'm calling with a question," I said. "You mentioned that one of your boys saw a suspicious blue pickup in South Lake Tahoe, but it didn't match Paco's first description, so your officer let it go."

"Yeah."

"Where was that sighting?"

"You think that could matter?"

"I'm desperate."

"Hold on. I'll see if it's in a report."

He put me on hold. I was coming down the West Shore from Tahoe City, going past the neighborhood where Paco had been kidnapped a couple of hours before. My fatigue was overwhelming. I'd thought I was being so clever. Even had Paco help set the crazy trap. But I put the boy at risk and lost him. No amount of rationalizing would change that simple fact. I'd used terrible judgment, and Garcia was possibly going to take a scalpel to a little boy and take his organs as a result. Maybe he had already cut the boy open.

Mallory came back on the line. "I talked to the officer who saw the two big men. He said they were parked over on Third, a couple of blocks toward the lake from Highway Fifty."

"He say what the men were doing?"

"That's what was strange. He said it looked like they were on a stakeout."

"What happened?"

"He watched them for a bit, called it in, the men saw him, and they drove away."

"Thanks."

FORTY-NINE

I drove into heavy rain as I went around Emerald Bay. The rain continued into South Lake Tahoe.

At the "Y" intersection, I turned toward Stateline, drove a couple of long blocks and took a left on Third. The street goes into an area of warehouse buildings before it curves into the residential neighborhoods closer to the lake.

I went down two blocks and parked.

I grabbed my cell phone, got out into steady rain, and took Spot with me. I wanted stealth in the dark, and a Harlequin Great Dane does not aid stealth. But Spot was a formidable foe against bad guys.

The area was dark, the businesses closed. We walked down one very long block, turned the corner, walked the next short block, turned and repeated. The rain was steady, making all the surfaces shine, reflecting distant car lights on Lake Tahoe Blvd.

There was no animal hospital listed for this area, so I didn't know what I was looking for. But I had nowhere else to look.

When we completed the circle and came back to our starting point, we went in a different direction. There was an auto repair shop, a metal fabricator, the garbage collection facility. I passed the recycling center, multiple construction contractors, a dance studio, and a newspaper office. There was a small storefront that was closed up, a fenced storage yard for heavy equipment, a lighting showroom, another auto repair shop, a cluster of rental storage garages.

I tried not to rush, tried to be a thorough observer and use all of my senses.

I looked for the odd light glowing in the back of a business that was closed, a sound that didn't fit with a place where the people had all left for the night, a smell that was out of place. But I succeeded at nothing except getting myself soaked. I'd wasted a lot of time.

But I had nothing else to do. All the law enforcement agencies were looking for Dr. Garcia, too. I had no better idea about where to look.

Then I realized that I'd been thinking wrong about searching this dark commercial district.

Whenever I walked Spot at night, he always noticed a hundred things that eluded me. Most of the time, I had no idea what they were. But he would turn and stare into the dark. Sometimes he stopped, forcing me to stop, while he sniffed the breeze. Often, I couldn't tell if what he noticed was a sound, a sight, or a smell. Regardless of the sense, he was much more perceptive than I was.

My mistake was paying attention to my perceptions when I should have been paying attention to Spot's.

We started making another circuit of the area, walking all the same blocks. This time, I stopped looking at the buildings and just watched Spot. Spot looked and turned and pulled and focused here and there at places where we'd already been. I couldn't imagine what all his questions and thoughts were about. After a time, he'd turn away from whatever had caught his attention and resume walking.

We had retraced most of our steps when Spot came to a full stop in front of the abandoned storefront. He stood in the wet dark, staring at it, nose held high, air scenting.

The building was long and narrow and made of concrete block. The front had a window that was covered on the inside to make it opaque. Next to it was a glass door, also covered on the back side.

I let go of Spot's collar. "What is it, boy?"

He swung his head up to look at me, then turned back toward the storefront.

I gave him a little pat on his shoulder. "Go look. Show me what you're smelling."

Spot walked toward the door, lowering and then raising his

head, sniffing the air. He turned away from the door and went to the right, down along the side of the dark building. I followed.

Spot sniffed the ground a bit, but mostly focused on the air, moving his head around almost like a slow-waving flag.

We went past several small, dark windows, set high up in the concrete block wall.

At the rear corner, Spot turned the corner and walked along the back side of the building.

There was a loading dock up at the tailgate height of delivery trucks. Next to the dock was a short stairway that rose to a double doorway. The right door was new, made of metal. It was wet with rain, and it shined, reflecting distant vehicle lights from Highway 50, two blocks away. The left door was old and corroded with rust and was too rough to show a reflection. Just visible in the night were old painted letters that came to the edge of the door, the beginnings of words that were interrupted when the right door was replaced years after the words were painted.

GA

TA

AN

HO

Spot sniffed his way over to the far rear corner of the building. Then he came back and investigated the stairway.

As Spot began to walk up the stairs, I figured out what the painted words might possibly have once said.

GARCIA'S

TAHOE

ANIMAL

HOSPITAL

If so, this would be where Andrew Garcia had his veterinary practice before he retired.

At the top of the stairs, Spot put his nose to the center joint where the new right door met the old left door.

He wagged.

My heart thumped.

Paco!

FIFTY

My first thought was to call 911, but I knew the routine. Cops would come, then more cops. They'd pound on the door. They'd ask why I thought a kidnapped boy was inside of a dark building, and when I said that I knew because my dog wagged at the door, they'd think I was nuts. They wouldn't be able to break in without probable cause and a warrant or some indication of an emergency within the building. Whatever terrible thing Dr. Garcia was doing could go on for hours uninterrupted.

I had to go in now.

I had to have surprise.

I had to do it alone.

I tiptoed up the stairway to check the door. There was no handle. It was designed to be opened from the inside only.

The tiny crack between the doors was dark. I put my ear next to it. Nothing. I sniffed as Spot had done. Nothing. But I knew not to put any stock in not being able to detect odors that were obvious to Spot. A human's nose compared to a dog's nose is like an ant's eyeball compared to the Hubble Space Telescope.

I took hold of Spot's collar and gently pulled him down the stairs. We ran around the far side of the building. There was no side door. Other than the double metal door at the back, the only way in was the front door.

I went back to the front of the building and gently pulled on the front door. It was locked. It was a standard commercial door, solid metal frame with a metal rim around heavy tempered glass. It would be difficult at best to breach. Even the glass would be nearly impossible to break with any force less than a well-swung baseball bat.

The building's front show window was large and would be even stronger than the door.

I looked at the edges of the glass, trying to see if there were any gaps in whatever opaque material was behind the glass. But I could see nothing. No telltale hints of light at the edges of either window or the edge of the door.

Any attempt I made to break in would make a lot of noise. In the time it took me to find Paco inside the building, Dr. Garcia would gain a huge advantage.

Maybe I could get in from the roof.

I looked around for a way up, a dumpster or something that I could climb. There was nothing. The concrete block wall looked about a dozen feet tall with no handholds. I could search around nearby businesses and see if someone had left a ladder out back, but that might take hours and still yield nothing.

I saw a garage across the street that I hadn't noticed before. The door was up. Parked inside was a van, facing out. It was hard to see in the dark, but it looked like a white Ford van, like the van Whitehall had said Dr. Garcia used to haul his son Martin in his wheelchair.

Still holding Spot's collar, I ran to the garage with the Ford van. The key I'd taken from Garcia's kitchen drawer fit in the lock. I ushered Spot into the back on top of the lift platform. At the rear of the van was the spare tire compartment. I opened the tire cover, felt around in the dark, and removed the tire iron. Then I got in the front and started the van.

The big engine roared loud in the enclosed space.

I put the van in drive, rolled out into the street, waited until I thought I had enough momentum, then turned off the engine.

The van went silent as we rolled. Without engine power, I had no power steering or brakes, but I didn't have to turn. I guided the van alongside the building, then stepped hard on the brakes to stop.

"You stay inside here, boy," I said to Spot as I got out and gave him a pet, then put my finger across his nose, the signal not to bark.

With the door open, I stood on the driver's seat, and, holding the tire iron, boosted myself up onto the roof of the van and used my foot to gently shut the van door.

The top of the wall was now at face level. I grabbed the edge and boosted myself up, swung my foot over the edge, and pulled myself onto the roof.

Like many commercial buildings, the roof was flat and coated with small gravel. The rocks made crunching noises as I walked. Despite my rush to find Paco, I tried to move gently to minimize the sound.

There were several places where the flat roof was interrupted. There was a large exhaust vent near the back of the building and a small exhaust vent to one side. In the middle of the roof was a built-up skirt, and on its top a skylight mounted at an angle. I tiptoed over to look.

In the dim light from distant buildings, I could see that the skylight was an old model, hinged at the high end with a latch at the low end. From inside, a person could use a special rod to open the skylight for fresh air. From the outside, there was no way to unhook the latch except to break it.

I peered through the glass. Nothing but darkness below.

I thought of Paco. Maybe he was already cut open, his organs being carved out. Or maybe Garcia hadn't gotten to that point. Paco might still be conscious, waiting his fate with indescribable terror. There was no time to find a better way in.

I took the tire iron and put the tip at what looked like the most vulnerable point on the window-jamb. Tensing my muscles and grunting with effort, I rammed it in as far as it could go, then levered it up and down with ferocious force.

The metal skylight latch tore and popped with a screeching sound loud enough to be heard a block away.

I jerked the skylight up. Stepped over the skylight skirt and lowered myself through. Hung for a moment from the edge of the skylight. Based on the height of the wall, I guessed the drop to be maybe six feet. But when you can't anticipate, you can't land with any skill. I let go and fell.

FIFTY-ONE

My feet hit, and I crumpled to the floor, startled but unbroken. I got up. Going on Spot's tail wag at the double door at the back of the building, I turned that direction. I put my arms out, moved in the darkness, feeling for something, anything.

My hands hit a wall. I followed it sideways. Came to a door. Found the knob, turned it, yanked it open.

I was in some kind of room, mostly dark but with little green and red lights here and there. LEDs from high-tech equipment.

I felt a stabbing prick in my neck. I jerked sideways and down, hitting some kind of bench.

Lights went on. I reached up and pulled a syringe out of my neck. I looked at it and saw that the plunger was half-way in.

"I'm sorry you had to intrude, Mr. Owen McKenna," a man's voice said from behind me.

My elbows were on the top of a low, wide cabinet. My knees were on the floor. My hand still gripped the syringe.

I felt dizzy, and I started to sink down. I gently stuck the syringe's needle into the loose fabric of my shirt. I pushed the plunger in the rest of the way, allowing the remaining liquid to squirt out under my clothing where it wouldn't be seen. Then I collapsed onto the cabinet. As I lay helpless, my last significant move was to drop the spent syringe on the floor where the man would see it and notice that the plunger was depressed all the way. I wanted him to think that I'd gotten the full dose.

"I could tell when I met you that you were dedicated," the man said. "But this time your dedication has reached its end thanks to a shot of ketamine.

"Lovely stuff, I think you'll agree. It's sold on the street in small diluted quantities. Special K, its devotees call it. Makes for a wonderful escape from the real world.

"In full strength, it's a great anesthetic for vets operating on animals because it doesn't impair respiration as much as most other drugs. Pediatric physicians use it, too, because it works so well with children. Not so good with adults, though. With the dose I just gave you, it anesthetizes so thoroughly that the body eventually shuts down and turns off. But before you die, you'll experience double vision and hearing problems and then something like nightmares. Finally, just minutes before you expire, you'll get to enjoy severe hallucinations. It's not a pretty sight, let me tell you. But don't despair, it doesn't take all that long, even though I injected it into your muscle instead of your vein."

I gritted my teeth, grunted again, and rolled so I could see him.

Dr. Andrew Garcia stood between two gurneys. On one was his son Martin, covered with a sheet, a gas mask of some kind over his face. There was an IV pole with a bag and a tube running down to his arm. He looked to be unconscious.

Above were large flood lights, turned off.

On the other gurney was Paco, immobilized by straps at his ankles, wrists and across his chest. There was tape over his mouth. He strained, lifting his head and moaning. His eyes were huge, his lower lids raised and twitching.

I tried to call out to Paco, to reassure him, but my words were garbled. It felt like my entire mouth had been shot with Novocaine.

"Of course," Garcia continued, "because I'm all by myself and can't monitor Martin's respiration while I operate, I'm using ketamine on him as well. But he has been gradually building up an adaptive comfort level with the drug, taking it in small amounts, adjusting his body and brain to its effects. He's already part way under. I need only increase his dose a touch before I begin operating."

Garcia held his arm out and turned around in a circle. He looked blurry, and his movement seemed to warp and shift in my vision.

"Do you like my little operating room? It's not as sterile as you would find in a human hospital, and of course I don't have the luxury of the latest medical equipment. But this place served me well for countless operations in years past. Mostly dogs and cats, of course. But also rabbits and guinea pigs, parrots and pigeons and hawks. I've operated on a pig and a cow. Why, I've even operated on a snake and an iguana.

"This operation on my son is a bit heavy with emotional involvement, but it is no more complicated than what I've done before."

Garcia turned and looked at a computer screen.

"The time is near," he said. "It's been a long time waiting for the perfect donor match, struggling with the idiotic health protocols in this country. We came close with a good donor a year ago, but bureaucratic red tape prevented it from going through. So I took matters into my own hands. Fortunately, I had the sense to follow those stupid thugs when they followed you to your trap.

"For three days I've been giving Martin chemo in preparation for this moment. And just today his final, most powerful dose. I've just taken his blood sample and put it on one of those new biochemical assessment chips. It's the latest miniaturized method for analyzing blood. I put a drop of blood on it and connected it to the computer. It looks for markers that indicate the existence or absence of the item we're seeking. In this case, we need to know if all of Martin's cancer cells have been killed. The result will be up on the computer soon. When I know that we've killed the last of his cancer, I can proceed to give him the bone marrow and kidney transplants that will give him back his life."

I watched as two Garcias sat down at the computer, clicked two mouses in perfect synchronized movement.

My head throbbed. My tongue felt so swollen that it took up the entire inside of my mouth.

Both Garcias swiveled in their chairs to face me.

"A few more minutes," they said, voices not quite in synch, echoing in my head.

"You know, when I was a child, my mother was prone to a terrible melancholy. She should have had anti-depressant medication. But she was not the kind to go to a doctor for such a thing. She called it la oscuridad. The darkness. I remember when it would get bad. She'd sit up in the night, her tears invisible to me except by touch. Sometimes she'd sob out loud. She told me about her own teenage years in Spain during the Depression and during the Civil War in the land.

"My mother asked her parents, my grandparents, if they would be safe, and they told her yes, there was nothing to worry about. Then came the bombing at Guernica. You've probably heard about it. One of the most cowardly atrocities ever, committed by Hitler and Mussolini and ordered by the despicable dictator General Franco.

"My grandparents told my mother that it was a terrible thing that Franco had done, bombing women and children. The Basque men who came back to Guernica were understandably outraged. But some of them – instead of focusing their anger on General Franco – they took out their passions on anyone that they felt were Franco sympathizers.

"My parents had always kept out of politics. When accosted by people who were angry, they said that they were neutral. But after Guernica, some people didn't believe them. One day, some Basque teenagers accused them of being Nationalists, of being Franco supporters. My grandparents explained that they were neutral. Nevertheless, that night their house was lit on fire."

Garcia's voice got very quiet. "The family had a dog, a terrier named Ruidoso. The dog slept in my mother's bedroom. When the fire began to roar, he barked and woke my mother. They got out of the house. But my grandparents died, burned alive in their own home.

"While my mother lived, she said that it was only her body that escaped. The rest of her, her heart, her love, her life, burned up with her parents."

Garcia stopped talking as if all energy had gone out of him. But I saw his chest rise and fall with heavy breathing. The red in his cheeks intensified. The color pulsed in my vision, and his face changed shape like it was melting, like in a Dali painting.

"I grew up in California. I had a good childhood. But when

I was eight, my mother took her life. And with her life she took most of me. Ever since, I've felt as if I was only going through the motions. I've suffered the same darkness as she did. I would give my life to have her back for one day. Even in my veterinary practice, I was consumed with my loss. Every little dog or cat that I saved, I pretended it was my mother I was saving.

"I've never been to Europe, never been to the Basque country. But those Basque teenagers destroyed my life just as thoroughly as they destroyed my mother.

"Then along came Martin. Ironically, his mother was Basque. Our marriage didn't last. But Martin made it worth it. Finally, I had some joy back in my life. And he was the embodiment of my mother. He looked like her. He talked like her. He moved like her. He smelled like her.

"Then he got cancer. This time, the darkness came for me worse than before. A bone marrow transplant was the only thing that could save him. But there was no match. We scoured the data banks. We hired a blood research lab to focus on our problem. The blood researchers told us that the best marrow donor would be type O negative, which is somewhat rare among most people but very common among the Basque.

"The researchers also identified several other specific components we had to match if Martin was to have the best chance of survival.

"So my genius was to talk Robert Whitehall into medical philanthropy. I told him about how Basque people had unusual blood and unusual DNA, different than all the people of the world. I told him that if researchers had more information about Basque people, it would hugely expand science and benefit all of mankind. I suggested that Whitehall fund medical services in communities where Basque lived. The stipulation to participating doctors was that they had to forward blood work information as part of the research project.

"When Whitehall agreed, I picked the communities where his foundation would offer his services. I even worked with his foundation's secretary and helped him send out the proposals. We focused on several communities that had a good number of

Basque people.

"Then, when we began to receive the blood work information on large numbers of people, I forwarded it on to the blood researchers we'd hired.

"Whitehall's foundation performed an enormous service to the medical world. Not only did we find Paco, who is a perfect match for Martin, but we provided valuable information to the medical research community.

"I was able to strike up a relationship with Paco's mother, become one of her customers, and learn more about her and the boy.

"Of course, hiring a research lab took a lot of money, but I figured out a great way to play the stock market by learning where Tahoe business people traveled and then researching what that might indicate about their companies. I had Cassie include information on Robert Whitehall's movements. Of course, I already knew his travel plans, but it seemed a good way to keep me above suspicion. I made a lot of money playing the market with Cassie's information, enough to pay for all of Martin's medical care.

"It could have been so simple. After I'd developed a relationship with Cassie, I pretended to be one of the researchers and contacted her about further testing for Paco. She said that the research data that Dr. Mendoza forwarded to the foundation was supposed to be anonymous. So I explained that a person's life was at stake. Even so, she evaded me. I knew the real reason why. She worried that Paco would be identified as an illegal alien and deported.

"That woman put immigration issues in the way of saving a man's life!"

Garcia was panting. He took a deep breath, held it, let it out slowly.

The room wavered. It looked like he would fall off his chair.

"So my choice was simple. After Franco killed so many Basque, the Basque took my grandparents' lives and in the process destroyed my mother's and mine. Now the Basque will give life back by saving Martin.

"At every step, people have gotten in the way, tried to keep me from having the most basic thing, life for my loved ones. Now I have taken control. I will do what I have to do.

"You should know that I offered Cassie a very large sum of money. All she had to do was let Paco be a donor. The operation would have been done by the best surgeons and taken place in the best hospital.

"But she said no. She didn't trust me. She didn't trust the immigration police. She didn't trust our country.

"I didn't want Cassie to die. But she left me no choice. So, using my travel/investment pseudonym of John Mitchell, I called her and set up a meeting. Then I had those men go to that meeting in place of me. They were to take care of her and bring me Paco. What a joke. I found out that the boy was more than a match for the men I hired. Good genes in that boy!" Garcia looked over at Paco who squirmed on the gurney. "But now I finally have him."

I tried to speak, tried to say something that might slow him down, give me and Paco a little more time, but it came out as a long grunt with saliva sputtering off my buzzing lips.

"Martin is dying," Garcia said as if in response to my gibberish. "There is no time left to wait and do yet more paperwork and get permissions and find an appropriate treatment facility. I've done bone marrow transplants on dogs. I've done kidney transplants. It is one of the simpler organ transplants. The internal organs of humans are quite similar to those of dogs.

"Unfortunately, Mr. McKenna, you have gotten in my way. But you will be gone, soon. The amount of ketamine in your system is fatal. And no one will find your body.

"I know a very nasty secret about a man who is the manager of a rendering plant. In exchange for my silence, he will arrange for you to join the cattle carcasses and other euthanized animals that are the supply line for his factory. They make a special meat and bone meal that is used in fuel for power plants. The efficiency achieved in burning this material is right up there with fossil fuels, yet it's all recycled. It's a really marvelous way to utilize a resource that is normally wasted. Your dried tissues and ground bones will eventually help run our electric lights and charge our smart phones.

"And, while I'm hoping that the boy survives this operation, the risk is substantial. If he doesn't make it, he will join you, recycled for a better world."

The computer printer made the sudden soft noise of pulling a sheet into the machinery. It began printing. Garcia picked up the sheet as it came out of the printer. He angled it toward the light to read it.

"Excellent," he said. "The test results on Martin." He looked at the paper. "Perfect. His cancer is gone, destroyed by the massive chemo treatment. Of course, that means his bone marrow is destroyed, too. This is the break point. From this point, Martin either lives and gets better, or he dies soon. No more purgatory. It is time to begin the process of saving his life.

"In the hospital, they begin the transfer of bone marrow as they are simultaneously doing the kidney transplant. However, I am just one doctor. So I'll remove the boy's bone marrow first, put it into Martin's drip, and then remove the boy's kidney.

"First, I'll prepare the boy."

Garcia rolled Paco's gurney over near Martin's. Paco strained at the straps holding him, his eyes frantic, his panicked cries barely coming through the tape over his mouth.

Garcia raised Paco's gurney up several inches. He opened a drawer in a rolling cart and pulled out a 5 inch-long needle as thick as a 16-penny nail. It had a red plastic, pistol-grip handle. Garcia set it on a tray. Next to it he set a syringe without a needle attached.

He reached into another drawer, pulled out a bottle and checked the label. From the same drawer, he took a small syringe with needle attached. He inserted the needle into the bottle and drew out liquid.

This was the moment. I needed to rise beyond the constraints of the drug in my body. I couldn't talk, and my eyes saw everything in two images that wouldn't come together. But I thought I could roll off the cabinet and let my upper body fall to the floor.

Maybe I could make it a controlled fall. A fall with forward momentum. If I could will my legs to make one or two steps, I might make it to Paco. But I was so light-headed that I thought I'd faint.

I remembered from my cop days something a medical instructor said. She told us that if you are wounded and suffering from trauma, you can sometimes avoid passing out by simply bearing down and clenching your abdominal muscles as if you're about to cough. The tension keeps your blood pressure up and helps maintain blood flow to your brain.

One other thought came through from a decade or more in the past. A fight instructor had spoken about the power of a roar. His example was lions and elephants who can immobilize most creatures with a simple thundering vocalization. Although I couldn't speak, if I could make a loud noise while I made some kind of movement, maybe I could distract Garcia from his deed.

I shut my eyes and tried to contract my core muscles like I was doing abdominal crunches. Then I twisted my legs, rolled off the cabinet, and fell to the floor.

FIFTY-TWO

I landed with my left foot forward and my right foot back. My right knee smashed onto concrete. I spread my arms out and down, fingers splayed, hoping to catch myself if I fell sideways. Yet I had no clue whether I was listing sideways or not. My focus was on clenching my gut, keeping up the inner tension, trying to maintain consciousness.

With the focus that comes from outrage, I pulled my arms in and tightened my muscles as if to prepare for the most intense cough of my life. In an explosion of movement, I shot up with a roar.

Garcia jerked back, fear in his eyes. He raised his arms in defense. I slammed into him like a thrown hay bale. He was knocked back. The syringe and bottle flew out of his hands. He hit a counter, spun, and fell to the floor.

The impact bounced me toward Paco. I had no balance, no strength in my legs. My momentum pushed Paco's gurney to the side, and I fell across him, my body draping his. I knew he couldn't breathe with two hundred-plus pounds on his chest and belly. But I didn't attempt to push up, didn't even think I could push up. The most important thing was to unstrap Paco's wrists.

I squinted, trying to see, rolling on Paco's little ribs, crushing him, feeling for his arm.

My hands found Paco's wrist. I couldn't focus on the strap. Couldn't see. My fingers were frantic blind crabs, grasping, groping, feeling for the catch. I got it unhooked, pulled the strap away.

Again I clenched my gut, trying to send blood pressure to my brain, trying to stay conscious. I shifted, reached toward Paco's other wrist. Found the strap.

Other hands grabbed mine.

Garcia's fingers were like steel claws digging into the backs of my hands. I worked the catch as Garcia raked my skin with his fingernails. The strap on Paco's other wrist felt different than the first. It wouldn't come free. I realized I was facing the other way. I was pulling it the wrong direction.

My vision went dark. I clenched and tensed and coughed out another bark, and it brought me back just a bit. My hands were dark red. Garcia was gouging me down to the bone.

The catch came free.

I summoned one last roar as I slid off Paco. My hands found Garcia's clothes. I grabbed through slippery fabric, gripped the flesh of Garcia's thigh as if to tear it from bone.

The darkness came back. I couldn't see. But I could feel the pull of gravity as I slid off of Paco. I weighed a thousand pounds. I had no more strength to resist my fall. But I could still hang onto Garcia. I could take him down with me. Give Paco a moment to free himself from the other straps and the tape on his mouth...

I never felt the impact of the floor, but I became aware of it, cold and hard against my cheek. The salty taste of blood was on my tongue where I'd bit through it. The left sides of my lips were smashed.

My hands were empty. No fabric. No hard marathon runner's muscles under my fingers.

I clenched my gut and coughed, tried to hang onto fleeting consciousness.

Soft sounds of struggle came from behind me. I managed to roll. The rushed slaps of small shoes on concrete made a staccato rhythm, mimicked by heavier footsteps. A door opened to the distant sounds of traffic out on Lake Tahoe Boulevard.

I turned and saw Paco pushing the latch on the heavy double door, his tiny weight barely able to budge it. Garcia was running toward him, syringe raised in the air. Paco turned sideways to slip through the narrow opening. As Garcia lunged toward Paco, his arm bumped the light switch. The room went black except for the dim glow coming in from the wet street.

I summoned a last, shouted, garbled exhalation.

"DODGE, PACO! DODGE!"

Paco got through the door.

Garcia reached it, pushed it open, and stabbed the needle into Paco's back as Paco spun away. Garcia slipped and fell on the wet concrete. Paco bolted toward the street. Garcia pushed up with the spring of a much younger man and sprinted after him.

The footsteps receded. The door shut with a blast of cold air washing over me. The room went black, replaced by the vision of the old man sticking the syringe into the little boy as the boy got away. I tried to visualize, tried to remember if Garcia had been able to push the syringe's plunger in or not. But my brain was shrouded in fog.

My crawl across the floor was the movement of a snail. Small, pathetic contortions. I oozed forward. Slid my hands on the concrete. Regrouped my legs and body. Oozed again. Repeated.

Clench the gut. Get blood to the brain. Reach the hands. Push the paralyzed legs. Pull the arms back. Ooze another six inches forward.

The door was as far away as a distant galaxy. I was a tiny snail-ship lost in the galactic blackness of space.

Eons later, I hit the door, pushed myself into new, strange contortions, got a hand on the latch and pushed. The door opened.

The light of dark night was dazzling compared to the blackness of the room. My vision was weak, but I saw Paco in the distance, just visible as I peered between two buildings.

Paco was out on Highway 50. He was running down the middle of the street in the rain. All four lanes had traffic, moving fast, headlights reflecting off wet pavement. Close behind Paco was Garcia. The little boy was tiny compared to the marathon runner.

An SUV swerved. Paco gave it a hard hand-smack on its side. Paco spun around its tailgate as it went by.

The big runner behind him tried to follow.

Paco sprinted into the oncoming lanes. A small car was next

to a bus. The approaching vehicles didn't slow, didn't see the little boy against the night. Paco turned sideways, stood still on the dotted white line as the car and bus went on either side of him. Both drivers saw him at the last moment, veering away, giving him space.

Garcia stayed on the double yellow center line, the safest spot between the pulsing, rushing flow of traffic.

Paco saw an opportunity. He sprinted toward a break in the traffic, and he was able to make some distance down an empty stretch of asphalt.

Garcia saw the movement, anticipated Paco's intention, gave pursuit. It only took a few seconds for Garcia to close the gap.

Five or six cars were coming one way, close on each other, making an impassible obstruction on both lanes of eastbound traffic. In the westbound lanes were two motorcycles followed by a pair of pickups side-by-side. All were speeding at 40 or 45 miles-per-hour.

Paco sprinted through a moving corridor between the motor-cycles and the pickups. There was just enough room to make it. Garcia followed.

Paco stayed in the moving corridor as Garcia charged forward with confidence, the big runner about to grab the little kid.

Then Paco made an instantaneous turn, darted between the motorcycles, stiff-arming the closest rider. The big cyclist on his heavy machine barely swerved, but Paco used the blow like a rico-chet changing his direction. He shot backward against the traffic, heading for the narrow space between the onrushing pickups.

He was still moving at an angle, and he had too much iner-tia to avoid being hit. But he raised his arm up across his chest and shoulder-slammed the rear fender of the pickup. The blow bounced him off the truck and back into an open area of the highway where there were no vehicles.

Garcia jerked his head to see where Paco was going. But that movement caused him to lose his position. One pickup caught him, the corner of its bumper square in Garcia's thigh. Garcia bounced, screaming, to the pavement, and he rolled under the rear wheel of the other pickup.

Paco jogged to the side of the highway, reached over his shoulder and pulled the syringe out of his back. His energy and the time elapsed told me that Garcia hadn't gotten the plunger pushed in.

I collapsed on the floor.

EPILOGUE

Ten days later, we gathered at Aggie's Green early in the morning. Pam Sagan coordinated the process and made sure that, at the appointed time, José Castillo's family and Rafael Vargas's family were there, along with the local auto dealer who delivered the two used vans, the purchase of which Sagan had arranged.

We put everybody into the vans. José's father Ernesto drove the Ford with his four kids, and Rafael's mother Palma drove the Chevy with her two kids. The kids, especially Ernesto's, were a robust group, laughing and joking as one might expect with children who ranged in age from a bit younger than Paco up to maybe fourteen or fifteen.

Paco wanted to ride with Palma's family, and Pam Sagan joined them, so Street and Spot and I got some quality time as a threesome in the Jeep.

"Is that veterinarian's son still alive?" Street asked me as we led the caravan up into the Sierra.

I nodded. "Doc Lee talked to the guys in Reno. The donor they found wasn't a perfect match, but the drugs to help prevent rejection are working. Sounds like he might make it. If so, he will get to spend most of his life in prison for complicity in Paco's kidnapping. Who knows, maybe his cell mates will be Salt and Pepper."

"How's Paco dealing with it?" Street asked.

"He's still emotionally shut down, but he's thawing a bit. I think he's coming to realize that it was his ideas that allowed us to trap Salt and Pepper. And it was his running and dodging ability that allowed him to escape a strong, experienced runner."

"He learned that he has some control over his day-to-day life as well as his future," Street said.

"Let's hope so," I said.

The drive to Tahoe's North Shore took three and a half hours. Robert Whitehall's gate was open, and he was waiting with Diamond. I led the caravan into the big paving-stone drive with its multiple parking areas surrounded by Jeffrey pines.

The Castillos and the Vargases had wide eyes as they walked into the concrete-and-glass mansion on the beach. Except for soft murmured exclamations, the children were now silent.

I introduced Diamond to all of them. He was in his civilian clothes, so nobody seemed intimidated. He and I chatted with Pam over by the lakeside windows. The rain had paused, and we could see all the way to the mountains of the South Shore.

Whitehall directed everybody to sit and relax. They sat. They did not relax.

Paco was the exception. He lounged on the blue hearth of the fireplace looking very cool with his new replacement Oakleys perched on the top of his head. Street sat next to him.

Spot trotted around sniffing everybody and everything. Whitehall pet him with both hands, then raised up his hands and looked at all the little white and black hairs. Whitehall shrugged, then wiped his hands off on his expensive slacks. Impressive.

Whitehall had brought in a catering company, and one of their young women, a Hispanic girl who chatted in Spanish with the assembled crowd, served soft drinks.

Then Whitehall stood to the side of the fireplace, ready to speak. The worried stress of a defeated old man that permeated his being when I was last at his house was gone, replaced by the vigor of a man in charge of a small but important part of the world. A vigor that I hoped would stay with him for another decade or more.

"Hi, I'm Robert Whitehall, and I'm very pleased to meet all of you. I know you're hungry, so we'll get to lunch soon. We've only just met now, but I've had the pleasure of speaking with Ernesto Castillo and Palma Vargas over the last several days. We've assembled here today so that I can tell you the results of our inquiries.

"I have a foundation that funds some things here and there, and the best part of my job is that I get to pick which things those are. Today, we're here because Paco and his foster mother Cassie created a business that I felt was worth funding. Although I should add that I didn't have to fund much beyond a little of my time and those used vans you came in. You can think of me as more of a facilitator.

"Some time back, I signed up for Cassie's Field To Fridge delivery program," Whitehall continued, "and for months, I've enjoyed the best vegetables anyone could imagine."

Paco sat up a bit straighter and raised his hand.

"Yes, sir?" Whitehall said.

"Everything we brought you was fruit," Paco said in a voice that, if not strong, wasn't meek, either.

"Fruit? Really?"

Paco nodded.

"How does one tell?"

"Vegetables are like onions, and carrots, and spinach. Stuff without seeds."

Whitehall thought about. "Certainly, if you say so, it must be. All the produce I get has seeds, so it's fruit."

Paco nodded again.

A sudden little shriek of surprise came from one of the catering women working back in the kitchen. We all turned to see Spot come trotting back from the direction of the kitchen, licking his chops. Whitehall's eyes did that aimless wander in space that meant he was suddenly reassessing his house from the perspective of what a very tall dog might find. But he didn't express concern.

Whitehall's eyes refocused on the assembled crowd, and he continued to speak.

"We were all deeply saddened that Cassie Moreno died. This meant that Paco lost the only family he had. It turns out that Cassie left no will, but the most valuable thing she owned was the Field To Fridge business. Because Paco helped her build it, and because Paco was her only family, and..." Whitehall paused to give emphasis to his next point, "because Paco is the only one who really knows what is involved in running the business and keeping the customers happy, the Field To Fridge business logically belongs to him.

"With Paco's permission, I've had a lawyer put together business papers and file the forms with the state of California. Field To Fridge is now part of an official corporation, and Paco is the majority owner with fifty-one percent. He will acquire the power to make all decisions when he turns twenty-one.

"It turns out that one of the most valuable items that Field To Fridge sells is a wonderful tomato that Cassie and Paco developed called Cassie's Amazement. One of their customers over on the West Shore owns a restaurant chain and a produce distribution company. I spoke to the owner. Now, with Paco's permission, that company has purchased the rights to market Cassie's Amazements nationwide."

Next to me, Pam Sagan was beaming.

"In the meantime, because of Cassie's death, Paco lost his place to live. However, it turns out that the farm and the two houses on it were for sale.

"With the proceeds from the sale of the rights to Cassie's Amazements, we were able to purchase that farm in Paco's name. I won't bore you with the details. But the lawyer arranged the paperwork so that Ernesto and his family can live in the front house, while Palma and her family can live in the back house with Paco. Ernesto and Palma have agreed to take over management of the Field To Fridge business, and, after some years, they will own forty-nine percent of the corporation. All of you children will be able to help as your parents see fit."

Spot appeared by Paco's side and lay down on the hard concrete floor. Paco shifted on the hearth, lifted his legs in the air, and rested his shoes on Spot's back. A couple of the other kids giggled.

Whitehall said, "I would also like you to know that Paco told me a little secret. He's given me permission to tell it to you."

Both parents and kids were suddenly very focused on Whitehall, their eyes darting from him to Paco and back.

Whitehall grinned. "It turns out that there is money in this produce business. Even though Paco has been going to school, he's also been earning money for his work with Field To Fridge.

"Do you kids want to know how much Paco saved from his work in the last year and a half?"

Several of the kids nodded. Some said, "Yeah."

"Over four thousand dollars," Whitehall said. "How would you like to make that kind of money?"

They stared at Paco with astonishment. Paco couldn't have played it more cool. No big deal on his face.

"And there's another side to the money. We've set up a system where a certain percentage of earnings gets put aside for an education account for each of you kids.

"My foundation is going to match those contributions three to one. In other words, for every thousand dollars that goes into each child's education account, my foundation adds three more. Those accounts get invested in various markets. The results depend on the returns, but by the time you kids graduate high school, there should be substantial funds available for college.

"So," Whitehall continued, excitement in his voice. "Let me tell you about your business!

"Mr. McKenna gave me the list of Cassie's clients. I called them all and explained that Paco and his friends' families were going to continue Field To Fridge, and I asked if they would like to continue being clients. Do you know what they said?"

Whitehall grinned. Tahoe's local rock star and ball player and TV talk show host couldn't have found a more rapt audience.

"Every one of them said that they would like to continue. Five of them said that they wanted to increase their weekly orders. And seven of them said that they knew multiple other people who wanted in. So I called those people, and the Field To Fridge client list is now double what it was before. That's why you need two vans."

The kids were still looking at Paco, probably dreaming of his bank account, which was actually still a wad of cash that I was holding for him.

"Oh, one more thing," Whitehall said. "I learned from Principal Pam Sagan that there is a question about proper paperwork to keep our government happy regarding Paco's residency, and, it turns out, Ernesto and Palma's residency, too. So I collected the information on how long you've all been in this country, and I got statements from your employers. I took these to some friends of mine who happen to be senators and congressmen. Now here is where it gets a bit tricky to explain.

"As you know, in this country, right or wrong – just like in most countries – money buys influence. I'm a little uncomfortable with that. So I didn't say that I was going to give any money to any re-election campaigns. I simply explained that I've been looking to expand my company's manufacturing operations, and I decided that instead of outsourcing my needs to Chinese companies, I'm going to build a new plant in the Central Valley where there is a work force with a good work ethic. I let my friends know that doing the right thing is very important to me.

"The end result is that yesterday I got a call from a senator's office. I was told that they found a way to get the three of you into a program that leads to citizenship."

Whitehall turned to Paco. "We all know that this is the only country you've ever known and that you are as American in spirit and deed and experience as I am. Indeed, you're even working your own business, and nothing is more American than that. Are you okay with becoming an official American citizen?"

"Yeah," Paco said. He slowly stood up, looked at everyone and said, "Cassie always said that the only thing that overcomes hard luck is hard work. So if we grow a lot of tomatoes and peppers, we'll probably be okay."

Spot rolled over onto his side and sighed.

About the Author

Todd Borg and his wife live in Lake Tahoe, where they write and paint. To contact Todd or learn more about the Owen McKenna mysteries, please visit toddborg.com